FIRST STRIKE

"Listen!" someone shouted. When the patrons of the Chicken Coop had quieted down, the bartender turned up the volume on the television.

"*. . . has just learned that the government of Egypt has used a nuclear weapon against a force of Libyan troops that crossed the Egyptian border to attack an army garrison in the town of Qattara. A small nuclear warhead of less than one megaton apparently was fired into the Libyans from an artillery battery located some eight miles from its target. A mushroom cloud from the explosion can be seen from as far away as fifty miles.*

"*CBS has learned that the U.S. government does not know at this time how Egypt obtained a nuclear weapon. CBS will return at eleven with a full report . . .*"

"What does this mean?" Maggie turned to Ansel.

"It means the genie is out of the bottle."

BLOOD STRIPE

BLOOD STRIPE

WILLIAM D. BLANKENSHIP

AVON
PUBLISHERS OF BARD, CAMELOT, DISCUS AND FLARE BOOKS

BLOOD STRIPE is an original publication of Avon Books. This work
has never before appeared in book form. This work is a novel. Any
similarity to actual persons or events is purely coincidental.

AVON BOOKS
A division of
The Hearst Corporation
1790 Broadway
New York, New York 10019

Copyright © 1987 by William D. Blankenship
Published by arrangement with the author
Library of Congress Catalog Card Number: 86-90996
ISBN: 0-380-75284-0

First Avon Printing: April 1987

AVON TRADEMARK REG. U.S. PAT. OFF. AND IN OTHER COUNTRIES, MARCA
REGISTRADA. HECHO EN U.S.A.

Printed in the U.S.A.

K–R   10   9   8   7   6   5   4   3   2   1

For Heidi

MONDAY, MAY 26

Chapter 1

A blue dune buggy pulled into the service station outside the town of Puma, New Mexico, and a muscular young man jumped out as if eager for exercise. "Hi, can you tell me how far we are from Hassayampa Creek?"

Harry Williamson, a barrel-chested man with a permanently red face and wrinkles of fat along the back of his neck, rose with the lumbering grace of a sumo wrestler from the chair he had placed carefully in the shade. "The Hassayampa's just a couple of miles ahead. Fill her up for you?"

"No thanks, I topped off my tank in Albuquerque."

"Well, let me check that water bag anyway. You can't take chances with water out here, y'know. Not with the thermometer over ninety." Williamson unhooked the canvas liter bag strapped to the dune buggy's hood and carried it to his water hose.

"That's nice of you," the young man said. "Thanks."

A beautiful blond girl stepped out of the dune buggy and stretched languidly. She and her companion walked around the vehicle from opposite sides and leaned into each other with purring sounds.

Williamson watched with a smile. "Newlyweds?"

"I didn't think it still showed," the young man said. "We've been married for two weeks."

"New Mexico gets a lot of newlyweds, mostly kids like you, who like the outdoors. You picked a good season. May's the best month around here."

"Yes, it's beautiful." The young man's arm slid around his wife's waist. "I'm Bob Halliday. This is Rosemary."

Williamson didn't bother to introduce himself. "There you go." He recapped the bag and attached it to the hood.

Halliday had brought out a surveyor's map and was tracing one of the squiggly red lines with his fingertip. "If the Hassayampa is just ahead, then that mountain to the south must be the one we want."

"I'd say so." Rosemary Halliday looked toward the sand-colored rock spear that rose from the desert five miles in the distance.

"You folks mountain climbers?"

"Not exactly. Rosemary and I are spelunkers."

Although he knew exactly what the word meant, Williamson said in a serious voice, "I mostly steer clear of religion."

The Hallidays laughed, well accustomed to such misunderstandings.

"Spelunkers are people who like to explore caves," Bob Halliday explained. "That's our hobby. As a matter of fact, Rosemary and I met while we were both exploring a cave in Tennessee."

Williamson shook his head, embellishing his impersonation of an earnest dunce. "Spelunkers. I'll be damned. That's a new one on me, and I've been all over this world."

"You have?" Halliday seemed surprised that a gas station attendant could be so widely traveled.

"Sure. This isn't my living, ya know. I'm in the army. Staff sergeant over at Fort Powell. I only help out here because the owner's a buddy of mine. He's a soldier, too." While he talked, Williamson cleaned their windshield and looked at the profusion of neatly stacked equipment in the rear of the dune buggy: rope; two helmets rigged with lamps; cable ladder; hammer, pitons and caribiners; first aid kit; backpacks. They were equipped to go fairly deep into the mountain. "If you're looking for caves around here, you'll be disappointed. There aren't any that I know of."

"These mountains are honeycombed with tunnels and caves." Halliday pointed south. "According to this geological survey, that peak may have a network of caves that's never been fully mapped."

"Well, I wouldn't go into them if I were you. This country's overrun with rattlers."

The girl met his warning with cheerful resolve. "We know how to handle snakes."

Williamson made a final effort to dissuade them: "That's private property out there. It's posted 'No Trespassing.' "

"We never disturb the environment," Halliday replied, as if any sort of trespassing were made acceptable by that fact.

"Suit yourselves." Williamson stepped back and dropped his squeegee into a bucket of water. "Have a nice day."

The Hallidays thanked him and drove away.

Williamson watched as Halliday drove slowly down the highway, looking for an easy cut into the desert. There was nothing dumb about the kid. He knew how to pick his terrain. The dune buggy had gone only about a quarter of a mile before Halliday found a narrow natural rock bridge abutting the shoulder, and used it as a crossover into the desert.

For several minutes Williamson stood in front of the service station watching the dust raised by the dune buggy. It went like an arrow toward the distant peak. When he was certain the Hallidays weren't going to turn back or head for one of the other mountains in the distance, Williamson walked quickly to a small bungalow behind the station.

He picked up the phone in the bungalow and dialed a number at Fort Powell.

"Hank? This is Harry. We've got a problem."

"What's wrong?" a deep voice inquired calmly.

"We've got two people on their way to the mountain. Spelunkers. Honeymooners, for Christ's sake. Kids in their early twenties, probably staying at a hotel in Albuquerque. They stopped here five minutes ago in a blue dune buggy with New Mexico plates and a rental agency sticker. I don't know where they're from, but I'd guess the Midwest. They've got enough gear to penetrate the seven-hundred-foot level."

"It'll take them at least an hour to find the high entrance, if that's where they're headed. I'll be there in forty-five minutes. Keep your eye on the display."

"Will do."

Williamson put down the phone and went into the kitchenette. He took a beer from the refrigerator, popped the tab, and returned to the parlor. One wall of the parlor was decorated with a painting of the Grand Canyon so indifferently done as to make that magnificent sight look like nothing more than a hole in the ground. He pressed a button recessed into the wall and the picture slid silently aside.

Set into the wall behind the panel was a computer screen displaying a diagram of the mountain's cave system from the fifteen-hundred-foot elevation down into the bowels of the mountain. Concealed throughout the caves were heat sensors that triggered light and audio alarms through the computer should any creature large enough to be a man or woman enter the cave.

Williamson settled into an easy chair. Waiting didn't bother him. And if the Hallidays had to be canceled out, that wouldn't upset him either. Maybe Roper would let him have the girl for a few minutes first. She had a sweet little ass.

Forty-eight minutes later Hank Roper strode into the bungalow, still in uniform. "Any action?"

"Not yet."

"I'm going to change."

Roper went into the bedroom and stripped off his army uniform. The shirt sleeves bore the wide stripes of a sergeant major and a row of hash marks. He changed into an old pair of khaki pants, a well-worn safari jacket, and a pair of climbing boots.

Hank Roper was a man of medium height who looked tall because he was thick through the chest. His shoulders too were heavy with pads of muscle. Years ago he'd been a middleweight with good speed and better-than-average reach. A flattened nose and a patch of faded scar tissue under his left eye were his only visible souvenirs of those days.

Then the Vietnam War came along and Roper found that killing was even more satisfying than the ring. That discovery led him to stay in the army when the war ended and make the business of killing his lifelong pursuit—a smart decision. Everyone agreed that Sergeant Major Hank Roper was a top practitioner of a demanding profession.

As he was lacing up his boots, he heard the first audio signal from the computer. The Hallidays were inside the cave.

"We won't go deep today. If the cave looks interesting we'll come back tomorrow for a full-scale survey." Bob Halliday strapped on his backpack and adjusted the shoulder harness to distribute the weight equally across his back.

"I wish we'd find a bathtub," Rosemary said. "I hate those slimy underground pools, but it's so hot out here I'd be willing to take a dip in just about anything cool and wet."

They were standing inside the entrance to what their practiced eyes told them was an extensive cave system. The entrance was two-thirds of the way up the mountain. Access was good. It had taken less than an hour to climb up here carrying minimal equipment for an exploratory survey. They could look far out over the desert from here, out past the isolated speck on the highway that was the service station where they had stopped for directions.

Bob was methodically checking his equipment, quite unaware of Rosemary's admiring gaze. Even now, a year after their first meeting, the very sight of Bob thrilled her. His ruggedness and quiet decency were powerful attractions. She loved him completely. When Rosemary marveled at how perfectly her life had worked out, she became almost frightened. She was a no-nonsense girl who refused to believe in fairy tales. Better to have a few blemishes on her happiness than a marriage that could evaporate in a mist of unreality.

"Ready." She slipped on a pair of lightweight coveralls and adjusted the kneepads that were an absolute necessity for long crawls through narrow spaces.

Bob adjusted her backpack and kissed her lightly. "You're fantastic, you know that? Not many brides would spend their honeymoon prowling around some dirty old cave."

"And don't you forget it."

They switched on helmet lamps and started ahead at a crouch. Bob went only a few feet before stopping abruptly. "Damn, the safety note's still in the glove compartment. I meant to leave it under the windshield wiper. Too preoccupied with the equipment, I guess."

"Shall we go back?"

Bob considered doing just that. He always followed the standard safety precaution of leaving a note on his car windshield detailing the names of the people in his party, the date and hour he expected to enter the cave under exploration, the location of the cave, and the approximate hour he expected to return. He'd written the note, but left it inside the car. "No, it would take an hour to get back down to the car and another hour to climb back up here. That'd shoot the morning. We're only going partway in today. Let's push on."

"For a minute there I thought they were going to turn back," Williamson said.

"Spelunkers are stubborn. Stupid too, crawling around a dark hole with a bunch of bats and snakes."

"Why do they do it?" Williamson wondered, scratching the back of his fat neck.

"Two years ago the big sport was racquetball. Last year it was the marathon. This year it's spelunking. Our bad luck."

"Can't we at least seal off the high entrance to the caves? We've got our own access below."

"No way. The caves are the mountain's ventilation system."

They watched as the computer's blinking lights chronicled the Hallidays' descent into the cave. They were making good progress, moving much faster than Roper had expected.

A car pulled up to the gas pumps and Williamson frowned as he looked out the window. "Hank, it's Sheriff Perkins. What do you suppose that asshole wants?"

Roper saw Sheriff Leonard Perkins step down from a Chevy pickup truck dressed in hunting clothes instead of his uniform. "Relax, Len's only off on one of his hunting trips. Probably wants a free fill-up. You track those kids while I get rid of him." Roper left the bungalow and walked to the front of the service station to find Perkins peering into the office. "Mornin', Lou."

"Hello, Hank. I didn't think you pumped gas yourself. Important fella like you."

"Harry Williamson's not feeling so good, so I came out. Fill her up for you? High test?"

"High test'll be fine." Perkins followed Roper to the pumps and watched him with open curiosity. "I've been wondering why a smart guy like you bought a gas station way out here. Off the beaten track, like they say. Doesn't hardly seem to be enough traffic on this old road to make the place pay. That's why Ed Warner sold out to you, he said."

"I'm not pumping a hell of a lot of gas," Roper admitted. "I really bought the place for the six hundred acres that came along with the station."

"Six hundred acres of the worst real estate God ever created," Perkins declared. "No water. Alkali flats as far as the eye can see. I'll tell you something, Hank: God was pissed off at somebody the day he made this place."

"Well, I've got a hunch the town of Puma's going to grow in this direction, Len. And I bet my hunches."

"Why does a guy with your brains stay in the army?"

"It's a good life for a man like me. All I know is what I've learned in the army. I've got no family, no responsibilities. For a guy who started out with nothing except a pair of fast hands, I've done okay. The service has been good to me."

Perkins's shrewd little eyes took Roper's measure. "I hear you do better than okay. People tell me you've got every racket on the post sewed up. Loan sharking, gambling—all the good stuff."

Roper changed the subject. "Where you headed today?"

"Up to Laramie. Goin' deer hunting with my brother."

Roper capped the gas tank and hung up the hose. "The gas is on the house. Have a good trip."

"Thanks, Hank. I'll pay double next time." Perkins climbed into the pickup. "See you soon," he said, and drove away.

Watching the sheriff head his big Chevy pickup north toward Laramie, Roper found himself annoyed by the man's nickel-and-dime thievery. Perkins always said, 'I'll pay double next time,' but of course he never did. That was just a little fiction to allow him to feel he wasn't doing anything wrong. Roper didn't mind dealing with larcenous men. He was one himself. But he despised cheap crooks whose horizons were limited to cadging tanks of gas from service stations and chicken croquette lunches from diners.

When he returned to the bungalow Williamson told him, "These kids are good, Hank. They've already penetrated the six-hundred-foot level."

"Yeah, I can see that. For their own sake, I hope they turn back soon."

"Careful, that floor looks slippery."

"I'm watching," Rosemary assured him.

They stopped while Bob drew a notebook and pencil from the pocket of his coveralls. Lowering his head so the helmet light shown down at waist level, he added the chamber they were now in to the map he'd been sketching since they entered the cave. The map showed a classic phreatic formation, a cave system that had been subjected to heavy faulting and folding millions of years ago. As a result, there were enough twists, turns, and "snakes" to satisfy any spelunker.

Despite all the "snakes," plus a difficult bell squeeze that had taken twenty minutes to negotiate, they had made excellent time. The batteries on their helmet lights would last at least four more hours, so they could safely spend another hour in exploration.

"Okay, let's go." Bob shoved the notebook into his pocket and took the lead as they entered a smaller passageway almost cramped enough to be considered a squeeze. Within seconds they were crawling on hands and knees through a downgrade passage no more than three feet high.

"Bob, do you smell something?"

"Yeah."

"Water?" Rosemary asked.

"You're right. It's damp in here. But that doesn't make sense. These caves are as dry as old bones. No stalactites or other speleothems." Bob shook his head. "I think this squeeze is about to end. Maybe then we'll find out what that smell is."

Soon they emerged into the largest chamber they had yet discovered. There were still no stalactites, even though the dampness was more pervasive than ever. Bob paused to record the squeeze they had just passed through. Then they stood and began exploring this new chamber, both of them fascinated by its jet black walls.

"I've never seen cave walls like these." Bob removed his gloves and rubbed the walls with the palms of his hands. "So smooth. Almost as if they've been painted black. See how the black stops right here where the walls meet the floor?"

"Weird," Rosemary agreed. She shone her lamp around the chamber. "Bob, look at that! A pit!"

"Where?"

She held the light steady to guide him.

"Jesus! Rosemary, come here!"

She knelt beside him at the pit, which covered about a quarter of the chamber floor. Bob unzipped his coveralls to fumble in his pants pocket. He pulled out a quarter and dropped it into the pit. While he straightened his clothes, he listened for the quarter to hit bottom.

There was no sound at all.

"This is a hell of a deep one, Rosemary."

She was staring at the walls again. "You know what? I think someone actually did paint these walls black."

"That's impossible. Why would anyone do such a thing?"

"I don't know." She seized on a wild idea. "Maybe so that anyone coming into this chamber might miss the pit. It sort of blends into the wall, doesn't it? We almost missed it ourselves, despite its size."

"No, hon, that doesn't make sense. It's a unique formation, that's all."

"I suppose so." Rosemary checked her watch. "Bob, we should be backtracking."

"Yeah . . . sure." He was reluctant to leave. "Okay, we'll come back tomorrow with cameras and pit gear. I want to get this place on film. Wait, do you hear that?" He lay flat on his stomach and lowered his head into the pit.

"Bob, be careful."

"Ssshhh. Be quiet and listen. Do you hear something down there?"

Gingerly, she lay down next to him and cocked her head. In the silence there did seem to be a humming sound.

"What is it?" Bob wondered.

"A motor of some kind?" Rosemary suggested.

"Down there? No." Bob ticked off the possibilities in his mind. "Water. There's an underground stream at the bottom of this pit, I'd bet on it." He was more excited than ever. "This place has never been mapped. It's worth five pages in *The Speleological Review.*" He took out his notebook and carefully drew a diagram of the chamber, noting the location of the pit and tracing the route they had taken into the chamber. He wanted to be able to find the pit tomorrow without any trouble. A deep pit was an incredible find, the spelunker's equivalent of Mount Everest.

Rosemary was still mulling over the sounds from below. "That hum almost sounds like an air-conditioning system."

Bob laughed. "An air conditioner inside a mountain?" He rapped his knuckles on her helmet. "Anyone home in there?"

She laughed, too. An air conditioner. What a silly idea.

The computer display showed two red blips in the chamber eight hundred feet below the opening to the cave system.

"They're too fucking close," Roper said.

"Let's move. We don't know how long they'll stay down there."

While Williamson hung a PUMPS CLOSED sign on the front of the station, Roper drew two Walther PPKs from the armory hidden under the floor of the bungalow. He didn't expect to use the weapons; they were only for backup. Still, from Williamson's description, Halliday was no pimply teenager like the last spelunker who'd decided to explore that cave. He sounded like a well-muscled young man who'd probably put up a good fight, given the chance.

Before locking the bungalow, Roper also pressed the recessed button that slid the painting of the Grand Canyon back in place so that it hid the computer display and turned off the audio alarm.

He gave one of the handguns to Williamson and they climbed into a four-wheel-drive jeep van that waited behind the bungalow. Within two minutes of the decision to cancel and remove, the van was heading into the desert.

Their helmet lights began to dim as they reached the last chamber before the cave entrance. Bob carried spare batteries in his backpack, but didn't like to use them except in a genuine emergency. Instead, he urged Rosemary to move faster.

She did so readily. "I'll be glad to get out of here. The more I think about that pit, the funnier I feel. There's something wrong in there, Bob. Something really strange. Maybe we should ask around about this mountain before we come back."

"You'll feel better when we're in that nice cool hotel swimming pool. Hey, I just realized—we've been married two weeks *today*. It's our anniversary!"

"Do I get a present?"

"Yeah, sure. I'm going to do one of my perfect swan dives for you."

"My hero."

"I mean it. I'll do an all-time-perfect-Tarzan-eat-your-heart-out swan dive. That's a promise."

Bob emerged blinking into the desert sunlight. He

was removing his helmet when two pairs of hands grasped his arms from either side. "Hey—" He was yanked away from the cave entrance. "What the hell is this?" He dug in his feet and wrenched backward, but the hands propelled him forward at a quickening pace.

As his eyes adjusted to the light, he saw to his left the beefy face of the gas station attendant straining in grim determination. To his right was a shorter but more muscular man with a flat, menacing profile. "What is this, a robbery?"

Directly ahead, the ground fell away to a straight drop of about five hundred feet.

"No!" Bob struggled harder as their purpose became clear. "Rosemary, run! For God's sake, run!"

He was pushed forward and the hands released him. He twisted around, but his feet found no purchase. Gray rocks whizzed past his face. His body revolved effortlessly in the air. The realization that he was falling headfirst with his arms outstretched brought a shriek of hysterical laughter from his throat. This was it! The perfect swan dive he'd promised Rosemary. Absolutely perf—

The shriek died with him as he hit an outcropping of granite near the foot of the mountain.

"Bob?" A man seized her and Rosemary was too frightened to struggle. Something terrible had happened to Bob. There had been a horrible cry in his distinct voice. A chilling sound. But the sun was so bright . . . the rising desert heat so intense . . . she couldn't function.

"Come on, sweet thing. Let's see what you got for old Harry." A pair of rough hands pulled down the zipper of her coveralls and slid into her pants, thrusting for her crotch.

"Where's Bob?" she asked in a tremulous voice. "Where's my husband?"

"Knock it off." Roper shoved Williamson aside and zipped up Rosemary's coveralls. "This is supposed to look like an accident, remember?" He took Rosemary's arm and walked her to the edge without Williamson's help. Even now, as she looked down the mountain at the crumpled body of her husband, she uttered no sound and made no effort to struggle. She was in shock, her body trembling like a newborn lamb's.

Roper felt a twinge of pity for the girl. So young, and just married. To spare her the horror of a long fall, he grasped Rosemary Halliday's jaw and gave her head a brutal snap. Her neck broke with a brittle sound and she slumped forward. He allowed the lifeless body to plunge to the rocks below.

"Waste of good ass," Williamson declared.

"You're pussy-whipped anyway. Come on, I don't want to be at this all day."

They made their way back down the mountainside to the spot where the Hallidays lay within a few feet of each other. It took only a few minutes to conduct a thorough search of the Hallidays' clothing. The only items they removed from either body were the map Bob Halliday had drawn of the cave system and the keys to his rented dune buggy. Then they rolled each of the still forms into separate plastic body bags and loaded the bags into their van.

Williamson drove the van. Roper used Halliday's keys to start the dune buggy and followed the van to the main road, where Williamson turned north.

They drove forty miles to a mountainous area at the opposite end of Puma County. Williamson turned off the main road and drove into the desert with Roper following. The sun was now very low, casting enormous shadows between the mountains of central New Mexico. At a flat piece of ground near the base of a sheer mountainside, they stopped and unloaded the body bags. Roper unzipped the bags and arranged the Hallidays to look as if they'd fallen together from near the top. He left the keys in the dune buggy and climbed into the van with Williamson. Then they drove off.

As the van bumped along over the rocky ground, Roper tried to shake off the feeling that he'd made a serious mistake. Canceling out the Hallidays didn't bother him. That was all in a day's work and exactly what Control had ordained for anyone penetrating the six-hundred-foot level. He supposed it was his moment

of pity for the girl that troubled him. Pity was an
emotion he never allowed himself. You start feeling
sorry for people and the next thing that happens is
you're no good at your job. The memory of that mo-
mentary weakness annoyed him so much that he turned
to making small talk with Williamson. "Those kids
should've taken up racquetball."

"You're right. They say that game's real good for the
cardiovascular system."

"Got to be better for you than cave crawling."

Roper tried to purge the Hallidays from his mind,
but couldn't dispel the feeling that somewhere along
the line he'd moved just a little too fast.

A few hours later a phone rang in Langley, Virginia, on the desk of a man who already had put in a
twelve-hour day.

"Sir," said the man's secretary, "Bluebird is calling
in with a voice message."

"Put him on my private line and scramble the call."

"Yes, sir."

After a few moments of static, a voice said: "This is
Bluebird? Are we secure?"

"Yes."

"We've had a little problem here."

"Oh?" The man behind the desk hunched forward
anxiously. "Has the site been compromised?"

"It was. The intruders have been canceled out. They
were only spelunkers."

"Who handled the cancellation?"

"Roper and one of his thugs."

"Then I assume the matter is closed."

"Yes," Bluebird replied. "But I thought you should
know about the incident, considering how close we are
to launching the project."

"We should have thought about spelunkers in the
planning stage."

"No one can foresee everything," Bluebird said. "Not
even you."

"Delivery in three days, " the man in Langley, Virginia, continued. "Are you ready?"

"Affirmative." Bluebird chuckled. "Just like the old days, isn't it?"

"Better than the old days. You'll check in again tomorrow?"

"I will. Good night."

"Good night, Bluebird." The man in Langley put down the phone with a sense of satisfaction he hadn't felt in a long time.

WEDNESDAY, JUNE 11

Chapter 2

He lay on the bunk with arms and legs akimbo, sleeping hard, when a thick set of knuckles rapped on the door.

"Sergeant Major? It's five hundred hours."

Ansel Burke snorted and raised his head. "Say again?"

"Five . . . hundred . . . hours!"

"Okay, you don't have to shout." Burke swung his legs over the bunk and planted them solidly on the hardwood floor. The cool polished wood curled his toes. "Yeah, I'm up. Thanks, Lou."

"Anytime, Sergeant Major."

Lou Brodsky was an old-timer, a sergeant first class who talked nostalgically about "the brown shoe army" and got ritualistically drunk every payday. He never called Burke "Sarge." It was always the full rank: "Sergeant Major." Brodsky was also the only man left in America with a crew cut.

Burke stared blearily around, trying to recall what it was he had to do this morning. Then he remembered that he was scheduled to testify at Corporal Feeney's court-martial. Poor Feeney. He was certain to draw a minimum of two years in Leavenworth, no matter how artfully Burke might be able to shade his testimony.

He rose with a complaining groan and raised the shades on the two windows in his small room, flooding it with pale dawn light. The best features of the room—the only features, for that matter—were two huge

21

windows overlooking the main parade grounds of Fort Powell, New Mexico. Because he was a senior noncom, Burke occupied a spacious corner room on the second floor of the barracks. The building was adobe, one of the first structures built when the post was established in 1884 to protect settlers from Apache raiders from Mexico. For an army barracks it had a rough charm.

An easel had been placed directly in front of one of the windows with such care that it might have been a prop in a play. Burke lifted the cover from a large canvas and frowned at half-formed images. "Shit-oh-dear," he muttered. "Still too much yellow. When will I learn?"

He threw the cloth over the canvas and reached for his shaving kit.

Twenty minutes later Sergeant Major Ansel Burke left his cubicle in the south wing of the Military Police barracks and walked through the squad room between rows of sleeping soldiers toward the mess hall in the opposite wing. He was dressed in his best Class A summers, and his shoes were polished to a high, black gloss. The brass on his collars, MP brass with the crossed pistols insignia, gleamed. On his sleeves Burke wore the rank of a sergeant major; three stripes above three rockers with a diamond in the center. Each was a blood stripe, earned in combat.

He loved the feel of an army barracks in the last few minutes before the CQ turned on the overhead lights and blew his shrill whistle. He loved the rows of neatly aligned footlockers; the aroma of the first coffee of the day drifting into the squad rooms from the mess hall; the snores and wistful dream-sighs of the sleeping troopers. Above all, he loved the feeling of being in the one place in the world where he fully belonged.

Ansel Burke looked as if he belonged in the army. He was big and imposing in a way that drew stares from men as well as women—six-foot two with a craggy Mount Rushmore head, prideful eyes, enormous worn hands, oxen shoulders, and stubborn features weathered by combat and his thirty-eight years, nineteen of them as a soldier.

The mess hall Burke entered was frantic with prep-
arations for breakfast. In the kitchen the cooks in
fresh whites shouted at each other as they broke doz-
ens of eggs into steel pots and lined up loaves of bread
for toast. KPs filled stainless steel coolers with milk
and lugged heavy containers of silverware into the
dining room. Burke made his way through the bedlam
of the kitchen to help himself to a cup of coffee from
one of several enormous pots on the stove.

"Mornin', Ansel," said Mess Sergeant Jacob Winkler.
"I got some nice sausage for ya. Or I can put a steak
on the grill. Steak and eggs. How's that sound?"

"Steak and eggs for the troops too?"

"Nah, the taxpayers ain't that generous. But the
troops get sausage with their eggs today. That ain't
too bad, is it? Don't worry, I always got a prime New
York strip for the sergeant major."

"Maybe later. I just came by to remind you we've got
a new CO. If he gets a good breakfast, maybe he won't
break my hump on his first day."

"I don't need no remindin'. I've handled more new
COs than I got hairs on my ass." Jake took Burke's
arm and led him into the dining room out of the KPs'
earshot. "I been askin' around about our new CO.
First Lieutenant Walter Sloane is a West Point man.
Graduated just two years ago near the bottom of his
class. No wife. Spent the last year as an instructor in
the artillery school at Fort Sill. Got his silver bar just
last week, along with a transfer here. Didn't want a
transfer into the MPs, but he had to take the billet
because his last efficiency report didn't smell too sweet.
Oh, he's gonna be a proper bastard, Ansel. A prick
with ears. Mark what I say."

"I'll bet you can even tell me what he likes for
breakfast."

"Eggs and sausage," Jake said triumphantly.

"Your coffee's awfully good this morning."

"I bought a pound of gold reserve with my own
money. Start a new CO off with his favorite breakfast
and a great cup of coffee, and he's yours for life. That's
the secret of my success."

"You're the last of the great suck artists, Jake. But

I've been collecting background on the man myself. It seems Sloane likes his eggs sunny-side up, not scrambled."

Jake gaped at him. "You certain of that?"

"I got it from a buddy at Sill. He told me everything there is to know about Sloane, right down to his shoe size: ten and a half."

The mess sergeant wheeled and charged into his kitchen. "Corporal, hold them eggs! You ain't broken them all, have you? Sweet Jesus. Run over to A Company and borrow a dozen, and move your lazy ass!"

Burke left the mess sergeant screaming at his cooks and went across the quadrangle to the provost marshal's headquarters in the post stockade. A desk sergeant was stationed just inside the building to book prisoners and take phone complaints from the civilian police in Puma, the town nearest to Fort Powell. Farther down the corridor were the communications center, the armory where MPs checked out their .45s before going on duty, and the offices of the provost marshal and the sergeant major. The provost marshal also served as the Military Police company commander.

Burke's office was standard GI issue—metal desks and chairs, a row of green filing cabinets, photo of the President on the wall next to a huge map of Fort Powell, and in the corner an American flag and company guidon in upright holders.

He greeted Brodsky more civilly than he had earlier and went to his desk, where a stack of night patrol reports awaited him. He scanned them to see what antics the troops of Fort Powell had been up to overnight. The first item that caught his eye was the arrest report on a Private First Class Jeanette Knox, who had been picked up on the main post stark naked and in a drunk-and-disorderly condition. Somehow Pfc. Knox had managed to shinny up to the top of the flagpole in front of the PX, where she was found howling at the moon. The MPs coaxed her down, wrapped her in a blanket, and took her to the stockade.

He flipped through the next reports, which were more routine. Someone had stolen the batteries out of four jeeps in the Camp Funston motor pool. Two

A.W.O.L. recruits had been picked up on Route 41 trying to hitchhike to Albuquerque. Several gunshots had been heard up on Custer Hill, but the MP patrol in the area had not been able to determine where the shots came from, or whether there really had been any "unauthorized target practice." Probably there had been, Burke decided. Soldiers love their guns. Especially infantrymen. And Custer Hill was headquarters for the 31st Infantry Division.

"Shit-oh-dear," he murmured. The last report in the stack meant real trouble. One of the historical displays at Fort Powell was an old World War I howitzer that sat on a hilltop in front of the post theater. During the night someone had removed the chocks that held the howitzer's wheels in place and pushed it downhill. It had careered along for more than a hundred yards before falling onto an auxiliary road below, where it lost a wheel and tipped over. No one saw the men who set loose the cannon, but the job would have taken at least two. The MP who discovered the artillery piece missing also found eleven empty beer cans at the top of the hill.

Unfortunately, the antique howitzer was the pride and joy of the post commander, Major General Claude Leland, who considered it a symbol of the past glories of the United States Army. The old cannon was cleaned and polished every day. Its original wooden wheels had been replaced by sparkling chrome, and a team of four matched white stallions had been trained to pull the howitzer and its caisson in parades. General Leland would foam at the mouth like a mad dog when he learned that his favorite toy had been trashed.

"Lou!"

"I already got Amos Biggs working on it, Sergeant Major. He said to tell you that you can have his stripes if he don't bring in the troopers who broke the general's toy by sixteen hundred hours."

"I'll *take* them, too. General Leland'll bust me down to E-1 if I don't throw *somebody* in the stockade, and I mean right away."

Private First Class Wilson Holland appeared at the desk and put his patrol report down in front of Burke.

"Here you go, Sarge. Another brilliant report from the most underrated soldier in this man's army."

"We don't say 'this man's army' anymore, Holland. Not since we got so many women in the ranks. And you can eighty-six the commercial message. Your promotion to corporal will come through when there's a T.O. and E. slot and not before." As he reviewed Holland's report, a ripple of anger rose in his throat. "What's this? You only patrolled thirty miles last night? I could do better on a bicycle."

"Quiet night, Sarge. What else can I say?"

Burke stared balefully at the young private first class. "Did you find a card game last night? Is that it?"

Holland opened his mouth, then shut it and said nothing.

"At least you're not a liar." Burke initialed the report while he considered what to do with Holland. "I'll let it slide just this once. But if you fuck off on me again I'll ship you over to Wolfe Heinzman in the Thirty-first Infantry. How'd you like to soldier for Wolfe? I might tell him to put you to work pulling targets on the firing range. Ever been down in the trench behind the targets?"

"No, Sergeant."

"It can be kind of exciting. You got rifle fire coming in about ten inches above your head. Most of the time you're safe enough down there in the trench. But once in a while, every six or eight weeks, a round hits one of those wooden target frames just wrong and then— ricochet. One young trooper lost an ear last month to a wild round. You heard about that?"

Holland nodded solemnly.

"You could loose more than an ear soldiering for Wolfe Heinzman. You might even lose that big swinging dick you like to brag about. Think about that the next time you feel like fucking off on patrol." He jerked his thumb at the door. "Dismissed."

When Holland had gone, Brodsky said, "I love the way you kick ass, Sergeant Major."

"Well, I've had plenty of practice." Burke looked at his watch. Almost 6:00 A.M. On impulse he picked up his phone and dialed an off-post number in Puma. The phone rang half a dozen times before it was answered.

"Mzzupfh . . . uh, hullo?" a sleepy voice said.

The sound of her voice made him idiotically happy. "Hi, Maggie."

"Ansel? Is that you? What time is it, anyway?"

"Almost six o'clock."

"In the morning? My God, what's wrong?"

"Nothing. I just wanted to tell you what a great time I had last night. You've got to be the sexiest woman in New Mexico."

Maggie Winston yawned sweetly. "Darling, why limit me?" She groaned. "Look, I appreciate the accolade, but couldn't you have saved it for a more civilized hour?"

"I had an idea. Let's drive into Albuquerque tonight and have dinner at Pancho's."

"Sounds good. Can I go back to sleep now?"

"Sure."

Maggie yawned again. "What's it like to be a soldier and be up and around every morning before six?"

"It's sort of like—"

"Never mind, I don't really want to know. I'm sure it's awful. See you tonight, lover."

Burke put down the receiver carefully, as if a moment's clumsiness might damage both the phone and his warm glow. He was suspicious of his happiness. Never in his life had good fortune lasted very long. Every decent year had been followed by a disastrous one. Things had been going well for eighteen months now. His run of luck had started the day he sold his first picture, the one of the Rancho de Taos church, followed up the next month when he met Maggie at an art gallery in Albuquerque. Too good, he thought morosely. *Things have been too good for too damned long. I'm in for a shitstorm any day now.*

The premonition made him shiver.

A shrill blast from the CQ's whistle called the MP company to reveille.

Brodsky picked up his clipboard and strode outdoors to the quadrangle in front of Military Police headquarters. Burke followed. As sergeant major he no longer

had to take reveille, but he always enjoyed Brodsky's
early morning performances. The grizzled old noncom
was smart and experienced, but on occasion he sounded
like Casey Stengel on an especially confused day.

About ninety MPs took reveille. They were standing
in two formations of four ranks each, yawning and
staring around with bleary eyes. Most were dressed in
green fatigues. Those who wore Class As would be
going on morning patrol. Or on prison chaser duty. Or
out to guard gates in the restricted areas of the post.
Their collective youth annoyed Burke, who lately had
begun to feel like the proverbial Old Soldier.

The sun was above the horizon, a red ball of fire
already starting to scorch the desert floor. On the
easel in his room stood the beginnings of a still life of
a mountain ranch house festooned with strings of chilies ripening in the sun. He'd been working on the
picture for two weeks and having a hell of a time
making it come alive. Now he saw why. The problem
was in the shade of red he was using for the chilies.
Seeing the exact color he needed made him itch to get
at his canvas, but that would have to wait.

"Ten-*hut!*" Brodsky barked. "Report."

"First platoon all present or accounted for."

"Second platoon all present or accounted for."

Brodsky made a notation on his clipboard. "Good
morning, gentlemens. Stand at ease. I got a complaint
here from Colonel Higgins's wife. She says somebody's
been pissing on the flowers in front of the Bachelor
Officers Quarters. She's sure that's why they're dying.
She thinks some junior officer is coming back to the
BOQ drunk every night and relieving himself on them
posies, which Mrs. Higgins planted herself. She wants
us to run a patrol by there every half hour between
twenty-one hundred and twenty-four hundred hours to
catch the guy who's hosing them down. Carmichael,
you got the piss patrol."

There was a single groan from the ranks and a lot of
laughter.

"Quiet down, gentlemens." Brodsky squinted at his
notes. "We lost the batteries out of four jeeps in the
Camp Funston motor pool last night, so let's double up

on patrols there. Meanwhile, I'm checking the service stations in Puma to see if anyone from Powell is trying to peddle batteries. I don't know what's wrong with the young troopers around here. In the old brown shoe army we didn't bother with batteries. We stole the whole fuckin' jeep."

Brodsky squinted at the next sheet on his clipboard.

"I got some complaints that too many troops on the main post are ignoring retreat. Now gentlemens, the loudspeakers on the main post call retreat every afternoon at seventeen hundred hours. When that happens, the troops are supposed to come to attention. We call retreat every day of the year in the U.S. Army. That's . . ." He groped for the correct number. "That's three hundred and twenty days a year! So I want'cha to write up any trooper who ignores retreat. You got that? Okay."

Brodsky consulted the duty roster.

"Today there'll be five patrols up on Custer Hill and four at Camp Funston. Ten on main post. Four in Puma. Seven men on the gates. Five working prison chaser. See me if you got any questions about the duty roster." Brodsky lowered his clipboard. "Now, listen up. You all know we got a new CO. He's gonna be taking a good look at everybody, so I want you troopers to stand tall. Anybody fucks up, they got the sergeant major to answer to. That's all for this morning, gentlemens. Atten-*hut!* Dismissed."

As they walked back into MP headquarters together, Brodsky seemed preoccupied. Finally he said, "How much stockade time d'ya think Feeney'll draw?"

Burke was aware that Brodsky and Feeney were old drinking buddies, which was one of the reasons Burke regretted having to testify at Feeney's court-martial. "A couple of years, and not in the stockade. They'll send him to the federal prison at Leavenworth."

"Bastards. They oughtta give Feeney a medal for what he did to Lulu's. That place was a clip joint from day one. But how do you know they'll send him to Leavenworth? Maybe they'll just dump Feeney in the Fort Powell stockade for a few months."

"Not this time. General Leland's taken a personal

interest in the case. He's even sitting on the court-
martial board."

"Then you're right," Brodsky said gloomily. "It's Leavenworth for Feeney."

Staff Sergeant Amos Biggs hated driving a jeep. His
beer belly, which had taken a lifetime to nurture into
its present magnificence, was jammed so tightly behind the steering wheel he could hardly breathe. And
he hated the desert almost as much as he hated driving a jeep. People kidded him about that. Everyone
thought he should be acclimated to hot weather because of his "African heritage." Which was bullshit.
Amos Biggs was raised on Amsterdam Avenue in Harlem and liked the New York winters better than the
summers. The colder the better, as far as he was concerned. So naturally the army sent him to New Mexico.

Biggs parked outside the squat adobe building hous-
ing the headquarters of the 31st Infantry Division,
unwedged himself from the jeep and went into the
division office. Sitting behind the desk making out his
morning report was Sergeant Major Wolfe Heinzman.
No one had ever looked less natural behind a desk. In
crisp fatigues and spit-shined field boots, Heinzman
most resembled a bear dressed up for a circus act.

His voice was bearlike, too. "Biggs! Vat you vant up
here on Custer Hill, you fat pig?"

Heinzman was an East German who had been drafted
into the army at eighteen and found that he loved the
life but hated his Russian masters. At the age of twenty-
three Heinzman deserted from the East German Army,
tunneled under the Berlin Wall, and asked the West
German government for political asylum. Later he
emigrated to America and joined the U.S. Army in
time for Vietnam, where he earned most of the decorations they were handing out over there.

Biggs wouldn't have cared to serve under Heinzman;
he gave the top soldier of the 31st Infantry a wide
berth except when he needed his help. This was one of
those times.

"You heard what happened to the general's howitzer? I'm investigating that little romp."

"You think somebody from the Thirty-first tip over that damned thing?"

"Could be." Biggs took out the notes he'd made. "We found a pile of empty Budweiser cans near the spot where the 105 was on display. They don't sell Bud at the PX or any of the N.C.O. or EM Clubs. The beer was bought off post in Puma. I checked the liquor stores there. Two guys in civilian clothes, but with Thirty-first Infantry pins on their shirt pockets, bought four six-packs of Bud last night. They were already a little high, which is why the store owner remembers them. I'd be interested to know which of your men checked out passes last night."

"I think I vant to know, too."

Heinzman picked up the phone and began calling each of the three regimental headquarters in his division. The pass system in the 31st Division was simple. Anyone who wanted to leave the post had to sign out at his regimental office. If a man's name wasn't on a duty roster, he was issued his pass. A soldier could stay off post all night, so long as he appeared at reveille the next morning. Through this system Heinzman could quickly learn the name of every trooper who had gone into town last night.

When he finished with his calls, Heinzman looked at Biggs with cold eyes. "I think ve got them. Two men in the Twenty-eighth Regiment check out passes last night. Pfc.s Hill and Selecki. The CQ in the Twenty-eighth tell me Hill and Selecki come in drunk last night. Raise hell in barracks. Don't say vere they been, but grin and laugh about something. Big secret."

Biggs was delighted. "You just turn them over to me, Wolfe. I'll find out what they've been up to."

Heinzman shook his bullet head. "I vant them first."

"No way! Ansel Burke will roast my balls if I don't bring in these guys."

"I vant them for one hour."

Biggs refused, but Heinzman was adamant. They were still arguing the matter when the two privates appeared in the doorway of Heinzman's office. Biggs took one look and knew he had his men. Both privates bore the telltale signs of a hangover and their eyes were jumpy with guilt.

"You two come here," Heinzman commanded. "Vere you go last night?"

The one with HILL on his name tag stuttered out an answer: "We just hung around the enlisted men's club, Sarge."

"Stupid lie. Everyone in barracks know you vent off post. And if you stay at fort, how come you check out passes?"

"We were gonna leave the post, but we changed our minds," Selecki insisted.

At first Biggs had felt sorry for them. Now that they were stonewalling, he lost all pity. "You guys went into town and bought beer, then came back to the main post and sat around on that old 105 drinking yourselves blind." He patted his massive belly. "I know because I've done the same myself a few times. Then you decided to have a little fun, push that old piece of iron downhill. Somebody shoulda told you young troopers how much General Leland loves his howitzer."

"We didn't do it!" Hill insisted.

Heinzman went to his office closet and took out two brooms from a supply of eight or ten that he kept in there. He thrust the brooms at Hill and Selecki. "Sveep the verevolf."

The two Pfc.s stared at him in horror.

"No, please," Selecki pleaded.

"Sveep the verevolf," Heinzman repeated.

"We wrecked the howitzer!" Selecki blurted out. "We're the ones."

Hill glared at his buddy. "Shut up, Tom!"

"I'm not going up there," Selecki declared.

"Yes you vill," Heinzman promised.

"But we did it," Selecki admitted. "I'll sign a statement."

"I know you vill. But first you sveep the verevolf." Heinzman forced the brooms on them. "Go." He pointed out the window at the rocky crest of Custer Hill, where the ferocious likeness of a werewolf, the symbol of the 31st Infantry, The 'Werewolf Division' was painted across the rocky ground.

Since Heinzman was ignoring him anyway, Biggs agreed to what he wanted. "Okay, you can have these two guys for now, but deliver them to me at the stockade by eleven hundred."

"Jah." Heinzman grinned.

As Biggs returned to his jeep, Hill and Selecki were beginning the long climb to the peak of Custer Hill. Once again Biggs reflected that he wouldn't care to serve under Wolfe Heinzman. When the German got hold of troublemakers he sent them up the hill to sweep any drifting sand from the werewolf's fierce likeness. The peak of Custer Hill swarmed with rattlesnakes as long as bullwhips. They lived in the fissures between the rocks and hated to be disturbed when they came out to warm themselves in the morning sun. Enough men had been bitten by snakes up there so that the words *sweep the verevolf* struck fear in the toughest troopers. Biggs just hoped Heinzman would be able to deliver Hill and Selecki to him, instead of to the hospital.

On the drive back to the main post Biggs noticed three turkey vultures circling in the air off to the south, which surprised him. Vultures were sort of rare. That was one of the few things he'd learned about the desert. Must be something bigger than a dead rabbit out there, he decided.

When he came to the unmarked dirt road leading out to the artillery range, a wasteland pocked with craters from fifty years of target practice by big guns, Biggs stopped the jeep and considered going out to see what the vultures had found. He had to kill about an hour anyway. If he showed up at the stockade too far ahead of his prisoners, Burke would scorch his ass for letting Heinzman have first crack at them. Besides, there were two cold beers on ice in a cooler under his seat and he needed a quiet place to drink them.

Biggs turned up the dirt road. He wasn't worried about artillery fire. On days that the range was in use, MPs were posted as guards on the access roads. He drove three miles, keeping an eye on the circling birds, until two of them dropped down to take a closer look at whatever was out there. Stopping, he climbed pon-

derously from the jeep and dragged the cooler out with
him. It was the smallest he could find, holding just
two cans of beer and enough ice to keep them cold for
several hours. He opened one of the beers and drank
deeply.

"Sheeit, that's good."

Biggs wiped his sweaty brow with his shirt sleeve
and peered across the desert. Those birds were getting
ready for a feast all right, and on something that lay
about a hundred yards out from the road. He took
another pull on the beer, almost emptying it.

Miserable fucking place. Thousands of square miles
of parched earth. The only thing in New Mexico he
admired were those mountains off to the north, the
Sangre de Cristos, which meant the Blood of Christ.
Biggs had been raised in the Abyssinian Baptist Church
and remained in awe of any object named for the
Saviour.

He took a pair of binoculars from the jeep and focused them on the towering mountains, trying to discern why the early Spanish settlers had given them
such a name. They certainly weren't red, at least not
this far south. Baffled, he lowered the binoculars and
refocused them on the spot where all the vultures
finally had settled. It looked to Biggs as if they were
just starting on their free lunch.

The image came into focus.

At first Biggs doubted his eyes. He dropped the beer
can and used both hands to focus the field glasses
more sharply.

"Holy shit—"

What he saw was a human arm and leg. Biggs
dragged his Colt .45 from its holster, flicked the safety
back with his thumb and fired the weapon into the air
twice.

The vultures reacted to the shots by taking to the
air with a panicky flapping of wings. When they were
clear, Biggs took a longer, more concentrated look. He
could see the whole body now, or what was left of it. A
woman's body, he thought. Bloody and blistered from
the sun. The white ground around the corpse glistened
red. The heat had caused the blood to coagulate in

shiny patches instead of soaking into the ground, creating a reddish halo that shimmered in the air above the corpse. The effect was so unearthly that Biggs thought he knew how those nearby mountains had gotten their name.

"*Sangre de Cristo,*" he said, reaching for the radio in his jeep.

Chapter 3

"Name and rank?"

"Ansel Burke. Sergeant Major. Fort Powell Military Police headquarters."

"Were you on duty at MP headquarters on the evening of April tenth?"

"Yes, sir, I was."

"And did you receive a call from the county sheriff's office on that evening regarding a disturbance near the Puma city limits?"

"I did."

"Sergeant Burke, please tell us the nature of the disturbance and the subsequent events related to the sheriff's phone call."

Burke wished he didn't have to give the evidence that would send Sean Feeney to Leavenworth. Feeney was a drunk and something of a disgrace to his uniform. But fifteen years ago Feeney had won two silver stars and a bronze star, so he must have been a helluva soldier in his time.

"Sergeant Burke, did you hear the question?"

The prosecutor stood over him, tapping his foot. The members of the court-martial board leaned forward. And Feeney's defense counsel, a pretty young woman with the rank of captain, frowned at him. She had to be new to the Fort Powell J.A.G. office since Burke didn't know her. Only Corporal Sean Feeney seemed indifferent to the proceedings. The slight, pug-nosed Irishman was staring out the window of the courtroom

with the wistful look of a man who knew his next
drink was a long time away.

"I'm sorry," Burke said at last. "I was just recon-
structing the events in my mind. Yes, I did receive a
call from the sheriff's office that night. I was told that
an army tank had been seen on Route 52 coming from
the direction of Fort Powell. Not only was the tank on
the highway, it was weaving all over the place and
running cars off the road.

"I was also told that the tank had turned off Route
52 onto Hastings Road just outside the town of Puma
and was reported to have attacked an establishment
on Hastings Road known as Lulu's Place. I might add
that Lulu's Place is—or was—a well-known house of
prostitution."

"Sergeant, define what you mean by the word
attacked," the prosecutor said.

Burke was beginning to enjoy the effect of his testimony on the court-martial board. A couple of the officers were squirming. General Leland had dropped his
eyes to the table. Everyone recognized that it would be
necessary to hear testimony about Corporal Feeney's
activities in order to convict him, but no one really
wanted to listen. Feeney's adventures had caused serious community relations problems for the post. Well,
fuck them, Burke thought. If they want to send Feeney
away, they'll have to listen to the embarrassing details.

"Yes, sir. Witnesses said the tank drove up onto the
porch of the whorehouse—"

"House of prostitution." The prosecutor was a newly
promoted captain with glittery eyes and obvious ambitions. He'd earned his bars by sending a soldier to
Leavenworth for stealing ten dollars from his bunkmate.

"All right. The tank drove up onto the porch, destroying most of the face of the building. The driver
then traversed his gun from left to right, knocking
down the beams supporting the second floor of the
building, which promptly collapsed, pretty much wreck-
ing the house."

"Sergeant Burke," said the prosecutor, "did you personally investigate this incident?"

"Yes, I did. Immediately after receiving the call I

drove to Lulu's Place. I found a lot of mostly undressed men and women either fleeing the house or attempting to free themselves from the wreckage." For Feeney's benefit, Burke added, "Fortunately, no one was hurt. Excuse me, that's not quite true. One whore—uh, prostitute—had a broken leg. She'd been in bed with this guy—I think he was a city councilman from Puma—when the floor shifted and the two of them—"

"There's no need to be anecdotal," General Leland said, invoking his position as president of the court-martial board.

"Yes, sir. As I was saying, six witnesses told me that an army tank had indeed caused the damage. They reported the tank had left Hastings Road and headed overland, instead of along the highway, back toward Fort Powell."

"Did you know at that time who was driving the tank?" the prosecutor asked.

"I talked to Lulu Watson, the proprietor of the house. She claimed that Sean Feeney, one of her regular customers, had been in her establishment earlier in the evening. Feeney had been drunk and complained about the quality of the service. It seems he'd paid for a round-the-world trip, but all the girl did was let him get his cock wet. Before leaving, he threatened to get even with Lulu."

"Sergeant Burke, I won't warn you again," General Leland said.

"I'm sorry, sir." Burke worked an aggrieved look onto his face. "I'm just trying to make the situation clear for everyone."

"Continue," the prosecutor said, "but bring out the facts without using objectionable language."

Burke shrugged. "Anyway, I knew Feeney from around the post. I knew he was a tank driver in the Thirty-ninth Armored Battalion, so I drove back to the post and headed for Camp Funston, where the Thirty-ninth is headquartered. The tanks are parked in a fenced-in area near the barracks. I noticed that the fence had been broken down in one section. There were tank tracks across the wreckage of the fence. On one tank"—Burke consulted his notes—"an Abrams

M1 tank, number 571, the engine cowling was still
warm.

"I went inside the barracks and located Corporal
Feeney asleep in his bunk. His clothes were still on.
He smelled of liquor. I woke him with some difficulty
and asked if he'd taken the tank off post. He said, 'Lulu
should've treated me better.' I went to the company
office and found out that Feeney's tank was number
571. After getting him sobered up enough to walk, I
placed him under arrest and took him to the stockade."

Burke closed his notebook and put it back in his
pocket.

"Thank you, Sergeant." The prosecutor turned triumphantly to the defense table. "Your witness, Captain Silk."

So her name was Silk. Burke approved of the name.
He liked her looks too. Captain Silk was a lively little
redhead with a freckled face and the quick, confident
movements of an athlete. She advanced on Burke as if
he were a rabbit already in her snare. "Sergeant, did
Corporal Feeney say anything to you other than 'Lulu
should've treated me better'?"

"No, he didn't. Once I got him sober enough to walk,
he shut his mouth completely."

"Then at no time has Corporal Feeney admitted that
he drove a tank off post and used it to destroy Lulu's
Place?"

"That's correct."

"Sergeant Burke, did you check the engine cowling
on every tank in the Thirty-ninth Armored Battalion?"

Shit-oh-dear, he thought. She's got me there. "No,
Captain, I didn't. I checked maybe six out of the twenty
tanks in the compound. When I found one with a hot
engine, I figured I'd found the tank that flattened
Lulu's."

"Then a tank other than the one for which Corporal
Feeney had the key could have been used?"

"Yes, I suppose that's possible."

"And none of the witnesses to the destruction of
Lulu's Place saw who was driving the tank or noticed
the serial number painted so prominently on the side
of every armored vehicle on this post?"

"No, they sure didn't."

Captain Silk seemed to have a sudden thought. "Then perhaps, Sergeant, the tank could even have come from somewhere other than Fort Powell. Would you say that's possible?"

Burke chuckled along with the court-martial board, which was clearly delighted to see Captain Silk doing such an inept job of defending Sean Feeney. "Maybe the Mexican army sent a tank over the border to attack Lulu's Place, but that doesn't seem very likely."

Captain Silk went to the defense table and picked up a bound blue document that Burke recognized as an Army Corps of Engineers survey. "You testified that the tank left Fort Powell and went toward Puma on Route 52."

"Yes, ma'am. Every witness I talked with confirmed that."

"But, Sergeant, according to this report from the Army Corps of Engineers, the one bridge that exists between Fort Powell and Route 52 *will under no circumstances support the weight of a tank or armored personnel carrier.*" She turned to the court-martial board. "General Leland, I'd like to enter this report in evidence for the defense."

"I don't see the relevance," General Leland snapped.

"Sir, the relevance is obvious," Captain Silk countered. "Last year the General Services Administration complained that you've wasted millions of dollars in fuel by negligently routing tanks around the bridge that crosses Zuni Creek on the way to the armored firing range. You solicited a report from the Corps of Engineers showing that the detours were necessary because the bridge won't support the weight of tanks. If Sean Feeney did drive a tank into Puma, then the report is wrong and the General Services Administration's accusations are true.

"I'm entering this report in evidence to show that Corporal Feeney could not have driven a tank into Puma. According to the army's own Corps of Engineers, the one bridge leading into town will not support the weight of a tank."

Burke couldn't believe his ears. This young lawyer

was issuing a direct threat to General Leland. If he
convicted Feeney, she'd sic the GSA on him. There
was nothing the board could do. They had to accept
the report in evidence. But from the way General
Leland was looking at Captain Silk, Burke knew she
had no future at Fort Powell.

Captain Silk turned back to him. "Thank you, Sergeant. I have no more questions."

Instead of returning to his office as he'd planned,
Burke took a seat at the rear of the courtroom. He
wanted to see if the little redhead could twist the
general's nose and get away with it.

The proceedings were concluded soon afterward. The
prosecutor called only one more witness, the CQ who
was on duty in the 39th Armored on the night Burke
arrested Feeney. He testified that Feeney usually turned
in the ignition key to his tank when he went off duty,
but that he'd kept it the night Lulu lost her whorehouse. When Captain Silk chose not to put Feeney on
the stand, the court-martial board closed the proceedings and adjourned to reach a verdict.

Because Feeney was under guard he wasn't allowed
to leave the courtroom. When Captain Silk offered to
get him a cup of coffee from the machine down the
hall, Burke fell into step beside her.

"That was a gutsy defense, Captain."

"Why, thank you, Sergeant Burke."

"Do you realize that you just put yourself on General Leland's permanent blacklist?"

"Yes, I know that." She shrugged in a languid way
that Burke found appealing. "But I don't intend to
make a career out of the army, so I don't much care
what he thinks." She looked at Burke with more than
casual interest. "So you're top sergeant of the MPs.
You certainly look the part."

"If you're not RA, then you must have come in
through an R.O.T.C. program," Burke guessed.

"That's right. I'm from New York, but I got an
R.O.T.C. scholarship to the University of Michigan. I
couldn't afford law school any other way."

"How do you like the army?"

"I hate it. Thank God I only have two more years of

active service, then five in the reserve. It's a good trade-off for a law degree." They came to the coffee machine. "Damn, I forgot to ask Feeney if he takes his coffee with cream and sugar."

"I'm pretty sure he drinks it black." Burke dropped a quarter in the machine. "I'll get it."

"Thanks. You seem to know a lot about Feeney."

"It's my job to know the people on this post. That's why I was surprised to see you defending Feeney. Usually I hear right away when we get a new Wac—I mean, female officer—as good looking as you."

"Wac." Captain Silk made a face. "I hate that word. It makes us sound like a bunch of airheads. And do you know what they call the womens barracks here?"

"They call it the Wac Shack," Burke said with a grin. "Female personnel aren't officially known as Wacs anymore, but the name's hung on. Do you mind if I ask your first name?"

"Jean," she said promptly. "And yours is Ansel?"

"That's right."

"Ansel Burke. You're Irish, of course."

"My father was Irish, but my mother's people came from Norway. I grew up in San Francisco."

"Norwegian. That must be where you get your size."

At that moment Captain Jean Silk's red hair caught the light in a way that made Burke catch his breath.

"You must be aware that enlisted men aren't supposed to stare longingly at female officers. At least, not in public."

"I'm sorry," Burke shifted the hot cup of coffee from one hand to the other.

"I'm not telling you to stop. I rather like the way you look at me. I just don't want you to get in trouble for it." Her eyes lit up. "Do you know why I was sent to this godforsaken place?"

"I can only assume that the prayers of thirty thousand Fort Powell soldiers were answered."

"What a nice thing to say. But if that's true, then God does work in mysterious ways. I was in the legal section at the Pentagon until my commanding officer discovered I was going out with an enlisted man. That's *verboten* in the Pentagon, you know. The next day I received orders for Fort Powell." They had almost reached the doors of the courtroom. Jean Silk stopped and said, "Does that give you any ideas?"

Burke had seldom been surprised in so many ways by one woman. "It would. Except that I'm involved with someone right now."

She made a sound that was partly a sigh, partly a chuckle. "Then I guess I've been batting my big blues at you for nothing."

They went inside. Jean Silk gave Feeney his coffee and began telling him in her animated way what a mess the Uniform Code of Military Justice was. From his seat in the rear, Burke heard her complaining that, unlike the U.S. Constitution, the Uniform Code gave every advantage to the police and none to the suspect. She explained to Feeney that the Military Police didn't even have to advise him of his rights and that in a court-martial the judge and jury were one and the same. As she railed against the Uniform Code, Burke began to suspect that the Pentagon had more than one reason for shipping her out to Fort Powell. A lawyer with so many negative opinions about military justice would be about as welcome in the Pentagon as a Russian adviser.

The side door opened and the five members of the court-martial board returned to their places. General Claude Leland was at the center of the group. He was tall and ramrod straight. His arrogant face, all clean lines and smooth planes, was twisted into an expression of disgust.

"Corporal Feeney, please stand," he said.

Feeney rose.

General Leland looked at a sheet of paper in front of him and bit his lip. Then he fixed Sean Feeney with an implacable glare. "The court-martial board finds insufficient evidence to convict you of the charges of willful destruction of private property and theft of government property."

Feeney wheezed out his relief and glanced gratefully at Jean Silk.

"However, we do find that your conduct on the evening of April tenth—the drunkenness and ugly behav-

ior at the public establishment in Puma—to be counter
to the standards of conduct expected from a noncommissioned officer. And so you are hereby reduced in
rank from corporal to private first class." General Leland banged his gavel. "This court-martial board is
adjourned." He stood and left the room before the
other officers could rise from their chairs.

Feeney had enough sense to wait until they were
well outside the courtroom to whoop with joy and
wring Jean Silk's hand. "Captain, you're the best
damned lawyer in the army! You'll get all my business
from now on. That's a promise."

"Do me a bigger favor. Stay out of trouble. You
won't be so lucky next time."

"That's a deal, sir. Uh, ma'am. Ansel, can I buy you
a drink at the N.C.O. Club? I go some celebratin' to
do."

"You sure you want to do that? My testimony almost sent you to Leavenworth."

"Hell, that's your job. You weren't happy about it. I
could see that, and so could his nibs."

"I'll have a drink with you some other time."

"C'mon."

"The N.C.O. Club isn't open yet. And you can't go
into it, anyway. You're a private first class again."

"Oh yeah." Feeney shrugged. "Well, I been busted
before. I'll get those stripes back."

"Not at Fort Powell."

Feeney laughed and licked his lips, his thirst a pal-
pable thing. "I'll see ya both later then. Thanks again,
Captain."

When he left them, Jean Silk seemed dejected. "I've
got a terrible feeling my 'gutsy defense' was all in
vain. Feeney will go to Leavenworth yet. Or at least to
the stockade. He was born for it."

"You're probably right. Feeney's career already in-
cludes two stretches in the stockade. And you'd better
watch out for yourself too. You made a powerful enemy today."

"General Leland? What could he do to me? I'm just
passing through his army."

"Take care of yourself anyway." Burke touched the

bill of his cap. "It was a pleasure watching you work, Captain. See you soon, I hope."

Jean Silk watched Burke walk away, thinking he was an itch she'd never have a chance to scratch.

Burke cut across the quadrangle toward the stockade with his eyes on the flagpole in front of the PX.

"I know you're patriotic, Ansel. But I didn't think you were a fanatic. Keep on watching that flag and you'll walk into a wall."

He dropped his eyes to discover Hank Roper walking in step next to him. "It's not the flag: it's the *pole*. One of our Wacs got drunk last night and shinnied up to the top. I was just wondering how she managed it."

"All female soldiers come equipped with rubberized pussies. Didn't you know that?"

"No, that one slipped past me. What are you doing up so early, Hank? I thought you always stayed in your bunk till noon."

"I'm turning over a new leaf," Roper announced. "Up every morning before eleven and take a thirty-yard walk, whether I need it or not."

Burke only grunted. He didn't like Roper, Roper didn't like him. Most people assumed their antagonism was based on the fact that they were both sergeant majors. He and Roper and Wolfe Heinzman were the only sergeant majors on post. As the highest-ranking noncommissioned officers at Fort Powell, there was bound to be a certain amount of tension between them. There's only room for one king-of-the-hill in any game.

But Burke disliked Roper for a different reason: Roper was a crook. He operated a network of rackets that permeated every unit at Fort Powell. Every payday Roper's shylocks collected money they had loaned out to soldiers at interest rates of 50 percent per month. Burke also suspected that Roper sold transfers to some of the world's more desirable U.S. Army posts. It was rumored that for three thousand dollars Roper could get a man transferred to Schoofield Barracks in Hawaii or the Presidio in San Francisco. If that was true, Roper had a partner in the personnel office. Burke had been trying to identify Roper's accomplice, so far without success.

Roper's primary duty was running the Fort Powell Noncommissioned Officers Club. Burke knew, but again couldn't prove, that Roper also took kickbacks from the liquor dealers who supplied booze to the N.C.O. Club.

"Hey, you interested in the stock market?" Roper took a *Wall Street Journal* from under his arm and pointed out the name of a company he'd underlined in red. "Keep an eye on Shieldstone Enterprises. Surgical equipment. They've invented some kind of new apparatus that makes it safer to do bypass operations. Every surgeon in the country wants one. Put a few bucks into it. You can't go wrong."

"No thanks."

"Why not? You've got some money now, I hear. Sold some of your paintings?"

"That's right."

"How much do you get for one?"

Burke didn't like talking to Roper about that. On the other hand, he couldn't help wanting Roper to know that he was successful, too. Egos, he thought. Everybody's got one, I'm no exception. "Last month my dealer sold one of my paintings for five thousand dollars."

"No shit?" Roper was genuinely impressed. "Way to go. Say, maybe I should buy one myself. Put it away in a vault until you're famous. Quadruple my money. Would you sell me one of your paintings?"

"No."

Roper laughed. "I gotta hand it to you, Ansel. Everything's up front. When you hate a guy's guts, you let him know it."

"That's right. And one of these days I'm going to throw your ass in the stockade. You've got a right to know that too."

Roper ignored the threat. "Take care of yourself, Ansel. And good luck with your painting. I respect a guy who can make money out of a piece of canvas and a tube of paint. I really do."

Burke watched Roper walk off in his cocky gait.

Nobody's perfect, he thought. Roper makes mistakes, too. And the next time he does, I want to be there.

When Burke walked into his office, Brodsky told him, "We got a corpse out on the artillery range. A woman, says Biggs. He's the one who found her."

"Where exactly?"

"Three miles off Custer Hill Road. I've called the Puma sheriff's office and our photo lab. The county coroner's on the way, too."

"Does Biggs think it was an accident?"

"From what he said, it looks like someone killed her."

"Then you'd better call the FBI office in Albuquerque. When there's a murder on a government reservation, they've got the jurisdiction."

"I know the drill. And you know the FBI. They don't give a shit how many people get themselves killed on an army post. We won't see those bastards till Christmas."

"Call them anyway."

As Burke was going out the door, Brodsky said, "How many years did Feeney draw?"

"They found him not guilty."

"Not guilty? That's impossible."

"He had a great lawyer. All they did was bust him one grade."

Brodsky gaped. "I once got busted a grade for not saluting some shavetail lieutenant. Now Feeney gets the same for stealing a tank and knocking down an entire whorehouse. There ain't no sense to it."

"I won't argue with you there.

"Get Biggs on the radio and tell him I'm on my way. Make sure he doesn't touch anything or disturb the area around the body."

"He won't even go near it. She's out in the desert and Biggs is scared of snakes."

Burke pushed his jeep up the road to Custer Hill for all the speed that was in it. He hoped to beat Sheriff Leonard Perkins to the site because the man was a moron who usually mishandled whatever physical evidence he found. Unfortunately, Perkins had little to do except sit in his air-conditioned office drinking Dr.

Pepper and listening to radio calls. Burke arrived to find Perkins's black-and-white police cruiser already parked behind Biggs's jeep.

"What's the story, Amos?"

Biggs hitched up his belt and said, "I noticed a bunch of vultures going round and round up there and decided to see what they found so interesting. There's a dead woman out there and she's naked as the day she was born."

Burke looked out onto the desert floor and saw the portly form of Sheriff Perkins squatting in front of the corpse. "Didn't you get my message to keep the area clear?"

"I'm sorry, Sarge. I told Perkins you didn't want anyone stomping around out there. 'I don't take orders from soldier boys,' he said."

"Okay, you stay put. Corporal Willie Ray, the post photographer, will be here soon. And the coroner. And an ambulance. You make sure everybody circles around and comes up to the crime scene from the opposite side. I don't want people tramping around in the desert between the corpse and the road."

"Got it."

Burke was trying to picture Amos Biggs taking a deep interest in the activities of a few vultures. "What were you really doing out here?"

"Like I said, I was curious about the vultures."

"Sure. And I'm Secretary of the Army." Burke went to Biggs's jeep and looked under the front seat. "Well, now. What have we got here?" He pulled out a small Igloo cooler, pushed back the lid and took out two empty beer cans. "Refreshments?"

"I'm not built for hot weather," Biggs said miserably. "I gotta find ways to stay cool. You see, I nailed the guys who busted up the general's artillery piece, but they belong to Wolfe Heinzman. He wanted to give them his *sveep-the-verevolf* routine before shipping them off to the stockade, so I decided to kill a little time out here." He retreated from Burke's withering look. "Paid off, didn't it?"

"That's the only reason you're not going up on an Article Fifteen. Next time take a thermos of iced tea. I won't have my MPs drinking while they tool around in jeeps. You read me?"

"Whatever you say, Sarge."

Burke nailed him with one more silver-bullet glare, then went out onto the desert. He followed his own instructions, circling around to come up on the corpse from the rear.

"What'sa matter?" Sheriff Perkins called. "You got something against walking in a straight line?"

"You tramped all over the path between the body and the road, Len."

"So what?"

"There might be footprints."

Perkins jiggled his double chin in annoyance. "That's a lotta crap. This is hardpan."

"It's sandier near the road." The hell with you, Burke thought. "What've we got here?"

He looked down on the body of a naked woman so drenched in her own blood that it was difficult at first to locate her wounds. But Burke had seen a lot of death in his time, so he didn't flinch or look away or gag on the stench of rotting flesh. Looking closer, he identified multiple gunshot wounds in her chest, and saw that her throat had been cut. A colony of red ants had started to explore the cavity between her legs and she was covered with insect bites.

"What's that in her mouth?" Perkins asked.

"Her left ear." Burke pointed to the spot where the girl's ear should have been. "It's been cut off and stuffed in her mouth."

"Jesus, why would someone do that?"

"I don't know."

"You fuckin' soldiers, you'll do anything."

"Don't be so damned sanctimonious. Civilians kill each other, too."

"Yeah, but you people got a flare for it." The sheriff rose up from his squatting position and stepped back a pace or two. "I seen more psycho shit at Fort Powell than I care to think about. Remember the warrant officer that cut off his CO's whanger with a trench knife?"

"Sure I do. That was almost as bad as the housewife in Puma who set fire to her own baby."

"One in a million." Perkins nodded at the corpse in front of them. "Do you recognize her?"

"No."

"I'd say she's twenty to twenty-five years old, about the age of most the Wacs I see around town. She's one of yours, all right. How long do you think she's been out here?"

"Not very long." Burke remembered the night patrol reports on his desk. "I'm guessing she was killed about 1:00 A.M. Someone reported hearing gunshots up here on Custer Hill about that time."

"Lucky she was found so soon. A couple of days out here and there wouldn't have been much left of her."

Perkins gestured toward the road. "Here come the coroner and the meat wagon. And your photographer."

Biggs was directing everyone along the same circuitous route Burke had taken. When they arrived, Perkins took charge of the civilians and Burke issued his instructions to the post photographer.

"I want photos from all angles, Willie. What have you got in your camera, black-and-white or color?"

"I can do either or both."

"Color."

"Okay."

Burke walked back along the path the killer or killers must have taken when they brought the girl out here. He stayed far enough to the side to avoid ruining any footprints there might be. Sheriff Perkins's size twelves had made deep impressions in the softer ground close to the road and they were all over the place. Burke had about given up hope of finding anything else when he spotted a few footprints that definitely weren't the sheriff's.

"Army boots," he said out loud. After nineteen years, he knew the imprint of an army boot as well as he knew his own face. He knelt for a closer look. There were about six impressions distinct enough to be called footprints. Of the six, only one was good enough to constitute physical evidence. On close inspection he found a diamond-shaped mark on that one. "Amos!"

"What is it, Sarge?"

"Get Brodsky on the radio. Tell him to bring some plaster of Paris out here. I want him to make a cast of a footprint."

"Right."

"And toss me that cooler of yours. Empty it first."

Biggs took out the beer cans and tossed the cooler to Burke, who opened the top and carefully laid it upside down over the footprint. "Don't let anyone near this." He went back to the crime scene and told Perkins about the footprint and the casting he was having made.

"Keep your casting," Perkins said in his most sarcastic voice. "Better yet, give it to the FBI. They love that shit." His voice brightened. "Hey, that's right. This case ain't mine. A murder on government property belongs to the feds."

"That's right. You lucked out," Burke said.

"I've got some luck coming. Lately we've been finding stiffs all over the county, which has played hell with my work load."

Burke smiled.

"Don't look down your nose at me, Ansel. I'm plenty busy. Did you hear about that couple found dead out near Red Cliff?"

"Sure, I read about them. But that was an accident, not a murder. They were hiking on the cliffs and fell."

"Even so, there was a helluva lot of paperwork to that case. And they weren't the only ones. We've had one accident after another in the mountains this year."

"You've got a tough life, Len. But your coroner still has to do the autopsy. That's the law."

"I know the law."

"Sarge?" Willie Ray had been moving around the corpse, shooting with a motorized Nikon. Now his camera was dangling from his hand. "I think I know this girl."

"You do? Who is she?"

"I can't be sure. Her face is so—"

"Just give me a name. I'll find out whether you're right."

"Well, she sort of looks like Betsy Palermo. Corporal

Betsy Palermo, a records clerk over in the storage depot." The longer Willie Ray looked at the dead girl, the more pale he became. "I don't feel so good. Can I take off now? I got plenty of pictures."

"Yeah, go ahead." Burke had a second thought. "Wait a minute. You know anything about this Betsy Palermo?"

"Not much. I tried to hit on her once at the N.C.O. Club and she brushed me off. She was with Hank Roper. If I'd known that, I wouldn't have made a move on her. It doesn't pay to get Hank sore at you."

"She was with Hank?" That didn't make sense. Hank Roper said all Wacs were pigs. No exceptions. Recalling Hank's "rubberized pussy" remark, Burke wondered why Roper'd made an exception to his rule—if this was, in fact, Betsy Palermo. "Thanks, Willie. Take off, but I want color prints by four o'clock."

"Sarge—"

"Four o'clock."

The coroner finished his preliminary examination and announced that the victim was a dark-haired, female Caucasian, approximately twenty-five years of age, who evidently had died as a result either of multiple gunshot wounds or a slashed throat. The autopsy would determine which wounds had actually killed her. That pronouncement was hardly news to anyone, but Burke took more interest in the coroner's opinion that the girl might have been raped.

"I won't know that for certain until I get her on the table, but the discharge of blood from the vagina is consistent with rape," the coroner said.

"Amos!" Burke called. "Get on the horn to the Wac Shack. Find out if a Corporal Betsy Palermo reported for duty this morning." He spelled out the name.

"Will do, Sarge."

Sheriff Perkins looked at his watch. "Hey, I'd better get going. I'm speaking at the Rotary Club today."

"If I weren't so busy, I'd come and listen to you," Burke said.

"My subject is 'Standing Up for the American Way of Life.' Hell of a speech. I hired Sam Gibbs over at the Puma *Union* to write it for me."

"They'll probably throw money."

Perkins fixed Burke with his bright little eyes. "You soldier boys don't hold the patent on patriotism, you know. This country means everything to me and I don't mind saying so in public."

"Knock 'em dead, Len."

"Fuck you, Ansel."

Amos Biggs came jogging across the desert, his eyes sharp for snakes. "Hey, Sarge, I just talked to Major Seward at the Wac Shack. Betsy Palermo didn't make reveille this morning. She's A.W.O.L."

Burke looked down at the swollen corpse at his feet. "Not anymore."

Chapter 4

Maggie Winston opened the gallery at ten o'clock
and then settled down at her desk with last Sunday's
edition of the *New York Times*. The paper arrived by
mail in New Mexico on Monday, but Maggie seldom
could bring herself to read it until the following morning. Sometimes she felt like pitching it into the wastebasket, but she never did. Though she harbored a deep
resentment toward New York's art establishment for
the way they had gloated over her downfall, she had to
know what was happening there.

So it was with nettlesome feelings that Maggie turned
to the last pages of the 'Arts and Leisure' section,
where the big galleries and auction houses advertised
their wares.

She saw that Christie's was announcing an auction
of fine Japanese netsuke and inro and that the William Doyle galleries were featuring old master and
modern prints, including a signed lithograph of Grant
Wood's "Approaching Storm." There was an article on
"Spain's Great Masters" and a review of a new show at
the IBM Gallery of Science and Art.

But what caught her eye were the number of smaller
galleries advertising the work of Western artists. The
artists ranged from Frederic Remington to Jack Kilgore,
who had committed suicide on his Wyoming ranch just
two years ago. The publicity resulting from the suicide, combined with the scarcity of his work, had pushed

the sales price for a Kilgore oil into the six-figure
arena.

I was right, Maggie gloated. Suddenly Western artists are in. Pretty soon now the price of fine contempo-
rary Western art will double. Maybe triple, if the New
York collectors come into the market in a big way.
That doesn't mean my gamble here will automatically
pay off, but at least I'm ahead of the market.

"Damn!" She threw down the paper, jumped up from
her desk and stamped her foot on a story that offended
her. The two-paragraph item concerned the sale of a
Marshall Vogel painting to the Harvard University
collection for $208,000, a record sale for the young
New York artist.

Maggie moved quickly around the gallery, straightening pictures and changing the lighting on them, but
that kind of busywork didn't help to take her mind off
the item. It was so unfair. Marshall Vogel had been
her discovery. She had arranged his first one-man
show and nurtured his reputation. Then, just when he
was starting to sell, the disagreement over the size
and disbursement of her commissions erupted and he
signed with another dealer. After losing the lawsuit
he brought against her, she didn't even have enough
money left to pay the rent on her gallery space in
Soho—never mind the elegant space on Fifty-seventh
Street she'd been negotiating for.

I didn't leave New York, Maggie thought with lingering bitterness. I *fled*. And I'm not going back until
I can do it in style.

A man in brand-new Western togs came into the
gallery. Maggie smoothed her skirt and substituted a
smile for the churlish look generated by the *Times*.

"Good morning, can I help you?"

"I'm only browsing," the visitor replied.

"Go right ahead and enjoy yourself. Are you a New
Mexican, or are you visiting the area?"

"Just a tourist." The man waved his hand vaguely
to the south. "Spending a couple of weeks at the X-Bar
Ranch. Great country out here."

"Yes, it's lovely. Don't let me disturb you, but please
speak up if I can be of help."

"Thanks."

Maggie returned to her desk and went to work on
her books. She gave the visitor no more thought. He
was a looker, not a buyer. Of that she was certain.
Maggie's greatest gift as an art dealer was her ability
to tell the browsers from the serious collectors. However, this particular browser was exactly the type of
person she wanted in her gallery. From his clothes
and manner Maggie could tell that he had both money
and the willingness to spend it.

After slinking out of New York, Maggie had been
unsure of where to settle, but she meant to stay in the
art business—to conquer it, in fact. That meant making a new start somewhere else. She considered all the
obvious places to open a new gallery—Carmel, Scotts-
dale, Palm Beach, Sedalia, Rockport, Santa Fe—and
rejected them. In each of those places Maggie would
have been just one more gallery owner in a sea of such
creatures. Besides, all the best artists in those areas
were already signed up by someone. So she bet everything she owned on the town of Puma, which was just
beginning to draw wealthy tourists to its dude ranches
in the surrounding mountains. In a few years Puma
would become another Santa Fe.

Because Puma and the market in Western art were
both on the verge of a boom, Maggie had gambled that
she could make it big here and return to New York
with five or six highly marketable artists in her sta-
ble. And her strategy was beginning to work. The
gallery was making a modest profit and she had two
new artists whose reputations were building rather
quickly. Ansel Burke was so good that Maggie was
testing the market for his work in New York. She had
sent two of his paintings to a Fifty-seventh Street
gallery on consignment.

As the browser departed, Maggie said, "Thank you
for coming in," and gave him one of her most charming smiles. Well-to-do browsers often had collectors for
friends. As the visitor left he held the door open for an
elderly couple entering the shop.

Maggie's antennae immediately began to quiver.

These are *buyers,* she decided. What a splendid way to start the day.

She stood and smoothed her skirt, giving the couple a few moments to look around and, more important, giving Maggie an opportunity to confirm her judgment. They were in their sixties, dressed in casually expensive clothes. The man wore a gold Rolex and the woman a pair of earrings Maggie recognized as original Paloma Picassos, which meant she had purchased them at Tiffany's in New York. Buyers, no doubt about it.

Maggie glanced into the mirror behind her desk. Her hair was in place and her dress impeccable. Fortunately, the desert sun hadn't coarsened her skin in the eighteen months she'd spent here. It had bleached her hair to a lighter shade of brown, but she rather liked that. As always, Maggie was reassured by the image in the mirror. She saw a tall, thirtyish woman, almost slim and beautiful enough to be a model. A good part of her success, past and future, depended on her appearance. Using her looks for business purposes came naturally to her. She had only contempt for those who complained that she sometimes did so in an unethical manner.

"Good morning." Maggie approached them slowly. Never make buyers feel they're being rushed. "Welcome to the Winston Gallery," she said, extending her hand. "I'm Maggie Winston."

"How do you do." The man took her hand in an old-world way. "I'm Charles Elliott and this is my wife, Sandra. I understand this is the place to see the work of Ansel Burke."

"Yes, I'm his dealer." Maggie was genuinely excited now. When they ask about a specific artist, they're definitely in the market. "I have several of his paintings."

She led them to the area of the gallery where her best paintings were featured. The wall was directly below a skylight, giving the paintings the advantage of natural light. "Here they are." Maggie picked up a brochure from a small side table. "This will tell you something about Sergeant Burke."

Sandra Elliott glanced at the photo of Ansel on the front of the brochure. "Fierce-looking fellow, for an artist."

"He's been a professional soldier for nineteen years."

"What made him decide to take up a brush so late in life?" Elliot asked.

"Actually, Ansel began painting when he was only a boy. He went into the army during the Vietnam War and sort of lost touch with the artist in himself. A few years ago he started painting again. Last fall I was lucky enough to see his work and become his dealer. It's all in the brochure." She backed off a pace. "I'll leave you alone now, but please let me know if you have any other questions."

Maggie returned to her desk. From long experience she knew that serious collectors demand time and silence when they're evaluating art. And these two were serious collectors. Maggie had identified the Elliotts' accents as Bostonian. From their lack of tans she knew they weren't staying at one of the several dude ranches in the area. She suspected they had come to Puma specifically to see Ansel's work, which meant they somehow had heard of him in the east. But how?

The phone rang and Maggie, still deep in thought, picked it up. "Winston Gallery."

"Maggie, darling. So wonderful to hear your voice."

"Donald?"

"Of course it's Donald. Who else in New York is mad enough to be up and around after only two hours sleep?"

"Poor dear," Maggie murmured, wondering what in the world Donald Hillary wanted from her.

"Two hours," Donald Hillary repeated, as if no one had ever before suffered so deeply.

"You deserve a medal, or at least a free dinner at your favorite sushi bar."

"I've given up sushi," he clucked. "No one eats that dreck anymore. Everyone's into TexMex now. You've been away from New York too long."

Maggie let that pass.

"How are all the dear little coyotes and foxes and wild things out there?"

"Oh, they're making meals out of each other, just as people do in New York."

Donald laughed girlishly. "How I miss your droll tongue."

"What are you calling about, Donald?"

"Just to thank you for sending me those two Ansel Burkes. He has a crude power that I rather like."

Maggie's pulse quickened. "Have you sold them?"

"As a matter of fact, I have."

"Full price?"

"Better than that. I had one of my inspirations: marked them up to twelve thousand apiece and sold them both."

"Wonderful!" Numbers and ideas rolled through Maggie's mind. Donald Hillary was one of the shrewdest art dealers in New York. Only the prospect of a very big deal would ever justify his inconveniencing himself. "As I told you when I sent the paintings, I have a very good contract with Ansel. My commission is 50 percent, so you and I will split six thousand on each painting."

"Yes, I know. How in the world did you negotiate such a favorable contract? Burke must be a monumental rube."

"He's a sweet, simple man who trusts me implicitly."

Donald laughed over that. "Poor fellow. But I'm glad you have a contract. I wouldn't want to see you lose him." He paused, then went ahead with what was in his mind. "As you did Marshall Vogel."

"Don't worry about that." Maggie was certain now that Donald wanted more of Ansel's work. "Ansel and I are joined at the hip, legally and otherwise."

"Ah. Got him into your busy little bed, did you?"

"Don't be loathsome, Donald."

"I'm not. I have only admiration for the way you use that supple body of yours. I used to do the same with my young artists, until my pectorals fell. Now let's talk business. The check for both sales is on its way to you and I'd like to have more of Ansel Burke's work—as much as you can provide. I might even be willing to

buy a few pieces, instead of taking them on consignment."

"What's going on?"

"I like to encourage new talent, darling. You know
that."

Maggie was watching the Elliotts, who were studying Ansel's paintings with rapt interest. "Two collectors walked into my gallery just a few minutes ago.
They're looking at some of Ansel's work right now. Is
that a coincidence, or do you and these people know
something that I don't?"

"Who are they?" Donald asked quickly.

"Charles and Sandra Elliott."

"I know them. The Elliotts are from Boston. I sold
them a William Hopper a few years ago for their
summer place in Marblehead. They have a quality
collection of American contemporaries. Maggie, don't
let them walk out with anything today."

"Why not?"

Donald gave a bleat of exasperation. "I might as
well tell you. The Museum of Modern Art bought the
Burke canvas titled 'Ghost Dancers.' One of the Gettys
picked up the other one. They worked through another
dealer, so I don't as yet know what part of that charmed
family it went to. If I'd had any idea I was selling to a
Getty, I'd have asked forty thousand without blinking
an eye."

"My God." Maggie was transported, first with joy
and then with rage. "You bloodsucking weasel. You'd
have bought Ansel's work from me for rock-bottom
prices and sold them for a fortune. The Museum of
Modern Art *and* the Gettys? That's unheard of."

"Yes, we're sitting on a gold mine, darling."

"We're sitting on a gold mine?"

"You'll need to work through a New York dealer
and I'm your logical choice. In fact, people will wonder
if Ansel Burke is really that good if I drop him."

"I see. If I go to another dealer, you'll tell everyone
that *you* dropped *him.*"

"Of course."

Donald is right, Maggie thought. I do need him. "All

right, we'll continue under our present arrangement. You and I will split my 50 percent commission."

"That's acceptable. Now, how much of his work is available, and how good is it?"

"I'm holding twenty canvases." She ran them visually through her mind. "Fifteen are excellent. The other five are either too derivative or not up to his best."

"I'll accept your judgment. You've always had a good eye. Finding Burke only confirms that." There was an interval of silence while Donald Hillary plotted strategy. "We can hold a one-man show in my gallery next month. Do you have a calendar? June thirtieth through July twenty-fourth. Mark it down. Crate the fifteen canvases and send them Federal Express. I'll also need photos of Burke and a biography. He's really a soldier?"

"Ansel is macho personified."

"How deliciously kinky."

"What kind of a floor shall we set?"

"My dear, we musn't price anything at less than thirty thousand. If we hold the show at the end of June, everyone will have a chance to talk about Burke during July and August in the Hamptons. The major buyers will make their moves in September. We should be able to clear the walls before the frost is on the pumpkin."

Maggie felt a beautiful warmth spread outward from her bosom. Her share would be more than enough to finance a triumphant return to New York. "I want the invitations and all advertising to read 'Hillary House and the Winston Gallery Present the Work of Ansel Burke.' "

"Never!"

"Then I'll take my chances with someone else."

"You vile bitch." Donald could be heard making pouting sounds while he considered Maggie's ultimatum. "Oh, very well. But you'll pay half the cost of mounting and advertising the show."

"Agreed."

"And, darling, you must keep Burke under control. We can't have him waltzing away from you the way Marshall did."

"Don't worry about that. I'll marry him if I have to."

"Marriage? What a brilliant coup. Then you'd have 75 percent of the profits. I'm limp with envy."

"I'll call you when I have the weigh bill number for the shipment. Good-bye, Donald, and thank you."

"Good-bye, darling. It's refreshing to do business with you. You've restored my faith in the innate greed of the human animal."

Maggie laughed and put down the phone. The Elliotts apparently had made a decision, because they were waiting impatiently for the end of her conversation.

"We've decided to take two of Mr. Burke's paintings," Elliott said. "The one of the little girl against the sky and the still life of the old Colt revolver. He's really very good. I've never seen such menace in an inanimate object."

"And he has a wonderful sense of color," Mrs. Elliott added.

"I'm very sorry," Maggie said, "but none of these paintings are available just now. I've been asked to withdraw them from the market temporarily."

Charles Elliott drew himself up. "That's ridiculous. I'm prepared to make a legitimate offer and I expect to have it accepted."

"You were preempted by Donald Hillary."

The Elliotts glanced at each other more in defeat than surprise.

"That was Donald on the phone. We've decided to hold a show of Ansel's work in New York next month at Hillary House. If you're really interested in those two paintings, you can bid on them at that time."

"I should have guessed." Elliott dropped his belligerence, which had been nothing more than a bargaining ploy. "When we heard yesterday that the Gettys and the Museum of Modern Art both had purchased Burke's work, we caught a plane and tried to steal a march on the New York dealers."

"Congratulations. You almost succeeded." Give the old goat a compliment, Maggie thought. He may still be a buyer. "I hope you'll pass on your good impression of Ansel Burke's talent to your friends."

"Oh, no," Mrs. Elliott laughed. "We're not going to
drive the price up until we own one ourselves."

"Does that mean I'll see you at the show in New
York?"

"Possibly," Elliott conceded. "Meanwhile, we'll have
to content ourselves with enjoying the desert sun. Good
day, Miss Winston."

When they were gone Maggie sat down and tried to
pull her thoughts together. She was trembling with
excitement. She had known Ansel was good, but this
reaction to his work was incredible. The fifteen paintings were just a start. The future body of his work
might be worth *millions*.

I *will* marry him, she decided. And get him out of
the damned army, too.

The walls of Hank Roper's office at the N.C.O. Club
were decorated with photos of boxers. Some were of
recent champions; others went all the way back to
Willie Pep and Jack Johnson and the great John L.
Sullivan. His favorite was the photo of Joe Louis in a
half crouch, his fists raised and ready, his face empty
of emotion.

Roper often talked about Joe Louis. "Louis was the
toughest nigger that ever lived," he liked to say. "He
was a great champion because he never lost his cool.
No matter how strong and fast the other guy was,
Louis always came straight in at him. The man had a
block of ice in his gut."

Privately, Roper liked to compare himself with Joe
Louis. He had proven in Vietnam that he could stay
cool in a fight and since then he'd shown some championship footwork of his own in building his "business."
Roper's business was based on a simple principle—
everything is for sale. Each day from noon until two
o'clock Roper made himself available to those who
wanted to buy his wares. At precisely 11:55 John the
bartender automatically placed a pot of coffee on the
credenza behind Roper's desk and turned up the air
conditioner to a comfortable level. At noon Roper settled himself behind his desk, poured a cup of coffee,

and hit a buzzer that signaled John to send in his first customer.

The first man who came through the door today was dressed in medic whites. "Sergeant Roper?"

"Right."

"I'm Sergeant Whitson. Ed Whitson. I'm in charge of the ambulance drivers over at the post hospital."

"Sit down, Ed. What's on your mind?"

Whitson squirmed in his chair until he made up his mind what to say. "I hate this post."

"Sorry to hear it. I kind of like the desert air, myself."

"Oh, I don't mind the desert. It's the chief medical officer who's driving me nuts. He's on my ass every minute. Nothing I do is good enough for him. I'm due to get promoted to E-7, but do you think I'll get it? Shit, no. I put in for a transfer five times but nothing's come through."

"And you want a little help," Roper coaxed.

"Yeah, that's it." Whitson leaned forward and dropped his voice. "I was wondering . . ."

"You don't have to whisper."

"Oh. Okay. Look, I hear you've got good connections. Is there any way you could get me a transfer to Fort Polk?"

Roper almost spilled his coffee. "You want to go to *Fort Polk?* Louisiana?"

Whitson nodded.

"What the hell for? There's about ten thousand troops trying to *get out* of Fort Polk. That place is the asshole of the universe."

Whitson looked offended. "I don't think so. I've got family near Fort Polk. So does my wife. We'd like to get back there."

Roper shrugged. "Hey, it's your life. You want to go to Fort Polk? That's easy. I got a bargain price for that kind of transfer. Fifteen hundred bucks."

"Fifteen hundred? That's a pretty steep bargain."

"You want to play? You gotta pay."

"I don't have that much in the bank."

"Sell your car. Put your wife out on the street. Do whatever you have to do, or stop wasting my time."

"You're certain you can get me the transfer?"

"Put fifteen hundred bucks in my hand and I'll have you on the next levy out of here."

"Okay," Whitson finally said. "I'll get the money somewhere. It's a deal."

When Whitson had gone, Roper picked up his phone and dialed a number at the post personnel office.

"Warrant Officer Manuel Garcia speaking."

"Oh, I thought thees waas the Frito Bandito speeeking."

"Goddammit, Hank. Knock off that racist shit."

"Oh, don't get a bug up you ass, Manny. I've got a customer for you."

"I don't know. We've been doing too much business lately. I'm only the assistant personnel officer. Captain Scott reviews my levies. If I send one more trooper to Hawaii or Europe this month, he's liable to get suspicious."

"Relax. I've got a noncom who's willing to pay for a transfer to Fort Polk. Nobody would believe you could sell that one."

"Polk? Why would he want to go there?"

"Because he's an asshole. The asshole's name is Staff Sergeant Ed Whitson. I'll let you know when he comes up with the money. Meanwhile, put his papers in the pipeline."

"How much is he paying?"

"Fifteen hundred. You'll get your half when I collect. Eees okay weeth you, Frito Bandito?"

"Go shove a cactus up your ass, Hank."

Roper was laughing as Garcia hung up on him. "Man's got no sense of humor at all," he said, and pressed the buzzer to signal John to send in the next customer.

Over the next hour he collected his percentage of the monthly take from two loan sharks operating under his protection and arranged for the sale of twenty dozen Class A uniforms stolen from the 31st Infantry supply room. He was toting up figures on a sheet of lined yellow paper when his phone rang and he answered with, "Sergeant Major Roper speaking."

"Can you talk?"

At the sound of Control's voice, Roper put aside his pencil. "Sure."

"I've just heard that the body of a young woman has been found on the artillery range. That wouldn't be our little friend, would it?"

"I hope to hell not."

"Then you aren't certain?"

Roper hated to sound equivocal, but he had no choice. "No, I'm not."

"Then find out," Control ordered.

"I will."

"If you paid more attention to serious business and less to your penny-ante rackets, you'd know these things."

"I can't just drop all this small stuff. Everyone would wonder why. You agreed to that when we went into business together."

"Yes, but it occupies your mind and your time more than is necessary. Do you read me?"

"Yeah."

"Good. Now listen. We have two clients coming into town tomorrow. They want to see the merchandise before making a commitment."

"I don't like that."

"Neither do I, but our backers have approved the arrangement."

"Fuck them. They won't be there if this turns out to be a rip-off. Neither will you. What are you asking for one unit now? Three million dollars? Your clients could save a lot of money by pumping lead into me."

"You're a resourceful man. That's why I made you my partner."

"Junior partner."

"Don't poor-mouth. You're making more money with me than you ever dreamed of with your stupid little rackets."

"When do your friends want to see the merchandise?"

"I don't know. As soon as I have the details, I'll be in touch."

"Make it soon."

His caller broke the connection.

Roper was seething as he sat back and replayed the

conversation in his mind. Control thought of him in much the same way he thought of Sheriff Leonard Perkins—as a nickel-and-dime chiseler. That wasn't right, not after everything he'd done for Control. And done right, too. There hadn't been any trouble until now.

Williamson! The sloppy pig just couldn't take the time to do the job right. Lack of professionalism, that's what it amounted to. Roper looked again at the photo of Joe Louis. You and me know what professionalism is, don't we, Joe? And so does Ansel Burke. He'll dig and probe and ask a thousand questions about Betsy Palermo. And sooner or later he'll come up with a few answers. No use trying to warn him off or buy him off. Ansel's a hardhead. Always has been.

Roper knotted his right hand into a fist and studied it with uncritical pride. So what? If old Ansel crowds me, I'll put him down for that long count.

Chapter 5

Burke returned to MP headquarters to find Mess Sergeant Jake Winkler slumped in a chair outside the CO's office.

"What's the problem?"

"Sloane busted me down a grade." Jake's voice was hoarse with misery. "He inspected my kitchen after breakfast and said it was a cesspool. My kitchen! A cesspool! I'm supposed to see him in a few minutes about my menus too."

"Maybe I can talk to him. You run a clean kitchen and everyone knows it."

"Thanks, but you'd best watch out for your own stripes. He's been asking for you all morning with blood in his eye." Jake looked nostalgically at the third rocker on his sergeant's stripes. "Took me five years to earn that fucker."

"You'll get it back."

"Yeah, in *another* five years."

When Burke walked into his office Brodsky told him, "The new CO wants to see you right away. Do you know what he did to Jake?"

"I heard. How did the impression of the footprint come out?"

"Here it is. Looks good to me."

Burke picked up a large hunk of plaster of Paris and examined the impression. The diamond-shaped mark on the sole stood out in fine detail, so at least one thing had come out right this morning.

"What'll we do with it?" Brodsky asked. "Give it to the FBI, when and if they show up?"

"I don't think so." Burke opened the bottom drawer to his desk, put the casting inside, and closed and locked the drawer. "The FBI won't use anything we turn up. We're just a bunch of clowns to them. I'll hold on to it for now and hope I can find the boot it matches."

"You'd better report in to Sloane. He's asked for you a dozen times."

"How do you read him?"

Brodsky rolled his eyes. "Section Eight."

After checking his appearance in the mirrored surface of a window, Burke crossed the hall and rapped his knuckles three times on the CO's door.

"Who is it?"

"Sergeant Major Burke, sir."

"Come in."

Burke played it by the book. He opened the door, stepped briskly inside, closed the door behind him, marched to a spot directly in front of the CO's desk, saluted, and remained at attention.

"At ease."

He clasped his hands behind his back and moved his feet apart.

"So you're Sergeant Major Burke. I've been hearing about you every five minutes since I arrived at Fort Powell. You're a legend in your own time, Sergeant. Did you know that?"

"No, sir. I didn't." Burke lowered his eyes and looked at First Lieutenant Walter Sloane with as neutral an expression as he could manage. What he saw wasn't encouraging. Sloane looked even younger than his twenty-five years. Though his uniform was as crisp and correct as one would expect of a West Point man, he looked vaguely uncomfortable in it. He had thin shoulders and a hairline that was already beginning to recede. His mouth was too firm; it had the pouting rigidity of a child's. But what struck him first were Lieutenant Sloane's extraordinary eyes. They were large, wild, and dangerous. They reminded Burke of a video game going over two hundred thousand points.

"It's customary for the ranking noncom to greet a

new commanding officer on his first morning in a new unit and introduce him around, but you weren't here this morning. Why not?"

"I intended to be, sir. But we've had a murder on the post. A young girl—I'm pretty sure she's one of our Wacs—was found shot to death on the artillery range. I had to call in the county sheriff and coroner and take charge of the removal of the body."

"Isn't it the FBI's responsibility to investigate a homicide on a military installation?"

"Yes, sir, technically. In practice, the FBI doesn't much care what happens to soldiers. They feel they've got more important work to do. The last time we had a killing on post, the resident agent from Albuquerque didn't show up until three weeks later. Then he only rubber-stamped our paperwork."

Sloane didn't appear to be listening to Burke's reply. His unusual eyes were going in and out of focus. His firm mouth became tighter and his hands, which had been resting loosely on his desk, began to tremble. He hastily put them in his lap. "That does not mitigate your *inexcusable lack of courtesy!*"

"I apologize, sir. No disrespect was intended. I might add that I also had to testify at a court-martial this morning."

"Oh, I've heard all about that too." Sloane jumped to his feet and began striding back and forth behind his desk. "General Leland personally called to say how angered he was about your attitude on the witness stand. And to chew me out—*me*—for some vandalism that occurred last night. Something about damage to a historic monument."

"A couple of drunken troopers tipped over an old artillery piece," Burke explained. "They were arrested this morning by one of my men."

"I suppose you expect a medal and promotion. That's your *job*, Sergeant. And what about your testimony at this morning's court-martial? According to General Leland, you're at least partially responsible for letting a dangerously unbalanced man go free."

"I only testified to what I knew, sir."

"Sergeant Major, don't you realize what a blow it is

to me, personally and professionally, to be reprimanded by the post commander on the very morning that I take command of this unit?"

"That's unfortunate, sir. But I didn't wreck that artillery piece and my testimony this morning was accurate and impartial. In fact, I was a prosecution witness."

"General Leland says you did your best to sabotage the prosecution's case."

Sloane sat down and clasped his hands together on the desk. He fixed his eyes on Burke and tried to stare him into a more humble attitude, which was a mistake. Ansel Burke had been a top sergeant for too many years to be intimidated by a mere lieutenant. He returned Sloane's gaze coolly. There was no disrespect in his manner, but Burke had nineteen years of soldiering in his bearing, and eyes that had seen it all. And so it was Sloane who broke off eye contact.

"I'd like to be shown around the company now, and then I want to look over the company records."

"Yes, sir."

For the next hour Burke took him through the company, from the dayroom to the armory, introducing him to as many of the troops as possible. He explained that a number of men were asleep in their bunks because they had worked night patrol. Sloane asked intelligent questions and was quietly cordial with the men he met. At one point he commented, "My father always said Fort Powell was a charming old post. Now I can see what he meant. The adobe buildings are really quite striking."

"Your father is in the army, sir?"

"Uh, yes. Brigadier General Stanton Sloane. He's serving at NATO headquarters in Brussels right now."

"Then you come from a service family."

"I'm fourth generation West Point," Sloane said, and quickly changed the subject.

By the end of the tour Burke had Sloane figured out: he was another army brat packed off to West Point by his father, whether he wanted to go or not. Sloane might have preferred to be a banker or doctor. No matter. His father had decided to turn his boy into a soldier and Sloane was trying like hell to live up to his old man's expectations.

The clincher was the swagger stick he carried in his left hand. The two-foot-long baton with the .30 caliber bullet at the tip was something older officers carried. Young officers considered swagger sticks old-fashioned and embarrassingly macho. Burke would have bet money that Brigadier General Sloane had told his son, "A real officer always carries a swagger stick. It lends additional authority."

Burke thought Sloane deserved a chance to make a good start here, so he said, "Lieutenant, it's my job to see that the troops carry out your orders. Above and beyond that, I'm ready to do anything I can to make your tour with the MPs a success. You can trust me to keep my mouth shut when you want something kept confidential and to make sure you aren't blindsided by some other officer trying to make a name for himself."

The severe features softened just a bit. "Thank you, Sergeant. I appreciate that. Do you have any suggestions for getting off to a good start with the troops?"

"Yes, sir. I think that busting Winkler down a grade on your first day is unnecessary. Why don't you give him an Article Fifteen instead."

Sloane stiffened and slapped the swagger stick against the palm of his hand. "My father says the worst thing an officer can do is to back down in front of his men. If that's the best suggestion you can offer, I won't be calling on you for advice very often."

"Whatever you say, sir. I'll send in the company clerk with the records now."

Burke returned to his office and sent the clerk across the hall with a full month's worth of morning reports and the company inventory. Sloane would have to sign for every piece of equipment in the barracks, from the .45s the MPs carried to the mattresses they slept on. He'd want to count everything he was signing for, which meant he'd be out of Burke's hair for possibly two days.

"Do any good for Jake?" Brodsky asked.

"Sloane wouldn't budge. What about the girl? Do we have a positive ID?"

"Not yet. Major Seward has gone to the coroner's office in Puma to look at the body. She'll call here to let us know whether the girl is Corporal Palermo."

"I'm going to my room for a while. Ask Jake to send one of the KPs up with a steak sandwich and a cup of coffee. And tell him I'm sorry I couldn't do anything about his stripes."

Burke changed from his Class A uniform into fatigues. When the KP delivered the steak sandwich and coffee, he put them on a tray next to his easel and uncovered the canvas. He studied the mountain ranch house in detail while eating his lunch. Then he mixed various dabs until he got the exact shade of red he wanted and taped a piece of plain white paper to the canvas.

For ten minutes he practiced drawing chilies on the sheet of paper. He worked out a three-stroke motion for each chilie. When the motion was perfected, he threw the sheet of paper on the floor and started to work on the canvas.

The red was exactly what he wanted. The strings of chilies began to come alive just as he'd visualized them: a lush red. You could almost feel the sun nurturing their incredible strength. Pop one in your mouth and you'd breathe fire for an hour.

Burke allowed himself a smile. Most of the time he doubted that he had any talent at all. Then he'd make a breakthrough like this and for a while he'd be incredibly productive. Those periods seldom lasted very long. His hours in front of the canvas were a series of peaks and valleys—mostly valleys. Every session ended with the conviction that he wasn't an artist at all. Just a soldier with a hobby.

But right now all he wanted out of life was the chance to finish this picture while he still had the touch, and so he took a deep breath and began to work on the sky behind the house. Soon he was so engrossed in his work that none of the sounds of the outside world, from a helicopter that flew over the barracks to the footbeat of troops taking close order drill on the parade ground, reached him.

Ansel Burke had always been able to lose himself in

colors and shapes. The first color he remembered was the brilliant red of a San Francisco cable car. His father had been a grip on a cable car, driving the colorful little trolley up and down the steep hills of San Francisco with gleeful disregard for the law of gravity.

As a child, his mother often took him down to the Powell Street turntable and put him on the cable car with his father while she did her shopping. She was a big-boned Norwegian woman with a square jaw and a ready smile, who loved the thick San Francisco fogs as much as the clear blue days. His father was tall, with shoulders and arms splendidly developed from pulling and pushing all day long on the long-handled cable car grip. Burke remembered his home as a happy and even raucous place until he was eleven. Then it became as quiet as a library.

In his eleventh year his father died. He was going up Powell Street toward the top of Nob Hill when a truck coming downhill lost its brakes. It careered down Powell like a loose cannon. Shouting to the passengers to jump, his father held on to his grip so the cable car wouldn't move while they scrambled to safety. The truck rammed the little cable car head-on and demolished it.

From that day on his mother seldom smiled and never laughed. She found a job in the bookkeeping department at the Emporium on Market Street and left Ansel pretty much to his own devices.

With no one to tell him otherwise, Ansel would toss aside his books after school and head for North Beach, where all sorts of exotic wonders could be seen. He sneaked into topless bars through back doors and watched beautiful girls swinging their breasts to the rhythm of music. He stood in the corners of poolrooms and watched some of the best hustlers on the West Coast lure suckers into money games. But his favorite pastime was watching the street artists at the Embarcadero or Fisherman's Wharf. He was fascinated by what could be done with a brush and a few dabs of color. When he was thirteen he stole a set of paints and joined San Francisco's legion of street artists.

What amazed young Ansel Burke was how quickly
he learned the rudiments of drawing. Shapes came
easily to him. In a matter of weeks he was earning
pocket money by selling cute little paintings of the
Golden Gate Bridge to tourists. But the secret of creating subtler images remained a mystery to him.

Two years later the school authorities complained to
Mrs. Burke that her son was neglecting all other stud-
ies to concentrate on his art. Their complaints fell on
uninterested ears. Lena Burke didn't really care what
her son was doing. By then she was living in a perpet-
ual alcoholic daze. Her only concern was to stay sober
enough during business hours to keep her job and pay
for her booze. Controlling a son was something for
which she no longer had either ability or desire.

The other boys his age often joked about Ansel's
preoccupation with art, but never within his earshot.
Ansel had grown as tall and strong as his father. And
while he had an even temper, he rather enjoyed a good
fight now and then.

In the end the San Francisco public high school
system decided to graduate Ansel Burke despite his
terrible grades and uncooperative attitude. It was not
an act of charity—Ansel's art had brought credit to his
school. He won several state competitions and was up
for a scholarship to the California School of Fine Arts.
Ansel desperately wanted that scholarship. There was
so much to learn about form and perspective, and so
few who could teach it well. Ten scholarships were
available and he was certain one would go to him.

He was wrong. The ten scholarships went to young
men and women who were not only talented, but who
had "well-rounded interests and personalities."

The rejection was a crushing blow for an eighteen-
year-old. The first thing he did after reading the letter
from the scholarship board was to collect his paints
and canvases, carry them down to Pier 45, and throw
them into the San Francisco Bay. Then he went to the
recruiting office at the Presidio and joined the U.S.
Army.

Six months later he was lying on a ridge outside
Saigon, shaking with fright and firing his rifle at

every sound and shadow in the forbidding jungle below. He was trigger-happy until he learned that you gave away your position by firing long bursts. So he forced himself to settle down and began to study the soldier's trade with the same quiet zeal he had given to his art.

To his own amazement Ansel Burke discovered that he had a natural ability to command men and that he enjoyed putting that ability to use. Soldiers many years his senior responded to his crisp orders issued in a voice that remained steady no matter how desperate events became. Within two years Burke earned his sergeant's stripes as well as his first purple heart and bronze star for valor.

Every stripe on his arm was a "blood stripe"—a promotion resulting from the death of the noncom just above him.

Gradually Burke gave up any idea of becoming an artist and elected to make the army his career. After Vietnam he married a girl he met at a roadhouse outside Fort Bragg, North Carolina. She was tiny and cute and giggly and loved rock and roll played loud enough to break glass. Her name was Luanne. She couldn't cook and she refused to keep house. Burke was twenty-four, too young to realize he'd made a terrible mistake. Luanne did come to that conclusion. A year after they were married, she divorced him to go on the road with a musician who played steel guitar when he wasn't too stoned to function.

Ten years later Ansel Burke, by then a seasoned sergeant major with additional stripes and decorations earned in skirmishes from Lebanon to Grenada, was assigned to the MP headquarters at Fort Powell. The vivid hues of the desert and the stark shapes of the military post's adobe walls and buildings awakened old instincts. He found himself staring at everything with new eyes. Now and then he would take out a pencil and sheet of paper and make a quick sketch of an unusual face or object. His dreams were haunted by powerful images.

Finally he bought some paints and brushes and sat down to see if, after so many years, he could put anything at all on canvas. What happened seemed a miracle. The technique was still there. In fact, it was better than on that day so many years ago when he threw all his brushes and paintings into the San Francisco Bay. More important, he glimpsed what he suspected to be genuine power and richness in his work. After so many years, how could that be? He could only guess that now he was bringing to the canvas some of the pain and loneliness and knowledge accumulated during nineteen years of soldiering.

". . . hear me?"

"What?"

"I said, Don'tcha hear me?"

Burke looked over his shoulder to find Brodsky standing behind him, arms crossed.

"You really get caught up in that stuff. I've been talking to you for a minute or more."

"Sorry. What's going on?"

"Major Seward called from the coroner's office. The stiff in the desert was Betsy Palermo, all right. I talked to the coroner too. She was raped. And the slugs they took out of her were .45 caliber."

"From an army Colt?"

"I wouldn't be surprised."

Burke studied the painting while he cleaned his brush. The sky behind the ranch house was developing nicely. It had a brooding quality at counterpoint to the brightness of the chilies. Soon he'd be ready to show it to Maggie.

Maggie.

The thought of her made him horny.

"Is it finished?" Brodsky asked.

"Not quite."

"You know, Ansel, some of the troops think drawing pictures is kind of a weird thing for you to do. Not me," he added hastily. "I know you too well. But I'll tell ya, this artsy-fartsy stuff ain't doing your reputation any good down at the N.C.O. Club."

"I can live with that."

"I'm just saying be careful. One of the guys might call you out, y'know? See if you still got the guts for a fight."

"If anybody tries that, I'll hit him with my purse."

"Now, don't joke around! That's just the kinda talk gives people the wrong idea." Brodsky followed Burke out of his room grumbling. "Ain't no use making trouble for yourself. Or me, for that matter. I had to lay a beer bottle up alongside the head of one fella already."

"Defending my honor? Hey, you don't have to do that."

"I know. I just get antsy sometimes. There's lots of guys got their knives out for you, including our new CO. So watch your back."

"I always do," Burke said.

The Wac Shack was actually a compound of buildings consisting of three barracks and a company headquarters on the southern perimeter of the main post. About half the women at Fort Powell were unmarried personnel who lived on post. The other half lived in apartments in Puma.

As Burke went up the walkway to the headquarters building, he passed a platoon of women in fatigues who were taking close order drill. The drill master was a wide, weathered woman with staff sergeant stripes on her sleeves. The platoon was marching in such a ragged manner that the drillmaster finally called them to a halt.

"This is the worst close order drill I've ever seen," she complained in a jackhammer voice. "If you 'ladies' don't shape up fast, you ain't going on pass this weekend. And you know what that means. The men on post will have to spend Saturday night playing with their own whangers. So let's try it again." She waited while the ranks dressed right and left, then called out, "Atten-*hut!*"

The platoon again came slackly to attention.

"That was no damned good at all!" the drillmaster shouted. "When I call this platoon to attention, I want to hear thirty pussies suck air! Do you understand me? Let me hear it!"

"Yes, *Sergeant!*" the platoon answered in unison.

Burke kept his thoughts off his face as he went into

the headquarters and told the company clerk he was here to talk to the commanding officer.

Major Seward saw him at once. She was the exact opposite of the drillmaster, a handsome woman with a severe and carefully made-up face edged with sadness.

"Sit down, Sergeant Burke. Please excuse me if I seem distant. I'm still very upset. I've been in the army twenty-seven years. You know what an army post is like; this isn't the first time one of my girls has been killed. But whoever did that to Betsy was less than human. Do you think she was killed by one of the men here on post?"

"Yes, I do. I found footprints from an army boot nearby and the job was done with a .45." Burke took out his notebook. "What can you tell me about Betsy Palermo?"

Major Seward opened a manila personnel file. "Betsy joined the army three years ago in Cleveland. High school graduate with one year of college. Studied music at Cleveland State College. Twenty-three years old last January. Just a couple of months ago Betsy took a leave and went to Austria for the Salzburg Music Festival. She was so excited and happy. I enjoy classical music myself and we had a long talk about the festival when she came back. Betsy was no ordinary girl. She joined up to save money through the army scholarship fund."

"If Betsy was saving money for college, where did she get the cash for a trip to Austria?"

"I don't know." Major Seward opened a cigarette case and lit one up without asking Burke if he minded or offering him one. She was a major and he was a sergeant. Those little courtesies were unnecessary. "I assume Betsy went to Austria on a low-cost charter flight."

"What was her job?"

"She worked in the supply depot at Camp Funston." Major Seward consulted the records again. "Records clerk in the Restricted Materiel Center. In fact, Betsy had a Top Secret clearance, which means I have to notify the Department of Defense of her death." She made a note to do that.

"Top Secret? What kind of records did she handle?"

"I don't know. And I doubt that the R.M.C. people will tell you. But as her clearance implies, Betsy worked with both classified documents and material."

"Did she have a boyfriend?"

"None that I know of."

"Was she gay?"

Major Seward took no offense at the question. She knew better than anyone that a high percentage of the girls in her unit were lesbians, a given among army women. "No, Betsy occasionally went out with men. It's just that she had no boyfriend in particular on— Wait a minute." She took a drag on her cigarette. "Betsy did have several dates with Sergeant Major Roper. You know him, of course."

"Yes, I know Hank Roper."

"I was surprised to see him with Betsy. You probably know that Sergeant Roper never has anything good to say about army women."

Burke nodded. "The only time I ever saw Corporal Palermo was this morning. I couldn't really tell what she looked like alive. Was she a pretty girl?"

"Not especially."

Which made Hank Roper's interest in her even more puzzling. "Well, thank you for your help, Major Seward."

"I just hope you find the butcher who killed her."

"We will. Meanwhile, I'd like to collect Corporal Palermo's things and take them back to MP headquarters. There may be something in them that will help us."

"All right. I'll have to send her personal belongings to her family, but you can hold on to them for now."

Burke stood up.

"My clerk will take you to Betsy's locker. Oh, there's a sergeant from the Restricted Materiel Center going through her things right now. They want to make certain she didn't take any classified documents from the R.M.C. That's just a routine procedure, of course."

"Fine. I'll sort things out with him."

A clerk led Burke across the parade ground to the barracks where Betsy Palermo had lived. The Wac drillmaster was still marching her girls back and forth and yelling at the top of her impressive voice. It sounded like there wouldn't be any weekend passes after all.

As Burke climbed to the second floor, he heard a pair of masculine voices talking and laughing.

They came up into the long squad room that made up the entire second floor. Two men were going through a locker at the far end of the room.

"That's Betsy's locker and those guys are from the R.M.C." The clerk's chin trembled. "Betsy was a nice girl—real nice. Do you need me anymore?"

"No. And thanks." Burke walked down the center aisle of the squad room, hoping there was a logical explanation for what he was seeing and hearing. The two men at Betsy Palermo's locker were a staff sergeant and a young corporal. He recognized the older man as Harry Williamson, another pal of Hank Roper.

Williamson had thrown clothing, cosmetics, and personal papers from the locker onto a bunk. He was sitting on the edge of the bunk reading out loud in a mincing voice for the corporal's amusement.

" '. . . wish you could be here, Betsy darling.' " Williamson snickered and rolled his eyes, causing the corporal to throw back his head and laugh. " 'You are so sweet and lovely. Cleveland just isn't the same without you.' " Williamson stopped to laugh himself. "Hey, Benny, listen to this. 'All I want out of life is to make a home for you and to be a good husband someday and maybe, if we're lucky, a good father to our kids, too. The extra money you're making is wonderful. But all I really need for happiness is you.' Ain't that a load of shit?"

"What are you men doing?" Burke demanded. "Is that a letter to Corporal Palermo?"

The grins vanished. Harry Williamson stood up, his huge form dwarfing that of the corporal. "What we're doing is none of your fucking business, Ansel."

"You've got no right to read her personal letters, Harry. And having a big laugh over them is pretty low, even for a turd like you."

"Listen, I work over in the R.M.C., just like Palermo did. Captain Miller sent me to check out her locker. Make sure there ain't no classified papers lying around.

So I got as much right to be here as you do." Williamson squared his solid shoulders. "Benny and me are taking her things with us, so you just run along."

"Going through her gear is an MP responsibility. If she had any classified papers, I'll send them over to Captain Miller myself."

Williamson crumpled the letter in his fist. "Don't fuck with me, Ansel."

The corporal, not eager to get caught between two such large and powerful men, eased aside.

Burke approached Williamson, who stood his ground. When they were a few feet apart Williamson dropped the letter and braced himself for a rush. Burke smiled, which put Williamson briefly off guard. At that moment Burke clubbed the side of Williamson's head with his fist. Williamson staggered and grabbed for Burke's shirtfront. Burke slipped underneath the sweeping arm and hit Williamson in the gut with a quick right. Then he drove a knee into his balls and, as Williamson sagged, chopped another right into the bulge of his Adam's apple, sending the burly sergeant crashing to the floor.

As Williamson lay gasping for breath, the little corporal backed against a wall. "I'm not looking for trouble."

"Then get this piece of pig meat out of here. And keep your mouth shut about whatever you read in the girl's letters. She deserves better than that from men who served with her."

"I will, I promise."

It took the corporal several minutes to get Williamson on his feet. He was pale and shaky and had to be supported by the corporal as he walked the length of the squad room. Before going down the steps he looked over his shoulder at Ansel Burke with murderous intent.

Burke hardly noticed. He was packing Betsy Palermo's things neatly into a barracks bag.

Chapter 6

Burke decided to pull Amos Biggs and Jack Rittmaster off patrol and put them on the Palermo case full-time. Neither man could be described as detectives. There were no detectives, as such, in the Military Police. Any investigative work was supposed to go through the army's Criminal Investigation Division or the FBI. But both those agencies would be useless in a case like this. They concentrated their military activities almost exclusively on espionage, vying with each other to uncover spies and grab headlines. The murder of a corporal would interest them about as much as a shoplifter in the PX.

Biggs and Rittmaster were good choices for this detail. Amos Biggs moved slowly and consumed more beer than the state of Rhode Island, but he got results. He'd certainly been fast to nail the troopers who tipped over the general's cannon. And Biggs was a master of intimidation. He had a routine for questioning suspects that worked very well. For starters, Biggs would back a suspect into a corner and put his huge beer belly up against him. Then he'd ask a string of hectoring questions that had little to do with whatever crime he was investigating. When the suspect looked sufficiently confused and uncomfortable, Biggs would lift him bodily off the floor and shake him like a baby's rattle while he asked the important questions on his mind.

Burke was amazed that civilian cops got any confes-

sions at all, considering the many restraints imposed
on them. By contrast, the Military Police can do just
about anything they want. They can question a suspect without explaining his rights, for the simple reason that a soldier has few rights. A soldier can be
questioned without having an attorney present. His
locker, desk, car, or person can be searched without a
warrant. And most evidence is admissible in a court-
martial, often regardless of the methods used to obtain
it.

Free from all those pesky Constitutional restraints,
Biggs and his investigative techniques would be
invaluable.

Jack Rittmaster would be a solid addition to the
team for other reasons. Sergeant Rittmaster was a
student of sin. Every book he had ever read was pornographic. Every movie he saw was X-rated. The only
women he went out with were tramps or whores. As a
boy he had slept with both of his sisters, and bragged
about it. He knew every prostitute and pimp in central
New Mexico and kept himself well informed about the
sexual habits of his fellow troopers. Burke avoided
Rittmaster's company, even as he acknowledged that
Rittmaster was the most useful MP on post when it
came to a case with sexual overtones.

He told the communications center to call in Biggs
and Rittmaster, then placed a phone call to Puma.

"Winston Gallery."

"Hi, Maggie."

"Ansell I'm just about to close the gallery. If you
pick me up at six-thirty, we can be in Albuquerque
sipping margaritas by seven-thirty."

"I'm sorry, I'm going to be late. I don't think we can
make Albuquerque tonight."

"Oh, that's a shame. I've got *wonderful* news for
you. Can we have dinner in Puma?"

"Sure. I can be at your place by eight-thirty."

"I have a terrific idea," Maggie said. "Why don't you
take me to that place where all your army friends go?"

"The Chicken Coop?" Burke couldn't imagine Maggie
in the Chicken Coop.

"I've always been curious about the place. Didn't

you tell me that Waylon Jennings and Willie Nelson
used to play there?"

"Well, sure. But it's a soldier's hangout: loud country music, pitchers of beer, sawdust on the floor. That
kind of thing."

"Darling, I'm not a porcelain doll. And I'd really like
to meet some of your army friends. I'm beginning to
think you're ashamed of me."

"That's ridiculous. It's just that you're so different
from anyone else I know." He realized she was serious,
so he said, "Okay, the Chicken Coop it is. But don't
say I didn't warn you."

"See you at eight-thirty, darling."

Maggie was smiling as she put down the phone. The
idea of going to some grimy roadhouse called the
Chicken Coop filled her with disgust. But it would be
worth the sacrifice to meet some of Ansel's friends. To
break him loose from the army, she first had to understand why he loved the service so much.

One of the things about Ansel that irritated her was
the way he talked about his friends—as if they shared
some mystical secret about life, denied to mere civilians.

They can't be that special, she thought. Not a bunch
of moronic soldiers. I only have to show Ansel that
there's a whole different world out there full of more
interesting, more intelligent, more tasteful people.

Of course, she would have to choose her words carefully. Ansel would resent any direct attack on his
buddies. No problem. There were subtle ways to point
out how little he had now in comparison with how
much he could have if he left the army.

Maggie glanced sidelong at her profile in the mirror
above her desk. And, she thought, the centerpiece of
all he could have is me.

Burke met with Amos Biggs and Jack Rittmaster at
seventeen hundred hours in his office. Together they
began going through all the personal belongings and
army gear he had taken from Betsy Palermo's locker.

"At least she was neat," Rittmaster observed. "Most
army broads are pigs. Don't wash their underwear

often enough, not to mention their pussies. But Palermo's stuff is so clean you'd think it was new." He turned his head and coughed until a bit of phlegm cleared his throat. Rittmaster had the doughy complexion and raspy voice that came from six packs of cigarettes a day. He was in his late thirties and already gray-haired. He called cigarettes "cancer sticks" with the cheerful nonchalance of a man who at least knows how he's going to die. "Hey, this stuff *is* new."

"You're right." Biggs was going through the girl's papers. "There are a lot of receipts here for new clothes. She's been to some pricey women's stores in Albuquerque. If my wife spent this much money on bras and underpants, I wouldn't let her wear anything else."

Burke was looking at the airline ticket stubs from Betsy Palermo's recent trip to Austria. "She's been spending a *ton* of money lately. She flew *first-class* to Austria and back for the Salzburg Music Festival. From the receipts, the trip cost her at least five thousand dollars. She had a checking account at Albuquerque First Federal. Even after paying for the trip and all these new clothes, her balance is more than eleven thousand dollars. And look at this: she had a savings account in a different bank. It's in another name: Elizabeth Prince. Same initials—E.P. The handwriting is definitely hers. The balance in this account is over sixty-five thousand dollars."

The figure drew a whistle from Amos Biggs. "Betsy must've been doing some hooking on the side."

"No way," Rittmaster declared. "Number one, she didn't look good enough to make that much money on her back. Number two, I would've heard if Palermo was on the circuit. We got about ten female personnel at Fort Powell who do some hooking. She wasn't one of them."

"Are you sure?" Burke asked.

"Look at it this way," Rittmaster said. "She'd have to fuck two-thirds of the post to bank this much loot."

"Then where did she get all her money?" Amos Biggs scratched his belly and wished there were beer in it. "And how much more is there that we haven't found yet? Look at this." He showed Burke and Rittmaster

the same letter Harry Williamson had been reading
out loud for the entertainment of his buddy. "Betsy
had a boyfriend back home in Cleveland. They were
planning on getting married. Betsy told him she had a
great part-time job off post 'selling cosmetics.' She sent
him thirty thousand dollars over the last year. They
were gonna open a record store specializing in classical music when Betsy got out of the army."

Burke opened another envelope full of papers. "Let's
see what else there is."

Betsy Palermo's other papers raised additional questions. There was a blank application from a Swiss
bank to which Betsy had applied for an account. Apparently, she had died before opening it. However, on
her last tax form she had declared only a little more
than fifteen thousand dollars for the year, which
matched her army pay. They also found a diamond
bracelet in her jewelry box, with a receipt from
Fortunoff's in New York—she had paid $2,600 for the
jewelry—in cash.

"This broad went through money like a rich widow."
Rittmaster sat back and toted up figures in his head.
"She spent and banked more than a hundred thousand
dollars last year. Didn't pay taxes on any of it, I'll
bet."

"And she expected to have more big bucks soon."
Burke held up the blank application from the Swiss
bank as proof of that assumption. "Where did all that
come from?"

Finally Rittmaster said, "This isn't a case of a guy
raping a broad and then shutting her up with a .45.
Palermo was killed because she was into something
heavier than she could handle."

"Drugs?" Amos Biggs speculated.

"Maybe," Rittmaster said.

"There's another interesting thing about this girl,"
Burke told them. "She's been going out with Hank
Roper."

Biggs and Rittmaster registered disbelief.

"Hank *hates* those broads. He wouldn't walk across
the street to watch a Wac fuck a monkey." Rittmaster
looked to Biggs for confirmation. "Isn't that right?"

"I've never heard Hank say one good word about army women," Biggs agreed. He had a second thought: "Or blacks."

"Now don't go NAACP on us," Rittmaster said. "We've got other fish to fry."

"I'm only saying you're right," Biggs pointed out. "There's a lot of people Hank Roper don't like. At the top of the list are Wacs, blacks, and Orientals." Biggs was married to a Vietnamese girl. Roper had baited him more than once about his "yellow pussy." Because Roper outranked him, there was not much Biggs could do about it—except remember. "I'll tell you this: Hank ain't a man to change his spots; if he went out with Betsy Palermo, he wanted something besides her body."

"I'll go along with that." Rittmaster drummed his fingers on Burke's desk. "Did you guys know that Roper bought a gas station out in the sticks?"

"I heard something about it," Burke said. "Hank's into a lot of shady deals, but that struck me as a strange business for him."

"At first I thought he might be using it to run a string of whores, so I checked out the place: no women there. But he's got some of his buddies pumping gas on their days off. Guys you'd never expect to see pumping gas."

"What's your point?" Burke asked, though he knew where Rittmaster was headed.

"My point is that Hank Roper has done two things completely out of character: dated a Wac and bought a gas station. The station is in the middle of nowhere and a run-down old place besides—not that Hank would buy a gas station even if he could get Mr. Goodwrench to run it for him." Rittmaster had a coughing spell that gave everyone time to think.

"Okay," Burke said. "We need to find out more about Betsy and Hank. Amos, talk to her friends at the Wac Shack. See if you can find out where she and Hank went together. What they did. Whether Hank was sleeping with Betsy. She had a Top Secret clearance. Could that be why Hank was attracted to her? Another thing. She worked in the Restricted Materiel Center. See if you can find out what her job was. The people over there are pretty closemouthed, but do your best."

"Will do."

Rittmaster, breathing regularly again, grinned. "I get Hank?"

"You get Hank. See if any of his friends know why he was going out with Betsy Palermo. And get me more on that gas station. Which of his buddies work there?" Burke had an inspiration. "There's a Staff Sergeant Harry Williamson attached to the R.M.C. Another buddy of Hank's. He tried to stop me from impounding this stuff."

Biggs and Rittmaster smiled at each other as they speculated about the extent of Williamson's injuries.

"Find out if Williamson works at that gas station."

Rittmaster moistened the tip of a pencil with his tongue and wrote Williamson's name in his notebook. "This'll be fun. I've been curious about Hank's buddies for a long time."

"Don't get too close to him," Burke warned. "Hank's a rattlesnake in every way but one: he doesn't make a warning noise before he kills."

The barracks buildings at Camp Funston had none of the charm of those at the main post. They were clapboard instead of adobe. The wind came off the desert along the ridge on which Camp Funston was built like a freight train, stripping paint off the buildings and occasionally flattening the CAMP FUNSTON sign at the entrance to the complex.

Because Harry Williamson held the rank of staff sergeant, he was entitled to a small room to himself. He was lying naked on his bunk holding an ice bag to his testicles, which were swollen to twice their normal size. The left side of his face was also puffed out and a red welt ran across his throat.

Roper smiled down on him. "I hear Ansel doesn't have a mark on him."

"He jumped me from behind," Williamson croaked.

"That's funny. Ansel's tall, but I didn't think his legs were long enough to kick you in the balls from behind."

"Fucking bastard." Williamson pushed a finger into his mouth to explore a tooth that felt loose. "He won't be so lucky next time."

"Ansel doesn't need luck. He's a total professional."

"You think he's so hot, why don'tcha marry him?"

Roper looked at Williamson without pity. "If Ansel hadn't whipped your ass, I'd have done it myself. You screwed up. First you left Betsy where she could be found. Then you let Ansel take her stuff away from you. You were supposed to grab her things before anyone else could. Who knows what kind of notes and records Betsy might have kept." He took another look at Williamson's testicles and laughed. "I've never seen anything like those things. Grapefruits! That's what they look like to me."

Williamson, glowering, tried to shift himself to a more comfortable position.

Roper paced the narrow room. "Okay, I'll get hold of Control. He'll find a way to get Betsy's stuff out of Burke's hands. I hear that Burke has brought Rittmaster and Biggs into the case. Jack is smart and that nigger knows a few things, too. I don't like the idea of the three of them digging into this."

"So what are you gonna do about it?"

"If Ansel gets too close to us, we may have to cancel him out."

For the first time since his balls doubled in size, Harry Williamson smiled.

You could hear the Chicken Coop before you could see it. The *twang* of amplified steel guitars came off the desert like rolling thunder. Burke turned off the highway onto a dirt road and said, "Don't expect too much. This is just a roadhouse." He was annoyed with himself for sounding anxious.

Maggie slipped a hand under his arm. "Don't worry so much. I've been to places like this before. In fact, I went to the Lone Star Cafe in New York twice. It was delightful."

"That was New York. This is a different kind of place altogether."

"As long as the food is good."

The Chicken Coop sat a quarter of a mile back from the road. The building was a rambling, old, clay brick structure patched here and there with adobe. The roof was tar paper over tin. There was no parking lot. People more or less abandoned their cars in random patterns on the surrounding flat desert floor. A majority of the cars had Fort Powell bumper stickers.

Burke parked and came around to help Maggie out of the car. "Watch your step. There are prairie dog holes all over the place." He took her arm and escorted her across the rough ground to the entrance.

They were greeted inside the door by country music played at maniacal sound levels and the overpowering stench of beer and sawdust, causing Maggie to reel under the assault on her senses.

"Are you okay?"

"I'm fine, darling. Can you find us a table? I'd like very much to sit down." Maggie looked at her foot. A large dab of prairie dog goop was stuck firmly to the bottom of one of her hand-sewn Italian leather boots. Shuddering, she scraped the sole of the boot along the floor. Instead of coming loose, the goop increased in size as it picked up sawdust.

A man with iron gray hair worn in an old-fashioned crew cut waved at them. "Hey, Ansel! Over here!"

Burke led her through the tables to the place where the graying man waited. As they approached, he shouted at the others at his table, "Clear the table, gentlemens. We got Sergeant Major Burke and his lady with us tonight."

The others moved out smartly, leaving the table clear.

Ansel made the introduction. "This is Lou Brodsky, the man who really runs the MP barracks. Lou, meet Maggie Winston."

"I'm honored to meet you, ma'am."

"How do you do. You must tell me all about Ansel. He hates to talk about himself, you know."

"Oh, yes ma'am. That's a fact. Just sit down and I'll tell you anything you want to know." Brodsky picked up a large pitcher of beer and began pouring some into a glass for her. "But first you'd best drink up. Gets damned hot in this joint."

"Why is this beer green?" Maggie asked.

"Mexican beer," Brodsky explained. "Cheap but good." He filled Burke's glass and raised his own. "To your health."

Maggie drank a mouthful and almost gagged. The beer tasted *noxious*. She glanced to her left and was appalled to see Ansel enjoying his.

"I told you it was good," Brodsky beamed.

"Lovely." Maggie pretended to take another sip and then placed the glass on the table at arm's length. Green beer. What would the food be like?

Brodsky leaned close to her. "Ansel tells me you sell his pictures for him."

"Yes, dealing in art is my profession."

"I gotta tell you something."

He leaned even closer, which alarmed Maggie.

"Because Ansel spends so much time at his paint box, some of the troops think he might be going Asiatic. I mean, they see Ansel busting heads in the morning and drawing pictures in the afternoon. It's confusing for them, y'know? And he's so good at busting heads, they can't see why he'd want to do the other. What I want to tell ya is this: I understand." He winked at their shared secret. "Ansel . . . has got . . . to paint. Am I right?"

She was so relieved when he pulled back that she said, "You're very observant, Mr. Brodsky."

"And you aro ono good looking woman. I'd buy a paint box myself if it'd get me next to someone like you."

"How sweet," Maggie said, without moving her lips.

"Where'd you get them jeans?"

"Uh . . . Bloomingdale's."

"What's that, one of them discount centers?"

"No, it's a department store in New York."

"I never seen pants like that—so many stitches and all. Nice."

"Thank you." How does Ansel *stand* this man? she wondered.

During their conversation a waitress had put a sec-

ond pitcher of green beer and a platter of nachos on
the table and Ansel had ordered dinner for them.

Brodsky thumped Ansel on the back and said,
"Maggie's all right, Sergeant Major. You got a real
woman here."

"Hey, vat you doing here tonight, Ansel?"

"Wolfe! Come over here." A barrel-chested man with
a bald head shaped like a bullet plopped down in a
chair across the table from them. "Maggie, I want you
to meet one of my oldest army buddies—Sergeant Major Wolfe Heinzman. We served in 'Nam together. Wolfe,
this is Maggie Winston."

"Miss Vinston, I am honored. You like this big ape?
Vell, so do I. Ansel save my life two, maybe three,
times. You own the gallery downtown?"

"Yes."

"I go in there one day to see Ansel's pictures, stand
there vith my mouth open. This man can really paint,
I think."

"Yes, he's wonderful. In fact, I've just arranged for a
show of his work at one of the best galleries in New
York."

Heinzman and Brodsky were astute enough to be
impressed. Ansel only shrugged. "She just told me
about it on the way over here. Looks like I'll have to
start combing my hair forward and wearing a beret."

"There you go again!" Brodsky wailed. "Miss Winston, stop him from talking like that, will ya?"

The food arrived and turned out to be better than
Maggie had expected, even though everything was
drenched in hot sauce. She had hoped that Lou Brodsky
and Wolfe Heinzman would leave when the food came,
but they stayed and dug noisily into the nachos and
beer. The music became even louder, if that was possible, making conversation difficult. But Maggie appreciated the interlude: it gave her time to watch and
think.

What impressed her was the effect Ansel had on
others. Throughout dinner a steady stream of men
came up to the table to say hello. He introduced each
of them to Maggie. They left looking smug about the
fact that Ansel thought enough of them to introduce

them to his "new lady." It was obvious that being a
friend of Sergeant Major Ansel Burke was a mark of
distinction. Some felt otherwise: Maggie saw a few
men come in the door, spot Ansel at the center table
near the dance floor, then turn right around and leave.
No one seemed indifferent to him.

Maggie was pleased by the jealous looks she received from the other women in the Chicken Coop.
Ansel was considered a prize around here, as well he
might be. Little did they know how big a prize he was.
Still, when Maggie had told Ansel about the New
York show, she had deliberately downplayed the amount
of money it would put in his pocket. No sense making
him feel too rich and important. That was how she'd
lost Marshall Vogel.

Mercifully, the music stopped and the bandleader
announced that his group would take a short break.

In the relative silence, a woman's voice said, "Hi
there, Ansel."

Maggie looked up from her enchiladas and refried
beans to find a pert little redhead in a cowboy shirt
and old denims standing by the table with a lanky
young man who was trying to keep his arm around
her waist.

Burke stood and smiled at her. "Hello, Captain."

"It's Jean, remember?"

"Sure. Jean Silk, this is Maggie Winston, Wolfe
Heinzman, and Lou Brodsky." Ansel looked at the
crowd around them. "We've got a couple of extra chairs.
Would you like to join us?"

"Love to," Jean Silk said, to the annoyance of her
escort. "Oh, this is Captain Bill Manning, who's almost as new to Fort Powell as I am. Bill, meet Ansel
Burke. He's the sergeant major of the Military Police."

Manning sat down without shaking Ansel's hand.
"You didn't tell me this was an enlisted man's hangout," he complained.

"Oh, what's the difference." Jean pushed away the
hand that Manning continued trying to put around
her. "The music's good and the food smells delicious.
But green beer?" She hailed a waitress. "Can I have a
stinger on the rocks, please?"

"A stinger?" Ansel raised his eyebrows. "I haven't heard anybody order one of those in years."

"When I was a kid my father drank stingers while he read to me from his law books. Before he died, he asked me to help keep the stinger alive after he was gone. I've been fighting a one-woman battle for it ever since."

"A noble tribute," Wolfe Heinzman said. "Vaitress, bring me a stinger, too."

"The same for Maggie and me," Ansel said.

"Hell, I'll drink anything." Brodsky grinned. "Count me in."

Only Manning declined to order a stinger.

"Ma'am, are you the lawyer who got Sean Feeney off at this morning's court-martial?" Brodsky asked.

"I am."

"That was a hell of a job, Captain. I been in this army thirty-one years and I never seen an enlisted man win one like that."

Maggie didn't like the way this girl looked at Ansel. The little bitch obviously had her eye on him. An army lawyer? She looked more like a prostitute with that cowboy shirt worn tight to show off her tits. Maggie slid an arm inside Ansel's, just to let Jean Silk know the ground rules. There are times, she thought, when subtlety is totally inappropriate.

Jean understood. "Maggie Winston. You own the Winston Gallery on Colorado Boulevard."

"Yes, I do."

"I went in there my second day in Puma. I would have spoken to you then, but you were with a customer. I saw some striking paintings in your gallery. It wasn't until this afternoon that I learned they were painted by Ansel." She looked at him with open admiration. "Why didn't you tell me you're an artist? A very fine artist, at that."

He shrugged uncomfortably. "It's not the kind of thing I know how to talk about."

"Well, I can understand that." Jean immediately changed the subject. "Hey, I was handed an interesting case today. I'm going to defend two soldiers who got drunk and pushed some old cannon down a hill."

"Well, that's one case you won't win. Those guys are dead-bang guilty."

"So was Sean Feeney," Jean countered, "but I got him off. And I think I've got a defense for these two idiots. Do you know how much money General Leland has spent on that stupid cannon? One hundred and eighty thousand of the taxpayers' dollars. That's for all the chrome; the daily upkeep; the horses that pull the caisson in local parades; and the shipping charges to send the whole thing off to parades in other states. I don't think General Leland would like that to come out in court any more than he wanted that business about the tanks to come out this morning. My defense is going to be that those two boys did a fiscal service to their country by putting out of action an expensive, unnecessary, and ridiculous anachronism."

To Maggie's intense irritation, Ansel leaned forward anxiously. "Jean, you can't win every case by threatening to make your commanding officer look bad to the General Services Administration. Leland won't stand for it. Underneath that gentlemanly manner he's a vicious bastard. And remember that *he's* the law on this post, not you."

"I'll be all right," Jean assured him.

"You're being foolish," Manning said. "Leland is a brigadier general. Antagonizing him would be a bad career move."

"General Leland wants to send those two boys to prison for five years for a drunken prank in which no one was hurt and nothing of any real value was damaged," Jean retorted. "I can't let that happen."

"You've got the makings of a modern Joan of Arc," Burke said, "and you know how *she* ended up."

Maggie didn't like to hear Ansel comparing this little trollop to Joan of Arc. Admiration, she believed, was only one step from lust.

"Hey! Hey! Is it you? ... By God, it *is* you! Hot damn, I been wantin' to buy you a drink all day." Sean Feeney stumbled up to the table and grinned down at Jean Silk. He was still in the uniform he'd worn to his court-martial, though it was now in considerable disarray. His Irish pug face was lit with pleasure. "This little lady is the best damned lawyer in the U.S. Army, and don't ever let anyone say different. Not in my—" He belched. "In my presence."

"Pull up a chair," Ansel said. "Sean, I'd like you to meet Maggie Winston."

"Please to meet'cha, pretty lady."

"Jean defended Sean at his court-martial this morning. Got him off with only a one-grade bust."

"How clever of her." Maggie had no idea what a one-grade bust was, and in addition was completely revolted by the man's unkempt appearance, ripe aroma, and drunken behavior. "Why were you court-martialed, Mr. Feeney?"

"They said I knocked down a whorehouse with my tank."

"You're the man who did that?"

"So they tried to prove." Feeney winked at her. "But my lawyer here was too smart for 'em."

Maggie glanced at Ansel, expecting him to share her disgust. He was, after all, a policeman. But Ansel was laughing right along with the beastly little man. *Knocked down a whorehouse.* How could Feeney have been acquitted when he was all but bragging that he'd committed the crime? She looked around the table and saw that only Jean Silk's date appeared as uncomfortable as she felt.

The waitress delivered a round of stingers and Feeney scattered dollar bills across her tray. "These are on me." He leaned across the table until his face was only a few inches from Maggie's. "I'm thirty-seven years old and I ain't got a hair on my ass."

"I beg your pardon?"

"Feeney likes you," Burke whispered. "That's his way of getting acquainted."

"Charming." Maggie picked up her stinger and drank off a healthy portion. She was beginning to understand the army's attraction to Ansel. He had a wild side to him and these friends of his were not only untutored, they were untamed. Their company provided a rough kind of excitement that Ansel apparently needed.

New York, she thought. What I must do is get Ansel

to come with me to New York for his one-man show.
I'll make sure he gets all the excitement he can handle, including the company of some really bright and
interesting people. When I've shown him New York,
he won't want anything to do with these losers.

"Ansel," Jean was saying, "I heard a rumor this
afternoon that the body of a Fort Powell girl named
Betsy Palermo was found on the desert today. Is that
true?"

"I'm afraid so. And it wasn't an accidental death.
She was murdered."

Jean sipped her drink pensively. "Betsy Palermo
came to see me just a few days ago to talk over a legal
problem. She was one of the first people I met here."

Ansel pushed aside the beer pitcher standing between them. "What kind of legal problem? Tell me
everything she said. This could be important."

"Well, Betsy seemed worried—"

Their conversation was interrupted by a commotion
at the bar. "Listen up!" someone commanded. "Everybody quiet down and pay attention!"

A Royals–Yankees baseball game had been running
on the television set above the bar. No one had paid
much attention to it, except when the band went on its
break. The game had been interrupted by a news bul-
letin. The CBS anchorman was speaking from behind
his desk, looking grim.

"Listen!" someone shouted again. When the patrons
of the Chicken Coop had quieted down, the bartender
turned up the volume on the television.

". . . has just learned," the anchorman was saying,
"that the government of Egypt has used a nuclear
weapon against a force of Libyan troops that crossed
the Egyptian border to attack an army garrison in the
town of Qattara. A small nuclear warhead of less than
one megaton force apparently was fired into the Libyans from an artillery battery located some eight miles
from its target. More than four thousand Libyan troops
were reported killed and wounded and the remnants of
their force have retreated back over the border. A
mushroom cloud from the explosion could be seen from
as far away as fifty miles."

"Holy shit." Brodsky buried his face in his hands.

"In response, President Walter Bryant has severed diplomatic relations with Egypt and recalled our ambassador," the anchorman continued. "CBS has learned that the U.S. government does not know at this time how Egypt obtained a nuclear weapon. Some experts say that country has the materials and expertise to build its own nuclear device. Others claim that the delivery system used today was too sophisticated to have been developed within Egypt. And the apparent small size of the weapon also indicates that it was developed elsewhere. Only major nuclear powers currently have the ability to deploy small tactical nuclear warheads.

"CBS News will return tonight at eleven with a full report on this tragic story—the first use of nuclear weapons against a human population since the bombing of Hiroshima and Nagasaki in 1945."

The Chicken Coop's raucous atmosphere had been transformed into quiet gloom.

"Four thousand troopers wiped out by a single artillery round," said Sean Feeney, momentarily sobered. "A man wouldn't have survived in a tank, either."

Maggie, more frightened by the apprehension of those around her than by the newscast itself, moved her chair closer to Ansel's. "What does this mean?"

"It means the genie is out of the bottle."

"I think I'm gonna be sick," Brodsky said.

Burke put his arm around his friend's shoulder and patted his back, which Maggie deeply resented. I'm upset, she thought, and he puts his arm around that old fool's shoulder.

People were leaving in twos and threes. A few were crying. Jean Silk sat with her fists clenched, looking into her drink.

"Only thing I ever vant to be is a soldier," Wolfe Heinzman said. "No more. My next re-up date is November. By God, I don't think I vill re-up. I think I go find a hole and crawl in." The German left.

Ansel leaned across the table and patted one of Jean's clenched fists. "We'll talk about Besty Palermo tomorrow."

"All right." She continued to stare at her glass through unblinking eyes. "The murder of one girl seems almost unimportant now. That's the greatest tragedy, isn't it? The way mass murder makes individual lives seem insignificant."

Maggie searched for something to say. "They were only Libyans, weren't they? Maybe this was all for the best." She was alarmed by the hostile looks she received, even from Ansel. "I mean, we don't know the whole story yet. The Libyans could have accidentally exploded a nuclear device against themselves. That's a possibility, isn't it? And perhaps this will make everyone finally buckle down and ban nuclear weapons."

"Maybe." Burke downed the rest of his stinger. "It's possible that only something like this can stop the politicians from playing king-of-the-hill with bombs and missiles."

"That's what I meant," Maggie insisted.

Bill Manning stood and took Jean's arm. "Come on, let's go back to the post."

She rose like a zombie.

"I'll call you tomorrow," Ansel promised.

"Yes," she answered vaguely.

Feeney was drinking again, aiming this time for complete stupor. Burke and Maggie left him to his single-minded goal along with a few other serious drinkers and those too frozen with fear to move.

Maggie took Ansel to her apartment, a Spanish-style villa with large and airy rooms, smooth white walls, and high ceilings. Two of his paintings graced the walls of the living room.

She fixed drinks and then took him into her bedroom. The windows faced the Sangre de Cristos and the walls were decorated with brilliantly colored Mexican rugs.

"Sit down, darling." She gave him a gentle push.

Burke sat down on the edge of the bed, put his glass on the floor, and encircled Maggie's waist with his large, rough hands. She smiled and moved her fingertips gently along the back of his neck.

"I know exactly what you want," she whispered.

"Tonight I just want to forget everything. Except you."

"Let's make ourselves cool and clean first. The Chicken Coop leaves one a little soiled." She unbuttoned Ansel's shirt, then knelt in front of him and, her fingers teasing, unzipped his pants. Then she pulled off his shirt, shoes, and pants and stood back just out of arm's length to undress herself. As she loosened her clothes and let them drop to the floor, she caressed her own body here and there: along the curve of a breast; over the flat planes of her stomach; down the inside of her thigh.

When they were both naked, she took Ansel's hand and led him to the bathroom. She turned on the shower and they stepped inside.

Maggie picked up a bar of perfumed soap and lathered her hands. They were standing face-to-face under the showerhead with water running over their bodies in rivers. She began soaping his chest and he did the same for her shoulders and breasts. Presently Ansel lowered his head and began licking her rigid nipples. She pulled him hard against her, giving him the full blossom of her breasts with a sigh of pleasure.

He raised up and drew her mouth to his.

Ansel's hands moved between her legs, soaping her thighs and moving around to do the same for her buttocks. After a while she reached down and grasped him gently, guiding him up and into her. He backed her against the tile wall, lifting her off the floor. Her legs went around him and she threw her wet hair back from her head.

"Now then . . ."

The soapy surfaces brought them together smoothly. Maggie reached around and stroked him from underneath and behind. Ansel sucked in his breath and moved against her. The water poured over and across them. Her thighs enveloped him. They went rigid, kneading each other with their hands, murmuring, biting at the air around each other's ears like cats. Ansel gasped and Maggie, calculating to please him, cried out as he exploded inside her. His climax lasted so long that Maggie almost begged him to stop.

At last they came apart and slid down the tile wall until they sat together on the shower floor, as wet and exhausted as Olympic swimmers after a race.

"Jesus." Ansel raised his face to the rushing water. "That's the best shower I've ever had."

Maggie chuckled against his shoulder. "I've always hated all the bother of cleaning up after sex. This makes it unnecessary."

"From now on I won't be able to take a shower without getting a hard-on." He grinned down at her. "Which is going to make life very embarrassing for me back in the barracks."

Maggie laid her head on his chest and gave herself over to the soothing drumbeat of the running water. I've done it, she exulted. He's mine for as long as I want him.

THURSDAY, JUNE 12

Chapter 7

Throughout the morning, limousines had been depositing official visitors at the south entrance of the White House. In front, on Pennsylvania Avenue, lines of protestors walked up and down with hastily made placards hoisted high on the ends of sticks and broom handles. Often the signs of protestors were professionally done, the letters big enough to be easily picked up by the television cameras. But this demonstration had the earmarks of genuine spontaneity. No single contingent appeared to be in control of the crowd. The faces were angry and scared. Women clutched the hands of their children, who were there in surprising numbers. A group of perhaps two hundred people stood in a circle around a clergyman leading them in prayer.

Each limousine that approached the south entrance had to breach the mass of people with the help of a squad of uniformed policemen hastily assembled for crowd control duty. The occupants were subjected to intense heckling as their cars inched through the crowd.

Luther Amstel's plain black Chrysler attracted somewhat less attention than the more ostentatious limos. Only a professional eye could tell that the Chrysler's body was armor-plated and its windows bulletproof. It was allowed to proceed somewhat more quickly.

Amstel sat in the rear with half a dozen morning papers spread out around him: the *New York Times; Boston Globe; Washington Post; Los Angeles Times; Dallas Morning Herald; Baltimore Sun.* "Drivel," he muttered, dropping the last of the papers to the floor of the car. "It's no wonder most people only read the sports and 'Dear Abby.' "

The limo was almost within the White House grounds when one of the demonstrators recognized Amstel through the smoked glass.

"Amstel!" he screamed. "Where did the warhead come from? You know! You know!"

The crowd immediately made the accusation a chant: "You KNOW, you KNOW, you KNOW, you KNOW."

Luther Amstel stared stonily ahead, ignoring the cacophony.

He did not provoke such a violent reaction because of an unsavory reputation or sinister looks. To the contrary. Amstel's probity was well known and his round face, large paunch, and snow white hair lent him a Kris Kringle look. It was his position as Director of the Central Intelligence Agency that made him a target of some protest or another wherever he went. After three years as Director of the CIA, Amstel was accustomed to such theatrics and made a point of ignoring them.

Luther Amstel was a man whose corpulence, gained from years of sitting behind the chairman's desk at one of Wall Street's largest brokerage houses, hid the fiery passions of a patriot. As a young army lieutenant he had fought in the Korean War. There was, in fact, a small spot on the beach at Inchon that he felt belonged to him rather than to the Republic of South Korea. It was there that a North Korean machine gun cut him down at the legs as he charged its emplacement with his own carbine barking away on rapid fire. He had walked with a limp ever since.

But that was a century ago, or so it seemed. In more recent years Amstel, comfortably fixed with money made on Wall Street, had satisfied his patriotic instincts through public service. His posts had included Under Secretary of Commerce and Special Assistant to the President for Economic Affairs. Then, when President Walter Bryant came into office, he was tapped for the most demanding job of his public life.

Difficult as the job was, Amstel relished his role as

Director of the CIA. He saw the CIA as America's first line of defense against the Soviet Union. The agency could do things to protect the country that Congress and the President could not, or would not. The Congress, especially, was packed with sparrows too busy lining their own nests to watch for hawks in the sky.

The limo at last emerged into the courtyard. Stepping from the car, Amstel pushed away the hand of a White House guard who tried to help him. "I've only got a limp, young man," he snapped. "I'm not a cripple."

He walked briskly into the White House with his usual rolling gait and showed his pass to the guard inside the door.

"You're going directly to the President's office, Mr. Amstel?" the guard asked.

"No, I'd like to see Jim Canon first. I'm sure he's in."

"Oh, yes. It's liable to be a week or more before he sees the outside world again. In fact, Mr. Canon sent home for extra suits and shirts this morning."

Amstel returned the pass to his wallet and limped off toward the office of the President's press secretary. He found Jim Canon in his cubbyhole behind the spacious room where press conferences are held, typing away on an old Underwood with two fingers. "Good God, Jim. When are you going to get rid of that relic?"

"It'll be buried with me," Canon replied without looking up from the keyboard.

"You ought to get yourself a word processor."

"*I'm* the word processor around here." He continued pounding the keys, his two index fingers moving so fast they were a blur. Suddenly he stopped and ripped the sheet of paper out of the ancient typewriter. "Luther, listen to this and tell me what you think. 'President Walter Bryant today reported that a complete audit of the nation's nuclear arsenal is being undertaken. He is confident the inventory will prove that the warhead used by Egypt against the Libyan army did not come from the U.S. The audit is expected to be completed within three days. Meanwhile, President Bryant plans to cooperate fully with the special United Nations commission convened to investigate the tragedy in Qattara.' " Canon looked up expectantly. "What do you think?"

Amstel shrugged. "Fine as far as it goes. But no one's going to believe the inventory unless it's been blessed by the U.N. commission, and the U.N. isn't about to do that." He paused to analyze the press secretary's state of mind. Jim Canon had been up all night fielding questions from the press. He was unshaven, rumpled, and exhausted. The dark bags under his eyes were pouchier than usual. As a newspaperman with thirty years experience on political beats, Jim Canon's word carried substantial weight with his colleagues in the press. But it was clear that he was out of his depth on this one and that the press was not giving him their usual kid-glove treatment. "Have you given any more thought to my suggestion?"

"No." Canon ran a hand through his thinning hair and pushed himself away from the Underwood. "This is not the time for the President to say anything supportive of the Egyptians. For Christ's sake, Luther. They used an *atom bomb* yesterday. Even the Arab League has denounced them for that."

"It wasn't an atom bomb," Amstel said quietly. "The weapon was an artillery shell loaded with an extremely low-level nuclear charge. Our scientific team has just concluded that the radioactive fallout from the blast will be minimal."

"I wish the same could be said for the political fallout." Canon rubbed his tired eyes. "Everyone seems to think the weapon came from the U.S., and that means the President is on the spot."

"That's why it's so important to shift the focus of the public debate away from the President," Amstel insisted. "Remind people that the Libyans were attacking Egypt. My God, that army of theirs was headed for the Aswân Dam! If the Russians, through the Libyans, got control of the Aswân, the Egyptian economy would fail in six months. Swiftly followed by the fall of the Egyptian government."

Canon made no response. He was editing the draft of the statement he had just finished.

"Have you at least brought my recommendation to the President?"

"I mentioned it. He agreed with me that this is no time to make waffling statements about the use of nuclear weapons. The Egyptians were wrong. Period. He doesn't care if Libya was about to turn the Aswân into a car wash for camels."

"I see." Amstel wasn't surprised, only disappointed. But at least he knew the President's thinking, which would make him better prepared for their ten o'clock meeting. He put a hand on Jim Canon's thin shoulder. "Better get some rest, Jim. This is going to be a long siege."

"Yeah, I know. And if it goes past a week, my wife will probably divorce me."

Amstel left Canon pounding his two-fingered drumbeat on the Underwood and went upstairs to meet with the President.

In the oval office, President Walter Bryant was for once alone with his thoughts. He had shooed the ever-present aides and executive assistants away so that he could have a few minutes to himself to contemplate his meeting with Luther Amstel. He knew what Amstel's advice would be. Amstel had prepared him by sending in a suggested statement via Jim Canon.

Bryant was a plain-faced man with big knotty hands that seemed to be made up mostly of knuckles. His plainness was often compared with Abraham Lincoln's, a fact that had contributed to his upset election to the presidency. Like Lincoln, Bryant came from the Midwest. He was a Kansas farmer who also held degrees in law and economics. At this time of year he longed for the flat plains of his home state and the smell of spring wheat. He hoped the manager he had put in charge of his farm would get the wheat in early this year. Farmers who waited too long to harvest sometimes lost their wheat to summer lightning.

But the thought of wheat only floated through his mind. What occupied him was the audacity of Egyptian President Raqui Zamal in using a nuclear weapon against Libya. That single act had upset the delicate balance of power between Russia and the U.S. And Walter Bryant could see no easy way to put it right again.

An aide knocked discreetly on the door, then opened it. "Director Amstel is here, sir."

"Send him in."

Bryant sat up, trying to look aggressive and in control of events. He didn't want Amstel to know how helpless he felt. Despite his Father Christmas appearance, Amstel was a street fighter who went straight for the throat of anyone he sensed to be weaker than himself.

"Good morning, Mr. President." Amstel limped into the office and paused, as he always did, to gaze admiringly at the presidential seal painted on the ceiling of the Oval Office. Then he took a seat across the desk from Bryant. "Are we meeting alone today? I thought the Secretary of State was going to join us."

"Henry flew down to New York for the first meeting of the U.N. special commission."

"Ah."

"Do I hear a note of derision in that *ah*, Luther?"

"You have a fine ear, Mr. President. But I wasn't deriding Henry Flowers. It's the U.N. to which I object."

"I know how you feel. But the U.N. is a fact of life. We can't ignore the General Assembly's point of view, especially in this case."

"Sir, in my opinion we can and should ignore the U.N. The General Assembly is stacked against us on every issue. Even the small ones. On an issue this big, we stand alone. But I'm sure you know that."

Wheat, Bryant thought tiredly. I must get back to the farm for a few days of rest. "Do you have any new information for me, Luther?"

Amstel carried a thin black briefcase, which he put across his knees and opened. He took a single sheet of paper from the case and leaned forward to put it on the desk in front of the President. "This is a report from the deep-cover agent in Moscow we identify by the code name Jupiter. As you know, he is a member of the Central Committee and sees the Russian Premier at least twice a week. I want you to know, Mr.

President, that Jupiter gambled his life to pass this message to you. He says—and I will quote from the paper in front of you—'No retaliatory action is contemplated. The Committee views Egypt's use of the nuclear weapon as a clear signal from the U.S. that further aggression in the Mideast will not be tolerated. Rorchov impressed and intimidated. Brave work. Stand firm.'"

Bryant stared in shock at the sheet of paper. "Jupiter and the rest of the Central Committee think we gave the nuke to Egypt? And that Egypt's use of it against Libya was a U.S. power play?"

"Yes, sir. That's correct."

"My God." Bryant's mind was spinning. He realized half the world thought that the U.S. was responsible for this tragedy. But until now he had been convinced Russia's leaders understood that Egypt had acted on its own. In a daze, he turned to the paper shredder next to his desk and fed the message from Jupiter into it. "This is a disaster."

"No, sir," Amstel said firmly. "It's a triumph." He thrust his head forward. "Don't you see? Russia has been stopped in its tracks in the Mideast because they believe you stood up to them there. Not Egypt. You! Instead of condemning Egypt, you must support them. That will give Moscow more reason to believe that Egypt acted on your orders. Choose judicious words, of course. Condemn the use of nuclear weapons in general, but express sympathy and understanding for Egypt's plight. After all, the Libyan army was rolling toward the Aswân Dam. And not just to 'wash their camels.'"

The President wished Jim Canon hadn't relayed his exact words to Amstel. Feeling cornered by the Director of the CIA, he abruptly changed the subject: "Where did that nuke come from, Luther?"

"The trail is cold in my part of the world. Our station head in Cairo says his sources claim the warhead was bought through an arms dealer. No one seems to know where it was manufactured."

"And the FBI hasn't yet found evidence that any of the warheads in our U.S. storage depots are missing."

Bryant's carefully controlled temper finally flared. "Goddammit, that nuke came from *somewhere!* Do you mean to say that with billions of dollars to spend you can't find the answer to that simple question?"

"It's not such a simple question. To keep our nuclear arsenal from becoming vulnerable to attack, our warheads are stored in small numbers in special depots in fifteen foreign countries and three hundred and eighty-six sites here in the U.S. Most warheads are larger than the one used by Egypt. But that doesn't help us. The explosive elements from one large warhead could have been redesigned for use in multiple small artillery shells. I won't say we're looking for a needle in a haystack, but the proliferation of nuclear weapons makes it difficult to keep track of our own, much less those of other powers."

"What a nightmare." A wave of agonized despair swept over Bryant. He had sought and won the presidency believing that he could bring about a sizable reduction in nuclear weapons. Instead he found himself under attack for allowing—many said encouraging—a U.S. ally to use one of those weapons. And the arsenal was now so big he couldn't even guarantee that the weapon had not originated in the U.S.

Amstel was watching the President closely. When he thought the moment was right he said, "As difficult as it may be for you to accept, Egypt's adventurism may be to your advantage. As Jupiter says, Moscow is impressed and intimidated. Now is the time to begin serious negotiations with the Russians on a whole raft of issues from nuclear disarmament to human rights and trade agreements. But first you must strengthen your hand by supporting Egypt's decision to use a nuclear warhead against the Libyan invaders. Otherwise the Russians will realize that you did not provide Egypt with that nuke."

The director's argument was convincing. Bryant almost accepted it. Like every president since Harry Truman, he craved approval as a man who can "stand up to the Russians." But after a moment he shook his head firmly in the negative. "Egypt had other options. The use of a nuclear weapon was wrong, Luther. I can't support it, even indirectly. That would only open the door for more of the same." His voice grew stronger as he spoke. "Henry Flowers and I are considering a variety of responses to Egypt. I may send the Sixth Fleet to patrol the Mediterranean and let Egypt know we'll destroy the Aswân ourselves if they try to use another nuke."

Amstel was shocked. "They're one of our few allies in that part of the world."

"Allies come and go, Luther. I'd rather lose a friend than see another nuclear weapon used." Bryant felt more comfortable with himself now that he had made a decision. "And your station chief in Cairo had better come up with something tangible about the source of that nuke. If he doesn't deliver, replace him." He chose his words carefully. "Anyone can be replaced, Luther. You. Me. Anyone. Only those who get the job done will survive this debacle. Remember that."

"I understand, sir." Amstel could hardly believe that he was being threatened with the loss of his job. Walter Bryant was notorious for his inability to fire people with whom he worked closely. The Egyptian incident obviously had struck a deep chord of anger within him. "I'll call you as soon as I have any new information." He snapped shut the locks on his briefcase and left the oval office.

On the drive back to CIA headquarters, in Virginia, Amstel huddled in the sealed rear of the limo and thought back over the conversation with Bryant. He decided he'd pushed him too hard and too fast. The President would have to be led more slowly to the correct decision.

The car phone rang and he answered it to find his executive assistant at Langley on the other end. "I have an urgent call from one of your private sources, sir. The code name he gave is Bluebird."

"Put the call on the scrambler and patch it through to me."

There were several seconds of electronic noise as the call went through the scrambling procedure and was transferred to the limo. Then a familiar voice said, "This is Bluebird. Am I on a secure line?"

Amstel smiled at the sound of the voice. "We're secure, Bluebird. How are you?"

"Just fine. And how's the project going on your end?"

"Slowly. The President has not yet come around to our way of thinking."

"He's a fool."

"No, not a fool. Just a bright Kansas farmer with a simplistic view of the world."

"The customer you sent my way intends to look at the merchandise tonight. If he's satisfied, he may want to take two units away with him. Should I proceed?"

Amstel allowed himself only a split second of doubt. "Yes. We've gone too far to stop now. And I sincerely believe our plan is working. The other side already feels checkmated. I have that information from an inside source."

"Wonderful!"

"We must keep the pressure on. Are there any problems on your end?"

"A minor problem: one of our people had second thoughts and had to be eliminated; the Military Police are looking into the matter. Could you ask the FBI to get hold of the physical evidence the MPs have assembled? That would cut the ground out from under the Military Police without drawing any attention to me."

"Certainly. I'll tell the FBI the victim was one of our stringers and we intend to investigate the killing ourselves. What's this person's name?"

"Corporal Elizabeth Palermo."

"A woman?" Amstel was briefly saddened. Then he reminded himself that this was a war—a real war, not a cold war—and casualties were inevitable. "Consider it done." He took out a small notebook and wrote down the name with a gold Cross pen.

"I'm sorry to put this additional burden on you," Bluebird said.

"Don't be ridiculous. That's what friends are for." Amstel succumbed to a rush of nostalgia. "Things were much simpler in the old days, weren't they?"

"Yes. I often wish we could go back to those times."

"So do I. But there's no retreat. We must go forward."

"I know. You're a brave man, Luther. Someday this country will appreciate all you've done."

"Will they? I'm not so sure."

"Someone had to act. Thank God you're in a position to do so."

"You're taking the greater risk," Amstel insisted.

"No, we're in this together," Bluebird said. "As always."

Amstel's confidence surged, as it always did when he spoke with his oldest friend. "Good luck with your customers."

"Thank you. Good luck with the politicians."

As he put down the phone, Amstel glanced out the window and saw the sun shining off the Capitol dome. The politicians are gathered in there right now, he thought, collecting tax money with one hand and throwing it out the window with the other. Do they have any comprehension of how much they've weakened this country? Can't they see how indecisive and redundant they've become? Worse yet, they've infected the executive branch with their own dithering ways.

I was right to act, he told himself. The nation will have a difficult month or two, but we'll come out of it stronger and once again in charge of our own destiny.

A saying his mother often repeated came back to him: "Strong medicine. Lasting cure."

He hoped to God she was right.

Chapter 8

Burke rose before dawn so that he could be at his canvas at first light. The picture of the ranch house had changed in his mind. Now he saw a child's face in one of the windows. He sketched it in with pencil just to get the proportions right, then erased the sketch and began to work in oil.

Where the face came from he didn't know, though he did seem to recognize it as someone from his past. He only knew the face belonged in the leftmost window. His hand moved as if under its own control, something that had never happened to him before. When the face was done it added a new dimension to the painting. Though small in relation to the other elements, it dominated the picture. The expression on the child's face was one of blank terror.

"Who the hell are you?" he wondered. "And why are you so scared?"

Shortly after six hundred hours he finished the sky behind the ranch house and added his signature at the bottom. He was surprised that the picture had made a ninety degree turn on him from a pastoral scene to a moody study of a terrified child trapped in an isolated place. Even so, the overall effect satisfied him.

He put the painting in the corner to dry and went across the quad to his office. Before he reached his desk Brodsky said, "Did you hear the news? The Thirty-first Infantry's shipping out. They say we're gonna invade Egypt and kick some Arab ass."

"Is that news or rumor?"

"Well . . ."

"Because Jake Winkler stopped me on the quad with the news that the Thirty-first is shipping out to fight *with* Egypt against Libya."

"Yeah? Hey, I gotta tell Feeney that one." Brodsky picked up the phone and dialed the headquarters of the 39th Armored Battalion.

Burke sat down and tried to read the night patrol reports but was soon distracted by visitors and callers with additional rumors to peddle. Most of the rumors fell into one of four categories. One: the 31st was shipping out to fight Egypt. Two: the 31st was shipping out to fight Libya. Three: the 31st was shipping out to fight Russia. Four: the 31st was shipping out to fight Cuba. All he knew for certain was that on this particular morning the same rumors would be circulating through every combat unit in the army.

Finally he received a call that was not just another rumor. Jean Silk was on the line wanting to know if he'd like to meet her for breakfast.

"Where?" he asked.

"The coffee shop across from the PX?"

"I'll see you there in twenty minutes."

Before going to meet Jean he checked the morning report and saw that two of his MPs had been absent from reveille: Pfc. Joey Mascowiz and Sergeant Carl Lane. "I hate to send a morning report into Sloane that shows two of our MPs A.W.O.L. He'll want to bring them up on charges."

"I can carry them present. We done it before when one of the boys missed reveille because of a *vino* attack."

"What do you know about Lane and Mascowiz?"

"Lane's got a girl in Puma." Brodsky tried to remember her name. "Rita or Lita, something like that. He probably slept over there and forgot to set the alarm. I'll get the girl's phone number and call him. Tell him to get his ass on post or kiss one of his stripes good-bye. Mascowiz is due back from a three-day pass. I think he went home to Phoenix." He pondered the problem of Mascowiz. "Maybe his plane is late. I'll check that out."

"Okay, let's carry them both present for now. But I want to see those guys when they show up. Having two men A.W.O.L. would give Sloane an excuse to make life miserable for the whole company."

"I'll hold them," Brodsky volunteered. "You kick the shit out of 'em."

Burke laughed and picked up his hat. "I'm going over to the PX coffee shop for an hour or so. Call me if Sloane starts to act up. And make sure Biggs and Rittmaster check in with me before lunch. I want to know what they've learned about Betsy Palermo."

"You got it, Sergeant Major."

"You have some very strange ideas about food and drink," Burke observed.

"My mother's fault." Jean had taken a bottle of ketchup and poured several ounces into a glass of water and stirred the water with a spoon until it resembled tomato juice. She drank some of the concoction, then began to eat a sandwich she had made by putting a sliced onion, an order of hash brown potatoes, and some pickles between the two halves of an English muffin. "My father made so little money practicing law that my mother had to work. I was left alone to make my own breakfasts and lunches. Dinners too, now that I think about it. So I used my imagination. Still do." She grinned at Burke as she bit into the sandwich. "Yumm."

Burke watched her with a sense of wonder. "I thought all lawyers made a lot of money."

"Not my dad. He spent weeks on cases that didn't pay any fees at all. Defending elderly indigents who were being evicted from their rooms. Trying to get the city of New York to prosecute gamblers who stage dogfights for money; they goad the dogs into killing each other, you know. He nailed some of them, too. Drove them out of the city. They didn't go out of business, of course. Just moved their dogfights over to New Jersey."

"Sounds like an interesting man."

"Oh, he was wonderful. The law and stingers on the rocks. Those were his two big passions." Some of the sparkle faded from her eyes. "My mother finally left him. She just couldn't compete."

"That's too bad." Burke continued to be fascinated by the onion, pickle, hashed brown potato, and English muffin sandwich. "Is that your regular breakfast?"

"No. Yesterday I had— Uh, oh yes! A banana, a plate of sliced tomatoes, and a box of animal crackers. And a glass of ketchup and water, of course. I'm hooked on that."

"Well, it's inexpensive, anyway. I know people who spend a lot of money on Perrier."

"They're crazy. There's nothing better than ketchup and water." She took a long swallow to prove her point—and to provoke a reaction from Burke.

Then she became serious: "Are any of the stories I've heard this morning true? God, there are a hundred of them. I've never seen anything like the army's rumor mill."

Burke stirred his coffee. "Nobody ever tells a soldier anything, so we have to do a lot of guesswork. In this case every rumor you've heard is probably wrong."

Jean finished the last morsel of her unique sandwich and pushed her plate aside. "I was sort of surprised last night that all the army men in the Chicken Coop were as upset about the news from Egypt as I was. I thought they'd ... well, maybe not cheer ... but sort of relish the idea of a war."

"Some soldiers do," Burke admitted. "So do a few civilians. But most of us have seen too much killing already. We're not in the army because we want to fight anyone."

"Then why are you here?"

"Lots of reasons. Some guys just like to be in uniform. Others are kind of lazy. Many have never felt at home anywhere else. Quite a few stay in because the retirement deal is good, if you live to collect it. And a few are genuine patriots. There are as many reasons as there are men."

"What about you?"

Burke had expected that. "It's a good feeling to be at the top of your profession, whatever it is. And I'm one

of the best sergeant majors in the army. Does that
sound egotistical?"

"Not at all. In fact, you remind me—" She broke off
the thought and dropped her eyes.

"Of what?"

"Nothing."

"Come on."

The words crept out of her: "My father."

That sounded like such an enormous compliment
that Burke didn't know what to say. He opted for the
simplest reply: "Thank you."

She pushed around her empty plate to cover her
embarrassment. "Actually, I didn't ask you to breakfast to tell you about myself. I want to talk about
Besty Palermo."

"So do I." Burke took out his notebook. "When exactly did you see her? And where?"

Jean tapped the Formica surface of their table. "Right
here in the PX coffee shop on Tuesday morning. Betsy
called me at my office in the J.A.G. headquarters
about 9:00 A.M. She introduced herself over the phone
and said there was something confidential she needed
to discuss with a lawyer. Someone had told her about
me. That I was new to Fort Powell and the only woman
on the J.A.G. staff. I invited her to come to my office,
but she wanted me to meet here instead."

"Why?"

"She said she didn't want to do anything official.
Just wanted to talk. So I came over and we had coffee
together at this very table."

Burke supposed Betsy Palermo wanted to size up
Jean before sharing anything personal with her. "What
was your impression of Betsy?"

Jean mulled over the question before answering.
"She was a rather ordinary-looking girl who went to
great lengths to make herself attractive. It was obvious that she spent a lot of money on makeup. And
somehow she managed to make her uniform look better than the average."

"She had tailored uniforms made for her at a shop in
Albuquerque," Burke explained. "What did she talk
about?"

"Music mostly. She was very knowledgeable about classical music. I gathered she spent most of her leaves going to music festivals and concerts. In fact, she mentioned that she'd gone to hear the Albuquerque Symphony last Saturday night. I remember she said the musicians were 'adequate.' I think she was a snob in that respect."

"Did she say who took her to the symphony?"

"No. It wasn't until her second cup of coffee that she mentioned a man."

"Who?"

Jean reached for the bottle of PX ketchup. "I hope you don't mind if I mix myself another ketchup and water."

"This time I won't even gag."

"The man," Jean said, as she went about making herself an ersatz tomato juice, "was never named. Betsy used the words *he* and *him* reverently. As if this person had extraordinary powers."

"You mean she was terrified of him."

"Exactly. What she said was—and I'll try to come close to her exact words—'I'm involved with this man. Not in a sexual way. But he found my weak spot. Talked me into doing something I shouldn't. Now I want to break away, but I don't know how. The only way out is to go to authorities and I can't do that. I don't want to go to prison. And besides, he'd kill me.' " She stopped to sip her drink. "That all came out in a rush after we'd been talking for a while."

Burke had been scribbling in his book. "Can you give me the last couple of sentences again, a little more slowly?"

She repeated them.

"Did she go back to the subject? Say anything more about the kind of trouble she was in? Or the man?"

Jean propped her chin up on her hand and thought back. "No, not really. It took her about twenty minutes to feel comfortable with me. Then she got what she wanted to say out of her system very fast. Afterward she just stared at me as if I could wave a magic wand and make her problems disappear."

"What did you tell her?"

"I said she hadn't told me enough for me to be able to do anything for her. Because her name was Palermo, I asked if she was Catholic. She said yes, but she hadn't practiced her religion in years. I suggested she see the Catholic chaplain anyway and tell him the entire story. He'd be bound by his vows to keep silent, but he'd be able to give her better advice than I could with so little information at hand."

Burke wondered if Betsy had made it to the office of Father Riley, the Catholic chaplain, before she died.

Evidently Jean could read minds. "She didn't see him. As soon as I heard that she was dead, I called Father Riley and asked."

"Too bad."

Jean felt Burke's disappointment keenly. "Tell me something. How was Betsy killed?"

"She was shot twice with a .45. In addition, her killer slit her throat, cut off her left ear, and stuffed it in her mouth. She was raped too."

Jean regretted having asked. Then she remembered the scrap of paper in her purse. "Hey, guess what—I've got an actual clue." She reached into her purse and brought out a crumpled piece of pink paper. Smoothed out, it was a six-inch square from one of the paper place mats used by the PX coffee shop. "Betsy took out a pen and started to doodle while we were talking. You know—nervous doodles. But I noticed that the doodles changed after she started telling me about her fear of this man. So when she excused herself and left, which she did very suddenly, I tore off this piece of the place mat and kept it."

Burke turned the scrap of paper over in his hands. Arrows and concentric circles and crude daisies made up most of the doodles. But here and there she had repeatedly scribbled the same set of initials: F.D.N.W.

"What does F.D.N.W. mean?" Jean wondered.

"I don't know. But I can tell you what it is: A military abbreviation."

"Are you sure?"

"I've seen a million of them. Haven't you? How long have you been in the army? Two years?"

"Three."

"Then you must know what I mean. Hell, you're even an acronym: you're a Wac."

"Okay, but there must be a way to tell what this one means."

"When I said there are a million military abbreviations, I wasn't exaggerating. F.D.N.W. could mean anything."

"Isn't there one place you can go to find out?"

"Like to the Keeper of the Acronyms—who would be called the K.O.T.A.? No, he doesn't exist. But *somebody* has to know what these particular four initials mean. I'll start asking around."

"Can I help?"

Burke was slow to reply. He wanted her help . . . and he didn't. The more they saw of each other, the more involved they would become. He knew that for sure. She was cute and gutsy and smart. If he started seeing a lot of her, there was no way he could leave her alone. Looking into her eyes, it was obvious she was aware of that. But what about Maggie? He couldn't turn away from Maggie. She'd done too much for him. Helped to establish him as an artist, opened up a whole new world to him. Hell, more than that—given him *herself.* "No," he said finally. "I'll have to take it from here."

Her disappointment lingered in the air between them.

"Well . . ." Jean's eyes moved from side to side, avoiding Burke's. "I'd better get back to my office. Lots of work to do."

"I'll let you know how the case is going," he said, reluctant to cut her out completely.

"That's not necessary." Her face was set in a stubborn expression. "I've got plenty to keep me occupied."

Burke asked the waitress for a check. She toted up his bill for bacon and eggs but wasn't sure how to charge for the few odd bits of food Jean had asked for, so she added only a dollar to the check.

"You must save a lot of money on food," Burke remarked.

"That's why all you guys like me. I'm a cheap date." It gave her satisfaction to see that she'd wounded him. "Good-bye, Sergeant Major."

*   *   *

Roper had called a meeting for 10:00 A.M. in the basement of the N.C.O. Club. While waiting for his men to arrive, he put an inventory sheet on a clipboard and began checking the cases of whiskey stored in the basement.

Joe Briscoe arrived first. Briscoe was a sergeant in the 31st Infantry, a much-decorated Vietnam vet who wore a big handlebar mustache and liked to show off the tattoos on his arms.

"Morning, Joe. Will you look at this? Somebody's been down here and lifted six bottles of Johnnie Walker Black from my stock. I don't know what the fuck this world's coming to when you can't trust the guys you soldier with."

"Yeah, people are shit," Briscoe said cheerfully.

Soon they were joined by four other Fort Powell troopers. Briscoe knew each of them: Louie Sanchez, who always carried a knife up his shirt sleeve; Arnie Arkolotti, a guy who liked to tie up women and play with their tits; Frank Craymore, the big-nosed, barrel-chested winner of the 5th Army pistol championship for the past three years; and Nels Jansen, who seldom talked because he was the only one who wasn't a noncom with years of service.

The only man missing was Sam Veck, who would be taking his turn on duty at the service station.

"Can we make this quick?" Arnie said. "My CO's got a bug up his ass this morning. I can't be away from the company for very long."

"This won't take long." Roper took a piece of chalk out of his pocket and started drawing lines on the basement wall. "First, nobody's got duty tonight, right? You're all available?"

They murmured assent, watching the map that was slowly taking shape on the wall.

"Okay, we've got two customers coming in tonight. Argentinians, I'm told. Control has made a deal for two units at three million per. Our cut's gonna be the usual 10 percent. Six hundred thousand," he said, for the benefit of those who had a problem with long division. "We'll use this plateau fifteen miles west of the storage site for the meeting." He chalked in the plateau and indicated the nearest road, New Mexico State Highway 34. "Sanchez is gonna make the contact in Puma because he speaks Spanish. These guys are supposed to speak English, but nobody knows how good. Sanchez, make the contact at ten hundred hours at the Burger King on Mercy Street. Take the jeep wagon with the phony plates. The guys you want will both be wearing blue Levi jackets with blue cotton shirts. One will be wearing a cowboy hat with a yellow feather in the band. The other will wear a red baseball hat with a Cubs emblem. You got that?"

Sanchez nodded.

"Just go up to them and say, 'I'm a Cubs fan, too.' Then go on outside and wait. They'll come out and get into their own vehicle. It'll be a pickup truck, I don't know what make or model. You leave and they'll follow. Go west on 34 for seven miles. Go past the cutoff for the plateau. When you get to the overpass for that little creek that runs along there, turn around and head back towards town. On the way back you can check to see if anybody besides our customers makes a U-turn. If so, scrub the mission and head for home. If everything looks kosher, lead them to the plateau."

Arkolotti's hand went up. "Hank, what if somebody's planted a beeper in their vehicle?"

"I'll have the all-frequency monitor. If they're carrying a beeper, I'll know it by the time they reach the plateau. Craymore, you'll be on the ridge behind me. If the monitor says they're wired, kill both of them when they step down from the truck. Then everybody evacuates over the escape route."

Roper began drawing X's in a circular pattern around the perimeter of the plateau. "Briscoe, dig in here. Craymore here. Jansen here, on the floodlight. Arkolotti, I want you here to make sure our customers exit in the right direction. Don't turn it on until I give you the signal."

"How much time are you giving them to inspect the merchandise?" Briscoe asked.

"Five minutes. And they'll probably use less than that. After all, this stuff comes with a pedigree. Con-

trol has got them presold or they wouldn't be here.
Five minutes should do it. While they're checking the
merchandise, I'll be checking their money. Now, I can't
count six million bucks in five minutes. But again,
Control says these guys are legit and he hasn't been
wrong yet. They have to trust us on the merchandise
and we have to trust them on the money count." He
grinned wolfishly. "But keep your MAC-10s locked on
automatic just in case." He looked around. "Any
questions?"

"What time do we meet to move the merchandise
from the vault to the plateau?" Craymore asked.

"We'll meet at the service station at eight hundred
hours. Weapons will be issued there. Anything else?"
No one had any additional questions. "Okay," Roper
said, pleased with the cool professionalism of his team.
"This deal's gonna work just like the last one. But
everyone should stay on their toes because we're short
a man. Williamson's still nursing a pair of swollen
balls."

Everybody laughed.

"Shut up!" Roper glared around the basement. "Williamson's flat on his back, courtesy of Ansel Burke.
The last thing we need is Ansel poking his nose into
our business. He's trouble. So stay sharp tonight if you
want to live to spend your money."

The meeting broke up on a more subdued note.

Chapter 9

Throughout the MP barracks portable TVs were turned on to catch the news bulletins about the Egyptian crisis. The rumors continued to multiply. When it was announced that the President had scheduled a news conference for later that afternoon, the story immediately began to spread that he intended to declare war on Egypt. The older men in the company took that one cynically, but the young troopers began cleaning their weapons and checking their field equipment.

"Do you think the President'll do it?" Brodsky asked.

"Do what?"

Brodsky stared at Burke. "Declare war on Egypt!"

"No, I don't."

"Well, shit. He's got to do something."

"He'll make a speech. That's what he's good at."

Lieutenant Walter Sloane strode into the office. His face was red. He was carrying his swagger stick and slapping it into the palm of his hand with the regularity of a metronome. Behind him trailed Corporal Fellows, the company clerk, misery written across his face. "Sergeant Burke, the company inventory is a *disaster*. I've got a three-page list of missing property. I *will not* sign the inventory until these items are found."

Burke came slowly to his feet. He had decided to handle Sloane with exaggerated courtesy, if only to blunt his wildness. "May I see the list, sir?"

It was practically thrown in his face. He smoothed out the paper and studied the list. Nothing he saw surprised him. Every company in the army would be short a few pieces of this kind of equipment. Mattress covers; helmet liners; entrenching tools; holsters; brooms, silverware and mess kits; cans of linseed oil; fatigue hats: nothing big or expensive. If a weapon or a jeep had come up missing, Burke would have turned the company upside down himself. But this was nickel-and-dime stuff. Ordinary breakage.

"I can understand why you're upset, sir. I think I know where most of these things are. Give me an hour and I'll have them back in the supply room."

"You'd better." Sloane's voice was trembling. "My father warned me that you noncoms always try to get the new CO to sign for equipment you've lost or stolen. He was certainly right. They tried the same thing on me at Fort Sill. I didn't let them get away with it there, either."

"That's very wise, sir."

"You've got one hour to put this inventory right, soldier." Sloane spun on his heel and stalked out.

Fellows had been holding himself at rigid attention. As soon as Sloane left the office he deflated with a wheeze. "That guy's nuts!"

"Shut up," Burke ordered. "He's your commanding officer."

The corporal deflated still more. "Yeah, but he's been chewing on my ass since yesterday morning. And this stuff he's so ape-shit about is just *gone*. How're we gonna replace all of it in *an hour?*"

Burke picked up his phone and called the headquarters of the 31st Infantry Division.

Wolfe Heinzman took his call immediately. "Ansel, vat you think? Ve invade Egypt?"

"If we do, I want the Pepto Bismol concession. The water over there will turn the bowels of our young troopers into mush."

"Jah, most of them pretty soft, all right. Ve lose more to dysentery than to nukes."

"Wolfe, I need your help. Our new CO just finished the company inventory and he's all bent out of shape over a few missing things. Nothing important. Just the usual breakables."

"Vell, that's too bad. I hear your CO cannot find his cock vith both hands. Vat can I do?"

"I'm sending a man up to Custer Hill in a deuce-and-a-half with a list of the missing stuff. Let him have the run of your supply room. I'll return everything he borrows in a week or so, when Sloane's looking the other way."

"Send your man along. I take care of him."

"Thanks, Wolfe."

"Any time. Say, vich of those two girls from last night you like the best? The little redheaded lawyer or the voman from the gallery?"

"Well, I'm seeing a lot of Maggie."

"Good! I like that redhead who drinks the stingers. You give her to me?"

"She's not mine to give," Burke said, getting a little hot about it.

Wolfe chuckled. "I think she is. Yours, I mean. Such an embarrassment of riches. You must tell me your secret, Ansel."

"Yeah, one of these days. Thanks again." He put down the phone before Wolfe could pass another remark that would make him feel even worse about the way he had treated Jean. "You heard that?" he said to Fellows. "Take a deuce-and-a-half up to Custer Hill. Wolfe will lend us whatever we need to cover the inventory."

Fellows grinned at his sergeant major in admiration.

"Don't just stand there!" Burke bellowed. "Move!"

A few minutes later, as Fellows drove out of the quad in a two-and-a-half-ton truck, a civilian strolled into Burke's office, wearing an expensive tan gabardine suit and Italian shoes. After looking around the office as if it were a swamp that needed dredging, he plopped down in a chair and put his feet up on Burke's desk. "Good morning, old buddy," he drawled.

The sight of FBI Special Agent Al Devereaux frankly amazed Burke. "What the hell are you doing here?"

"You had a murder on post yesterday, didn't you? Well, the FBI is here to take that little problem off

your hands." Devereaux, a former linebacker from the
University of Alabama, braced his wide shoulders and
smiled.

"The Palermo murder?"

Devereaux laughed. "Was there more than one? Hey,
you'd better get these soldiers under control, old buddy.
Otherwise they're liable to take over this shit pot of a
place."

The last thing Burke had expected this morning was
an FBI agent. Especially Al Devereaux, the special
agent in charge of the Albuquerque office. Devereaux
usually sent one of his flunkies to handle any Fort
Powell business. He didn't like the army. He was a
former naval officer and a rising star in the FBI—
more of a politician than a cop, in Burke's opinion.
The Bureau had given him the Albuquerque office so
he'd have some field experience on his record. A year
from now he'd be back in Washington behind a ten-
foot-long desk. "You're taking personal charge of the
Palermo case?"

"No, I'll put a couple of my guys on it." His hazel
eyes locked onto Burke's. "I'm just here to pick up
whatever evidence you've got." His mouth twisted in-
solently. "Probably not worth my time, but let's see
what you've found."

Burke leaned back as if he had all the time in the
world. "I don't get it. The FBI never responds to a
crime on a military reservation this fast. The last time
we had a murder out here I never saw you. And your
'Junior G-men' didn't show up for weeks. What's so
different about Betsy Palermo?"

"She's got a Top Secret clearance, for one thing."

"How'd you know that?"

Devereaux frowned and took his feet down from the
desk. "It doesn't matter how I know. This case is mine."
He looked around the plain office with contempt. "You
call my guys 'Junior G-men,' but what the hell are the
MPs? Real cops? Don't make me laugh. You bums are
still back in the Dark Ages, beating confessions out of
people and shooting at anything that moves. Now,
let's cut this shit and get down to work."

"You'd never set foot on Fort Powell if you didn't

absolutely have to. Who sent you here? What makes
Betsy Palermo so important?"

The two questions went unanswered. "Are you going
to give me what I came for, old buddy? Or do I have to
talk to your superior officer?"

Burke didn't want Sloane anywhere near the case,
so he had no choice except to cooperate. Devereaux
held the better hand, the FBI always did. So he got up
and went next door to the storeroom and opened the
safe that held the evidence in military cases. He brought
back a pouch containing most of the evidence and
spread out the contents on his desk.

Devereaux picked up a color print of Betsy Palermo's
body and scrutinized it as if he were looking at a
pornographic photo. He even gave a suggestive whistle. "The killer must have an ear fetish, wouldn't you
say?"

Burke stood silently while Devereaux casually poked
around among the photos, scanned the coroner's report, turned over the .45 slugs taken from the girl's
body between his thick fingers, and leafed through the
bankbooks.

"Got any leads?"

"Not yet." He decided to try out Hank Roper's name
on Devereaux. "She's been seeing one of the ranking
noncoms on post—Sergeant Major Hank Roper." No
reaction. "And if you take a good look at those bankbooks you'll see that Betsy was into something very
profitable. And probably illegal."

"Yeah. Looks that way." Devereaux began shoveling
the evidence back into the pouch. "I'll take this stuff to
Albuquerque and put a team to work on it. If they
need any local help, they'll call you." When the pouch
was full, Devereaux hesitated before closing the clasp.
"Is this all of it?"

Burke thought about the footprint casting shoved
into the bottom of his desk. It wasn't much, but it
might be his best shot at finding the girl's killer. He
didn't want Devereaux to have it. "Yeah, that's everything."

Devereaux closed the pouch and planted himself in
front of Burke. "Before I go, I want you to understand

that you're out of this. Don't go poking around unless
one of my men asks for your help." He used his politician's smile. "Is that clear, old buddy?"

"I'll do anything you want," Burke said, "if you
promise to stop calling me 'old buddy.'"

The smile tightened. "I'll take that as a yes. But just
for insurance I'd better talk to your commanding
officer."

He left the pouch on Burke's desk and went across
the hall. Burke heard him introducing himself to Sloane.
Then the door closed.

Burke figured it would take Devereaux about five
minutes to wrap Sloane around his finger. At that, he
overestimated Sloane's backbone. Four minutes later
the FBI man left Sloane's office and came across the
hall. He picked up the pouch, smiled at Burke, and
left.

Both Brodsky and Burke looked at the intercom
speaker that connected the offices of the CO and the
sergeant major. Seconds later it crackled to life.

"Sergeant Burke, come in here."

"Yes, sir."

Sloane's wild eyes were darting everywhere. When
they settled on Burke they became as round as napkin
rings. "Sergeant, you know that we're required to cooperate with civil law enforcement authorities. Special
Agent Devereaux told me you were surly and uncooperative with him. What am I supposed to make of
that?"

"Devereaux isn't a cop, he's a politician. For some
reason the FBI doesn't want Betsy Palermo's murder
investigated. They sent Devereaux to confiscate the
evidence and shut down the case."

"That's a ridiculous accusation. Why, I know Devereaux. By name, anyway. He was an All-Southeast
Conference linebacker a few years ago."

There was simply no logical reply.

"Sir, we've got to continue this investigation. Palermo
was into something nasty. The girl may even have
asked for what she got. But she was *army*. It's up to us
to find the men who killed her. No one else will."

"The FBI has jurisdiction."

"On this post we're the law . . . sir."

"That was a very reluctant *sir*." Sloane looked Burke up and down. He held up a thumb and forefinger spread an inch apart. "You're about this far from being insubordinate. Those stripes aren't welded to your uniform, you know. They're only sewn on. I can take them away any time I want. And for any reason."

Sloane suddenly stood and began pacing behind his desk, as he had on the previous morning. He started talking about the historical difference in function between officers and noncoms, the need for strict loyalty by the noncom cadre. It sounded like a lecture he'd heard at the Point.

As he stood listening to the lecture, which was rapidly becoming gibberish, Burke found himself losing whatever pity or empathy he'd felt for Sloane. There were just too many Sloanes these days. Over the past ten years he'd watched the officer corps degenerate to a sad state. Incompetents. Glory hunters. Drug addicts. Head cases. Bureaucrats. Gradually the losers had become the rule instead of the exception.

Why am I here? he wondered. I'm an artist. Or so people say. I could kick back and do nothing but paint. Go to New York with Maggie. Why not?

Sloane was winding down. Looking confused. Probably so struck by his own eloquence that he forgot what triggered it.

"So . . . uh, the point here, Sergeant, is that . . . Oh, yes. The FBI has jurisdiction. I'm giving you an order—a direct order—to keep your hands off that case. Do you understand?"

"Yes, sir," Burke made himself say.

Sloane settled back into the chair behind his desk. For a moment he seemed unsure of how to conclude the meeting. Then he snapped out, "Dismissed."

Burke went straight across the hall and threw himself down behind his own desk. The anger in him was deep enough to mine. In the background he heard the deuce-and-a-half pull up behind the headquarters; Fellows began to unload the stuff he'd borrowed from the 31st.

"Lou, go out and help Flowers, will you? Make sure

the CO knows we've found the 'missing' equipment.
And close the door behind you. I've got a personal call
to make."

"Okay, Sergeant Major." Anyone could see that Ansel
was royally pissed off. Obviously Sloane had ordered
him to dump the Palermo case. Just as obviously, the
edge in Ansel's voice told Brodsky that the CO had
wasted his time. Brodsky liked hearing that edge.
When Ansel got mad he was fun to be around. Things
would start popping now.

It took four phone calls to Fort Sill, Oklahoma, before Burke reached the man he was looking for. He
finally located Master Sergeant Sam Reedy in the
artillery school headquarters, where he had just taken
on the job of teaching recruits how to fire heavy weapons without blowing themselves up in the bargain.

"Hello, Sammy. I didn't know you had ambitions to
be an artillery instructor."

"No choice," Reedy said. "The former master sergeant of the artillery school was buried yesterday, and
I was the handiest replacement. Seems that one of his
105 teams made a basic mistake in elevation and
trajectory. Instead of dropping a shell on a target two
miles away, they put it in their instructor's lap. Actually, there wasn't much left of him to bury. It was a
closed casket funeral."

"I'd rather go into combat than instruct recruits. I
wish you better luck than the guy you're replacing."

"Thanks. What's on your mind, Ansel? As if I didn't
know."

"First Lieutenant Walter Sloane."

Reedy chuckled. "I told you he was an asshole."

"He's even worse than your description. If I don't
stop him, he's going to ruin this company. I've been
told you had him eating out of your hand when he was
at Sill. How'd you do that, Sam?"

"I just kissed his ass every morning and told him
how sweet it tasted."

Sam Reedy was a tall, proud Kentuckian whose
large family had made a good living for years out of
illegal whiskey stills. Sam had learned to fight with

his fists when he was two and fire a rifle when he was
six. He joined the army at seventeen after wounding a
federal revenue agent in a gun battle at one of his
father's stills, and stayed in because he liked guns.
The bigger the guns, the better. Which is how he had
become an artilleryman. The image of Sam Reedy
kissing Sloane's ass was impossible to imagine. "That's
bullshit. You must have something on Sloane. Whatever it is, I need it."

"I can't help you, Ansel."

"Why not?"

"It's too dirty. I wouldn't have used it myself, except
that the man didn't leave me any choice."

"Sam, I'm in exactly the same position."

Reedy thought about that. "Suppose I gave you what
I've got. You use it to checkmate Sloane. That's fine. I
know you; we go back a long way. But someday Sloane'll
be transferred out of Powell, and his next topkick'll
call you. He'll want some ammunition against Sloane,
too. What'll you do? Give him what I gave you? Will
Sloane have to go through life being blackmailed by
his own top sergeants? Much as I hate the guy, I
wouldn't want to start something like that."

Burke appreciated Reedy's concern. All he could do
was tell him what had happened to Betsy Palermo and
about the wall of silence being built around the case.
Reedy wondered if he was exaggerating. Burke promised he wasn't. There were too many odd circumstances:
all that money in Betsy Palermo's accounts; her Top
Secret clearance; the FBI's sudden appearance, swoop-
ing down to scoop up the evidence.

Finally Reedy said, "Okay, I'll tell you what I've got.
Just a minute." Burke heard the sound of a match
being struck. Reedy drew on one of his cigars. "Are
there any extensions on your phone?"

"No, I have a direct line."

"Good. Because I wouldn't want anyone else to hear
this. It's bottom-of-the-barrel stuff."

Burke said nothing. He was only interested in
listening.

"Fort Sill was Sloane's first duty station. He came
here right out of the Point, so I expected him to be

green and sassy. I knew he'd want to remake Sill in
the image of the Point. That's okay, he's entitled. He's
got the bars on his shoulder, right?" Reedy sighed.
"But it was more than that. He doesn't connect with
reality. Doesn't trust anyone. His father— You've heard
about his old man by now, I imagine."

"Yeah."

"His father raised him to distrust noncoms and hate
enlisted men. So he was on my back every minute.
Little things, but a dozen an hour. And he'd bust
a sergeant without a second thought. I even started
to worry about my own stripes. The guy . . ." Reedy
groped for words. "He's in the wrong line of work. And
his eyes! Shit, I've seen guys with saner eyes go out on
Section Eight. Ansel, he was tearing the unit apart.
Morale was in the crapper. I had to do *something.*"

"You don't have to justify yourself to me, Sam. *I'm*
the one looking for a lever."

Reedy could be heard puffing on the cigar. "I looked
for a lever, too. I put a couple of men on Sloane. Had
him followed around. They didn't come up with much
for the first three weeks. Then, finally, they noticed
the dogs."

"What dogs?"

"Sloane's. How many dogs does he have right now?"

"I don't know that he has any."

"I'll bet you cash money he owns at least two. Probably got special permission to keep them at the BOQ.
He started out here with a collie, a terrier, and a
beagle. One day the collie was gone. Nobody knew
where. Just gone. Then the beagle disappeared, too—
nice little mutt. I had a bad feeling about those dogs,
Ansel. Especially when I saw a pattern. The day after
one of his dogs disappeared, Sloane always locked himself in his office and refused to see anyone or take any
calls except from a superior officer."

A chill crawled up Burke's spine. "Did you ever find
out what happened to the dogs?"

"Oh, yeah. I decided to have Sloane watched twenty-
four hours a day. And I took the late shifts myself. The
collie and the beagle had disappeared about four weeks
apart. Starting the third week, I lost a lot of sleep. Put

him to bed and got up with him in the morning. And I started carrying my camera. Remember my old Nikon, Ansel?"

"I sure do. I've still got that shot you took of me on the range at Fort Ord. You made me look almost civilized."

"It's a sweet camera. Especially with my new telephoto lens." He clicked his teeth. "One morning about 4:00 A.M., Sloane came out of the BOQ with the terrier. Instead of taking it for a walk, he put the terrier in his car and drove off. I followed. We went out in the country and Sloane pulled up a side road. I was worried he'd notice my car, but he was intent on what he was doing."

"What did that turn out to be?"

"Ansel . . . I knew, but I didn't know. Couldn't get my mind around it. By then it was dawn. Real quiet and private out there in the country. He took that dog off into the field. Tied its front legs and put on a muzzle. Then he spread its back legs and—Ansel, I swear this is true . . . He screwed that little dog. It was a bitch, you see. Then he untied the pooch and let it run off. That's what happened to every one of those dogs; he'd screw 'em and then set 'em free. For years I've been saying that all officers are motherfuckers. I didn't think they were dogfuckers, too."

Burke hadn't seen that one coming. It took his breath away. "You got pictures?"

"I got pictures. There wasn't much light, but my telephoto and the fast film I was using did the job."

"Why didn't you bring the pictures to Sloane's CO? They would have thrown his ass out of the army."

"I thought about that. Instead, I took the pictures to Sloane. Told him I thought he should resign his commission. The poor bastard went to pieces. Bawled his head off and begged me to sell him the pictures. He'd pay anything. When I refused, he turned to ice. Pulled a .45 out of a drawer. Ansel, I thought I was dead. But he put the piece to his own head and swore he'd kill himself if I showed those photos to anyone. He meant it, too. The man's crazy. So we cut a deal. He'd sit in his office and sign the morning reports while I ran the company. And the pictures would never be seen again."

"What about the dogs? Were there more after that?"

"Not that I know of. I told him I'd be watching him. If I saw him with any more dogs, I'd take my pictures to his CO. But who knows? He was always going off to Oklahoma City on weekends. Probably screwed every pooch in the pound."

"Do you still have the pictures?"

"Yeah, they're tucked away. After all, he's crazy. If he thought I'd gotten rid of them, he might come gunning for me just to protect his 'good name.' They're my insurance."

"I'll need a set of prints."

"The information won't do?"

"I'm afraid not."

He sighed painfully. "I'll send you a set by Federal Express."

"Thanks, Sam. I owe you a big one."

"Be careful how you use them. Sloane could be dangerous."

"I won't use the prints unless I'm forced to."

"You'll use them, just like I did." He paused. "Do me a favor in return—make sure Sloane knows I'm keeping another set of pictures for myself. I don't want that weirdo on my case."

A few minutes later Brodsky stuck his head in the door. "You through with your call?"

"Sure, come in." Burke was leaning back, staring out the window. "Lou, do you know if Sloane has a dog?"

Brodsky began to chuckle. "It's funny you should ask. D'you remember at reveille yesterday I assigned Carmichael to find out who was pissing on the flowers outside the BOQ? Colonel Higgins's wife wanted to know because she planted them?"

"I remember."

"This morning Carmichael told me he saw some dogs pissing on those flowers. And they belong to Sloane. Carmichael found out that Sloane walks them every night about twenty-two hundred hours. The dogs have been stopping right outside the BOQ door to relieve themselves by the flowers." Brodsky waited for Burke to comment. When he didn't, Brodsky said, "How did you know Sloane keeps dogs?"

Burke tried to smile. "Just a lucky guess."

Chapter 10

Roper was satisfied that his team was sufficiently rehearsed to handle tonight's job. He only regretted that Williamson was still nursing his swollen balls. One more man would have provided that extra margin of safety he liked. Roper believed devoutly in safety margins, fail-safe devices, and insurance policies. Only suckers and circus performers took unnecessary risks.

John the bartender came into his office. "Hank, you know that MP who's always coughing? Jack Rittmaster?"

"Yeah, what about him?"

"He's watching the club."

"What? From where?"

"He's in a civilian car parked across the road under the pepper tree."

Roper stood back from the window as he checked out the street. Sure enough, Jack Rittmaster was there. In civilian clothes. In a beat-up old Plymouth, probably his own car. "Son of a bitch. How long has he been sitting there?"

"Don't know. I just noticed him."

The meeting in the basement had ended half an hour ago, so Rittmaster had probably seen everyone who attended. "Call the shylocks and tell them to make their payoffs tomorrow. Get Warrant Officer Jenkins on the phone, too. Tell him I'm not interested in buying any speed this week."

John reached for the phone under the bar.

"Then bring me a beer."

Roper turned up the air conditioner and sat back to think. He was concerned about tonight's operation. What if Rittmaster tried to tail him? Should he be canceled out? The disappearance of an MP would bring down all kinds of shit from Ansel Burke.

He briefly considered dropping the problem in Control's lap. After all, Control had promised to see that Burke was slapped down. Taken off the Betsy Palermo case and put back on the drunks and A.W.O.L.s beat. That was bound to take a little time. Burke was probably getting his orders right now. Under those circumstances, Roper decided that a second appeal to Control would make him look weak.

"Here you go, Hank." John came in and put a frosted beer on the desk.

"Is Rittmaster still out there?"

"Yep."

"Let me know if he leaves."

He took a couple of slow drags on the beer while he considered different countermoves. Gradually an idea formed that made him smile.

"John! Go out back and uncover the Porsche. Bring it around front. And make sure Rittmaster notices you."

"You *want* him to see me?"

"That's right. Make a little show of it. Take a rag and polish the hood. I'll be out in a minute."

Roper opened the closet door and studied the collection of clothes, both uniform and civilian, that he kept at the club. From the wardrobe he selected beige slacks, a white sport shirt, a navy blue Pierre Cardin jacket, and a pair of black Italian loafers.

After dressing, he removed a brick from his office wall and took out a green metal box from the hiding place behind. He kept as much as fifty thousand dollars in cash there. "Fuck-you money," he called it. If things ever went sour he could always empty the box, tell the army "Fuck you," and take off. He took ten thousand, closed the box, and put it back behind the loose brick.

When he came out onto the street fronting the N.C.O. Club, John grinned at him. "Lookin' sharp, Hank." He

tossed the buffing rag on top of the tarp that had been
covering Roper's red Porsche and opened the door for
him.

"I'll be back by three." Roper turned over the engine
and gunned it a couple of times, then put it into gear
and accelerated down the street like a streak of red
lightning.

Rittmaster quickly pulled out to give chase. Roper
laughed as oily black smoke billowed out from behind
Rittmaster's Plymouth. The old junker needed a ring
job—no acceleration. He couldn't have stayed on the
Porsche's tail if Roper hadn't slowed down to let him
catch up.

Having had his fun, Roper kept the powerful sports
car at a sedate thirty-five miles an hour as he drove
through Fort Powell. He didn't like to attract too much
attention with the car, which is why he usually kept it
covered and out of sight behind the club. Too many
people liked to speculate about his money, both the
source and the amount.

Passing the main parade ground, he saw a sergeant
giving close order drill to his platoon under the white-
hot sun. Roper had absolutely no respect for the man:
sweating your guts out for sergeant's pay was stupid.
He couldn't remember the last time he'd given close
order drill or let himself be ordered around by some
chicken-necked officer. Over in the admin building
was a Captain Foster to whom he supposedly reported.
For a thousand dollars a month Captain Foster let
Roper make his own hours.

Roper waved a Class A pass under the nose of the
MP on the main gate as he drove off post and headed
for Puma. When Rittmaster's Plymouth disappeared
from his rearview mirror, Roper again slowed to let
him catch up. "Put the pedal to the metal," he grumped.
"I haven't got all day."

Maggie had spent the morning cataloguing Ansel's
paintings and lining them up against the gallery walls
for close inspection. She dared not send Donald Hillary anything but the best of Ansel's work.

In the end she selected not fifteen canvases, as she

had promised Donald, but fourteen. The painting she rejected was of a flat Indian face webbed with the tiny lines of age. The face itself was magnificent: fierce, tribal, weathered, authentic. But Ansel hadn't given proper attention to the background. The brushwork to the sides of the face was sloppy. Donald would see that immediately. It was one of Ansel's early paintings, done before he had perfected the technique she was sure would make both of them rich. She would point out the problem and have Ansel redo the background.

Her attention was distracted by a screech of tires. Looking out the window, she saw a red Porsche pull into a parking place on Colorado Boulevard. A thick-chested man emerged from the Porsche and came toward the gallery.

A thrill of anticipation fluttered through Maggie. He was attractive and obviously well off. Both his car and clothes were top quality. She smoothed her skirt and moistened her lips, but made a point of showing her back to the visitor as he came through the door.

"Hi, there."

Maggie turned slowly, keeping her chin down so that she appeared to be looking up at him even though he wasn't particularly tall. Men liked to have women look up at them. It inflated their egos. "Welcome to the Winston Gallery."

"I haven't been to this part of town in a while," he said. "It looks different. Very classy."

"A number of boutiques and good restaurants have opened up here over the last year," Maggie said. "And I like to think my little gallery adds a chic touch of its own."

"It certainly does."

He walked around the gallery, his eyes roving aggressively. His bearing confused Maggie. He was too rough-hewn to be an art collector. Yet he was showing intense interest in her paintings. "I specialize in Western artists. Is there any one artist or school that interests you?"

"I'd like to buy something by Ansel Burke. I've got a condominium up in Vail with lots of blank walls. One or two of Ansel's paintings might dress up the place."

"You say Ansel's name as if you know him."

He grinned in a way Maggie could only describe as barbarous.

"Ansel and me go back a long way. My name's Hank Roper."

"I'm pleased to meet you, Mr. Roper. I'm Maggie Winston, owner of the gallery."

"You're even smoother and sexier than I'd heard." Roper raised his eyebrows. "You don't mind my saying that, do you?"

"Not at all. Tell me, where did you meet Ansel?"

"Over in 'Nam. And then we ran into each other again a couple of years ago when he transferred into Fort Powell with the MPs."

"You're a soldier?" Maggie didn't even try to hide her surprise.

"That's right. Sergeant Major Hank Roper. Has Ansel ever mentioned me?"

"I'm afraid not."

"No, I guess he wouldn't. We're not exactly buddies. In fact, Ansel hates my guts." He smiled as if that pleased him. Noticing Ansel's signature on the paintings propped up against the wall, he walked over and looked down at them with his arms crossed. "These were all done by Ansel?"

"Yes, they were." Maggie felt off guard. She believed Hank Roper when he said that Ansel hated him. He had a callous manner that Ansel would despise, but which Maggie found appealing. She could picture the two of them butting heads at Fort Powell like rival bulls. But if Hank Roper disliked Ansel so much, why would he want to buy his paintings?

"Look at that." Roper was admiring Ansel's painting of the post headquarters building at Fort Powell. He had given the classic Spanish-style building extraordinary dignity through the use of somber colors. "It's the HQ! Jesus, it never looked that good before. Ansel's quite a painter, isn't he?"

"He's wonderful," Maggie replied.

"How much do you want for that one?"

"I'm sorry, it's not for sale. None of these paintings

are. They're about to be crated and shipped to New York."

"New York? Why?"

"I've arranged for a showing of Ansel's work at one of the major galleries there."

Roper produced a thick sheaf of cash folded once over. The bills on top were all in hundred-dollar denominations. "I'll give you ten thousand dollars for the painting of the HQ."

Maggie was duly impressed, as she knew she was meant to be. Where were buyers like this when you needed them? "I'm afraid I can't sell you one of Ansel's paintings right now."

"You mean they'll bring even more in New York?"

"I'm expecting that they will."

"How much more?"

"That's hard to say. We'll be testing the market with bids from institutions and major collectors. It will take some time to—"

"Cut the insider bullshit. Give me a figure."

Maggie hadn't wanted to do that because the information might reach Ansel. On reflection, she decided it was safe enough to tell Hank Roper. He would be the last person to congratulate Ansel. She recognized his jealousy because she had been jealous of successful people all her life. "I'm hoping to get an average of twenty-five thousand per canvas."

The statement came as an unpleasant shock. All Roper could think about were the risks he had to take for money, while Ansel was making a fortune out of some stupid dabs and daubs. "Maggie, all I can say is I hope you clip the son of a bitch for a big hunk of it."

His blatant animosity amused her. "I'll get mine. Don't worry about that."

"I'll bet you will." Roper was suddenly in a better mood. "Why don't you close up and let me take you to lunch?"

"I'm sorry." She gestured around the gallery. "As you can see, I have a great deal of work to do."

"You have to eat lunch. Come on."

"No thank you," Maggie said.

"Look, it doesn't matter to me that you're seeing

Ansel. And what the hell, Ansel's not exactly starving for lack of someone to eat with. I saw him having breakfast at the PX this morning with that new lawyer, Jean Silk."

"You did?"

Roper knew he'd touched a nerve. "They were as thick as thieves, and that's something I know about."

Maggie was so angry she could hardly speak. "There's a new place just down the street. They make a very good crab quiche."

"I'm game."

"Then let's go."

The luncheon worked out better than either of them expected. Roper told her a little about himself, embellishing his early years as a boxer with the assurance that she'd never look up his record in *Ring* magazine. She loosened up so much that he threw in the story about the first crooked deal he pulled off in the army—the sale of a jeep to a farmer outside Macon, Georgia. She laughed in all the right places and didn't pull back when he touched her leg under the table. He liked Maggie Winston. She was beautiful and venal, the two qualities he admired most in a woman.

Now and then Roper looked past Maggie at the gray Plymouth across the street. Despite the heat, Rittmaster continued to sit and watch. Roper considered sending a pitcher of margaritas out to him, but decided against any showboating. The idea was to make Burke think he was trying to move in on Maggie. Which, as it turned out, he was. If Burke got jealous, he wouldn't spend so much time thinking about Betsy Palermo.

"It's funny," he said. "I can't see you and Ansel together at all. He's army beer and you're New York champagne. I suppose it's the money that makes him irresistible."

"Ansel can be very good company. But yes, I'll admit the money is important. What you don't understand, Hank, is that Ansel is the kind of bonanza every gallery owner dreams about."

"Hey, I'm not putting you down. In your position, I'd go for the bucks, too."

Maggie wasn't offended. Hank Roper was one of the few men she'd ever met who seemed to understand her instantly—and to approve of what she was. She enjoyed dallying over lunch with an attractive man without having to preen and dissemble for him. It had been years since she'd allowed herself that luxury. She found herself doing the unthinkable—being honest with a man. "You see, I almost made it big a few years ago when I had a gallery in New York. I found another artist—Marshall Vogel. Have you ever heard of him?"

Roper shook his head.

"Marshall is very good. I built his reputation slowly and carefully. Yes, I took a generous commission, but I was entitled, considering all the time I'd spent building the market for his work. Then we had a disagreement just when his work was beginning to command important money, and he signed with another gallery. I was left broke and, worse yet, an object of ridicule in the only city in the world that matters. So I moved out here."

"Tough luck."

"Now I've found another important artist and I don't intend to lose him."

Roper saw in her an icy determination that matched his own. He set aside the glasses and empty plates that stood between them. "If it's just money, why don't you and me get together? I've got enough even for a woman like you."

It was Maggie's turn to shake her head.

"You don't believe me?"

"On the contrary, I think I do. Yes, I want money. Lots of it. But I have other needs as well. I want the museums and important collectors coming to *me* for Ansel's work." Her face was hot from unpleasant memories. "For years I took scraps from their tables. No more."

Roper couldn't believe what he was feeling: *disappointment*—over a *woman*. That wouldn't do at all. "Okay, I can appreciate what you're after, but you'd better move fast. That lady lawyer wasn't just having breakfast with Ansel; she was coming on to him like a heat wave."

"Oh?"

"I got burned just walking past the PX." He felt better about himself. Maggie's chin was trembling just a bit. Now that she was frightened of losing her meal ticket, she'd demand every spare minute of Burke's time. That's the key, he thought. Keep Burke off balance. Hit him with hooks and jabs. Save the knockout punch for another round. He signaled to the waitress. "Miss, can we have some coffee?"

Rittmaster's car was gone.

By the time Amos Biggs and Bill Rittmaster checked into company headquarters, Burke had been brooding for about an hour over the information he'd dug up on Lieutenant Sloane's sex life. He took out his bad temper on the N.C.O.s: "Where the hell have you two been? On leave? You're supposed to check in once in a while." Before they could answer, Burke came around his desk. "Let's go down to the armory."

Biggs let Rittmaster precede him down the hallway. He'd had three beers with his lunch and didn't want Burke to smell his breath.

Burke unlocked the armory, turned on the lights, and shoved some ammunition cases around to make seats for the three of them.

"What are we doing in here, Top?" Rittmaster looked at the racks of shining Colt .45s and long-barreled shotguns. "Somebody about to be executed?"

"It's a quiet place to talk. We could go to the dayroom if you want."

"This is fine." Biggs sat down solidly, making it plain that he didn't intend to move. The room smelled so pungently of gun oil that Burke wouldn't be able to catch even a whiff of beer.

Burke pushed the door closed with his foot. "I didn't want the CO walking in on us. He's given me a direct order to drop the Palermo case. Have either of you met Al Devereaux, the head of the FBI office in Albuquerque? He came in this morning to claim jurisdiction and impound the evidence. While he was at it, he stampeded Sloane into dumping the case." He looked from Biggs to Rittmaster. "You can bail out right now if you want. I won't ask any trooper to disobey a direct order for me."

After coughing behind his hand, Rittmaster said,
"Shit, I'll stick. I've had more fun today than a choir-
boy in a whorehouse."

Biggs stalled. He didn't like to take chances with his
stripes. On the other hand, Ansel Burke was one of
the few who hadn't laughed behind his back when he
married a Vietnamese girl. "I'll stick, too." Biggs opened
his notebook and flipped through the pages. "I've been
out to the Wac Shack to talk with some of the other
girls in Betsy's unit. She wasn't especially close to any
of them. Quiet little girl, everybody says. That's why
they were so surprised when she started seeing Hank
Roper. He made a big play for her about a year ago.
He may even have taken her up to that place he's
supposed to have in Vail."

"Was he fucking her?" asked Rittmaster, always
keen for sexual detail.

"Yeah, at first. Then she backed off, according to the
other girls in her barracks. You know about the boyfriend in Cleveland. She didn't want to lose him, the
girls say. But she didn't altogether stop seeing Hank,
either. According to one of the girls, their relationship
changed. It became"—he consulted the tortured loops
and whirls of his poor handwriting—" 'businesslike.' "

That confirmed Burke's theory. "Hank wanted something from Betsy, so he seduced her. Then he talked
her into doing whatever he was after, and paid her
well for it. Betsy started to have second thoughts and
he killed her, or had her killed."

Biggs flipped forward a few pages. "I also went out
to the Restricted Materiel Center. I got through the
gate because one of our own MPs is on duty there. But
inside they've got their own security. I talked to a
Captain Miller, who was Betsy's CO. About all he'd
tell me was that she was a records clerk dealing with
classified and hazardous supplies. Miller wouldn't even
let me look at her workplace." He pensively rubbed his
great belly. "Funny thing: there were a couple of FBI
men out there, too. I had to wait for them to leave
before I could talk to Miller. According to the company
clerk, they're helping out on some kind of inventory."

"Was Devereaux one of them?"

"Nope. I suppose he was here trying to shut down your investigation."

Burke shifted his weight around on the ammo case, not the most comfortable of seats. Three FBI agents visiting Fort Powell was unheard of. What the hell was going on? "That's good work, Amos." He looked to Rittmaster. "Jack, what have you got?"

Rittmaster had been quietly waiting his turn. What he had was dynamite and he didn't care to reveal it too quickly. Nor did he need to consult notes. "Plenty." He made them wait while he lit up a cigarette. "Don't worry." He followed Burke's eyes to the NO SMOKING sign on the wall. "I won't blow up the joint." He exhaled some smoke and picked a bit of tobacco off his tongue. Coughed. And was ready to tell his story.

"I staked out the N.C.O. Club this morning just to see what Roper might be up to. He had some kinda meeting in there. Several troopers. Most of them I recognized. You know Arnie Arkolotti? Little guy, scar on his chin, served in 'Nam with the First Cav?"

Burke placed him. "We had Arkolotti in the stockade last year. He beat up a girl in Puma and stripped her. Probably raped her, too, but she wouldn't testify. The post psychiatrist gave him a head check and kicked him loose."

"That's the guy. He was one of Hank's visitors. So were Joe Briscoe and Louie Sanchez."

"Sanchez." Biggs knew him. "Carries a knife up his sleeve, and not for opening his mail. But I don't know Briscoe."

"Handlebar mustache and lots of tattoos," Burke said. "Briscoe has a silver star. They love him at the recruiting office; send him out to the high schools to talk kids into enlisting. Briscoe flexes his tattoos and feeds the kids a line of bullshit about army life. He's a top soldier, but I've never liked him. Who else did you see?"

"The Nose."

"Frank Craymore? He's got credentials, too. The man's a genius with a .45."

"Hey!" Biggs thought he'd solved the Palermo case. "Betsy was shot with a .45."

"She was shot twice," Burke pointed out. "Frank

Craymore is a U.S. Army pistol champion. He'd never spend two rounds on someone."

"There was another man," Rittmaster said. "A young Pfc. Didn't recognize him, but I figure his name is Nels Jansen. I found out they all work for Hank at his gas station on their off hours: Nels Jansen, Harry Williamson, Arnie Arkolotti, Frank Craymore, Louie Sanchez, and Joe Briscoe."

"What do you suppose they were talking about in there?" Biggs wondered.

"They weren't trying to decide how much to charge for an oil change and lube job at Hank's station." Burke slid down from the ammo crate. "You're on the right track. Keep pressing. Amos, I just had an idea. Put in a call to Betsy's boyfriend in Cleveland. He's been informed of her death by now. Find out if he has any idea where Betsy's money really came from."

"Okay, Top."

Biggs left and Burke began to lock up the armory.

Rittmaster looked up and down the hall. "There's something I didn't want to mention while Biggs was around. I followed Hank into town this morning." He cleared his throat. "He went to that gallery your lady friend owns."

Burke looked at Rittmaster slantwise.

"He was in the gallery maybe fifteen minutes. Then he took her to lunch at a restaurant down the block." He chose his words as if picking his way through a minefield. "They had a table by the window and I was across the street in my car. I've got to tell you that Hank was using all his best moves."

After locking the door and testing it, Burke said, "Did Hank know you were watching him?"

"Probably."

"Then that's why he went to see Maggie."

"To rattle your cage?"

"And take my mind off whatever else he's doing." Although Burke believed that, it didn't give him much comfort. He hated the idea of Hank cozying up to Maggie. The bastard could turn on the charm when he wanted. "Stay with Hank. I've got a hunch you're making him a lot more nervous than he's making me."

Chapter 11

Harvey Wriston IV stopped the open Land Rover and stood up to survey his surroundings. The great western desert of Egypt stretched in gentle rolls for as far as Wriston could see. He took off his hat and mopped his brow, bewildered by the sheer sweep of his surroundings. He didn't want to be here. His natural habitat was the orderly atmosphere of the American embassy in Cairo, where he served as second secretary. I'm an office man, he thought. Don't they know that?

He was looking for the Qattara Depression, described to him as a gigantic pit-shaped area to the south of the Libyan plateau and about 200 miles west of Cairo. It might just as well have been on the moon. Wriston could see no pits from where he stood. Only sand and rocks.

"Got to be around here somewhere." He swept the horizon once more with the Zeiss binoculars loaned to him by the embassy's military attaché. The attaché, a man named Hood, had been crushed to see this plum go to a civilian. "Take my binoculars," he said. "I'll be grateful to play even a minor role in your assignment."

Wriston had shocked Hood by saying he could have the fucking assignment if it meant that much to him.

"Where the hell is it?" He threw the binoculars onto the front seat and settled back behind the wheel. He tried to come to grips with his anxieties but managed only to slide deeper into them. His guts were on fire with fear. Or perhaps he was only feeling the effects of the *kishke* he'd had for breakfast at the filthy *wadi* twenty miles behind him.

Wriston started the engine and continued to drive west. The road he was attempting to follow had none of the usual characteristics of a road; it wasn't flat or smooth, it had no discernible direction or any signs. He continued on anyway, at first anxious that he was heading toward either the Libyan or Sudanese border. After a while he didn't care. Getting lost might be the answer to all his problems.

His self-pity was interrupted by a mirage: another car in the wasteland ahead. No, it wasn't a mirage. As he drew nearer, he could see it was an abandoned Renault, the driver's door swinging wide open. The hood was up, too. Wriston peered into the car without finding any clues to its ownership. The fact that the driver of the Renault had been going the same direction he was headed gave Wriston pause. Why would anyone in his right mind be driving toward the Qattara Depression? He had expected to be the only lunatic on this road.

The gears clashed as he rolled forward, nursing the Land Rover's cranky engine.

He had expected to see refugees, a naive notion. The nuclear explosion had occurred in an area unpopulated except for a handful of *fellahin* and wandering *Bedouin*. Most of the dead would be Libyan troops. The survivors among them would be traveling west toward their homeland.

Wriston's mission was simple: find the site of the nuclear attack and bring back an eyewitness report. He knew he had been chosen for this assignment because of his family. The Wristons had served in the State Department for four generations. His great-grandfather, Harvey Hollis Wriston, had died in 1910 protecting the American embassy in Mexico City during the riots preceding Zapata's rise to power. His grandfather and father had defended other embassies in other lands. The Wristons were of heroic mold. Everyone in the foreign service knew that. Everyone

except Harvey Wriston IV, who carried the secret taint
of cowardice.

The contrails of jet fighters cut the blue sky above.
The Egyptian Air Force was patrolling its airspace,
determined to keep planes carrying reporters and TV
camera crews out of the war zone. Intruders would be
shot down. Rumors were flying around the bar at the
Cairo Hilton that a C-19 carrying members of the
Western press had been forced down near El Minya.

The only way to reach Qattara was overland. Wriston
had used his diplomatic passport to go through the
roadblocks at El Faiyûm and Babriyah, all the while
hoping he would be stopped. No luck—the power of
U.S. diplomatic standing had carried him forward.

About half an hour after he had passed the abandoned Renault, Wriston spotted someone ahead of him
on the road: a lone man walking at a surprisingly
brisk pace. At the sound of Wriston's car he turned
and waved. When Wriston saw that the man was neither Egyptian nor Libyan, he slowed and came to a
stop.

"G'day, mate. And congratulations. You're just in
time to save an Australian's life." Without waiting for
an invitation, he threw a large canvas camera bag
into the backseat and jumped in next to Wriston.

"You're Australian?" Wriston asked, knowing it was
a stupid question.

"Every bloody inch of me."

"How'd you get past the checkpoints? The Egyptians
have patrols everywhere."

"You must have come across my Renault. I took it
over the hills north of Birkat. Thought I was pretty
smart until I found I'd cracked the oil pan. How'd you
get here, mate?"

"I'm with the U.S. embassy in Cairo. The guards let
me through on my diplomatic passport. My name is
Harvey Wriston."

"Archie Cox. Sydney *Telegraph*."

"Photographer?"

"Photojournalist," Cox said with a grin. "That means
I have to stay sober long enough to get the story as

well as the pictures. Come on, mate. Goose her along. We'll want to reach the cliffs before dark."

Wriston coaxed the Land Rover into gear and picked up speed. It felt good to have an English-speaking companion. And Archie Cox seemed to know how to reach the site of the explosion. "What cliffs are you talking about?"

"Why, the northern cliffs of the Qattara."

"The Qattara Depression? How far is it?"

Archie Cox's laugh was so infectious that Wriston had to smile with it.

"Mate, you really are lost. This *is* the Qattara Depression. You're smack in the middle of the bloody place!"

"I thought it was a big hole in the ground, like the Grand Canyon."

"My word, you've got the wrong idea altogether. It's a depression. Not a canyon. Four hundred feet below sea level and seven thousand square miles, that's the Qattara. Look to your west. See how the horizon rises? And to the east too? In another hour we should see the cliffs that mark the northern rim."

It struck Wriston that he was totally unqualified for a mission of this importance. God knows what would have happened if he hadn't met this Australian. He snuck a sideways look at Archie Cox. The photojournalist, a compact little man with reddish ringlets of hair and a flat face, was lounging back in his seat as if on holiday. Wriston wished he had Cox's self-assured air.

"What are you doing out here, Harvey?"

"I've been sent to make sure there aren't any U.S. citizens in danger."

Cox laughed harshly. "Rubbish. Your CIA wants to know how well their toy worked."

"Not true," Wriston snapped.

Cox shrugged and began fishing through the camera bag. He took out a Nikon body and fitted a lens to it. Loaded the Nikon with film. Did the same with a second camera. Then he reached way to the bottom of the bag and dragged out a bottle of whiskey that had been carefully wrapped in a cotton rag. "Drink?"

"No thanks."

"All the more for yours truly." Without removing the wrappings, Cox unscrewed the bottle cap and helped himself to three quick swallows. He looked down the neck, then replaced the cap with regret. "Short rations, I'm afraid. You don't happen to have anything to drink, do you?"

"No, sorry."

"Bloody Yanks," Cox grumbled. "Not that I don't appreciate the ride. Tell me straight, Harvey. Did your chaps provide Egypt with the nuke?"

"Absolutely not. My government is as worried about this disaster as the rest of the world. The embassy is getting ten messages an hour from Washington. All hell's broken loose back there. They want to know what really happened. That's why I'm here."

"Don't want to be here, do you?"

Wriston was shocked that a perfect stranger could read him so well. "Who would?"

"Me," the Australian said happily. "The first photographer to reach the scene and get back alive with film and a story will make a fortune. And that man is going to be Archie Cox."

You're lucky, Wriston thought. You know exactly what you want out of life.

They drove in silence for another twenty minutes, Cox with his head back against the seat and Wriston straining to see the cliffs. But it was Cox who saw them first, despite his half-closed eyes and languid posture.

"We're almost there, mate. Dead ahead."

The cliffs rose like majestic stone steps. No trace remained of the huge mushroom cloud reported by the refugees who had fled east. The sky was so clear that Wriston began to think he had come so far only to find the wrong place. There was no sign of a nuclear explosion's destructive force because the area was so desolate to begin with—no buildings or trees to be destroyed, no forests to be denuded. Wriston began to wonder what he would put in his report.

Then they passed what seemed to be a lump of charcoal. It registered with Wriston a few moments

later that the object was a human body burned to a
crisp charcoal black.

"Bloody hell," Archie Cox breathed. "Keep going."

"That was—"

"I know." Cox advanced the film in both cameras
and held up a light meter. "No need to stop. The main
body is just ahead. See there? And there?"

More lumps of charcoal could be seen on the desert
floor. Wriston had to leave the road to steer around all
of them. Gradually the ground itself became a darker
color. Amber. Burnt orange. A grim and gritty burn
the same shade as the bottom of a scorched frying pan.

"Must have been an airburst," Cox said. "Those boyos
behind us were incinerated even as they were thrown
free of the blast. My word, it fair fried everything in
sight, didn't it."

Wriston halted the Land Rover at what must have
been ground zero.

"We can't stay here," Cox said. "Lord knows how
many roentgens we're taking. We don't want our bones
going to dust."

One of the things Wriston had meant to take with
him was a Geiger counter, but the Egyptian government had confiscated every one they could find. The
thought of lethal doses of radiation penetrating his
body chilled him despite the heat. He shook off his
fears and looked around. If he got back to Cairo—
correction—*when* he got back to Cairo, the ambassador would want a description of this.

An airburst, Cox had said. That would explain why
there was no crater. The desert was burned for perhaps a mile in all directions, indicating that the nuclear device was a small one. The cliffs were blackened,
too. Bodies of Libyan troops littered the area, but
Wriston wasn't as horrified by the sight as he'd expected to be. The corpses were twisted into such
unrecognizable shapes they didn't seem human. The
few radiation-scarred survivors he'd come across at
the roadblocks had been more revolting. I'd rather die
straight off, Wriston decided, than hobble away with
radiation burns.

Cox had been standing on the hood shooting photos

first with one camera and then the other. The whirring and clicking of the motorized Nikons stopped abruptly and Cox jumped down into his seat. "Let's go, chum! Get us the hell out of here!"

Wriston needed no urging. He gunned the engine, heading the Land Rover along the face of the cliffs toward higher ground.

"Go around and up," Cox said, loading fresh film. "I want some shots from the top of the cliffs."

"I'll try." Wriston wanted to get up there himself. It was far enough away to be safe but close enough to get an overall view of the battlefield. But the farther they went from ground zero the worse the carnage became. The corpses three and four miles from the blast were recognizable as human beings. Wriston could see faces from which flesh had melted, leaving visible patches of white bone. He wanted to empty his guts, and would have if he could have done so without stopping.

Cox shot more photographs.

It took almost an hour to drive past the cliffs, up a treacherous grade that only a four-wheel-drive vehicle could have climbed, and around to the top of the cliffs. Wriston stopped less than three feet from the edge and climbed out of the Land Rover. His legs were terribly weak. Fear or radiation?

"What a bloody mess," Cox said.

"Why aren't you taking pictures?"

For the first time Cox seemed shaken by what he'd seen. "I will." But he left the cameras dangling against his chest.

From the top of the cliffs Wriston could see exactly what had happened. The Libyans had been advancing eastward through the Qattara Depression in a convoy of open trucks. Their officers must have been very confident. The burnt-out remnants of the trucks were too close together.

The Egyptians must have been waiting up here on the cliffs. The nuclear device was reported to have been fired from a conventional artillery piece. Wriston began to walk along the cliffs, looking for the site from which the device was fired.

A quarter of a mile away he found what he was

looking for. Several heavy vehicles had been up here, leaving a confusion of tracks. The Egyptians had littered the area with trash, too—cigarette butts and food tins, mainly. In the midst of the tracks and trash were three deep depressions about six feet apart that made a triangular pattern in the sand. Wriston decided the artillery piece used to fire the nuclear device had been set up here.

The footprints and general disarray of the area suggested that after firing the device the Egyptians had cleared out at all possible speed. Which was what Wriston himself had decided to do.

An aluminum box lying on its side caught his eye. At first he was unsure of why that particular piece of trash should have attracted his attention. Then he realized that one corner bore in black the letters U.S.D.D.—United States Department of Defense.

He ran to the box and snatched it up. It was about three feet in length and eighteen inches deep. The inside of the box was lined with rubber foam with a section cut out in the shape of an artillery shell. The discovery made Wriston dizzy. It was true: the nuclear weapon used here had come from somewhere within the U.S. arsenal.

Cox had come along the cliffs behind him. "What have you got there, mate?"

"Nothing," Wriston said quickly. He tossed the box aside as if it were unimportant, hoping Cox wouldn't notice its markings.

"This lot cleared out right smart, didn't they. And left quite a mess." Cox went over to the box and picked it up. He turned it over and read the initials. "That's what I thought."

"Don't jump to conclusions," Wriston warned, employing his official voice.

"Come off it, Harvey. The wogs cleared out so fast they forgot to take this bit of evidence with them."

"I suppose you think I was sent to find and destroy it."

"No." Cox smiled at him. "That's my job."

Wriston wasn't sure he'd heard correctly. He was further confused by the sudden shift in Cox's personality. Cox was no longer the cheerful, hard-drinking

Australian of modern folklore. His smile had become
cruel and tight. A revolver appeared in his hand. It
fired twice and Wriston was knocked off his feet onto
his back. Pain convulsed him. He gripped his chest
with both hands, trying to stem the bleeding and pull
the torn muscles back together.

Cox's face appeared above him. "Sorry, mate." He
put the revolver six inches in front of Wriston's face
and slowly pulled the trigger. Wriston watched the
cylinders turn; saw the bullet that would kill him
rotate until it was under the revolver's hammer.

The last thing Wriston saw was a flash of light.

Archie Cox drove several miles into the high plateau above the Qattara. When he found a place where
the desert floor looked soft, he stopped and hauled the
gray metal box and the body of Harvey Wriston out of
the backseat.

The Land Rover was a rental car usually used by
visitors to Cairo who wanted to explore the desert. Its
trunk contained a short-handled shovel for motorists
who got themselves stuck in deep sand. With swift
strokes, Cox tore into the earth. The ground wasn't as
soft as it appeared and he was soon gasping for breath.

This was going to be a lucrative assignment. Cox
was a contract employee of the CIA, which meant he
was paid for each assignment according to its degree
of risk. In this instance his contact at CIA headquarters in Langley had offered him $100,000 to find and
hide the box left behind by the Egyptians. The photos
he'd taken would bring even more. His only worry was
the amount of radiation he'd taken at the blast site.
Langley said the weapon was designed to produce low
radiation levels, but all that CIA lot were bloody liars.

He went down seven feet. More than enough. He
pushed the box into the hole first, followed by Wriston's
body. Poor sod should never have been sent out here.

After filling in the hole, Cox sat down in the sliver
of shade provided by the Land Rover and finished the
few ounces of whiskey left in his bottle. He would have
nothing to drink on the way back to Cairo. My own
fault, he thought. Should have come better prepared.
This was definitely a two-bottle job.

Chapter 12

Jean made up her mind not to fall in love with
Ansel Burke. I will not allow myself to be so stupid,
she thought. No way. I've only known the man two
days, for God's sake. Never even had a date with him.
She groaned and allowed her shoulders to slump. But
Ansel is so *beautiful*. And he's the first man I've actually lost sleep over.

No, she thought, I really must get him out of my
system. After all, Ansel made it plain that he's quite
happy with Maggie Winston—although I'll *never* understand how any man could be taken in by a woman
with a forged smile and a laugh as shrill as the mat-
ing call of a hundred-dollar bill.

Just for fun she wrote *Mrs. Jean Burke* on a sheet of
paper. It looked so right she wanted to cry. Fearing
someone would come into her office and see it, she tore
the sheet into small pieces and concealed them under
some other papers at the bottom of her wastebasket—
which made her feel unbelievably girlish.

For the next few hours Jean threw herself into her
work, only to find that a furious expenditure of energy
was no help in sweeping a man out of your mind. By
midafternoon she had made a cold-blooded decision to
try to take Ansel away from Maggie.

There was no law against stealing a man, she was
lawyer enough to know that. And she thought she
stood a chance against Maggie Winston. After all,
what did Maggie have that she didn't? Sure, Maggie

had a sexier body. Magnificent breasts. Luscious hair. Sophistication. Beautiful clothes. But those qualities weren't everything.

Were they?

It occurred to her that one thing Maggie did lack was a connection with the U.S. Army. Ansel was a soldier first, an artist second. More than anything, he wanted to find Betsy Palermo's killer. Although he'd told her at breakfast that he needed no help, he'd be bound to appreciate any new information she provided.

Jean thought of Major Ben Harrison, a staff officer in the army intelligence "Green Unit" at the Pentagon. She wasn't sure what the Green Unit did, but Ben Harrison had a high security clearance and he'd been very attentive to her in Washington. Smitten, even. Jean enjoyed his company, though she'd never felt sparks fly in his presence.

She looked up his phone number at the Pentagon and placed a long-distance call. It would be after 6:00 P.M. in Washington, but Ben usually worked late. He was ambitious to trade his gold oak leaves for the silver leaves of a lieutenant colonel.

A stern voice answered: "Major Harrison speaking."

"Hi, Ben."

"Jean?"

"That's right."

"Hey, I'm glad you called." The stiffness melted away. "The old five-sided torture chamber just isn't the same without you. How do you like New Mexico?"

"Oh, it has a few attractions."

"Sounds like you've met someone." A trace of disappointment. "What's it like to practice law in a line infantry outfit?"

"Kind of fun. I got a corporal off with a one-grade bust yesterday in a general court."

"Hey, nice going. What did the corporal do?"

"He knocked down a whorehouse with a tank."

"You handled that case?" Harrison laughed. "I might have known. We heard about the Whore War all the way back here on the Potomac. Sounds like you're still sticking it to the brass."

"When necessary."

"In that case, I'm glad you aren't planning to stay in the army. What's up, Jean? I'd say you called because you miss my boyish face, if I didn't know better."

"I need a favor."

He sighed. "I figured. Okay, what is it?"

"An army abbreviation popped up in one of my cases and no one seems to know what it means. The funny thing is, this stupid thing might be central to the case. I hoped you could tell me what it means or find someone at the Pentagon who knows."

"What is this mysterious abbreviation?"

"F.D.N.W."

"F.D.N.W.? Never heard that one. I'll ask around, though—*if* you promise to have dinner with me the next time you're in Washington."

"That's a date."

"I really miss you, Jean." Harrison's voice almost broke. "We could have been good together."

"I'm sorry," she said gently.

"Oh, never mind. I was probably destined to be a bachelor."

"And a general."

"Yeah, then I could order you transferred back to the Pentagon. I'll check that out for you: F.D.N.W.?"

"That's it. Ben, I've always wanted to ask you something. What does the Green Unit do?"

He chuckled. "You know the army. We keep an eye on the Blue Unit. Call me tomorrow."

"Okay. Good-bye, Ben. And thanks."

"Any time. Talk to you later."

As Jean put down the phone, Major Porter, the post magistrate, appeared in her door. "General Leland wants you to report to his office." When she failed to pop out of her chair like a jack-in-the-box, he added, "Immediately!"

"Did he say what he wanted?"

"For God's sake, he doesn't have to say. He's the *post commander*."

"How nice for him." She took more time than she needed to gather up her things, rather enjoying Major Porter's agitation. Usually he was so somnolent she couldn't even be certain he was alive.

"I knew General Leland wouldn't stand for what you did in court yesterday." Porter's whine had the irritation level of fingernails across a blackboard. "Look, I don't know how to say this . . . Could you find a way to let him know I had nothing to do with the way you defended Corporal Feeney? I don't want him to think that it was my fault."

"There's no 'fault' in a lawyer's providing an aggressive defense for a client. I won't apologize." Porter's plaintive expression finally got to her. "But I won't let him blame you, either."

He looked so pathetically grateful that Jean couldn't stand to be in his presence for another second. She brushed past him and walked quickly out of the admin building and across the courtyard toward post headquarters. If Leland intended to chew her out, Jean was ready for him. This wouldn't be the first time a general officer had disapproved of her courtroom tactics. Her strategy for dealing with such situations was to be civil and correct, but never apologetic.

The general's outer office was as spacious as a theater lobby and almost as uncomfortable. The clerk told Jean she could go right in. She expected to find General Leland alone. Instead he was standing over a table in conversation with a pale civilian in tweeds, a most unlikely style of dress for New Mexico.

Leland looked up and smiled. "Captain Silk, thank you for coming." He inclined his head toward the civilian. "This is Prentice Hart, my architect. Don't mind his bizarre clothes. He flew in from Baltimore for a quick meeting."

"Hello." Jean was surprised by Leland's cordiality.

Hart offered a perfunctory greeting and turned back to a scale model of a graceful white mansion that sat in the middle of the table.

"Please excuse me, Captain," Leland said. "I'll be through here in just a minute. Have a seat."

Jean sat down and took a copy of the *Army Times* from a side table. While turning pages, she listened to General Leland take his architect to task for "lack of vision." Apparently Prentice Hart was restoring to its previous glory a run-down old mansion the general

had bought on the outskirts of Baltimore. Leland
wanted extensive landscaping of the grounds and top
quality fixtures within the house. Hart argued that
Leland would never recover all the money he was
sinking into the place if he someday decided to sell.
Leland didn't care. He demanded the best.

Gradually she lost interest in the talk of dormers
and cedar shingles. And in the *Army Times* too. She
put aside the weekly service paper to study the photos
on the general's wall. It was a typical celebrity wall:
Leland with a movie star; Leland with a congressman;
Leland with the U.S. Army Chief of Staff.

The only photo that interested her was of two young
military cadets standing at extreme attention, probably doing violent harm to their spines. It appeared to
have been taken thirty or more years ago. Jean recognized the insignia on the boys' uniforms—the Virginia
Military Institute.

Leland was one of the cadets. His handsome young
face was freshly scrubbed. Hawkish. Still showing a
few signs of teenage vulnerability. The second boy's
face was rounder and less stern. It looked familiar,
too. Almost more familiar than Leland's. She could
feel a name on her tongue. It rolled around there,
reluctant to come out. She had just about coaxed the
name to her lips when—

"I'm sorry, Captain. I thought my personal business
would be finished before you arrived." Leland sat down
behind his desk.

"I was just admiring your photographs."

"Ah, yes. My wife says they advertise my egomania.
She's right, of course. But I'm too old to try to hide
such things."

Jean didn't think he looked old at all. General Claude
Leland had reached late middle age in fine fashion. His
face was almost as unlined as in the picture. His eyes
were a youthful china blue. True, his hair had turned
white, but it was a white so pure as to look premature.

"What do you think of this?" Leland gestured at the
scale model of the house, which he had carried over
and put on the corner of his desk.

"A beautiful house."

"It will be when the renovation is complete." Leland beamed at the model. "That was my home. Do you see here, the little stream at the back of the property? Caught my first trout there." He went on to point out the tree where he had put up a swing and the window that belonged to the room he had slept in as a boy. Apparently every detail of his youth was to be lovingly recreated. "It was a wonderful place to grow up. Later on my father had business problems and we lost it. I bought back the house recently—the previous owners had let it decay to a shameful degree—and I intend to retire there in a few years. When I do, I want everything to be exactly as it was when I was a boy."

Jean had no idea why he was telling her all this. She had expected a chewing out. Not a chat.

Gradually General Leland turned his attention to Jean. "You're wondering what my boyhood home has to do with anything."

"Yes, sir."

"Very simple. Traditions and symbols are important. And I don't mean just to me. They're important to our nation and to the U.S. Army."

She still didn't understand.

"Yesterday you fought me in the courtroom and won. I was angry at the time because Corporal Feeney deserved to go to prison. But I respected your tenacity and imagination, so I put the matter from my mind." He picked up a pair of blue army personnel folders.

"Now I see you're defending the two young men who wrecked the antique howitzer that usually sits in front of the post theater. I've heard from a reliable source that you intend to make an issue at the court-martial of the amount of money spent on upkeep for the 105."

"That's right, sir." Jean spoke calmly, but she was ablaze with anger. Someone had told Leland about her strategy for defending those two boys. But who? Major Porter? No, she hadn't mentioned her plans to him. Who had she told? Well, everyone she sat with in the Chicken Coop: Ansel, Maggie, Lou Brodsky, Wolfe Heinzman ... Sean Feeney ... Bill Manning. *Yes!* Bill Manning! That ass-kissing son of a bitch must have gone straight to General Leland with her plans.

"I can't allow that to happen, Captain."

"Sir, I have an obligation to defend my clients with every sound argument at my disposal. In my opinion those two boys should not go to prison for a drunken prank. No one was hurt. The antique howitzer was damaged, but not beyond repair—although one of my arguments will be that too much taxpayer money has already been lavished on that archaic contraption."

Leland's china blue eyes flashed. "Archaic contraption? Would you consider the U.S. flag an archaic contraption? Suppose those young troopers had set fire to the flag? Could such a thing be allowed?"

"That's an entirely different kind of offense."

"No it isn't. The flag and the howitzer are symbols. The flag represents the spirit of the country, and the howitzer the pride of the army. When troops are allowed to attack important symbols with impunity, morale is quickly undermined. I've seen it before. You may not remember the flag burnings of the sixties. I do. Those so-called acts of civil disobedience nearly tore the country apart."

"Sir, Pfc.s Hill and Selecki didn't intend to *undermine* the army. They were so drunk they hardly knew what they were doing."

"It's the result I'm worried about, not the intent."

Jean made no attempt to respond. Leland's thinking on this subject had been set years ago. All she could do was wait for the trial and make her case before the entire court-martial board.

"I could have you removed from this case," Leland said. "But I wouldn't do that. I'm not a man who tries to circumvent the channels of military justice. However, I will make you a promise." He held up the folders containing the service records of the malefactors. "These troopers have confessed to destruction of government property. They are guilty and will be convicted. The severity of the punishment they receive depends on the type of defense you give them. I called you to my office to deliver a simple message: if you try again to use a court-martial as a forum for embarrassing me, I will bury these young men in Leavenworth until their hair is whiter than mine." The charming smile never wavered. "You're dismissed, Captain Silk."

Never in her life had Jean been so skillfully threatened. She could only rise, salute, and leave General Leland's office. The clerk in the outer office didn't even look up to mark her passing. It wasn't until Jean reached the corridor that she allowed herself to show her anger. She kicked the wall, startling a passerby, and punched the elevator button so viciously that it popped out of its brass holder.

I won't let those boys go to Leavenworth, she vowed. No matter what I have to do.

Chapter 13

Without sun the desert became as chilly as the high
country to the north. Roper had donned a light sweater
against the night air. The moon was so full he could
read his watch by it. He would have preferred a darker
night, but in this line of work you took what you got.

He was wearing a TALKMAN field communications
headset and microphone. The mike came around from
the headset to just in front of his mouth. He switched
on the transceiver and spoke into the mike with delib-
erate precision: "This is a test. I repeat: this is Hank
testing. If you can hear me, report in over my headset."

"Yo."

"Got'cha."

"I hear ya, Hank."

"Right above you."

"Coming in."

Roper looked at the dim moonlit ridges around him.
He had posted his men carefully. They had overlap-
ping fields of fire and good escape routes. Each of them
wore a TALKMAN identical to his. They could com-
municate and still have both hands free for their weapons. Frank Craymore, the best man on post with rifle
or pistol, was equipped with a silenced and laser-aimed
Ruger Mini-14. The others were carrying Ingram
MAC-10s capable of firing 950 rounds per minute and
also fitted with silencers. Anyone attempting a double
cross would die in a silent cross fire of lead.

For himself, Roper had selected only a boot knife

169

and a standard issue .45, customized with a rubber handgrip and a barrel extension fitted with a silencer. He called the powerful weapon Whispering Death. "Frank," he said into his mouthpiece, "do you read me?"

"Right here, Hank."

"I want you to put a red dot on The Man's chest and keep it there."

"How will I know which one is The Man?"

"Take my cue. I'll call him Number One."

"Will do."

"Listen up, everybody. Remember that these two guys come from Argentina. They probably don't speak English very well. If they try to pull a rip-off, cut 'em down. But I don't want anybody shot just because they get their English confused and make a stupid move. Got it?"

A chorus of affirmatives came over his headset.

Roper paced back and forth behind a jeep van carrying the merchandise he was there to deliver. He felt ready for anything. So ready, that when his headset crackled to life, it didn't make him jump at all.

"Sanchez to base. Do you read me, base?"

"I read you," Roper replied. "You got our customers?"

"They're right behind me," Louie Sanchez confirmed.

"Everything kosher? No tail?"

"It's just like Control told you. Two Spanish-speaking dudes, one in a cowboy hat, one in a baseball cap. Actually, they look kinda dumb. I picked 'em up at the Durger King on Moroy Street. No guns showing. They're driving a Dodge pickup. Shall I bring 'em in?"

"Yeah, bring them in, Louie." To the others listening on the TALKMAN, he said, "Get set, everybody."

Roper busied himself by checking the ammo clip in his .45 and switching on the all-frequency monitor in the back of the van. Soon he heard the two vehicles approaching and saw their headlights. Louie Sanchez drove up onto the plateau, stopped the jeep, cut the lights, and trotted out into the darkness to take his place on the perimeter of defense.

The second vehicle, a heavy Dodge pickup with four-wheel drive, approached more tentatively. The man behind the wheel was evidently unused to that type of vehicle because he ground the gears noisily on the final hill leading to the plateau.

The all-frequency monitor hummed steadily. Roper moved the directional mike so that it was pointed straight at the pickup. When the needle stayed in the green zone, he said over the TALKMAN, "The monitor's not picking up any signals, so they aren't wired. Or if they are, they haven't switched on their system. Stay loose. I'll sing out if anything changes."

The pickup stopped about twenty feet from Roper, who was almost blinded by its headlights. "Cut those damned lights!" he barked as soon as the driver turned off the engine. When the lights were turned off, he whispered into the TALKMAN, "Jansen—hit the floods."

A thirty-square-yard area of the plateau was instantly bathed in harsh blue floodlight.

Roper motioned to the two men in the car to come forward. They did, and Roper had to grin. Louie Sanchez was right. The hats and blue denim jackets looked ridiculous on these two. Both were dark-complexioned men in their forties who carried themselves with stiff Latin dignity. The one who had been driving was the taller and more muscular of the two. An army officer, Roper guessed. The other had a flabby midsection and wispy mustache, an office dweller of some kind.

They came to a stop a few feet from Roper.

"Can we dispose of these ridiculous hats now?" the taller man asked with only a faint Spanish accent.

"Suit yourselves."

The tall Argentinian took off his baseball cap and skimmed it into the darkness. The cowboy hat followed it closely.

"Number One to my right," Roper said into the TALKMAN.

A red pencil-point beam lanced out of the darkness and fastened on the tall Argentinian's chest.

"What is this?"

"Relax, Pancho. That's just my insurance policy. You know what a laser is? *El laser?*"

"I am quite familiar with lasers," the Argentinian

said dryly. "And I now understand. You have a laser-aimed rifle covering me, yes?"

"You got it, Pancho. One wrong move and you and your buddy are taco meat. There are other guns out there, too. Try to remember that."

"Do not call me Pancho in your patronizing way."

"Okay," Roper said. "You're Number One and your pal is Number Two. Which of you wants to inspect the merchandise?"

"My *compadre* is the scientist." He said something to his colleague in Spanish and pushed him forward.

Number Two glanced nervously over his shoulder, then came ahead to help Roper unload one of the gray metal boxes from the van. They opened it together.

"Does your man speak any English?" Roper asked Number One.

"*Poco*. Very little."

"Tell him that's dry ice around the container. He'll burn himself if he touches it."

Number One said a few words in Spanish and Number Two nodded as if to say he already knew that. Number Two was on his knees in front of the gray metal box, lifting out the cylinder with utmost care. The cylinder was a special alloy shaped into an artillery charge. He put it on the ground and began to unscrew the explosive charge from the body of the round.

"Do you need this?" Roper handed Number Two a technical manual stamped on the cover with the Department of Defense logo.

Number Two laid the manual on the ground and turned the pages quickly, ignoring the English text, but stopping to study a few of the diagrams. Satisfied that he understood the interaction of the complicated mechanisms, Number Two proceeded with his examination.

For Roper's money, Number Two was overconfident. "He's not gonna blow us up, is he? I mean, that's a sophisticated weapon he's playing with."

Number One smiled thinly. "We are not all *gauchos* in the Argentine. My colleague is a graduate of the

Sorbonne and the recipient of many international scientific awards. He will not make a mistake."

"Who are you gonna blow up with that thing?"

"That remains to be decided. First we must be certain it will work."

"Hey, it's worked before."

"Yes, I know."

For the next five minutes they watched the mustachioed man complete his examination and reassemble the device's two main components. Roper helped him slide the artillery round back into the foam-covered slot in the box. They brought out the second box and Number Two began a similar examination of that unit.

"Show me the money," Roper said.

Number One tapped his partner on the shoulder and asked a question, which was answered in an excited burst of Spanish.

"You may not only *see* the money, you may *have* it. My colleague assures me your merchandise is legitimate."

"You bet your ass it is." Roper followed Number One to his pickup truck. A suitcase was taken from the front seat. Roper laid the suitcase on the hood of the pickup and opened it. Packets of U.S. currency spilled out, giving Roper a warm glow. There was supposed to be six million dollars here. He had no intention of counting it; that would take half the night. Besides, Control was responsible for seeing that all financial arrangements were correctly carried out.

"This better be six million," he said. "If it isn't, you'll be one dead spic."

"And those devices had better work," Number One retorted, "or you will be one dead anglo."

"Just so we understand each other." Roper shoveled the packets back into the suitcase and snapped the locks. "I'll bet you're gonna use those things to make another grab for the Falklands. Am I right?"

"That is our business," the Argentinian said coldly.

"Sure it is. I was just making conversation."

Number One looked down at the red spot on his chest, which continued to follow him wherever he moved. "Please turn off the laser. It is very disconcerting to walk around with a death mark on one's breast."

"That's the idea," Roper said with a grin. But he added, speaking into the mike, "Frank, you can turn off the laser for now. But keep these bozos covered."

The pencil beam disappeared.

"Muy bien," said Number Two, returning the second artillery round to its metal case.

Roper threw the suitcase into the back of the van and helped the Argentinians load the two metal cases into their pickup and cover them with a tarp. "You've got to keep these babies cool," he warned. "If you don't, they could destabilize."

"We are aware of that."

"I hope you've got a good plan for getting them out of the country."

"That is not your concern."

"The hell it isn't! If you're picked up, these things could be traced back here."

"Arrangements have been made," Number One assured him. "We will be out of the country before dawn."

"Good. Don't drive too fast. The cops in our country are always on the lookout for speeders."

"If your police were better occupied, your country would not have so much crime." Number One started the engine of the pickup and turned it in a circle until he found the bumpy path leading back toward the road.

"Arnie, watch the road," Roper said into his mike. "Make sure they go west toward Puma."

"Right."

"Joe, come on down. You'll ride with me. Everyone else scatter. And nice work. We'll have a big payday tomorrow."

Joe Briscoe came trotting across the plateau with a MAC-10 slung over his shoulder and jumped into the van next to Roper, who drove down off the plateau toward the highway.

"They're headed west," Arnie Arkolotti reported.

"Okay. Take off, Arnie." Roper turned off his transceiver and pulled off the headset and mike. "We did it! Three million this time."

"Can I take a look?" Briscoe loved the sight of large amounts of cash.

"Let's get on the road first."

Roper tossed the suitcase into the van and slid behind the wheel. A minute later they were back on the highway, driving toward Puma.

"Now can I take a gander?" Briscoe asked.

"Help yourself."

Briscoe leaned over the seat and opened the suitcase. "God *damn,* but money's beautiful."

"It smells good, too. Hey, I didn't have a chance to ask about Rittmaster. How'd that go?"

"No problem. He never even knew what hit him."

"You didn't kill him, I hope."

"Naw, I just gave him a new place to part his hair. He'll be okay in a few days."

"I knew he'd try to follow me tonight. Stupid bastard should have stayed in his own patch."

"His tough luck that he didn't." Briscoe drew a flat black policeman's sap from his back pocket and slapped it against the palm of his hand. "That's exactly what this beauty sounds like when she does her thing—*splat!* Rittmaster hit the pavement like a hundred and eighty pounds of warm shit."

Roper, looking for landmarks, had put Rittmaster out of his mind. "What time is it?"

"Ten-fifteen. Don't worry, we've got plenty of time."

"I don't want to be late for our meeting with Control."

"No sweat, Hank. You want a smoke?" Briscoe offered Roper a cigarette.

"Yeah, why not."

"I knew you couldn't quit."

"Bullshit. I've quit smoking a thousand times."

They settled in with their cigarettes, trading stories about people they knew who had tried to give up smoking.

"I knew a sergeant at Fort Ord who bet his wife a thousand bucks he could quit smoking for six months," Roper recalled. "Five months and twenty-nine days went by and he hadn't touched a cigarette. Didn't even miss them—he thought. The night before he would have won the bet, his wife took him to a Bogart film festival over in Monterey. The first movie that night was *The Big Sleep*. Remember that one?"

"I don't think so."

"Bogie smokes two or three packs in just the first reel. The sergeant couldn't take it. After watching Bogie chain-smoke for almost an hour, he *had* to have a cigarette himself. So he told his wife he was gonna take a leak and went to the men's room. Five minutes later she came busting in there. Caught him trying to flush a butt down the toilet. That one smoke cost him a thousand bucks."

Briscoe was indignant. "The bitch had no right going into a men's room! I mean, some things are sacred."

"Yeah. A thousand *bucks* is sacred."

They were into the town of Puma now. Except for Front Street and Colorado Boulevard, where most of the good restaurants and night spots were located, the town was silent. McKinley Avenue looked especially quiet. Although it wasn't yet 11:00 P.M., most of the large Spanish-style homes were already dark. The citizens of Puma went to bed early and rose with the sun—a western trait.

At the end of McKinley Street stood John F. Kennedy High School. The flagpole in front of the school was Puma's premiere landmark. The distance from the ground to the top of the pole was exactly one hundred feet. You could see it from all over town. During the day a huge hand-sewn flag donated by the Lady's Auxiliary flew from it. The pole and its flag represented the pride of Puma.

Roper drove around the school to the rear parking lot, empty except for a single car parked in the very center of the lot. That car was a polished gray Mercedes.

Roper stopped behind it. Briscoe got out carrying the suitcase given to him by the Argentinian. The trunk of the Mercedes was ajar. He opened it, tossed in the suitcase, and closed the hatch.

Control sat behind the wheel of the Mercedes, hidden in shadows. Without acknowledging the presence of Briscoe and Roper, he turned over the engine and pulled away. The car's lights weren't switched on until Control turned onto McKinley Street. Then the finely tuned engine went into higher rpms as the Mercedes sped away.

Briscoe came back to the van. "Did you see that? The son of a bitch couldn't spare even a minute to talk to us. After everything we've done for him, all his fucking black work, he just drives off."

"Forget it," Roper advised. "He's a prick. So what? His money's good. That's all that matters." He started the van.

"Sometimes I just get tired of being Control's errand boy," Briscoe grumbled, stroking his handlebar mustache. "Don't you?"

"Yeah, sure I do. But tomorrow morning my Swiss bank account will be about a quarter of a million dollars fatter. So will yours. How many *errand boys* make that kind of loot?"

"The guy just pisses me off."

"Make a doll. Stick pins in it. Just don't mess with him otherwise." Roper smiled. "Like they say, he's got 'friends in high places.'"

Chapter 14

Five minutes after Burke arrived at Maggie's apartment they were in bed making love.

Afterward they lay close, each savoring the experience in a different way. For Maggie, sex was a proven method for retaining the upper hand in a relationship. Beds were battlefields and orgasms victory skyrockets. Burke's obvious pleasure in her body was her best guarantee that he wouldn't take his paintings elsewhere.

Ansel marveled at Maggie's athleticism. He had never encountered a woman so agile. Still, as much as he enjoyed their contests, which is how he sometimes thought of sex with Maggie, he always had the feeling he was taking part in an Olympic event.

Maggie rolled over and kissed the flat of his belly. "What happened at Fort Powell today?" She was determined to show more interest in his army career. "Did you find out who killed that poor girl?"

"Not yet." Burke stared at the ceiling, seeing Betsy Palermo's broken body on the desert floor. "I do have a few suspects." He looked from the ceiling to her. "One of them is Hank Roper."

He knows that Hank came to see me, she thought. "Hank Roper? But he's a friend of yours. At least he said he was when he came into the gallery today." How much should I tell him? "He even took me to lunch. I wouldn't have gone, of course, if he hadn't claimed to be your drinking buddy."

Burke snorted. "We've never been buddies. We served together in 'Nam, that's all. Hank can soldier when he wants to, I'll give him that. He didn't win those stripes in a poker game. But to Hank the army is just a money pot. He spends every waking hour figuring out ways to separate his 'buddies' from their pay. Doesn't give a damn about friends or the service or anything else except himself."

That's the only way to survive, Maggie thought.

"There are too many like him in the army these days."

"Ansel, how did you know Hank Roper came to see me?"

"I have a man watching him."

"Really?" Maggie saw it then. Knowing he was being followed, Hank came to the gallery and invited her to lunch as a way to taunt Ansel. Very smart. Very daring. She liked Hank's style more and more.

"Don't let him near you again, Maggie. He's dangerous."

"I won't. Good Lord, I had no idea he was that kind of man."

"What did he talk about?"

"Well, first he wanted to buy one of your paintings. I refused his offer, which made him a bit testy. He took me to lunch to try to change my mind. That didn't work, of course. Let's see, he also did a lot of bragging about his condo in Vail and all the places he's been. But I must tell you: he turned a *very* sour shade of green when he heard how well you're doing as an artist."

"I'd rather burn a painting than sell it to Hank."

The thought of a lot of money going up in flames made Maggie queasy. "Don't talk that way, darling. I hate to think of any piece of art being destroyed."

"Hey, guess what. This morning I finished the picture I've been telling you about—the ranch house."

"Wonderful! When can I see it?"

"Right now, if you want. It's in the car."

"Darling, get up and bring it in this minute. I'm *dying* to see it." Maggie slid out of bed and threw on her robe, urging Ansel to hurry up and dress. From the way he had been talking about this picture, she knew it was important. A breakthrough of some kind. If so, it might become the centerpiece for the New York show.

Burke dressed and went out to his car. As usual, he felt like a kid bringing a term paper to school. He carried the canvas into the apartment with a sheet thrown over it, more anxious about her reaction than he cared to admit.

"Put it down here." Maggie pointed to the best-lighted wall. As soon as Ansel had leaned the canvas against the wall, she snatched off the covering.

What she saw shocked her. It was magnificent—and terribly disappointing. A major departure from his previous work. Yes, the house festooned with strings of chilies was thrillingly real. People ate and slept there. Had babies. Raised them. Died and were buried high in those mountains. The house had personality and a history. You wanted to know the people who lived there. All of that was wonderful.

But the face at the window was a different story.

That face—small as it was in relation to the rest of the canvas—overshadowed everything. She couldn't discern whether it was the face of a man or woman, child or adult. But it bore a sadness that jarred Maggie's senses. It was the face of a person who has lost all hope.

"Well?" Ansel was waiting nervously for her opinion.

"Give me a minute." She didn't know quite what to say. As it stood, this painting could not be the centerpiece of the show. In fact, she would be reluctant even to send it to Donald Hillary. Because of that haunting face, this picture had a completely different feel from Ansel's other work. It was grittier, sadder, angrier: in a painting, those qualities don't sell. But she had to tell Ansel *something*.

"Darling, it's wonderful."

His relief was childlike. "You really think so?"

Maggie was pleased to be able to manipulate such a strong and capable man with ease. "Yes. It's definitely the best thing you've ever done."

"That's what I thought, too, but I didn't want to blow my own horn. Besides, you're the expert."

Which was exactly what Maggie wanted to hear.
"Where did the face come from?"

"I don't know."

"Why is it there?"

"I'm not sure about that, either. I started to finish
the picture and, before I knew what was happening,
there was that face at the window. I don't know who it
is, what it means, or why it's there. I hardly even
remember putting it there." He sighed. "This may
sound crazy—I think that somehow the face is connected with the nuclear attack in Egypt. I think I'm
trying to say something about that. I've seen plenty of
combat survivors. The eyes are pretty much the same,
no matter what kind of shit they've been through.
What I'm trying to say in this picture—maybe—is
that all of a sudden every one of us is a potential
casualty."

Maggie took him by the hand and led him to the
couch. "Sit down here, Ansel. Come on, get close. That's
better." Now she knew how to handle him. The whole
problem could be solved very easily. "Something mon-
strous happened and it affected your vision of this
picture. That's understandable. Very human. But that
face does not fit into the body of your work."

"I don't understand. I thought you liked the picture."

"Yes, of course I do. Except for the face. It throws
the whole canvas out of kilter."

"How?"

"Well, it distracts your attention from the house . . .
the chilies . . . the mountains in the background."

"I kind of thought the face unified those things."

"I'm afraid not." She patted his large, rough hands.
"Don't worry, there's an easy fix."

"Fix? The picture is already finished."

"Not necessarily. Darling, don't look so stricken.
Artists rework canvases every day. All you have to do
is paint out the face."

A certain stubbornness entrenched itself in Burke's
expression. "I'm not sure I want to do that."

"Give yourself some time to consider the idea." Maggie
jumped up from the couch. "Look, I'll show you what I
mean." She picked up a magazine and tore out a dark,

three-inch square from the background of an ad. "Come here."

Maggie laid the painting on the floor and placed the scrap of paper on the offending face, blotting it out and leaving just a dark window. "There! Isn't that an improvement?"

It didn't look like an improvement to Burke. "I hate it." He groped for better words. "All the life has gone out of the thing."

"Not at all. Look, in the beginning you never *intended* to have a person in this picture."

"Maggie, I never know exactly where I'm headed when I start a painting. I have a rough idea—the rest just grows."

"Now that you're in the big leagues, you'll just have to get used to taking some constructive criticism."

"What does that mean?"

"It means Donald Hillary won't take this picture as it is."

"So what?"

"You must consider his reactions. After all, he's putting on your show."

"Then we just won't include this canvas."

Oh, no, Maggie thought. It's time you learned the ground rules, mister. "Ansel, to become a successful artist, you must learn to adapt yourself to the public taste."

He laughed at that. "Hell, I don't know what the public taste is. Does anybody?"

"I know what it *isn't*." She lifted the folded swatch of paper from the face. "And this kind of morose theme just won't sell. You must stick to what you do best."

"Which is?"

Maggie was so intent on putting across her message that she missed the truculence built into his question. "Strong faces. Still lifes with powerful color. Landscapes with uplifting themes."

"Shit-oh-dear, you make me sound like a slot machine. Put in a quarter and watch the wheels turn. Bing! A strong face. Bing! A landscape. Bing! A still life. Wow! Jackpot! Maggie, I don't paint with other people in mind. I just try to dig out what's in my own head."

"That's not good enough for Donald Hillary," she snapped, a little more coldly than she'd intended. "Or for me."

They were at a point of impasse when the phone rang. Maggie answered it brusquely. "Yes?"

"Hello, Maggie," said Lou Brodsky. "Is Ansel there? I need to talk with him real fast."

"Yes, he's here." She handed him the receiver. "Your friend Brodsky. Duty calls," she added sarcastically.

Burke was glad for the interruption. He'd never argued with Maggie before. If he didn't know better, he'd say she was trying to exert some kind of control over him. "What's up, Lou?"

"I'm at the post hospital. Jack Rittmaster was brought in a couple of hours ago. He was found in the N.C.O. parking lot next to his car. Head all bloody. He's in bad shape. It's a fracture, not a concussion."

"Well, shit. Was it Hank?"

"I dunno. I haven't had a chance to talk to Jack. He's conscious now, they say, but the docs are working on him."

"I'll be right there. If you get a chance to talk to him before I get there, take it."

"Will do, Sergeant Major."

Burke put down the phone. "I'm sorry, I have to go. One of my men—the one who was following Hank this morning—has been hurt."

"That's a shame." Maggie wasn't surprised. Hank Roper didn't seem the type to let people spy on him.

"I'll take this with me." He tossed the sheet over the canvas and put it under his arm.

Maggie realized she had been too harsh. Some of the things she had said held echoes of her confrontations with Marshall Vogel. "Darling, I'm sorry if I sounded shrewish." She put her arms around his neck. I musn't try to win the war all at once, she thought. This will take time. What do they call it—a war of attrition? "I'm only trying to ensure your success. Forget everything I said. Be exactly the kind of artist you want to be."

"You had me worried," Burke admitted.

"Don't worry about *anything*. Go see how your friend is doing and call me in the morning." She smiled sweetly and kissed him. "I love you."

"You're incredible," Burke said, returning the kiss. "Good night."

He left with the painting under his arm. When he was out of earshot, Maggie picked up a piece of Murano glass she'd bought in Venice and smashed it against the wall.

Rittmaster was listed in serious condition. He looked critical. His doctor said they could talk to him, but didn't guarantee answers to their questions.

Burke and Brodsky were at Rittmaster's side for almost an hour before he opened his eyes. They fluttered and closed again almost immediately. Presently he turned his heavily bandaged head and looked at them.

"Uh . . . Ansel . . . what the fuck happened here?"

"Jack, don't move your head." Burke leaned over him. "You're in the hospital. Someone slugged you in the parking lot."

"Yeah? . . . don't remember."

"You've got a fractured skull."

"The doc says you'll make it," Brodsky put in.

With effort, Rittmaster smiled. "Sure I will. I'm due to die of cancer. Everybody knows that."

"Did you see who hit you?" Burke asked.

"Lung cancer." Rittmaster coughed painfully. "See what I mean?"

Burke and Brodsky waited.

"No, I can't remember much. Except Hank, that bastard . . . had something goin' tonight. Don't know what. I was gonna tail him." Another chest spasm. He cleared his throat. "Left the barracks . . . last I remember."

"Do you have *any* idea what Hank was planning for tonight?"

"No. Bastard's slick." Rittmaster licked his lips. "Can I have some water?"

Brodsky poured water from the container at the

bedside into a cup and dribbled a bit into Rittmaster's mouth.

"Thanks. Now if you'll just light me a cigarette . . ."

"You're crazy." Burke smiled.

"One drag is all I want."

"The doc would bring us up on charges," Brodsky said.

"Goddamn head hurts. Wish I remembered more." His eyelids began fluttering again. "Sorry."

Burke put his hand on Rittmaster's shoulder. "Get some rest, Jack." But Rittmaster already had slipped back into unconsciousness.

On the way out, Burke asked the nurse to call him if there was any change in Rittmaster's condition.

"What I'd like to do," he told Brodsky, "is drag Hank into the stockade and let Amos Biggs work on him until he tells us what he's up to."

"You'd never get away with it. We've got nothing on Hank; Jack didn't even see the guy who decked him."

"I realize that. And Hank's too smart to lean on Jack himself. I'm sure he sent one of his buddies."

"So what do we do?" Brodsky wondered. "Rittmaster's out of action and Biggs hasn't come up with anything new on the Palermo girl. He checked in a couple of hours ago; her boyfriend in Cleveland had no idea Betsy was banking so much money, he says. On top of that, the CO has pulled you off the goddamn case."

"I can handle Sloane."

"How?"

Burke didn't want Brodsky to become enmeshed in his private war with the CO, so his answer was indirect: "I'm expecting a Federal Express envelope tomorrow. If I'm not in the office when it arrives, lock it in your desk. Don't let anyone else touch it. As soon as I've got that envelope in my hands we can stop worrying about Lieutenant Walter Sloane."

Brodsky didn't pursue the subject any further. From Burke's expression, he wasn't sure he wanted to know the contents of that envelope.

On the way back to the barracks Burke stopped at his car and took the new painting out of the trunk.

Crossing the quad, he met Jean Silk coming back from the post theater.

"What was the movie tonight?" he asked her.

"A thriller about two women who agree to murder each other's husbands. Sort of a *Strangers on a Train* rip-off."

"Any good?"

Jean shook her head no. "What's that, one of your paintings?" When he appeared reluctant to answer, she said, "I'm not asking to see it, if that's what you're worried about." She held her watch up to the pale stream of light from the nearest lamppost. "I didn't realize it was so late. Good night."

"Wait a minute." Burke cursed himself for always acting like a klutz in her presence. "I'd like you to take a look."

"Don't bother." She threw her hair around. "I mean, I won't exactly die if I don't see it." Her natural good humor got the best of her, producing a wry smile. "I'm curious as hell, of course."

"Then come on." He took her to the coffee shop, which stayed open until midnight, and commandeered a quiet corner table. "I'll get us some coffee. Wait until I get back before you take off the cover, okay?"

While she waited, Jean decided to give her honest opinion of his work, even if she didn't like it. Feeding mindless flattery to a man was a debasing way to win his approval.

Burke sat down across from her and shoved one of the coffee cups across the table. "The canvas isn't quite dry, you'd better let me uncover it." He had set the painting on one of the extra chairs. With a nervous smile, he carefully removed the cover and pushed the chair back into better light.

To cover his anxiety, he added too much sugar to his coffee. Jean made him nervous. She was studying his work with the kind of single-minded intensity that cats give to strange new objects. After a while her silence began to nettle him. "Well, what do you think?"

"I think that for a man who didn't even want to show me his work, you're very anxious for an opinion."

"For Christ's sake."

"I like it very much. The house is striking. The sky is absolutely breathtaking. And that face in the window gives me cold chills. You can be very proud of this one, Ansel. It's a whole dimension above the work I saw at Maggie's gallery. That face makes me want to weep."

"You don't think the face might detract from the rest of the work?"

"God no! It's the very soul of the picture." The question astounded her. "Did someone suggest that?"

"No," Burke said quickly. "I just wondered if I was hitting a discordant note."

"Of course not." Jean realized she was coming on pretty strong. "But I'm the wrong person to ask. I don't have any training in art."

"You're from New York, which means you've probably been to a lot of galleries."

"Well, I've made the museum rounds: the Metropolitan; the Guggenheim; the Museum of Modern Art; the Whitney. That doesn't make me an expert."

"I've never been to any of those places," Burke said, a little wistfully. "Sometimes I feel like a fraud. I can't talk about art the way Maggie and her friends do. They're all so certain, so knowledgeable about everything to do with art. I can't even remember the dates of Picasso's blue period."

"Would knowing the dates make you a better artist?"

"Sometimes I think it would." He sat back and tried to cover the fact that he was admiring her. Jean was dressed in denims, running shoes, and a yellow T-shirt with a picture of Beethoven on the chest. She looked fetching, if that was still a word. "I don't have any perspective about what I'm doing. I don't even know where I fit in. What 'school' I belong to. Anything like that."

"Maybe that's important; I don't really know. I do know you have a lot of talent and a wonderful insight into people." She moved her shoulders restlessly, aware that she'd revealed too much about her own feelings. "I'm sure Maggie's already told you all that." She glanced at her watch. "I really should get back to the BOQ. Lots of work to do in the morning."

Burke said, "Thanks for looking at the painting. Your comments mean a lot to me."

Jean was touched by this new vulnerable side of Ansel. "I meant all of it," she said simply.

A few minutes later they went separate ways to their barracks, each pleased with the way the day had ended.

Chapter 15

At the top of President Walter Bryant's list of things he disliked was television. The constant yammering of the commercial pitchmen and the pompous posturing of the anchormen were almost more than he could bear. The best thing ever to appear on television was the old "Honeymooners" show with Jackie Gleason and Art Carney. There was no entertainment to match it today. The few times in recent years that he flipped through the channels to see what was on, he found only car chases and insipid family comedies.

Worse yet, his position constantly forced him to look at the tube. Every evening at 7:00 and 11:00 P.M., the senior members of his staff came into the Oval Office to watch the network news shows and evaluate their treatment of the administration. The set in the Oval Office was specially built: it contained three screens, each tuned to a different network.

Bryant had dubbed it the Three-Headed Monster.

Tonight the President had been joined for the eleven o'clock news by Secretary of State Henry Flowers, CIA Director Luther Amstel and Jim Canon, the press secretary. Together they watched a parade of tragically scarred survivors of Egypt's nuclear attack on the Libyan army. On each network, President Bryant was called to task for the proliferation that had made it possible for a relatively small country like Egypt to acquire a nuclear weapon. Several newscasters repeated their challenge to President Bryant to prove that the weapon did not come from the U.S. arsenal.

"We are in deep trouble," Secretary of State Henry Flowers announced as soon as the national news ended.

Jim Canon said, "I think we should—"

"Just a minute," the President said. "I'd like to see the sports."

The others in the oval office shut their mouths, though they were clearly surprised that Bryant would take time to watch the sports news at this crucial juncture in the nation's affairs.

For the first time since the sun had come up that day, President Bryant began to smile. "How about that! The Cardinals and Royals are both leading their divisions. Maybe we'll have another all-Missouri World Series this year. Okay, you can turn it off now. I'm sorry, gentlemen, I just felt the need of some relief from the day's events."

"Perfectly understandable," murmured Luther Amstel, trying to hide impatience.

"Now let's have your reports. Henry, how did it go at the U.N.?"

Henry Flowers came to Oval Office meetings with a stack of three-by-five cards on which he had written notes in his precise hand. He referred to the cards only when a stray fact escaped his sharp mind. "I'm sorry to say it was the disaster we expected. My presentation to the special committee was interrupted a dozen times by hoots and catcalls. Chairman Tsing did not have the temerity to call the audience to order," he concluded dryly.

Flowers's face reddened at the memory. "The U.N. is, as always, totally opposed to whatever position the United States takes. And the eastern bloc has convinced everyone, even France and the U.K., that the nuke came from us."

"France is always ready to believe the worst of us," Jim Canon scoffed.

"But not England," the President said sadly. "When the U.K. goes against us, we really do stand alone."

"Under present conditions," Flowers continued, "I believe that even a retaliatory strike by us against

Egypt will be viewed as a part of a cover-up of our own complicity."

Luther Amstel was overjoyed to hear that, though he was careful to maintain a solemn visage.

"The answer," Jim Canon said in his aggressive newsman's way, "is to find out where the fucking thing came from!"

The President knew that Canon's outspokenness was galling to many in his administration, but Bryant didn't care. He valued his press secretary's honesty. "Jim is right. How about it, Luther? Any more information?"

Amstel had been waiting for that question. "My people are coming to the reluctant conclusion that Egypt may have built the device itself from radioactive material salvaged from its nuclear power plant. However, we may not be able to prove that. Incidentally, just before leaving my office I received some photos from Cairo by telecopier." He opened his briefcase and handed them around. "One of our agents managed to reach the scene of the explosion and take these pictures."

"Jesus Christ," Canon muttered, staring at the charred remains of a Libyan soldier.

Bryant's stomach heaved, but he maintained his presidential demeanor. "How soon will photos like this make the newspapers?"

"Three or four days," Amstel estimated. "The Egyptians are trying to keep the Qattara clear of journalists, but sooner or later they'll get through."

"Who took these?" Flowers asked.

"The CIA station in Cairo sent in a contract agent, an Australian photographer."

"The Cairo embassy also sent a man into the Qattara," Flowers said. "Nothing has been heard from him."

Amstel used the melancholy pause that followed as an opportunity to put forth his case. "I continue to believe that we should allow the Soviet Union to think we provided Egypt with the weapon. I have hard evidence—you've seen it, Mr. President—that the Russians are ready to back down on their aggressive strategy in the face of what they perceive to be our tough stance."

"I disagree," Flowers said promptly. "If the rest of the world believes we set up Egypt to nuke the Libyans, that can only help Moscow achieve its aims."

President Bryant gave all opinions serious consideration. He had heard them before, but changing events often dictated new strategies. For the next half hour he allowed Amstel and Flowers to expand on their arguments and encouraged Jim Canon to take potshots at both of them. He wanted every idea, opinion, and scrap of information he could get hold of.

Finally, when both sides were argued out, he stepped in.

"Gentlemen, the fact is that we *still* don't have enough information to determine our course of action. We need to know where Egypt got that weapon." He looked deeply tired. "If in the next few days we cannot categorically prove that the weapon came from outside the U.S., then everyone will continue to believe we were working in collusion with Egypt. In which case we may have to follow Luther's advice and allow the Russians to think we're taking a hard new tack."

Henry Flowers's face went ashen and Jim Canon shook his head in abject disappointment.

"Perception is reality," Bryant said, feeling the need to defend himself.

Amstel remained diplomatically silent. But his heart was singing his favorite song: "I've won, I've won."

FRIDAY, JUNE 13

Chapter 16

The Federal Express envelope from Fort Sill arrived early in the morning while most of the troopers were still at chow. Brodsky handed it to Burke when he came in from the mess hall. Burke locked it in his desk without comment and picked up the phone. Something Sheriff Perkins had said while they were looking at Betsy Palermo's body had been nagging at him.

"Len Perkins here."

"Good morning, Len. This is Ansel Burke."

"Oh. What do you want?"

"Something you said when we were looking at Betsy Palermo has been bothering me."

"Look, the Palermo case isn't mine. I don't want anything to do with it. And you don't have jurisdiction, either. That smooth article from the FBI office in Albuquerque, Agent Devereaux, called specifically to tell me not to share any information about that case with you." Perkins sounded pleased. "Interservice rivalry, isn't that what you guys call it?"

"You should know. Devereaux wouldn't share a typhoid germ with a county sheriff. When we were out at the crime scene, you said something about having a big work load, finding a lot of corpses out in the desert. Could there be a connection between some of those deaths and the Palermo killing?"

"No way. Those were accidents, not murders."

"How many have there been?"

"How many what?"

"Accidents."

"Ten or more since the first of the year—a dirt biker who broke his neck, a kid bit by a rattler, a couple rock climbers who took a fall. That kinda thing."

"The couple who fell from the cliffs," Burke prompted. "What were their names?"

"The Hallidays. Honeymooners, for Christ's sake. I don't remember their first names."

"I recall the story now. The Puma *Union* said they were spelunkers, not rock climbers."

"So what?"

"Spelunkers don't climb mountains, they explore caves. Are you sure what happened to the Hallidays was an accident?"

"Of course I am."

"I'd like to send a man to your office to collect the records on all the accidents you've had out in the desert this year."

"What the hell for?"

"Morbid curiosity."

Perkins argued that it was a waste of time. His man had better things to do. Civilian accidents were out of Burke's jurisdiction anyway. And who'd reimburse the county for the expense of copying all those records?

But in the end it was easier to give in than to face Burke's persistent demands.

"I'll send a man over this morning. Make sure he gets what he needs."

"You're a pushy bastard, Ansel. And you've been riding high for a long time. But I got a hunch somebody's about to pull the plug on you. When you start to go down the drain, don't call on me for help."

"Just don't take me off your Christmas card list, Len. I don't think I could stand a shock like that."

They hung up simultaneously.

When Burke looked up, he found Amos Biggs standing over him.

"I just came from the hospital. The doc says Jack's gonna make it, but he may never soldier again." Biggs's hands were balled into fists. "Did Hank have Jack worked over?"

"I think so. But there's no proof." Although it was

only eight hundred hours, Burke smelled wintergreen on Biggs's breath. He wondered if the wintergreen was covering up something else. Like the smell of beer. It was awfully early for a beer, even for Biggs. He decided to ignore it. "I was just talking to Sheriff Perkins. There've been a number of stiffs found out in the desert lately. Accident, the sheriff says. Most of them are, I'm sure. But I've got a hunch Hank and his pals have been using the desert as their private cemetery. Go down to the sheriff's office and make copies of every file pertaining to a desert accident this year. Perkins is expecting you."

"I got a better idea," Biggs said. "Why don't we just grab Hank, take him somewhere quiet, and beat the shit out of him until he tells us what the fuck's going on around here."

"Wouldn't work." Burke didn't like the ugly expression on Biggs's face. "Hank's not the kind to spill his guts because of some pain. So don't try anything like that on your own." He added, "That's an order."

Biggs unballed his fists and slowly dropped his eyes. "Whatever you say, Top."

"I'm going out to the Restricted Materiel Center and talk to that officer who stonewalled you—Captain Miller."

"Good luck. Miller wouldn't tell me a damned thing."

"Get over to the sheriff's office fast, before Perkins decides he doesn't have to cooperate after all."

"I'll get right on it," Biggs said, patting his belly.

When he did that, Burke knew he was planning to take a beer break first.

A few minutes later Burke sneaked a look inside the package that had arrived from Fort Sill. There were a dozen eight-by-ten black-and-white photos, all grainy and of poor quality because they were shot just after dawn in poor light. Even so, they told a sickening story. Master Sergeant Sam Reedy had gotten just close enough with his telephoto lens to destroy First Lieutenant Walter Sloane.

In the medium shots Sloane was shown in an empty field with woods in the background. His pants were down around his ankles as he squatted over a small

dog that he was holding to the ground. The tighter
shots revealed him forcing himself into the bitch, his
expression full of sick ecstasy.

"Shit-oh-dear," Burke muttered. "You could go to
Leavenworth for that, Lieutenant."

He returned the photos to the envelope and resealed
it with Scotch tape. Keeping it in his desk would be
stupid. Sloane was the kind of officer who liked to
search through his men's belongings. "A snap inspection," Sloane would call it.

Burke went to the armory. The .45 caliber ammunition for side arms was kept in a steel locker at the
back of the armory. The locker weighed hundreds of
pounds and probably had not been moved in twenty
years. He slipped the envelope into the space between
the locker and the wall and let it fall to the floor. If he
ever needed the envelope, he could fish it out with a
yardstick.

With a little luck it would stay there for the next
twenty years.

The Restricted Materiel Center occupied forty acres
of desert land off a side road between Custer Hill and
Camp Funston. The entire forty acres was enclosed by
a twelve-foot barbed-wire fence monitored by closed
circuit TV. Inside the compound a dozen huge buff-
colored warehouse buildings stood side by side, half a
million square feet of climate-controlled storage space.
The air-conditioning units on the roofs were so powerful they could be heard from half a mile away.

The sentry on duty at the guard post was one of
Burke's own MPs, a Pfc. Wiley. When Wiley saw who
was behind the wheel of the approaching jeep, he
quickly disposed of a cigarette and came out of his
gatehouse.

"Mornin', Sarge."

"Hello, Wiley. Is Captain Miller in?"

"Yeah, he's here. I can let you through this check-
point, but they got their own security inside. They
screen everybody and they don't let many people past
the admin center."

"So I've heard." Burke put the jeep in gear without

letting out the clutch."You know my rule about smoking on guard duty. It's *verboten*. When you go off duty here report to Sergeant Brodsky. He's got some urinals that need cleaning."

Pfc. Wiley's shoulders sagged.

Burke drove up to the admin center, which provided the only pedestrian access to the warehouses. A separate drive led to the loading docks. He had to halt the jeep while a dust-covered eighteen-wheel semi with Texas license plates negotiated the turn. A sticker on the semi's rear bumper bore the title of a popular country and western tune: "Amarillo by Morning."

He left the jeep in a visitor's lot consisting of only two spaces—the army's subtle way of discouraging visitors—and went into the admin center. From behind a GI-issue metal desk, Staff Sergeant Harry Williamson looked up with his customary scowl.

"Hello, Harry. I heard you were up and hobbling around."

"What the hell do you want out here?"

"Somebody told me you were playing basketball with your testicles. I thought I'd come by and watch."

Williamson planted his hands on his desk as if to launch himself at Burke, then settled back in his chair. "Yeah, my balls were pretty swollen for a day or so. A lot of people got a big laugh out of that. Someday you're gonna pay for those laughs, Ansel."

"While I'm waiting for you to get real tough, I'd like to see Captain Miller."

"He ain't in."

"Come on. Wiley told me he's here."

"Why do you want to see Captain Miller?"

"That's none of your business."

Williamson stroked his block jaw and picked up the phone. "Captain, I know you said not to bother you. But you've got a visitor—Sergeant Major Burke from the Military Police. No, sir, he doesn't have an appointment. Yes, sir, I'll ask him to do that." He put down the phone. "The captain says he's very busy but he can spare a few minutes to talk to you."

Burke went through the door behind Williamson's desk and into a spacious office furnished very differently from the spartan atmosphere of the R.M.C. There were paintings on the walls, carpeting on the floor, and the desk was teak.

"Sergeant, could you move a little to the left?"

He stepped aside to allow Captain Miller an unimpeded view of a miniature putting green set up at the opposite end of the office.

The officer stood hunched over a putter, deep in concentration. "I'm about to sink my tenth straight putt, a new office record." He stroked the golf ball smoothly and watched it roll across the carpet. The ball went straight to the mechanical cup, teetered on the edge, then rolled past. "Shit!"

"Sorry, sir. I probably ruined your concentration."

"Don't worry about it." Miller laid the putter across his desk. "Silly game, but it's the only fun I can find in this boring place." He extended a hand and smiled. "Captain Dan Miller."

"Sergeant Major Ansel Burke."

"Burke? Are you the man who put my clerk out of action for the last two days?"

"I did have a little disagreement with Sergeant Williamson."

"Disagreement! From what I heard, you just about put Harry Williamson in the hospital. He wants to prefer charges against you."

Well, this was a mistake, Burke thought. I'll be lucky to get out of here with my stripes. "He asked for everything he got, sir."

"Of course he did. Williamson is a pig. I finally got him to admit that you jumped him because he was reading a love letter from Corporal Palermo's boyfriend out loud for the amusement of one of his buddies. Disgusting. You did the right thing, Sergeant. Relax, you aren't going up on charges. I'll see to that." He waved Burke into a chair and sat down himself. "What can I do for you?"

The response so surprised Burke that for a moment he couldn't speak. Miller wore a combat infantryman's badge, a bronze star for valor, a purple heart with cluster, and a Vietnam service ribbon. On his right shoulder was a First Infantry Division insignia, indicating he had served in combat with that unit. The First Division was famous for hard discipline. Burke had expected an officer trained in the First Division to at least chew out a sergeant major who had brawled with a lower-ranking noncom. "I wanted to ask a few questions about Corporal Palermo's work here at the R.M.C."

"What happened to Betsy was a terrible tragedy. Have you found the killer?"

"Not yet, sir. That's why I wanted to talk to you."

"Of course. What do you want to know?"

Burke began with routine questions. What was Corporal Palermo's assignment? Was she a good worker? Did she have any close friends on the R.M.C. staff? Had her co-workers noticed anything unusual in her attitude during the past month? Miller responded to each question with a quick, precise answer.

Captain Dan Miller was a breed of officer unfamiliar to Burke. Despite the ribbons, he couldn't imagine Miller commanding a combat infantry unit. He was a man of Burke's own age, late thirties, who looked as if he'd never seen a tough day. The word *sleek* came to mind. Miller's uniform was tailored, his nails manicured, his light brown hair razor cut and blown dry. The round face and guileless eyes were a touch too sincere. He had a little potbelly that perfectly fitted his golf-and-cocktails personality, but which would have gotten him instantly booted out of the First Infantry Division.

"Exactly what kind of work did Betsy Palermo do?"

"She was an 8100 operator." Miller reacted to the question in Burke's eyes. "The 8100 is the computer system we use to keep inventory on the materiel stored in the center."

"Why did she have a Top Secret clearance?"

"Most of the equipment stored here is classified. Only those with Top Secret clearances are allowed to access the system."

"What kind of equipment do you handle?"

"Sorry," Miller said with a little smile. "I'm not allowed to discuss that."

Burke had expected that answer. "Can I at least take a look at Corporal Palermo's workstation?"

Miller fiddled with the putter that lay across his desk while he considered the request. "I guess I can allow that, since you're the top cop around here." He stood up briskly. "Come on."

Burke followed him into the anteroom, where Harry Williamson was entering data into a computer with a slow two-fingered hunt-and-peck motion, like a gorilla playing with a toy.

"Sergeant Williamson, give Sergeant Burke a visitor's badge."

Williamson unlocked a desk drawer and selected one badge from a neat row of them. Each badge bore the word VISITOR in block letters and a three-digit number. A strip of magnetic tape ran diagonally across the badge.

"I'll take him through," Captain Miller said.

"Yes, sir." Williamson turned back to the computer terminal. "Just let me record his visit in the system first." When he had done his bureaucratic duty, he smiled sardonically at Burke. "You're all set, Sergeant Major."

"Thanks, Harry."

The first door they came to was steel set into a steel frame. Miller put his own badge into a slot next to the door. A magnetic reader scanned the badge's code and unlocked the door with a buzzing signal. They went through into a warehouse building five hundred feet long and thirty yards wide.

"Everything in here is automated." Miller pointed out the computer-controlled picking machine that moved noiselessly up and down the warehouse aisles plucking material from some bins and putting it into others. All sizes of boxes and metal containers, each stamped with a number and U.S. Defense Department identification, were stored in the bins.

"Sir, is everything stored here classified as Top Secret?"

Miller laughed. "You know the army—a lot of things are classified Secret or Top Secret for no really good reason. Let's say some of those crates hold spare parts for experimental weapons that are never going to be mass produced. Or manuals for computer systems used in Combat Information Centers. That sort of thing. I really can't be more specific. All I can say is that the U.S. Army spends a hell of a lot of money controlling some very ordinary stuff." He stopped at a desk. "This was Corporal Palermo's workstation."

The desk was one of seven positioned along one wall of the warehouse. Each desk had a computer workstation identical to the terminal Harry Williamson used. Betsy Palermo's desk was the only one vacant. Clerks, most of them female personnel like Betsy Palermo, were working at the other terminals.

"Corporal Palermo was responsible for the inventory control of about fourteen hundred different items. All the clerks use the 8100. Betsy was especially good on the terminal. She could even fix the printer when it jammed. It's going to be tough finding a comparable replacement." Miller blinked a few times. "I'm sorry, I guess that sounded callous."

"Not especially. Do you mind if I look through her desk?"

"Help yourself." Miller even opened the top drawer for Burke. "Her personal belongings are still in here, but Sergeant Williamson has already removed any classified documents and other work-related papers."

I'll bet he has, Burke thought.

He went through the desk and, as expected, found nothing of interest. No letters from home. No bankbooks. No snapshots. No notes. Nothing of a personal nature except for some cosmetics and a box of Tampax.

"Take anything that can help you."

Burke thought he detected a condescending note in Miller's otherwise helpful attitude. "Nothing much here. Did the FBI go through her desk, too?"

"Yes, they were here yesterday on another matter and asked me to brief them on Corporal Palermo. Then they looked through her desk, too. The agent in charge was a big fellow name of Devereaux. Didn't he play football for one of the major schools? I thought I recognized the name."

"Yes, sir. He was a star at Alabama. Now he's a star

at the FBI." Burke closed up the desk. "I guess there's nothing here that can help me."

"I'm sorry. Can I buy you a cup of coffee? You ought to get some kind of payback for coming all the way out here."

"Thank you, sir, but I have to get back to my HQ."

"Suit yourself."

As they walked behind the row of desks at which the clerks were working at their terminals, one of the screens caught Burke's eye. The letters F.D.N.W. appeared in green letters, followed by a group of numbers. Serial numbers, he guessed. The army stamped a serial number on everything it owned, including its troops. Burke didn't break stride. Out of the corner of his eye he checked to see whether Captain Miller had noticed or reacted to the abbreviation. Apparently not. His expression remained vacuously pleasant.

Miller personally escorted Burke to the parking lot. Outside, he contemplated the grim row of warehouse buildings with disgust. "This is the dullest duty I've had in ten years. Hope they find me a better billet one of these days, and the sooner the better."

"Would you take the Big Red One again?"

"The what?"

"The First Division."

The smooth smile asserted itself. "Yes, that was good duty. Look, I'm sorry I couldn't be of more help. Betsy was a nice girl. I want to see her killer thrown in Leavenworth for life. You'll keep me informed of your progress on that, won't you?"

"Yes, sir, you'll be the first to know."

As he drove out of the R.M.C., Burke wondered how Miller could have served in the First Infantry Division without learning that the division's nickname was the Big Red One.

When Captain Miller returned, Harry Williamson looked up from his terminal with more than his usual truculence. "That was a mistake," he growled, not bothering to add the required *sir*.

"Nobody asked your opinion." Miller went into his office and closed the door behind him. He picked up his golf club and tried another putt. This time the ball missed the mechanical hole by six inches. Miller tossed the putter in a corner, sat down behind his desk, and picked up the phone.

No one answered the first number he called. He dialed a second number and this time reached his party. "This is Control. Ansel Burke was just here. I thought you were going to get him off our backs." Miller listened. "Really? Well, it's not working. Is it so hard to put the screws to a *sergeant?* What do I have to do, call in a team from Langley?" He listened again, this time with a scowl. "I'm sorry, but I don't trust your people to handle this type of problem. They're fine for black work, but this is a Class Seven operation. And that's my field." He smiled without warmth. "We don't want to blow it now. Not when we're almost home."

Chapter 17

"Thank Christ you're back." Brodsky flourished a DOD 710 in Burke's face. "The CO's got me making out *court-martial* papers on you."

"What kind of charge did he dream up?"

"Refusing a direct order." Brodsky was so rattled he couldn't stop brandishing the paperwork. "Ansel, that means a general court. He wants to send you to Leavenworth!"

Burke gently removed the form from Brodsky's hand and walked the old trooper back to his desk. "Sit down and relax. If anyone goes to Leavenworth from this company, it won't be me."

"What do you mean?"

"I mean that Sloane isn't going to court-martial me or anyone else." He tore the DOD 710 into small pieces and consigned them to the nearest wastebasket. "Lou, how tight are you with the personnel office?"

"I've got friends there."

"Could you put your hands on a personnel package without going through channels?"

"Whose package do you want?"

"Captain Daniel Miller, adjutant of the R.M.C."

Brodsky wrote down the name. "So you got in to see him. Did he give you anything new on the Palermo girl?"

"No, but he gave me something else to think about."

"Like what?"

"When I went into his office, he shook my hand

instead of waiting to take my salute. On top of that, his office is decorated like a spread from *Architectural Digest* and he seems to spend most of his time putting golf balls across the carpet. And here's the really screwy part. Captain Dan Miller wears a Combat Infantryman's Badge and a First Infantry Division shoulder patch. But when I mentioned the Big Red One, he didn't know what I was talking about."

"Uh-oh." Brodsky drew a circle around Miller's name. "This guy sounds like a ringer."

"He sure as hell didn't serve with the First Division. I want to know where he really comes from. There's something weird going on out there. The adjutant isn't what he says he is, and the company clerk is Staff Sergeant Harry Williamson, who's never done a lick of paperwork in his life."

Brodsky picked up his hat. "I'm on my way to the personnel office." His worried old eyes shifted to the closed door across the hall. "Are you sure you can handle the CO?"

Burke thought about the stack of photos hidden in the armory. "Lieutenant Sloane is about to become my most vocal admirer."

He brought in Corporal Fellows to watch the phones and went to the armory, where he retrieved the envelope of photographs from behind the side-arm safe. He removed one of the photos, neither the best nor the worst, and returned the others to their hiding place. Then he knocked on Captain Sloane's door.

"Come in!"

He entered, marched up to the CO's desk, and saluted smartly.

"Well, finally . . ." Sloane leaned back in his chair, his electric eyes aglow with malice. "It's about goddamn time you reported in. Just who the hell do you think you are, making your own hours and your own rules? You're just a sergeant major, not the chief of staff!"

"I've been out of my office on business, sir."

"Yes, and I know what kind of business. You've been investigating the death of that girl even though I gave you a *direct order* to leave her case to the FBI."

"Yes, sir. That's true."

Sloane stared at him in wonder. "You brazen bastard. You've just convicted yourself out of your own mouth. Disobeying a direct order will get you about three years in a federal prison."

"No, sir, I don't think so." Burke had been holding back the photograph. Now he stepped forward and dropped it on Sloane's desk.

Sloane snatched it up irritably. He took a quick glance; then a longer look. His boyish face, so heavy with displeasure, went pale. He gulped and licked his lips. In a frenzy of energy, he leaped to his feet and tore the photo into a hundred pieces. That defiant act seemed to take everything out of him. He slumped into his chair, his arms falling loosely at his sides.

The litter of picture fragments on Sloane's desk top reminded Burke of parade confetti. "I have more photos."

"I'm sure you do," Sloane said bitterly. "I can only suppose that Sergeant Reedy at Fort Sill is one of your many 'buddies.' "

"Sam and I have done a lot of soldiering together."

"He promised me that he'd destroy those photos," Sloane whined.

"Sam doesn't trust you. He thinks you'd go after him if he gave up the negatives. For what it's worth, he didn't want to make any prints for me. I had to twist his arm."

"Don't give me that. You sergeants always stick together. My father warned me that all noncoms are scum.

That was just the kind of shit Burke no longer intended to take. "He would have done better to tell you not to go around fucking dogs."

Sloane winced. "I didn't— I never hurt them. It's not in me to hurt an animal. I just did . . . what I did, and then let them go." His chin trembled. "Never the same dog more than once. That's the truth."

"I don't want to hear it."

"It started when I was just a kid. My father never let me—"

"Shut up! That's something to tell a shrink. Not your sergeant major."

"A psychiatrist?" Sloane withdrew so deeply into his chair that he threatened to disappear. "I couldn't go to a psychiatrist. Word would get out. You know the army. My career would be threatened."

Burke's determination to destroy Sloane and get on with his own business wavered. "Lieutenant, forget about your career. You're sick. Get professional help."

"I can't do that." Sloane set his jaw stubbornly. "I *won't* do that."

"Suit yourself." Burke's sympathy for Sloane dissipated. "Meanwhile, you're going to do what I tell you about everything else. First, get rid of your dogs. You're not fucking any more of our canine friends at Fort Powell. If I hear that you've so much as scratched a dog behind the ears, I'll send the other pictures I have to the I.G. You know what that would mean—Leavenworth."

"You bastard," Sloane said hoarsely.

"Next I want you to give Jake Winkler's stripes back to him. He's the best mess sergeant on post. You only busted him to show the company what a tough CO you were going to be."

"His kitchen—"

"Is clean. Jake gets his stripes back. Subject closed." Sloane mumbled his reluctant agreement.

"My big problem is this case I'm investigating. It's connected with some very interesting people here at Fort Powell. That's why the FBI told you to yank my chain. I want to know who else has been complaining about me."

"General Leland." Sloane twitched like a steer touched by a cattle prod. "The general said my efficiency report depends on keeping you on your own reservation. He says you've been getting too big for your stripes and he'll support whatever disciplinary action I might decide to take against you."

Leland? Burke couldn't imagine the general having anything to do with the killings. It was more likely that Leland was still pissed about his testimony at Sean Feeney's court-martial. Either way, Burke didn't relish having a brigadier general's enmity. "No wonder you've been on my back."

"General Leland knows my family." Sloane was still using the whining voice he'd fallen into after seeing the photo. "He threatened to tell my father I'm not cutting it as an officer. I couldn't let that happen."

Burke was tired of hearing about Sloane's father. "There's only one other thing I want from you, Lieutenant. Leave me alone to do my job."

"General Leland—"

"Tell him you chewed me out until I shit in my pants. Tell him I'm in my barracks hiding under my bunk. All I need is a little breathing room. I don't care what you tell Leland or the FBI. Just buy me some time."

"I can't!"

Burke poked an index finger into the shreds of the photograph and stirred them around to expose some of the gamier sections. "You've got no choice."

He left Sloane behind a closed door, nursing his fears. Burke alternately despised and pitied the young officer. There was no way out for Sloane. If he stayed in, the army would crush him. If he left the service, his father would disown him.

Brodsky had returned from post headquarters with Captain Dan Miller's personnel package, but for the moment he was more concerned about Sloane. "What's the story? Did Sloane threaten you with a court-martial? What *happened?*"

"The CO and I are engaged. It'll be a June wedding. I even talked Sloane into giving Jake back his stripes."

"You're a goddamn magician. What the hell do you have on the bastard?"

"That's my business. Let me see Miller's jacket."

There was only a single sheet of paper in Miller's file, a DOD requisition form which read "For information on this personnel file contact the National Security Agency personnel office, Bethesda, Maryland."

"This guy doesn't even exist," Brodsky declared.

"He exists." Burke closed and resealed the package. "But he's not army. And Miller probably isn't his real name. He's a spook."

"What kinda spook? NSA? CIA? Army Intelligence? Shit, there's more kinds of spooks out there than I care to think about."

"I'm not sure." Burke doubted that Miller was NSA, even though the National Security Agency was holding his pay jacket. That would be too straightforward for the spook community. And Miller wasn't army intelligence because he just wasn't an army man. That left the CIA.

He returned the file to Brodsky. "Get this back to the personnel office. And make sure nobody knows we took a look at it."

"Right away, Sergeant Major." Brodsky stopped at the doorway, the file tucked tightly under his arm. "I almost forgot. Captain Silk called. Wants to know if you could come by her office. Says she's got some new information for you about the F.D.N.W. What's that mean, anyway?"

"I don't know. But don't mention that particular abbreviation to anyone. Betsy Palermo was scribbling it on a napkin when she talked to Jean."

"Jean?" Brodsky winked broadly. "Lately you've got more women than a sultan." He noted Burke's displeasure. "Okay! I'm going, I'm going! On my way back I'll stop at the hospital and see how Rittmaster's doing."

"Tell him we're closing the noose on Roper."

"Are we?"

Burke wasn't sure whether the noose was closing around Roper's throat or his own, but he wanted to cheer up Rittmaster and reassure Brodsky. "Hell, yes. We've got Hank on the run. He just doesn't realize it yet."

On the way to the admin building he went over every fact in the case and found himself running into one brick wall after another. Telling Brodsky that they had Hank Roper on the run was a flat-out lie. There wasn't one damned thing to connect Hank with the death of the Palermo girl. What made his skin crawl was the growing evidence that he was into something way over his head. Hank plus the FBI plus the CIA added up to some kind of high-level cover-up.

Although he still doubted that Leland was involved, it wouldn't hurt to check out any connections between Roper and the general.

All the clerks and officers in the admin building were away from their desks, gathered in various offices where TV sets were tuned in to a presidential news conference. Burke found Jean in the magistrate's office along with some of the other lawyers on the staff. She pulled him into the room. "Ansel, listen to this. The President is being incredibly evasive."

Major Porter, the magistrate, frowned over the comment, or perhaps at the familiarity Jean was showing to a mere sergeant.

President Walter Bryant was standing behind a White House lectern as if it were a barricade. ". . . can only repeat that no evidence exists to show that the nuclear warhead used by the Egyptians came from the U.S. stockpile. And, as you all know, President Zamal of Egypt has refused to say where his country acquired the weapon."

Many hands went up and President Bryant nodded in the direction of one of them. A woman in a yellow dress leaped to her feet. "Sir, have you spoken directly to President Zamal?"

"No, I haven't. He has refused to speak directly to me or my representatives. All we have to go on is his official statement that use of the weapon was justified by Libya's invasion of his country."

"Sir," the woman put in quickly, "a follow-up question. Do you agree with that statement by President Zamal?"

President Bryant answered aggressively: "I can neither agree nor disagree until all the facts about this tragic event are brought to light."

Every reporter in the room waved wildly. Bryant selected one of Washington's oldest and most prestigious correspondents, who rose with ponderous self-importance. "Mr. President, are you implying there are circumstances under which you would approve of Egypt's use of that nuclear weapon?"

"Tommy, that's not what I said. I'm only stating the

obvious fact that we need to know everything about this incident before we come to any final conclusions."

"Does that mean you do not intend to impose any sanctions or take any retaliatory measures against Egypt?"

"Not at this time."

"What about—"

"Only one follow-up question, Tommy. You know the ground rules. Next?"

A *Washington Post* columnist was awarded the next question. "Mr. President, are there any circumstances under which you *would* sanction Egypt's use of a nuclear weapon?"

"I can't conceive of any such circumstance at this time."

"Does that mean you aren't ruling out your approval at some future time?"

"I'll stand by what I've just said. Next?"

The press conference continued for another ten minutes. During that time the reporters tried to draw out Bryant on the reasons behind his refusal to issue an outright condemnation of Egypt, but the President continued to sidestep the issue. He concluded by repeating that absolutely no evidence existed that Egypt had access to a U.S. warhead. Then he concluded the press conference: "I think that's enough for now. Thank you for coming, ladies and gentlemen. You'll be kept informed of any new developments."

President Bryant stepped down from behind the lectern and walked briskly to the exit. Before going through the door, he turned to smile and wave.

Major Porter turned off the television. "Looks like we won't be sending troops to Egypt after all, so we'd all best get back to work now." Major Porter looked pointedly at his watch. "Plenty of cases on the books."

Burke followed Jean to her office, which bore little resemblance to the carefully ordered cubicles of the other lawyers on the J.A.G. staff. Books were stacked helter-skelter and piles of briefs threatened to topple from the credenza. A can of Yoo Hoo and a package of Malomar cookies stood open on the desk. The office looked as if she'd occupied it for years instead of days.

She swept a stack of newspapers from the chair opposite her desk and Burke sat down. He was concerned about Jean, who looked pale and anxious. "What's wrong?"

"I'm a little shaky today, that's all."

"Sure you are. Nobody can eat and drink the stuff you do and stay healthy. Yoo Hoo and Malomars? Was that your breakfast? Why don't you just shoot sugar into your veins?"

"Malomars are better for you than that stuff they call health food." A smile pulled at the corners of her mouth. "Have you ever been in a health-food store? The clerk is usually an asthmatic with gray skin and a nervous tic."

Burke laughed. She was right about that. "Okay, give me a Malomar." He put his feet up on the desk. "Now tell me what's bothering you."

Jean pushed the package of cookies over to him. "Yesterday I called a friend at the Pentagon and asked him to find out what F.D.N.W. stands for. He called back this morning. He found out what it means, but didn't want to tell me. It's the designation for a Top Secret weapons program." She expelled a moody sigh. "It took all my feminine wiles to coax the information out of him."

When she paused for a long stretch to make marks on the desk blotter with her thumbnail, Burke said, "So what does it mean?"

Jean answered slowly, enunciating each word. "Field Deployable Nuclear Warhead."

The first thing that came into Burke's mind was the truck he had seen at the R.M.C. with the Texas plates and an "Amarillo by Morning" bumper sticker. It was common knowledge that the Department of Defense assembled its nuclear weapons at a manufacturing center in Amarillo. And that truck had been making a delivery to the R.M.C. "I was out at the Restricted Materiel Center this morning. The adjutant showed me the desk where Betsy Palermo worked a computer screen as an inventory clerk. On one of the screens I caught a glimpse of the initials F.D.N.W."

"So nuclear warheads are stored here at Fort Powell." Jean shivered. "I feel like running for the hills."

"And part of Betsy Palermo's job was to keep the inventory for those warheads." Burke thought about all the implications to that fact. "Did your friend at the Pentagon tell you any more about the weapon?"

"Apparently it's a very small, specialized warhead. He said it may be the smallest tactical nuclear weapon ever made."

"Did he say anything about the delivery system?"

"What's a delivery system?"

"Is it carried by a rocket? Dropped from a plane as a bomb? How is an F.D.N.W. delivered to a target?"

"I didn't even ask."

A scenario had been forming in Burke's mind. Haltingly at first, and then with greater confidence, he began putting the pieces together for Jean: Betsy Palermo was involved in something illegal that netted hundreds of thousands of dollars. She got cold feet and was murdered. The FBI moved in to quash the investigation. Betsy was also tied to Hank Roper, whose affinity for easy money was well known. And a number of other troopers were involved with Hank, among them Harry Williamson, who worked with Betsy at the R.M.C. Burke also told Jean about Captain Dan Miller and his belief that Miller was a CIA spook.

He summed up his suspicions tersely: "I think Hank Roper and his friends may be selling warheads to foreign governments with backing from people high up in the government."

"I can't believe that." Jean shook her head emphatically. "President Bryant is a decent man. He'd never go along with such a thing."

"Maybe he doesn't know. A president has a lot of people around him. They go off on their own too often. Maybe," Burke suggested, "the people behind this wanted to help Egypt wipe out that Libyan force."

The possibility of the nuclear weapon used by Egypt originating at Fort Powell had already occurred to Jean. She couldn't deal with it. The idea was too fantastic—except for the fact that Betsy Palermo had been in a perfect position to conceal the theft of any missing warheads. "Ansel, what should we do?"

"First we have to find out whether we're on the right track. There could be a different explanation for every one of our suspicions." Burke realized he hadn't touched his Malomar. He bit into it and was surprised at how delicious it tasted. This was the first Malomar he'd eaten in years. It made him feel like a kid again. "Hank and his buddies are spending a lot of time at a gas station he bought way out in the desert. The station's a money-loser, which makes it a strange investment for Hank. I've got a hunch that station may be the key to this whole deal. I'm going out there tonight and look around."

"I'll go with you."

"No you won't."

"I'm going," she insisted. "This isn't just your case anymore, Ansel. I'm involved." She grinned spontaneously. "I'll be your decoy."

"I don't need a decoy."

"I'm going with you," she repeated stubbornly.

The phone on Jean's desk rang, interrupting their test of wills.

"Captain Silk here. Yes, I'll take the call." She put her hand over the mouthpiece. "It's Major Ben Harrison, my friend at the Pentagon." She removed her hand. "Ben? Hi. What's up?" Jean's expression became grim. "That's terrible! Can't you do anything? Go higher up the chain of command?" She looked contrite. "I'm so sorry. I had no idea anything like that would happen. Are you sure there's a connection? Yes, I wouldn't be surprised. Ben, please don't—" Jean looked at the phone in her hand, then slowly put it down.

"What's wrong?"

"Ben hung up on me."

"Why?"

"A few minutes ago he was told to pack his bags and take the first available air transportation to Fort Richardson, Alaska, where he's been put in command of the motor pool. *The motor pool.* Ansel, that doesn't make sense. Ben Harrison is an intelligence officer, and a good one."

"Don't expect the army to make sense. Does Harrison see a connection between his transfer and the questions he was asking about the F.D.N.W.?"

"Yes, he's sure the transfer is punishment for going out of channels for information about a Top Secret project. He's furious with me. This could be very damaging to Ben's army career, and his career means everything to him."

The idea of a high-level conspiracy was becoming more credible to Burke every minute. It was too bad about Harrison, but Burke had a policy of not worrying about the career problems of field-grade officers.

"Now you've *got* to take me with you tonight," Jean said. "You owe it to me—and to Ben Harrison."

They took up the argument where they'd left off and Burke soon realized that arguing with a trial lawyer could be a frustrating experience. Jean had a talent for twisting his words around and using them against him. First she finessed him into acknowledging that he did owe her a debt. Then he found himself admitting that it would be helpful if she distracted whoever might be on duty tonight at the gas station while he reconned the place. Finally he threw up his hands in exasperation and agreed to let her come along. "But you'll do exactly what I say," he warned. "And not one thing more."

"That's a deal. Come on, I'll walk out with you. I'm going over to the BOQ for lunch."

"Don't tell me what you're having for lunch. It would just depress me."

Maggie had crated each of Ansel's paintings separately and arranged for a Federal Express pickup at 10:00 A.M. When the paintings were on their way, she phoned Donald Hillary in New York to give him the shipping numbers.

"I'm looking forward to seeing them," Hillary said. "I expect to be sent into a *rapture*."

"Donald, I won't let you hold Ansel Burke responsible for your raptures. Have you had any more interest from major buyers?"

"No, and that's beginning to worry me. The word of

mouth is excellent and I'm arranging for publicity in the *Times,* but we need something more. We need to make this an event. A *cause célèbre.* Any ideas?"

"Not offhand. I sent along some photos and a bio of Ansel. The fact that he's a soldier with oodles of combat medals and citations should be good for some newspaper space."

"Yes, but that's not enough. These days every gallery has an artist with a strange pedigree. The Drake Gallery is showing the work of a hermaphrodite from Wales. And he's very good in the bargain. We need a gimmick, Maggie dear. And we need it rather badly."

Maggie sensed a new mood of pessimism in Hillary's tone. "Don't worry, Donald. I'll come up with a gimmick that'll buy us tons of space."

"Will you? I shall adore you for the rest of my life."

"Just give me a day or two to think of something."

"This is Friday," Donald Hillary said. "Call me on Monday morning."

That sounded very much like an ultimatum. "Donald, what's going on?"

"I'm just concerned about the gross that Mr. Burke will produce for us. Frankly, I'm beginning to have doubts that we can clear the walls of his paintings as quickly as I had hoped."

"You haven't even seen his new canvases yet."

"That's true. But I will have seen them by the time you call on Monday. If I'm suitably impressed—and if you've given me a gimmick to promote him—we'll proceed with the show. Otherwise . . ."

"Otherwise what?"

"Well, I've discovered a watercolorist from Cape Ann whose work also merits a show. And he happens to be related to the Rockefellers. That alone will guarantee the chap's success."

"You promised me a show!"

Donald Hillary's laugh was light and tinkly. "Darling, I never said *absolutely.* But there's no reason to sound so angry. My goodness, I can picture your lovely breasts all aquiver with righteous indignation. The show will proceed—*if* I like Burke's new paintings;

and *if* you give me something I can use to promote the show. Is that so much to ask?"

With great effort, Maggie brought herself under control. There was no point in arguing with Donald. He knew what he wanted and he expected her to deliver. It was that simple. She was certain he would admire the paintings she had sent. All she had to do was find that gimmick for him. "No, Donald, it isn't. Don't worry. I won't let you down."

"I'm sure you won't," he said soothingly. "By the way, how is your campaign to marry Burke coming along?"

"Right on schedule," she lied.

"Wonderful. Oh my, I just had an idea. Why don't we hold the wedding in my gallery as part of the opening of the show! Now *that* would be a gimmick worthy even of Maggie Winston."

"A human sacrifice," Maggie laughed. "I love it. But I may not be able to bring Ansel to the altar quite so soon."

"That's a pity. Well, let's talk again on Monday morning. *Ciao,* darling."

"Good-bye, Donald."

Maggie sat back with tremors of black anxiety. The walls of her gallery were almost bare, a testimony to how much she had riding on Ansel Burke. Marry him? That might not be so easy. Last night had been a disaster. She had said and done all the wrong things.

Why can't I learn? she thought angrily. I pushed him too hard, just as I pushed Marshall Vogel. I've got to ease off. No more business talk. No more ideas for changes to his paintings. I'll give him sex and laughter, in that order.

Her confidence restored, Maggie picked up the phone and called Ansel's number at Fort Powell.

"MP headquarters. Corporal Fellows speaking."

"Hello, this is Maggie Winston. I'd like to speak to Ansel Burke."

"Sorry, the sergeant major isn't in right now."

"When will he return?"

"I don't know, ma'am. He went over to Captain

Silk's office a while ago, but he didn't give me an ETR."

Maggie went rigid. "He's with Jean Silk?"

"That's right, ma'am. Do you want to leave a message?"

"No . . . thank you. No message." She put down the phone and rubbed her upper arms with crossed hands. Suddenly she was cold and afraid.

Chapter 18

After the press conference the President's advisers, anxious to hear what the commentators would have to say about Bryant's performance, gathered in the Oval Office for yet another session in front of the three-screen television set.

There were no real surprises. The network correspondents took the President to task for evading a direct answer about a U.S. condemnation of Egypt. Then they went on to compare Egypt's generally civilized behavior with Libya's many acts of aggression, which was exactly what the President and his team had hoped they would do. Of course, more than hope was involved. They had worked the phones all day providing the press with detailed reminders of the Libyans' warlike behavior: aircraft hijackings, attacks on neighbors, and the financing of terrorist activities.

When the comments were over and the TV turned off, the President's men settled back for a post mortem.

Secretary of State Henry Flowers led the discussion. "You came off very well, Mr. President. I think the nation is beginning to realize that we did not support the Egyptians in their adventure."

"I disagree." Jim Canon cast his belligerent eyes around the room. "When we don't condemn Zamal, we support him by default."

"Is that so bad?" Luther Amstel asked.

"Yes!"

Bryant spoke up quickly to dampen the acrimony

that had developed over the past few days between his press secretary and the Director of the CIA. "Let's not make a judgment until we see tomorrow morning's papers. The networks gave me the benefit of the doubt, but the print media may not be so generous."

"The *New York Times* is going to kill us," Canon predicted. "I've got that straight from the head of the Washington Bureau. I don't know what those fuckers at the *Post* are going to do."

Luther Amstel suppressed a smile. Jim Canon had just made a fatal mistake; he had sounded as if he almost relished seeing his boss attacked by the nation's most important newspaper. Amstel had watched a shadow cross the President's face. Very unusual. Jim Canon and Walter Bryant had been friends for more than twenty years. If this crisis caused a split between the President and his press secretary, Amstel would be delighted. He considered Canon a noisy vulgarian who had no business in the high councils of government.

"There are other newspapers in this country besides the *Post* and the *Times*," the President pointed out. "I want to know what the *St. Louis Globe-Democrat* and *Chicago Tribune* have to say. And the *Kansas City Star*, of course. Give me the Midwest papers anytime. That's where the real pulse of the country is found."

Amstel feared the President was about to break into one of his "I'm proud of America's heartland" speeches. Instead Bryant turned to Roy McCluskey, Director of the FBI. "Roy, did I tell the truth at that press conference? Can you guarantee the warhead came from outside the U.S.?"

McCluskey, a burly ex-cop with dark hollows under his eyes, puffed on his pipe and gave a typically cautious answer. "I don't have any evidence that Egypt put its hands on one of ours. My people have been auditing every depot where nukes are stored and they haven't found a single one missing."

"So we're clean," Canon said.

"Ostensibly."

"What the hell does that mean?" Canon demanded.

At that moment Roy McCluskey decided to resign at the end of the year. He hated his job. It was ruining

his health and destroying what once had been a satisfying marriage to a wonderful woman. McCluskey had
been named Director of the FBI three years before,
when Bryant came into office. Previously he had been
Chief of Police of San Francisco, a job he loved. Sure,
there were problems in running a big-city police force.
But the politics in San Francisco were reasonably
straightforward; if you left the gays alone and kept
the hookers off Nob Hill, you were a success. Washington was something else again. Every decision had political ramifications. Every working day was eighteen
hours long. And Russian spies and urban terrorists
were a lot harder to catch and convict than North
Beach muggers. The decision to resign lifted a huge
weight from McCluskey's shoulders. For the first time
in two years he felt able to speak his mind. "The
evidence says that nuke came from elsewhere. My gut
says it was made in the U.S.A."

"Your gut?" Luther Amstel all but sneered. "I thought
the FBI had reached a higher level of criminal science
than that."

"A cop's gut is worth all the criminal science in the
world," McCluskey growled.

The President was aware of an interesting change
in McCluskey's demeanor. "Go on, Roy."

McCluskey knew that Luther Amstel distrusted him
and that the Washington elite looked down on him.
Big dumb cop—that was their assessment. Now that
he no longer cared what they thought, he spoke rapidly instead of in the careful cadence of the past three
years. "Okay, here it is. The inventories at our storage
depots are in order, but so what? An inventory can be
rigged. So I said to myself, screw the numbers. Let's
look at the kind of weapon the Egyptians used: small
payload; low megaton; delivered in a conventional way
the Egyptians could handle. Then I went over the list
of warheads in our arsenal that fit that profile."

He had everyone's attention. They had never heard
McCluskey speak with such unrestrained authority.

"There are three weapons the Egyptians might have
used. The first is the Halo, a surface-to-air missile
used for aircraft carrier defense. By the way, whoever

gave it that name ought to be shot. The second is the Field Deployable Nuclear Warhead, or F.D.N.W., which hasn't even been announced. It's a battlefield nuke designed for tactical situations. The third is the Challenger, one of our oldest nukes. The Challenger was designed forty years ago to be dropped by B-47s on small concentrations of enemy troops. Gentlemen, I think the Egyptians got their hands on one of those three weapons."

Amstel was shaking his head even before McCluskey finished his pitch. "Roy, for the past two days I've had my experts analyzing the type of weapon that might have been used. They've come to the conclusion that the Egyptians probably broke down a larger weapon, a MIRV for example, to create smaller and more manageable warheads."

"I think your experts are full of shit," McCluskey answered. "They often are. That's why I'm sending my agents back into the field to make a physical count of every weapon in those three categories. That comes to about seven thousand warheads out of ninety thousand in our inventory. The count will take at least a week, but I consider that time well spent."

The President was shocked, and secretly pleased, to see Luther Amstel challenged so openly. As much as Bryant admired Amstel's sharp mind and devoted patriotism, he was often annoyed by his CIA director's arrogance.

To dissipate the heavy antagonism in the air, Henry Flowers cleared his throat and offered up smiles to both Amstel and McCluskey. "Roy, I can see you're committed to this course. But why don't you let the Defense Department help you make the count? And borrow some people from Luther. By combining forces, the job could be done in a couple of days."

"I don't trust the people at Defense. Or the CIA." McCluskey had been wanting to say that ever since he came to Washington.

"Ninety thousand warheads?" Jim Canon felt betrayed. "I've been telling the public that we have forty thousand." He looked at the President, his friend of twenty

years, as if seeing him for the first time. "Why wasn't
I given an accurate figure?"

"Because the true figure has never been made public." Bryant realized this meeting had altered forever
his relationship with Jim Canon. He was saddened.
But that was the price you paid to sit in the Oval
Office. He looked pointedly at Roy McCluskey. "And I
don't want it to come out now."

"Nobody will hear it from me," McCluskey promised. "I'm just outlining the size of the job and telling
you that I don't want any help from Defense or the
CIA. Internal security is an FBI responsibility."

Luther Amstel saw a chance to give McCluskey a
counterpunch. "If, for the sake of argument, the device
used by Egypt did come from inside the United States,
then the FBI would be guilty of criminal mismanagement of our internal security."

"If that turns out to be true, I'll resign." What the
hell, McCluskey thought. I'm going to resign anyway.

"Let's not have any talk of resignations," the Secretary of State said quickly.

"You're absolutely right," the President agreed. "Let's
get through this mess first. If it turns out that one of
our warheads was lost or stolen, there'll be plenty of
blame to go around." He sounded weary to his bones.

After a knock on the door, Jim Canon's assistant
stuck his head into the oval office. "Jim, I've got to see
you right now."

Canon went outside and closed the door behind him.

"Okay," the President said. "Do it your way, Roy.
Just do it right."

"I intend to."

Jim Canon came back into the office like a man in a
trance. He fell into his chair and pressed a hand to his
chest as if to supress a stab of pain.

"What's wrong, Jim?" the President asked.

"Argentina has just made a formal demand in the
U.N. They want Cuba to stop smuggling arms to revolutionary elements in Argentina and organizing guerrilla cadres in their country. Cuba is guilty of that, of
course. Argentina is Cuba's next target for revolution.
But the Argentinian ambassador to the U.N. said, and

I quote, 'If Cuba does not halt its efforts to destabilize our government, Argentina will use all available force, including nuclear weapons, to defend itself against Cuban aggression.' "

"Dear God," Henry Flowers whispered.

The President found his voice. "Could Argentina be bluffing? Using the Egyptian attack to make Cuba think they've got a nuclear weapon, too?"

Canon shrugged lamely and struggled to his feet. "I have to get back to my office. The press will be all over us on this one. They'll want to know if we're supplying Argentina with nukes, too."

"That's insane," Flowers scoffed. "Everyone knows we do not want proliferation of nuclear weapons."

When Canon had gone, Amstel said, "We also want to stop Russia and Cuba from spreading their net. What the Egyptians and, now, the Argentinians are doing may have that very effect. You can hardly blame the world for thinking we're behind all this when we're the chief beneficiary."

"Are we? Luther, find out whether Argentina is bluffing," the President ordered. "Commit every resource you have to that goal. Henry, reassure our allies that we have *nothing* to do with Argentina's threat against Cuba. Then get through to the Argentinian ambassador or President Reyes and find out whether they really have a nuke, and where they got it. Roy, I want that physical inventory completed in three days, not in a week."

"Yes, sir."

McCluskey rose along with Amstel and Canon. The meeting adjourned spontaneously. Everyone had a busy afternoon and evening ahead.

Upon returning to CIA headquarters in Langley, Virginia, Luther Amstel called a meeting of his top staff. He ordered them to squeeze every agent and paid informer in Argentina and to infiltrate new agents into the country from other areas of Latin America. There were also several excellent targets for blackmail in the Argentine government. He spent an hour discussing the matter with his staff, then sent them

out with the warning that President Bryant expected
to know by the next day whether Argentina really
possessed a nuclear weapon. If so, the President demanded to know where the hell it came from.

Later he sat back in his chair with a cup of tea and
ruminated over his meeting with the President. Amstel
considered Bryant the most dangerous President since
Jimmy Carter. Bryant had no iron in his backbone.
The Russians were stealing new pieces of the globe
every year with impunity.

Proof of Bryant's ineffectiveness was the quality of
most of his staff. Henry Flowers was a timid diplomat
with no taste for confrontation; the post of Secretary of
State demanded someone who could stand up to the
nation's enemies. Jim Canon, a pathetic example of
the undereducated newspaperman of the past, had no
business at all in politics. Roy McCluskey was a street
cop in the wrong job. And Miles Avery, Secretary of
Defense, was useless when it came to strategic thinking. All he knew about the Pentagon was its budget.

The only surprise that came out of the White House
meeting was Roy McCluskey's insight into the weaponry used by Egypt. McCluskey's decision to narrow
the search for missing warheads to three specific nuclear weapons was disturbing, but manageable.

When the tea was gone Amstel folded his hands
over his large midriff and waited for the call that was
due at 3:00 P.M., Eastern Daylight Savings Time. At
precisely that hour his secretary buzzed him and came
on the intercom. "Mr. Amstel, the call you were expecting just came in. Code name Bluebird. Shall I put
Bluebird on a secure line?"

"Yes, Blanche, thank you." Amstel picked up his
phone and waited for the double beep indicating that
his line was secure. Amstel was the first CIA director
since Richard Helms to personally run an agent. Those
of his staff who knew that fact often speculated about
who Bluebird was and what his mission might be.
Amstel offered no clues.

The phone beeped twice.

"Hello? This is Bluebird."

"Yes, Bluebird. I'm here."

"Is our line secure?"

"Absolutely."

"You've heard the news from Argentina?"

"I was with the President when the news broke. A very satisfying experience. Obviously, last night's transfer went successfully."

"Yes, it did. Our friends from Argentina were out of the country before the sun rose. The packages are already in Buenos Aires."

"I made that assumption when the Argentinian ambassador issued his statement. I've got every agent in Latin America trying to learn whether Argentina really has a nuke, and where they got it."

Bluebird chuckled. "Do you think your agents will be successful?"

"I have grave doubts."

"Do we take the next step?"

"Yes. We've finally got the Russians against the wall. Let's keep them there."

"My sentiments exactly," Bluebird said.

"Is the operation still secure on your end?"

"I have only one problem—an MP sergeant who's too smart for his own good."

"Terminate him," Amstel said immediately. "We're too far along to let some noncom cause us trouble."

"He'll be taken care of tonight."

"Your next delivery will be to our friends in Saudi Arabia. The royal family is very worried about the Iranians. I've been assured they will deal with the Iranian threat—if we provide the weapon."

"Better and better," Bluebird murmured. "It's all falling into place."

"Just as we planned." Amstel drummed his fingers on his desk. "I've had one problem on my end: Roy McCluskey isn't satisfied with his inventory. He's sending his agents back to make a physical count on three specific weapons, one of them the F.D.N.W. Can you handle that?"

"Yes, of course."

"I knew you could," Amstel said warmly. "By God, this is like old times! You and me against the world."

"You and me," Bluebird parroted, with equal feeling.

"Call me tomorrow at three."

"I will. Good-bye, Luther."

After the call, Amstel swung his chair around to look at a photo that stood in a silver frame on the credenza behind his desk. It was a picture of himself and Bluebird taken more than thirty years ago, when they were barely out of their teens.

My face was round and chubby even then, Amstel thought. But at least my belly was flat. I looked damned good in uniform. He patted his large midriff wistfully. I wouldn't have this Wall Street paunch if I'd stayed in the army. On the other hand, I wouldn't have become Director of the CIA. And my opportunity to save this country from itself would have been lost.

With a grunt of satisfaction, Amstel turned back to his desk and plunged into his paperwork.

Chapter 19

Jean was driving her Subaru because Roper's friends might recognize Burke's car. They were going west on Route 41 through the desert. It was after ten o'clock on a clear night well illuminated by the moon. The distant mountains were black monoliths. For the first time since her arrival in New Mexico, Jean found the desert romantic. She had to keep reminding herself that their purpose tonight was anything but romantic.

"Why did you stay in the army all these years? A man like you could have done so much more." Jean suddenly realized how terribly patronizing she was being. "I'm sorry. I didn't mean that the way it sounded."

"I'm used to it," Burke said. "Most people think the army is for people who can't do anything else."

Jean felt very small.

Burke smiled slowly. "You know, a lot of people rank lawyers even lower than soldiers."

"Including you?"

"I might have. Until lately. The fact is, I stayed in the army because I'm good at soldiering. It's satisfying to do something well, even if there's not a lot of money or prestige in it. Simple story."

"I guess that's why you remind me of my father." She gave him a sidelong glance, unsure of whether to ask the question that was on her mind. Why not? "I heard someone say, 'Don't get Ansel Burke sore at you. You're liable to become his next blood stripe.' What does that mean?"

"A blood stripe is a promotion you get when everybody around you has been killed and you're the only one left alive. I've had more than my share of blood stripes."

"Oh." She regretted asking.

"There it is." Burke pointed out a cluster of lights in the darkness ahead. "Drive past without slowing down. I want to look it over first."

"I'm surprised the station is still open. There doesn't seem to be much traffic on Route 41 at night."

"Or in the daytime. That's what makes Hank's interest in this place so strange. He never sticks with a losing proposition."

The station's lights only served to reveal its isolation and run-down condition. Driving past, they saw two old-fashioned gas pumps, an office, a garage that wasn't even equipped with a hydraulic lift, and a small bungalow set about twenty yards behind the office.

"Did you see any people?" Jean asked when the station was behind them.

"No, but there are half a dozen cars parked near that bungalow. One's a red sports car of some kind, and Hank owns a red Porsche."

"So he's here tonight?"

"Maybe. Go down the highway a little farther, then turn around and drive past again."

Mimicking Lou Brodsky with amazing accuracy, Jean barked, "Whatever you say, Sergeant Major."

Burke had to laugh. "Brodsky does tend to jump when I speak. But you don't have to. I'm the noncom, you're the officer. Why don't you just drop me off here and go back to the post."

"How would you get back?"

"I'll manage."

"No way. All my life I've wanted to be a decoy. I may never get another chance." She slowed to make a U-turn.

On the second pass they saw a smallish man standing near the gas pumps with a long pole, checking the fuel level in one of the underground storage tanks.

"I know him," Burke said. "That's Sergeant Louie Sanchez, one of Hank's buddies. Louie's a magician with a knife. He always wears long-sleeved shirts because he carries a stilleto up his right shirt sleeve and a throwing knife up the left one."

"Sounds like a charmer."

"Louie has his soft side. They say he's never left a man to bleed to death; he always puts his stilleto through the kidney because that's a killing blow."

Jean shivered over the casual way Ansel spoke about such things. She couldn't get used to that side of him. "You're trying to scare me off, but it won't work."

Burke was surprised at how accurately she could read him after just a couple of days. That's exactly what he'd been trying to do, although his description of Louie Sanchez's preoccupation with knives was accurate. "Okay, then pull up here and drop me off. Give me fifteen minutes to get into position behind the bungalow. Then drive into the station and ask Louie to fill the tank. Turn up the volume on your radio; that'll help to distract whoever's in the bungalow. When you've got your gas, have the oil checked, too. Then drive about a mile down the road and wait for me."

"How long will you be at the bungalow?"

"Just long enough to get some idea of the setup. Who knows, maybe Hank only uses the place to play poker and watch porno tapes with his pals. If there's more to it than that, I'll come back with some of the best head-busters in the MPs."

Jean stopped the car and switched off the lights. "Be careful."

"You too." Burke hated to leave her alone in the dark. "I don't want you in that station longer than five minutes."

"I understand."

Burke was wearing dark denim jeans, a blue knit pullover shirt, and gray sneakers. He slipped out of the car and immediately vanished into the darkness. Jean sat very still, feeling more alone than she had ever been and, finally, just a tad frightened about driving up to that lonely gas station.

The news that Argentina had threatened to use nuclear weapons against Cuba made this foray—this "recon," as Ansel called it—even more scary. The pace at which events were moving made them wonder if their suspicions were only a form of hysteria. The threat of nuclear annihilation was doing that to people; one of the demonstrators in front of the White House had set himself on fire this afternoon and a man in Omaha had shot his wife, two daughters, and himself to death in order to "save" his family from the coming nuclear holocaust. If the nation was coming unraveled, maybe they were, too.

In the end they had decided they weren't being hysterical. Betsy Palermo had been murdered. There was evidence of an official cover-up. And links kept coming up between the killing and a weapon called a Field Deployable Nuclear Warhead.

Also bothering Jean was the guilty knowledge that she had involved herself in all of this to impress Ansel rather than to make the world a safer place to live. God knew, she wanted him. The fact that he was being so loyal to Maggie Winston only made Jean want him more. One of these days, she thought, Ansel's going to wake up and realize that he's just a meal ticket to Maggie. That's when I want to be around.

"Here's the duty roster." Roper passed around sheets of paper to Jansen, Briscoe, Craymore, Arkolotti, and Williamson, who were gathered in the bungalow behind the service station. "Control wants to beef up site security, so from now on there'll be two men on duty here at all times. That means more hours out here for all of us."

There were groans from all around. Louie Sanchez came in and was handed one of the sheets, too.

"Stop bitching," Roper snapped.

"I'm not bitching," Arkolotti objected. "It's just that I'm already having a tough time justifying all the hours I spend away from the post. I don't have the freedom of movement some of you guys do. My company commander expects to see me in the ranks once in a while."

"That'll be taken care of," Roper assured him. "Start-

ing Monday you're all on 'detached duty' to the Restricted Materiel Center. Officially, you'll be reporting
to Captain Miller, the adjutant at the R.M.C. Unoffi-
cially, you're reporting to me. Your orders will be cut
tomorrow."

"That's more like it." Briscoe grinned around the
room. "I guess the fix goes way up, huh?"

"Don't worry yourself about those little things," Roper
said coldly. "Just take orders and bank your money.
Anybody got a problem with the duty roster now?"

There was no further discussion on that point.

"Item two," Roper went on, "is better news. Control
has decided that Ansel Burke is making too many
waves. He's gonna be canceled out." A craggy smile
softened Roper's hard features. "Tonight. I've got Sam
Veck waiting near Ansel's car right now with a fragmentation grenade. The minute Ansel gets into his
car, Sam is gonna frag him."

"Well, shit." Harry Williamson was acutely disappointed. "Why didn't you give me that job? I owe one
to that bastard."

Roper looked at Williamson skeptically. "Ansel already took you down once this week. Wasn't that
enough?"

Williamson, whose balls were still sore, could only
sulk.

"Won't it stir up a lot of trouble to frag Burke?"
Craymore asked. "Why not arrange another accident?"

"It would take time to set one up. Control would
rather take some heat about an out-and-out killing
than let Ansel keep on digging. Okay, let's talk about
our next deal. We've got two Arabs coming in to pick
up some merchandise next month. I don't want to use
the same transfer point again. Too risky. Anybody got
a suggestion for a new site?"

The office bell rang, indicating that someone had
driven up to the gas pumps.

Everyone looked at Louie Sanchez, who swore under
his breath as he rose. "I got a goddamn fortune tucked
away and I'm pumping gas like a *cholo*. That don't
make no sense at all."

"Hey, don't forget to clean the customer's windshield,"

Roper joked. "This is my station, I've got a reputation to protect."

"Sure, sure." Sanchez stomped out of the bungalow, annoyed by the laughter that followed him. His mood didn't improve until he saw that his customer was a good-looking piece of slash. A redhead, in fact. Sanchez loved girls with red hair. He had married one redhead and fathered two children by another.

He swaggered around to the driver's side and leaned in the window with a leering smile that he thought made him irresistible. "Hello there, *bonita*." This redhead even had freckles.

Jean Silk smiled back a little nervously. "Fill it up with unleaded, please."

"Sure, I fill you up. Anytime you want." Sanchez winked at her and went around to the pumps. While he was setting the nozzle, the redhead turned her radio up full blast, flooding the air with Waylon Jennings's voice and guitar.

With the pump filling the gas tank on automatic, Sanchez had time to come back around to talk to the girl. "Hey, you got a Fort Powell sticker on your window."

"Yes, I'm stationed there."

"Me too! I'm Sergeant Louie Sanchez. I see you got New York plates on your car. You from New York City or upstate?"

"New York City."

"Hey, I got family in Spanish Harlem. You ever go that far uptown?"

"Sure."

While Louie Sanchez talked about the delights of Spanish Harlem, which for him seemed to consist mainly of sex clubs and head shops, Jean began to regret her demand to accompany Ansel. Being a decoy was more unnerving than she'd anticipated, and Ansel's warnings about Louie Sanchez now seemed understated. As Ansel had predicted, Sanchez was wearing a long-sleeved shirt. Did he really carry a knife up each sleeve?

The gas pump made a belching noise and shut off.

"I think the tank is full. Would you please check the oil?"

"Sure thing." Sanchez's eyes dropped to Jean's breasts. "If you want, I'll even service your headlights."

"Just the oil," she said, a little more sharply than she'd intended.

"Okay, okay. Relax."

While Sanchez was capping the gas tank, Jean studied the bungalow, which was ablaze with light. One of the cars in front of the bungalow was definitely a Porsche, so Hank Roper must be in there. Where was Ansel? I hope he's being careful, she thought. This place has an evil chill to it. Or am I only imagining things?

Sanchez came back to the front of the Subaru and opened the hood, all the while leering at Jean through the windshield.

It's not my imagination, she decided. This is an evil place. Hurry, Ansel . . . *hurry.*

Burke moved cautiously into position, pausing often to be certain Roper hadn't posted sentries around the property. That seemed unlikely. But if the gas station was important, then Hank might have posted perimeter guards. Or perhaps he had installed a scanning system to detect intruders.

When he was convinced otherwise, Burke crept up to the rear of the bungalow and flattened himself against the wall. He could hear voices coming from the parlor, primarily Hank's. The brightness of the moon was unfortunate. Anyone glancing out the window or coming around the building was bound to see him.

He reached inside his shirt and drew out a nine-millimeter Browning that held an eleven-round magazine. In Burke's opinion the Browning was the only handgun worth owning. All others were unreliable or inaccurate or both. He pulled back the slide silently to make sure there was a round in the chamber, then moved close to the parlor window with the Browning held at the ready.

Snatches of conversation came to him. He recognized Joe Briscoe's voice: ". . . fix goes way up, huh?"

Then Hank Roper: "Don't worry yourself about those little things. Just take orders and bank your money. Anybody got a problem with the duty roster now?"

Duty roster? Burke wondered what the hell kind of duty these guys were pulling. By standing far back from the window, well out of the light, he could see the best collection of cutthroats ever assembled from the ranks of Fort Powell: Briscoe, Sanchez, Craymore, Arkolotti, Williamson. Not a straight soldier in the bunch.

"Item two is better news," Hank was saying. "Control has decided that Ansel Burke is making too many waves. He's gonna be canceled out. Tonight. I've got Sam Veck waiting near Ansel's car right now with a fragmentation grenade. The minute Ansel gets into his car, Sam is gonna frag him."

The inside of Burke's mouth dried up. Well now. If I'd decided to take *my* car instead of Jean's, I might be dead. So might Jean.

A red rage caught fire inside his head—hot, scalding, and under high pressure. He raised the Browning, flicked forward the safety, and lined up the front sight on Hank's chest.

You want blood? *We'll start with yours.*

He checked himself just in time. Jean would be driving her Subaru into the station any minute. If he started a firefight, she'd drive right into it.

Reluctantly, Burke lowered the Browning and slipped back into the shadows next to the window. You came here for information, he reminded himself. Get that first. Deal with Hank later. Control? Who or what is Control? What the hell's going on out here?

He heard Hank say that two Arabs would be coming next month to pick up some "merchandise." They needed a new place to make the transfer. Burke strained to hear every word, but nothing was said about F.D.N.W.s.

Just then Jean drove up to the gas pumps. Louie Sanchez went out to help her and Hank continued with his discussion. Jean's radio was turned up to a boisterous country music song, which encouraged Hank to speak louder. A number of new transfer sites were suggested: back roads, desert arroyos, mountain mesas, even the parking lot of Puma High School. None struck Hank as just right.

They were discussing the possibility of making the transfer of their merchandise—whatever it was—on a desolate stretch of the Fort Powell artillery range when suddenly a beeper went off somewhere within the bungalow.

The sound galvanized the group. They turned in unison to a rather amateurish painting of the Grand Canyon on the bungalow wall. Hank went to the painting and pressed a recessed button. The painting slid smoothly aside to reveal a large computer screen built into the wall. A scale drawing was etched on the face of the screen. Burke risked leaning close to the window for a better view.

The image on the screen appeared to be the inside of a building . . . or a mountain. Caves. Tunnels. Chambers. Vertical pits. At what appeared to be an entrance, two red lights were blinking.

"Not enough heat," Roper said. "Those images aren't people. Just a couple of coyotes."

"That's the third time this month we've had coyotes in the cave," Arkolotti pointed out. "I thought all the coyotes were supposed to be dying off."

"Not around here." Roper touched a reset button to kill the beeper, then slid the painting back across the face of the computer screen. "There're lots of coyotes in these mountains. A few wolves too."

"Fucking scavengers," Williamson growled. "I kill them whenever I can." He grinned around. "Hey, maybe it's not coyotes. Maybe those readings are the Hallidays, come back to haunt us."

Roper was annoyed. "I don't believe in ghosts. And I don't believe in talking about our cancellations, either." He switched back to the subject of the transfer point.

The Hallidays. Burke leaned against the wall and tried to put all these new pieces together. So Hank and his pals did kill that young couple. Just that afternoon he had been looking at the photos of the Hallidays' bodies provided by the Puma sheriff's office. The Hallidays had been spelunkers and that computer screen was linked to heat-activated surveillance monitors inside the cave system of a mountain.

Which mountain? Obviously, one of the peaks in this vicinity. The gas station was just a cover for a monitoring post. The Hallidays must have tried to explore the caves inside the mountain. They were picked up on the monitors. Then Hank, or some of his men, went to the mountain and grabbed the Hallidays, who were taken off to another part of Puma County where their "accidental" deaths would not be connected with the mountain.

What was important enough to hide inside a mountain? To guard with sophisticated electronic equipment? To kill for?

Field Deployable Nuclear Warheads was one answer. But no one had mentioned warheads. They only talked about *merchandise,* which could mean many things: other types of stolen army equipment, drugs, conventional weapons, or something else altogether. No matter: he now had enough evidence of illegal activity to bring a squad of MPs out here, and Sheriff Len Perkins too.

A phone rang inside the bungalow and Roper answered it. Burke again leaned close to the window to try to catch the gist of the conversation.

"Yeah, okay. Where the hell did he go? ... Sure, that's possible ... Yeah, just stay with it, but don't take any chances. I want this job done *right.* You can have more men if you need them."

He hung up. "That was Sam. It seems that Ansel didn't use his car tonight and no one knows where he went. He's not with the broad from the art gallery. Or at the Chicken Coop. Or the N.C.O. Club. Or in his quarters playing with his paint box." Roper paced the small parlor. "I don't like not knowing where Ansel Burke is."

Burke eased back from the window.

Roper walked to the bungalow door. "Who's playing the radio so loud?" He peered at the Subaru parked at the gas pumps. "Don't I know her? Isn't that the new lawyer from the J.A.G. office? Ansel's friend?"

Without waiting to hear more, Burke cocked the

Browning and sprinted through the darkness toward the rear of the garage.

"Louie!" Roper shouted. "Grab that broad! Don't let her drive away!"

Roper started out of the bungalow with a couple of his friends. Burke fired twice at them on the run and heard the bungalow's front window shatter. They dived back inside.

No point in concealment now. Burke cut into the open and headed for the Subaru on a dead run. "Jean, start the car!"

"What?"

"Go! Get out of here!"

Louie Sanchez had reached into the car to grab Jean's arm. He released her and jerked his head up. He saw Burke coming and shook his right arm. A black, seven-inch stilleto dropped into his hand. He threw it with a snapping motion. Burke dodged aside, but the blade sliced his right shoulder.

The car's engine turned over and Jean looked to him for guidance.

"Go!" he shouted.

Jean hurried to get the car in gear but was too late. Sanchez came flying out of the darkness like a panther, his backup knife thrust at Burke's throat. Burke fired once. The nine-millimeter round picked up Sanchez and slammed him against the side door of the Subaru, cracking the window. Sanchez slid down onto the ground, his chest an ugly mess of shattered bone and torn tissue.

Burke dove into the Subaru, yelling: "Move it, Jean! *Go,* for Christ's sake!"

She popped the clutch, sending the car lurching forward, then recovered and picked up speed. Burke leaned out the window and fired at the dark forms spilling out of the bungalow. The shots went wide because of the jerking motion of the Subaru, but at least he made the bastards dive for cover. Every second of confusion was precious.

With a sinking sensation, he saw two of the men rise to firing positions. They were aiming automatic weapons at the Subaru. Burke spun around and jammed his left foot down on top of Jean's right foot, forcing the accelerator pedal to the floor.

"Ow!" she objected.

The automatic weapons opened up and the noise became deafening. In the rearview mirror Burke and Jean saw a riotous flash of color from the muzzles of the weapons. A torrent of lead tore into the car. The Subaru swerved and shuddered like a wounded animal. Window glass flew up in their arms and faces. There was an explosion and the Subaru began to *bump, bump, bump* along the highway.

"A tire!" Jean gasped. "Ansel, we've got a flat tire!"

The firing tapered off as they pulled out of range, but that didn't make Burke feel better. There were cars back there. Cars without flat tires. They'd catch up to the Subaru in minutes. "Is this thing four-wheel drive?"

"Yes. In the winter—"

Burke reached across her and hit the headlight switch, plunging them into darkness.

"What are you doing?"

"Turn off the road into the desert. Go left toward the mountains."

"But—"

"Now!" He turned the wheel for her, forcing them off the road.

"God, I can't see where I'm *going*." Jean brushed hair from her eyes and gripped the wheel tightly.

"The moon's bright enough. Just stay on the flats. Avoid that dry creek ahead. That's it, bear left."

The Subaru lumbered along at a slow, uneven speed.

"I can only go about fifteen miles an hour."

"They won't be able to do much better. I saw two jeep vans in front of the bungalow. The others were sedans and Hank's Porsche. No good out here."

"Then they'll catch us in the vans."

"We've got a better chance out here than on the highway." He was scanning the desert floor. "Go right. Don't drive into deep sand. We'd never get out."

"I can't *tell* where the deep sand is. Ansel, did you kill— I mean, was that man dead?"

"Sanchez? Yeah, he's dead." Burke glanced at the

blood streaming from his shoulder. "I told you Louie
was a magician with a knife."

Jean was appalled. Ansel's voice revealed not a shred
of remorse over the man he had just killed. If anything, he sounded lighthearted. Or maybe he was just
light-headed. Jean knew that she was. Everything had
happened so fast that her head was spinning.

The Subaru hit something and bounced into the air,
then came crashing down. Jean heard a piece of metal
snap and the car seemed to lean sideways, though it
continued to move.

"I think we broke one of the shocks," Burke said.
"By the time we get out of here, the trade-in value on
this thing is going to break your heart."

"Don't joke!" Jean was starting to get mad. The
worse things became, the more relaxed and offhand
Ansel sounded.

"Sorry." Burke looked back over his shoulder. "Force
of habit. In combat you never talk about how slim
your chances are. You make jokes instead. Well, they
still haven't started after us. That's good and bad.
Hank's getting them organized. Giving them orders.
They'll be on our trail soon enough, and do just as
Hank says. At least we've bought a little time. Our
best chance is to put a few more miles behind us, then
stop and change the tire." He looked at her in alarm.
"You do carry a spare, don't you?"

"Of course I carry a spare." The question made Jean
unreasonably angry. "What do you think I am? Some
kind of airhead? The proverbial dizzy redhead? You
men really piss me off sometimes."

"I'd never accuse you of being a dizzy redhead. Not
after the way you hung in back there."

The warmth of his words affected Jean like a tonic.
Forgetting the cuts on her forearms and the fear in
her stomach, she settled down to drive. She was pleased
that Ansel didn't want to take the wheel himself.
Despite the jolting motion of the crippled Subaru and
the uncertainties about the terrain, he trusted her to
keep them going. That meant a lot to her. "How's your
shoulder?"

Burke had cleaned some of the blood from his upper

arm and tied a handkerchief around the wound. "Not bad. I'm lucky that Sanchez kept his knife clean. There's nothing worse than being cut with a dirty blade."

"Yes, you're very lucky," Jean said dryly. "My dad used to say, 'If I didn't have bad luck, I wouldn't have any luck at all.' I'm beginning to think I inherited that trait."

"Don't let yourself think that way. One of the few things I've learned in life is that the smartest people are usually the luckiest. We'll make our own luck."

Jean hoped he could do that.

Chapter 20

"Take the jeeps," Roper was saying. "Whatever you do, don't let them get out of the desert alive."

"The girl too?" Craymore asked.

"No, let the girl go," Roper snarled. "That's all we need—an army lawyer who can build a case against us. Jesus Christ, Frank, after what she saw tonight and what Ansel must have told her, she's *got* to go!"

"We'll take care of them," Williamson assured him.

They had gone into the armory beneath the bungalow floor for weapons and ammo. Arnie Arkolotti, Joe Briscoe, and Harry Williamson were carrying their Ingram MAC-10s and Frank Craymore had picked up his favorite weapon, the Ruger Mini-14 with the laser sight.

"Now listen up." Roper was putting himself in Ansel Burke's place, trying to guess his next move. "We hit that car with at least a dozen rounds. That's why Ansel killed the lights and turned off into the desert. If the car is in bad shape, he won't try to get back on the highway where you could outrun him. Instead he'll try to evade you in the desert, using only the moonlight. Pick up his tire tracks and force him north, away from Puma and Fort Powell. When you catch him, don't take any chances. You know he's armed."

Briscoe looked down at the body of Louie Sanchez, which lay crumpled by the pumps. "I always told Louie that knives are worthless. If you're close enough to stab a man, you're close enough to shoot him."

Roper had no more interest in Sanchez. "Forget Louie. I'll dump him out in the boondocks. Get going."

Craymore and Arkolotti climbed into one jeep. Williamson and Briscoe took the other. Roper watched them drive down the highway and turn off into the desert at approximately the same place where Ansel and the girl had left the highway. He looked at his watch. Ansel had a fifteen-minute lead. Not enough to do him much good, especially if his car was badly shot up.

Nevertheless, Roper was worried. You could never be sure what Ansel might do. Roper wished he could have gone along with his men, but he didn't have that luxury. His duty right now was to let Control know what had happened. Control would want to set up a contingency plan in the unlikely event Ansel or the girl got out of the desert alive.

Roper wasn't looking forward to telling his story. Control would go ape-shit. It was impossible to know exactly how long Ansel had been behind the bungalow, but he must have heard plenty.

What were we talking about? A new transfer point. The merchandise, but only in general terms. The two Arabs coming in next month. Oh yeah, and I told everyone that I'd sent Sam Veck to frag Ansel. Ansel must have *loved* hearing that. I'm surprised he didn't blow me away then and there.

Oh, shit!

The alarm went off, Roper reminded himself angrily, and I moved the painting to look at the display screen. Ansel must have seen that too. Could he have figured out what the display meant? No, he didn't know that much. Jesus Christ! Williamson—that asshole—had even mentioned the Hallidays! Good thing they'd dumped the Hallidays on the other side of Puma County. There was no possible way to connect those damned spelunkers with the mountain.

Roper took hold of Sanchez's ankles and dragged him into the desert. There was a sinkhole about two hundred yards behind the bungalow that he'd been using to dump trash. Good place for Sanchez.

*   *   *

Burke had never changed a tire so fast in his life:
three minutes and ten seconds. "If your Subaru holds
together, we may be able to shake them." Jean was
still driving while Burke picked out the terrain for her
to follow because, as he explained, "I spent four months
at the Desert Warfare School in Fort Huachuca, Ari-
zona. That doesn't mean I know everything there is to
know about the desert, but I did pick up a few tricks.
After the Desert Warfare School, of course, they sent
me to Fort Richardson, Alaska. A typical army foul-up."

"I can't understand why you persist in loving the
army," Jean said, keeping her eyes on the desert floor.

"The army's like a family," Burke explained. "It
never works just right, and it seems like somebody is
always getting screwed, but it's better than no family
at all. That's why guys like Hank piss me off. They
want all the benefits of being in the family, but
they won't put a damned thing back into it. Hank and
his kind are sucking the army dry." He pointed to the
right. "Bear that way and take us down into the dry
arroyo."

"I could go faster with the lights on."

"They'd find us faster, too."

"Maybe they aren't even following. We haven't seen
any headlights."

"They're coming." Burke, who had been watching
the rearview mirror closely, turned to look through
the rear window, which was pocked with bullet holes.
"As a matter of fact, there they are."

Jean caught her breath. Two pairs of headlights
could be seen several miles back. The vehicles behind
them seemed to be moving much faster, causing Jean
to push down harder on the accelerator.

"Ease up a little," Burke said gently. "We can't
outrun them. We have to be smarter, not faster. Get
into that arroyo and stop."

Jean did as she was told, though she desperately
wanted to gun the engine and try to put distance
between herself and the men behind them. When they
stopped, Burke climbed out of the Subaru and told her
to follow him. He jogged ahead of the car for a few

minutes, then suddenly raised his arm to signal her to stop.

He came back and leaned in the car. "There's deep sand ahead. Go up along the side of the arroyo as high as you can. I'll lead you. As long as we're down here out of sight, you can turn on the lights."

Having lights made all the difference. Jean easily followed Burke on a winding route around the area where he said the sand was deep, then again stopped the Subaru at his command.

He came back to the car and said, "Kill the lights and help me wipe out our tire tracks."

Together they returned to where they had left the bottom of the dry riverbed and began kicking sand over the tracks the Subaru had made around the deep sand. Then, going back again, she and Burke each placed their feet in one set of tracks and shuffled forward to make artificial tire tracks, as if the Subaru had gone forward. The sand was very deep. After a few yards Jean began to panic. "Ansel, I'm being swallowed up!"

"Grab my hand." He latched on and pulled her forward. It took enormous effort to extract themselves from the deep sand, which seemed to be sucking them in with every step. By the time they reached firm ground, both were panting.

"What is that stuff?" Jean gasped.

"Just loose, deep sand. These old, dry rivers have pockets like this created by flash floods during the rainy season. I'm hoping we can lead them into it. Come on, let's get back to the car."

Jean thought they would use this opportunity to get farther away from their pursuers. Instead, Burke rummaged in the trunk and came up with an old Coke bottle.

"What are you doing?"

"I want to cut them down in size." He began draining gasoline from the tank into the Coke bottle. "They'll have to follow our tire tracks down this riverbed single file. The arroyo is too narrow for them to do anything else. When they get stuck in that sand, I'm going to feed them a Molotov cocktail. Shit-oh-dear, I don't have any matches."

"I think Bill Manning left some in the glove compartment." She got them for him. "I hate to ask, but what if they don't follow the tire tracks? Or what if they do follow but don't get stuck?"

"Then they've got us."

Jean tried not to show how frightened she felt. "What can I do?"

"Pull the Subaru up another two hundred yards and wait for me with the motor running. We'll be leaving in kind of a hurry, like we did from the gas station. By the way, you were fantastic back there."

She tried to smile. "Good luck."

He put his hand on her cheek. "Thanks. Don't worry, I'll be back."

"I'm counting on that."

He went down the arroyo and Jean climbed into the car. She turned the ignition key, but the engine wouldn't start. Her heart sank. She fought down her panic and turned the ignition switch again. This time the engine caught and began to idle. Oh God, she thought, I'm not built for this kind of a fight. Give me a courtroom anytime.

Harry Williamson and Joe Briscoe were in the lead van, following the Subaru's tire tracks as fast as the bumpy terrain would allow. The other jeep was about twenty yards behind them.

When they entered the arroyo, Williamson slowed up.

"What's the matter?" Briscoe asked.

"Why would Burke go into a dry riverbed? There might not be an easy way out for him."

"Let's hope you're right."

"He's too smart to do that without a reason."

Briscoe was disdainful. "Don't let Hank spook you. He thinks too much of Burke."

"Yeah, I know, but I just had a run-in with Burke myself and I'm still in pain from it. So we'll go a little slow through here."

"Maybe that's what he expects us to do." Briscoe

hated to slow down when he knew they were close. "Gives him a chance to drive full out."

"He can't drive full out. Look at those tire tracks. You can tell his car is all slewed over. Must have lost his shocks."

Suddenly the jeep's front end dropped a foot or more and the engine began to labor.

"Shit!" Williamson threw the jeep in reverse. The vehicle jumped back several feet, then settled more deeply into the sand. The wheels spun uselessly while the engine raced. "The bastard suckered us in! Joe, make sure the other jeep doesn't follow."

Briscoe jumped out and waved Craymore and Arkolotti to a stop. He landed hard in the soft sand, which sucked him in halfway to his knees. Briscoe struggled back several yards to the hardpan, cursing loudly. Williamson tried to step more lightly across the bog, but he was a heavy man and his struggle was just as difficult.

"What the hell happened here?" Arkolotti demanded. "How did Burke drive his car across this stuff?"

"I don't think he did." Craymore pointed at the tire tracks they had been following. "Look there: the tire tracks stop; then those other marks go ahead into the deep sand. They probably made those tracks by dragging their damned feet. Burke led you guys right into it after he circled around."

Williamson surveyed the problem. "We can hook a rope to our jeep and pull it out of the sand, or we can abandon it and stay on their tail in one vehicle. What do you think?"

"Let's stay on the bastard," Craymore said.

Briscoe was angry with himself for falling into Burke's trap. "I vote the same way. Burke can't be more than a mile or two ahead. I want him *now*."

"Suits me," Arkolotti agreed.

An arc of flame climbed into the air and descended on them.

"Scatter!" Briscoe yelled.

Everyone dove in different directions.

The flaming object fell on the hood of the second jeep and exploded, showering glass and fiery gasoline in all directions. The front of the jeep was immediately engulfed in fire. Frank Craymore, who had hit the ground near the jeep, was splashed from head to foot with liquid flame. He screamed and leaped to his feet.

"Help me!" he shrieked. "Help me! I'm burning up!"

Williamson tackled Craymore and began shoveling loose sand onto Craymore's body with his hands.

Arkolotti and Briscoe raised their MAC-10s and fired short bursts at the ridge above them, where they judged Burke had been when he launched the Molotov cocktail.

"Cover me!" Briscoe jumped up and raced up the side of the arroyo while Arkolotti swept the ridge with longer bursts.

When Briscoe disappeared over the ridge, Arkolotti ran to Williamson's side and grabbed one of Frank Craymore's arms. "Let's get him out of here! The jeep's going to blow!"

Together Williamson and Arkolotti dragged Craymore fifty yards down the arroyo. The jeep was now totally engulfed in flames. It contained boxes of ammo for Craymore's Ruger and Arkolotti's MAC-10. When the jeep blew, there would be ammo flying everywhere. They hid behind a boulder and waited. Seconds later the jeep went up in a pillar of fire; followed by the popping sound of live rounds exploding in the inferno.

They didn't emerge until the live rounds stopped exploding.

Briscoe came out of the darkness to join them. "The fucker got away. I heard his car take off. He couldn't have been more than three hundred yards ahead of me."

"Burke really did a job on us." There was a trace of professional respect in Arkolotti's voice. "We lost one vehicle, one man, the Ruger with the laser sight, and part of our MAC-10 ammo. And the other jeep is stuck in the sand."

Briscoe was trying to ascertain Craymore's condition. "Frank's dying?"

"He might as well be," Williamson said.

Frank Craymore was lying on his back moaning and twitching. Most of his clothing was burnt off, as well as a good deal of his skin. His trademark, the large red nose, had been reduced to a black button.

Craymore's voice was a croak of pain: "Help me, Arnie." A hand groped upward. "Get me to the post, I need a doctor."

The three looked at one another. There was no way to get Frank Craymore to a doctor and catch up with Burke and the girl, too.

"Who's going to do it?" Briscoe asked.

Williamson looked at Arkolotti. "Arnie should."

"Why me?"

"You're Frank's buddy. Better to get it from a buddy than one of us. Joe and me hardly know the guy."

Arkolotti sighed and slipped off the safety on his MAC-10. "I guess that's right."

"Come on." Briscoe touched Williamson's arm. "Let's start pulling the other jeep out of the sand. Arnie, make it fast. I want to catch up with Burke before dawn."

As they hurried back down the arroyo, a short burst from Arkolotti's MAC-10 rattled through the still darkness.

The explosion made Jean jump. She held the wheel even tighter and kept her foot lightly on the gas pedal.

A minute later Burke dived into the car with an anxious glance over his shoulder. "Pull out, one of them's right behind me. But keep the lights off."

Jean didn't need to be told. She was already accelerating the Subaru as fast as it would go. Could there be another bog of shifting sand ahead? Ansel didn't seem worried, so she put the possibility out of her mind. For the moment she was more concerned about being shot at by whoever had followed Ansel.

When she did hear shots, they sounded far away.

"Relax," Burke reassured her. "Those weren't aimed at us."

"Then who?"

"One of them—from his size, I think it was Frank Craymore—was burned pretty badly. I imagine they put him out of his pain."

"That's inhuman."

"Yeah, but good for us. There are only three now, and I don't think Hank is one of them. I put one of their jeeps out of action, too. So the odds are better." He looked over his shoulder again. "You can put on your lights for a while."

"The explosion—that was the jeep?"

"Sure was. And the other's stuck in the sand. It'll take them about twenty minutes to pull it out."

"Should we turn back toward the highway?"

"We're more than thirty minutes from Route 41. How much speed can you goose out of this thing?"

"When I go over twenty the whole car shakes."

"That's not good enough. They'd catch up to us before we reached the highway."

"Aren't there any ranches around here? Any houses with telephones?"

"Not likely."

Jean searched in vain for a pinpoint of light in the black night. Black morning, she should say. According to her watch it was 3:12 A.M. "It's a good thing I filled the gas tank back there. But Ansel, sooner or later we're going to run out of gas."

"So will they, and your Subaru has more range than what they're driving. I think our best chance is to go deeper into the desert and try to run them out of gas." He thought Jean should know what he was getting her into. "That means we'll have to walk out of here, which is going to be rough. But that's the point: I want to make it rough on them too. They'll be more likely to make mistakes."

"Don't worry about me." Jean hoped she sounded braver than she felt.

They continued driving through the darkness, stopping only twice during the next two hours—once when the car stalled going up a rise, and again when they had trouble making headway through some deep sand. Both stops were brief. Jean got the stalled engine started by gently pumping the gas pedal and later on Burke put his good shoulder to the rear of the Subaru to push it out of the sand.

Burke had tried without success to find rocky ground. They were leaving tire tracks that Hank's men could follow as easily as a road map. He couldn't resist glancing over his shoulder every few minutes to see if they were there. He had told Jean to shut off the lights many miles back. They could be seen from too damned far out here.

The Subaru was sounding worse by the minute. There was still a quarter of a tank of gas left when dawn came, but that wouldn't help if the engine overheated in the sun and failed.

In the light, Burke realized for the first time just how exhausted Jean must be. Her face was drawn, her mouth set. "You've done all the driving. Why don't I take over for a while?"

"I'm fine."

"Do you have anything to eat in this car?"

"I think there's something under the driver's seat."

Burke rummaged around down there and came up with a box containing twelve Hostess Twinkies. "Twinkies? I don't believe it."

She grinned, pleased at having surprised him again.

"Do you ever eat vegetables? Or fresh fruit?"

"Only when I run out of Twinkies."

"When this is all over, you and I are going to have a long talk about nutrition."

"You want some tips on where to find the best selection of junk food? Always glad to help."

"I don't suppose you've got something to drink, too."

"I'm afraid not. Oh my. We can't survive out here for very long without water, can we?"

"Don't worry, this isn't the Mojave. There's water. It'll just take a little work to find some."

Jean promptly stopped worrying about water. Ansel Burke had that effect on her. She believed whatever he said. Ansel was not only the most capable man she had ever met; he was also the first to measure up to her father. She realized now that her life had been a search for just such a man.

The rising sun did nothing to lift the spirits of the three men in the jeep van. Their quarry was still out of sight even though they had been pushing their vehicle hard.

"We're almost out of gas," Arkolotti pointed out.

Briscoe kept his eyes on the Subaru's tire tracks. "They must be low on fuel, too, and there's no way they can get back to a highway now."

Harry Williamson said nothing, but his mood had become nasty. At first he thought Burke had made a mistake by not running for the highway when he had a chance. Now he understood Burke's strategy—suck them in and wear them down. Burke is making us play his game, Williamson thought.

"Hey! I just saw something up ahead." Arkolotti was straining to see through the dusty windshield. "Stop for a minute."

When Briscoe halted, Arkolotti jumped out and climbed up on the hood.

"I was right! That was the sun reflecting off their car. They're maybe three miles ahead on the upgrade."

Williamson felt relieved. There might be enough gasoline left to overtake them after all. "Keep your foot steady on the pedal, Joe. We can't afford to waste an ounce of gas."

"I know that," Briscoe snapped. "You just be ready with the MAC-10. Burke's only got a side arm, but he knows how to use it."

"I'm ready." Williamson recalled the incredible pain he'd suffered when Burke kicked him in the balls. Payback time, Ansel.

They had to stop again when the Subaru's right front wheel dropped precipitously through the surface into a prairie dog tunnel.

As Burke climbed out of the car he noticed a flash of light on the desert floor behind them. "If we go forward, we might sink deeper. There's a whole network of these damned tunnels. Jean, I want you to put it in reverse when I give the signal."

"I understand."

Burke put his left shoulder to the right front fender and braced himself as well as he could on the brittle ground. "Now!" He grunted as he pushed forward, all four of the Subaru's wheels spinning noisily. But instead of rolling back, the car dropped another few inches into the tunnel. "That's enough! Hold it!"

Twenty yards away, a prairie dog stuck his head up to see who was making such a mess of his carefully constructed passages.

"This isn't working," Burke said. "We've got to take a chance on going forward."

"Okay."

"How much gas do we have?"

"The needle's touching the red. That means we've got about a gallon left, maybe a little more."

Burke could now see a pall of dust behind them. Jean hadn't yet noticed it, which was just as well. "We'll try again. This time I'll be in the rear. As soon as the right front wheel comes free, veer to the left away from all those holes."

"Got it."

Burke tightened every sinew of muscle in his body as he braced himself against the rear of the Subaru. "Now!" He strained until his face reddened and his teeth clenched so tightly he could hardly breathe. The wheels spun and the Subaru's engine whined. Still he pushed, a terrible wail of pain rising from his throat, his leg and back muscles knotted, his feet clawing at the earth. The Subaru lurched ahead. Burke fell to his knees as Jean gunned the car forward and swung it to the left. One of the wheels fell into another tunnel, but bounced right out again.

When Jean was on firm ground she stopped and waited for Burke, who got up and ran for the car.

"Ansel, hurry up! I can see them behind us!"

He threw himself into the car as Jean accelerated, no longer caring how much the Subaru shook and rattled. In fact, the car was shaking itself to death. Jean was pushing it close to forty and still the vehicle behind them was gaining. For the moment Burke didn't care. Helping to free the Subaru had drained his strength and concentration.

There was a rattle of automatic fire as puffs of dust rose from the desert floor far behind them.

Burke roused himself. "They're testing the range. Sounds like a short-barreled weapon. A grease gun or

some other kind of submachine gun. That's good. They'll
have to get awfully close."

"They *are* close." For once Jean's fear showed in
her voice.

Burke checked his Browning. Five shots left in the
clip and another eleven-shot clip in his pocket. Not
much defense against three men with automatic weapons. He looked anxiously at the gas gauge and saw
that the needle had dropped well into the red.

"Hold her at forty if you can. I'll try to back them off
a little."

He used his foot to knock out what was left of the
rear window and lined up his sights on the jeep, giving
himself plenty of Kentucky windage. There was not
much chance of actually hitting the jeep, especially
with the Subaru bouncing and shaking so violently,
but at least he'd feel less helpless for a few moments.

Burke squeezed the trigger just twice. The Browning kicked like a mule and the smell of cordite stirred
his combative instincts. He was pleased to see the jeep
falter before coming on again. They weren't sure of
what to expect and the muzzle flash from the Browning had spooked them.

There was a wild spate of return fire from the jeep,
two automatic weapons opening up this time, just to
show they weren't intimidated. Burke now recognized
the distinctive slapping sound of the weapons. Ingram
MAC-10s—bad news. The MAC-10s would rip the
Subaru to pieces if the jeep closed to within seventy
yards.

"They're gaining!" Jean yelled.

"Keep your foot down." Burke looked ahead for a
place where they might make a stand, but the foothills
of the Sangre de Cristo mountains were still miles
away.

"Ansel, we can't outrun them. What shall we do?"

"I'll try to stop them. Just hold this thing as steady
as you can."

He braced his arms and aimed again at the jeep. It
now presented a much better target, having pulled to
within a hundred yards of them. The men in the jeep
fired again and this time one of their rounds thunked

into the chassis of the Subaru. Burke returned fire
with three spaced shots, emptying the Browning's clip.
None of the rounds seemed to do any damage to the
jeep, which was now almost close enough to put sustained fire into the Subaru.

As he reloaded, Burke's mouth was dry. He'd gambled and lost. Worse yet, he'd gambled away Jean's
life as well as his own. Still, he had eleven rounds left.
One round put into the jeep's radiator, or a tire, or
better yet into the driver, would stop them cold.

Before he could take aim, the jeep bucked and slowed,
bucked again, slowed even more, then gradually rolled
to a stop. Two men leaped from the jeep and knelt
with their weapons raised. The long bursts from their
MAC-10s fell uselessly short of the Subaru.

Burke heard himself laughing.

"What happened?" Jean called.

"We did it! We ran the bastards out of gas! Keep
going! Drive!"

"Ansel, we're almost out of gas ourselves."

"Every mile we put between us and them is gold."
He stuffed the Browning into his belt, yanked the rear
seat free of its bolts, opened the door, and tossed it out.
Then he started throwing every loose item he could
lay his hands on out the windows.

"What are you doing?"

"Getting rid of extra weight. Slow to twenty again.
The lighter and slower we travel, the longer our gas
will last. Head for those foothills. We might be able to
lose them up there."

"Yessir, Sergeant Major." Jean was amazed at her
own resilience. The cold knot of terror in her stomach
had virtually disappeared. For now.

Williamson stared morosely at the jeep, which sat
immobile on the flat desert floor. "Another quarter of
a gallon of gas and we'd have finished the job."

"No use thinking about it." Briscoe was unloading
the weapons, the extra ammo, two canteens of water,
and the packages of dehydrated food customarily carried in the jeep. "We've got a long walk ahead of us."

"And they've got themselves a big lead," Arkolotti observed.

"Maybe not." Williamson shook off his gloom. "Their car is about to fall apart. Did you see it shaking? And they can't have much gas left either."

Arkolotti was beginning to think Ansel Burke might be as tough as his reputation. "I hope Burke doesn't have any more surprises for us."

Briscoe, the ranking noncom now that Frank Craymore was dead, automatically had assumed command. As he distributed the guns and other gear in equal weights, the rapidly escalating temperature began matting his dark, curly hair with sweat. "Don't bunch up. I want ten-yard intervals between each man."

They checked the loads in their weapons and moved out at wide intervals in a modified skirmish line. So far Burke had been both smart and lucky. But soon he and the girl would be on foot, making them much more vulnerable. They had no doubts about their ability to catch up with Burke. Search-and-destroy was their business.

"We'll double-time for ten minutes, then walk for ten," Briscoe said.

The three men raised their weapons to port arms and broke into a trot with the disregard for heat and fatigue that stamped them as professionals.

SATURDAY, JUNE 14

Chapter 21

Hank Roper found the Pepper Tree coffee shop on the outskirts of Albuquerque and parked far away from all the other cars in the lot. This was just the kind of place he hated to leave his Porsche. The lot was full of old junkers and trucks. But Control had picked the meeting place and, under the circumstances, Roper couldn't very well object.

Only a few people were still lingering over Saturday morning breakfast. Control had chosen this place to avoid troopers from Fort Powell. Most of the patrons were truck drivers or residents of a nearby trailer park. The coffee smelled weak, the bacon and eggs on the grill reeked of grease, and the tables were only halfheartedly wiped clean.

Captain Dan Miller, dressed in slacks and a sport shirt, waved to Roper from a booth at the rear of the restaurant.

Roper worked his way through the maze of tables and slid in across from him. "Couldn't you think of a better place? Even the mess halls at Fort Powell are cleaner than this."

"The location is more important than the food. And besides—" Miller broke off as a waitress slouched up to the booth.

"What'll ya have?"

"Tea and toast," Miller said.

Roper ordered black coffee and scrambled eggs. "And tell your cook to lay off the grease," he added.

"Our chef is an outpatient from the psycho ward over at Albuquerque General Hospital," the waitress said. "Why don't *you* go tell him."

When she was out of earshot, Miller picked up his train of thought: "Besides that, I didn't pick this place. Someone else will be joining us. He chose the location."

Roper didn't like the sound of that. "You're my control. I don't want anybody else in on my business."

"You won't be compromised." Miller's eyes were leaden with anger. "This meeting wouldn't even be necessary if you'd done your job. Sergeant Major Burke is supposed to be *dead.*"

"Me? You're the one who said Burke was checkmated. The fucking FBI was supposed to put him in a box."

"Keep your voice down."

They fell into a cold mutual silence, the animosity hanging in the air between them like cigarette smoke. Roper considered Miller, with his country club manners and smooth edges, to be a lightweight. Like most of the CIA spooks Roper had met over the years, Miller needed lots of people and money and equipment to get a job done; he couldn't function on his own. For his part, Miller thought of Roper as a limited man who could do a few simple tasks well, just another in the long line of thugs he had run over the years. And now Roper had failed even at a simple physical task, the cancellation of Ansel Burke.

Roper finally spoke. "Who are we waiting for?"

"I'm not at liberty to say. He may decide to phone me here instead of putting in an appearance."

"Your boss?" Roper ventured.

"Yours too, Sergeant."

"I may not wait around."

"Fine. Go back to your dingy little cubicle at the N.C.O. Club. I'll call with your instructions when decisions have been made."

The waitress came with their coffee and food. As Roper had expected, the eggs were greasy and the coffee thin, but he was hungry. He'd had nothing to eat since yesterday afternoon, so he dug into the eggs, aware that Miller had scored a big one off him. To leave would be to put all further decisions about Ansel Burke in the hands of Miller and his mysterious superior.

They finished breakfast in belligerent silence and were lingering over coffee and tea when Brigadier General Claude Leland appeared.

"Gentlemen, may I join you?"

Roper's jaw fell as Leland slid into the booth next to Miller.

"General? Is this operation *yours?*"

"That's a reasonable deduction, Sergeant."

Leland too was dressed in civilian clothes. The attire of the three men made an interesting contrast in personal styles. Roper's civies were L.L. Bean, sturdy and serviceable. Miller dressed in color-coordinated sports clothes straight out of Macy's Young Executives department. General Leland, in cool denims and deck shoes, could have modeled for Abercrombie and Fitch.

The waitress grudgingly reappeared. "Y'want breakfast, too?"

"Absolutely not. Just bring me some water. In a clean glass—if you can find one."

"Well okay, you don't have to get on your goddamn high horse."

When she left, Leland chuckled. "There's a price to be paid for hiding among the masses." He quickly moved on to business. "Sergeant Roper, I'm here to find out just how badly we've botched the job on Burke. Relax, I'm not blaming you. We've all managed to underestimate the man. Our job now is to contain the damage. Tell me exactly what happened last night."

Roper pulled his thoughts together and began to recount the meeting he had held with his men at the gas station, stressing the subjects he'd been covering and the likelihood that Ansel Burke had heard everything and had seen the computer screen in the bungalow. He told them about the girl, Jean Silk, and how Ansel had come out of the darkness to kill Louie Sanchez and speed off with her. "I know we hit the car with a lot of rounds; we may have hit one or both of them too."

"But the car didn't slow down?" Leland probed. "It disappeared into the desert?"

"That's right, General."

"Don't use my rank in here." Leland looked around. He had chosen this place because it seemed safe from prying eyes and ears, but you couldn't be too careful. He kept silent as the waitress reappeared, set down a glass of cloudy water with a bang, and moved sullenly away. He moved the glass aside. "Have you heard anything from the men who went after them?"

"Not yet."

"Who did you send?"

"Craymore. Arkolotti. Briscoe. Williamson."

"How were they armed?"

"MAC-10s and a laser-equipped Ruger."

"The jeeps were equipped for desert travel?"

"Yes, sir."

All in all, the prospects for damage control were better than Leland had expected. "Those particular men should be able to do the job, despite Sergeant Burke's rather impressive talents. He's inadequately armed, compared with the MAC-10s and Ruger. His transportation is unreliable. And the girl will be a drain on him. I'd guess that right now Burke is taking some rather clever evasive action out on the desert, but his options are bound to run out."

"That's the way I see it," Miller agreed.

"Me too," Roper chimed in.

Leland raised a snow white eyebrow. "Have either of you bothered to look at Burke's service record?"

Roper and Miller shook their heads.

"If you had done that basic piece of intelligence work, you would have seen that a few years ago Ansel Burke graduated from the Desert Warfare School at Fort Huachuca—with commendations. He'll use that training to give your men a few surprises. By my estimate he has a one-in-ten chance of survival."

"One in ten is a little strong," Miller suggested. "Sounds to me more like one chance in fifty."

General Leland shared Roper's low opinion of Miller. The CIA man filled a necessary function as a conduit for passing orders and information to Roper and controlling the administrative aspects of the F.D.N.W. project, but he wasn't *army*. Miller just didn't understand how resourceful a soldier like Ansel Burke could be. "Even one in fifty would be too many, but I think the situation is more serious than that."

"Then we need a backup position in case Burke comes out alive," Miller said.

"Exactly." Leland had already developed a plan. "We must discredit him, whether he survives or not. Blacken Burke's name so thoroughly that nothing he could say, or has said, will be believed."

"How the hell are you gonna do that?" Roper asked.

"I'm not going to do it," Leland said. "You are."

He's got a job for me, Roper thought. And he didn't think I'd go along if Miller pitched it. That's why he's come out in the open with me. But why would a brigadier general get involved in a deal like this in the first place? Roper remembered hearing that Leland had bought back his family home, a run-down mansion somewhere in the Southeast, and was having the place rebuilt. So money could be the reason.

Yeah, that's it, Roper decided. Money makes his world go around, just like it does mine. "What sort of plan do you have in mind, sir?"

"A simple one." General Leland sat forward. "Listen closely. This is what I want you to do . . ."

After another seventeen miles, the Subaru ran out of gas and came to a final, jerking halt with what sounded to Jean like a groan of relief. They climbed out and studied the crippled auto.

"I wish we'd gotten fifteen more miles out of her," Burke said.

Jean had other regrets. "I wish she was paid for. I still owe almost five thousand dollars on that car—and look at it!"

"You'll have a tough time getting an insurance adjuster to come all the way out here."

She kicked a tire in frustration. "In New York I always used the subway. This was my first car and I really loved it."

"I'm sorry." He saw that Jean was really depressed,

and not just about the car. While they had been on the
move, escape had seemed possible, perhaps even prob-
able. Now they were stranded in the middle of nowhere with Hank's men certainly pursuing them on
foot. Under those circumstances she had a right to a
few moments of depression. But no more than that.
"Grab your Twinkies. We've got a long walk ahead of
us."

Jean straightened her shoulders and smoothed her
hair. "Where to?"

"Up there." Burke jerked his head at the foothills of
the Sangre de Cristos. "They'll have a harder time
following us in those hills."

"Can we lose them?"

"I doubt it. Arnie Arkolotti was a Ranger Scout.
He's probably a pretty good tracker."

"Great." She yanked open the Subaru door and
scrounged for her box of Twinkies while Burke went
through the trunk looking for anything that might be
of help to them. The only things he took were a screwdriver, a roll of friction tape, and a New York Mets
T-shirt. He pocketed the roll of tape, stuck the screwdriver in his belt, and began tearing the shirt into two
equal parts.

"Hey, don't!" Jean complained. "I bought that at
Shea Stadium."

"We need protection from the sun. Here, put this on
your head."

Jean skeptically examined the scrap of cloth he gave
her, then arranged it into a makeshift scarf which she
put on and tied under her chin. "How do I look?"

"Better than I will." Burke did the same with his
half of the shirt.

Jean couldn't help giggling. "No, I'm sorry, I didn't
mean that. You look *charming*."

"Come on, let's move out."

They started walking. Ten minutes later, when Burke
thought she was ready for it, he said: "We can't just
walk. We'll have to double-time."

"In this heat?"

"Double-timing isn't running."

"I don't know if I can. I'm not very athletic."

"Just until we reach the foothills."

"Ansel, I'm so *tired.*"

"The men behind us are moving fast, I can guarantee you that."

"Oh, all right." She stuffed the box of Twinkies under her arm and fell into step with Burke, who had begun to double-time.

The sky was a shade of blue that Burke wished he could match on a palette. Only here, on the desert, had he ever come across that particular blue, which seemed to be solely a morning color. By afternoon a cool white would overlay the red tones, altering the entire character of the landscape. He wondered if he would live to put those colors on canvas. Death was an inevitability he could deal with. Dying without finishing his work was harder to accept.

Jean, panting along at his side, said between gasps of breath: "Uh, Ansel . . . about the water you said was out here . . . I could sure use some."

"So could I. We won't find any until we reach higher ground."

She groaned and shifted the box to under her other arm. "I can't believe it . . . For the first time in my life . . . I don't want a Twinkie."

"Good girl."

"I just want to lie down . . . and try to breathe . . . like a normal person."

Burke looked at his watch. They had been double-timing for almost an hour. "Let's take a break."

They stopped and Jean threw herself on the ground. She lay fighting for breath, the sweat rolling from her body in rivers.

"My Aunt Florence—" She gasped. "Used to say . . . 'Men sweat. Women perspire.' She was . . . as usual . . . wrong."

"Don't talk. Rest."

He lay down next to her, shielding his eyes from the sun with a forearm. They would have to find water soon. You couldn't sweat for long in this climate without coming down with heatstroke. Fortunately the foothills were now only a mile or so ahead. The ground would begin to rise and they could walk instead of having to double-time because Hank's men would have to do the same. Burke estimated they were only an hour or two ahead of their trackers. If he were alone he could move fast enough to outdistance them. With Jean along, he would have to find a place to set a trap.

Slowly he climbed to his feet. "Come on, time to move again."

"We just stopped!"

"You've had a ten-minute rest. That's plenty."

Groaning, she struggled up. "Now I know why so many soldiers hate their sergeants."

"This is nothing." Burke grinned. "Usually I make a trooper who gets up so slowly carry heavy rocks in his backpack."

"You're a sadist."

"I hear that a lot." He gave her a gentle nudge. "We're almost to the hills. You only have to double-time for another fifteen minutes."

"Thank you, O Mighty One."

He took the box from under her arm.

"I can carry that," she protested. "It hardly weighs anything at all."

"I've got it." He was afraid he had driven her too hard. As she fell in next to him, her face was devoid of color and her leg muscles were trembling. "We'll walk instead of double-timing."

"No, I'm all right." Jean broke into a ragged trot.

Burke stayed shoulder to shoulder with her, afraid she might stumble. The heat was now so intense that it seared his lungs. Without the makeshift hats both of them would have been felled by the sun by now. Without water they soon would be unable to stay on their feet.

When they reached an upgrade, they stopped double-timing and began to walk. Soon Burke saw a flash of color and guided Jean in that direction. "We'll have something to drink in just a minute."

As they approached a rocky section of the hillside, Jean said through parched lips, "Oh, those flowers are beautiful. What are they?"

"Yucca plants." Burke helped Jean to sit down next to a large rock, sheltering her from the sun in its shade. "Now you can have a real rest. You've earned it. Just stay put while I get you something to eat and drink."

He used the screwdriver taken from the Subaru to chop away at the roots of a yucca plant. Its yellow flower trembled as Burke systematically dug a trench around the plant, then yanked it loose by the roots. He carried the plant to Jean like a trophy. "Here you are."

"Thanks. What am I supposed to do with it?"

"Chew the roots. There's lots of moisture in there." He tore off a piece and popped it into his mouth.

Jean followed his example. At first she chewed tentatively on the stringy brown stem. Then, with a smile spreading across her face, she set her teeth into it with more enthusiasm. "Not bad. But what's that funny taste? It's so familiar."

"Soap. The Indians used to grind up the roots of yucca plants and use the pulp for soap."

"That's it! When I used bad language, my father washed out my mouth with soap. It tasted just like this. I never thought I'd *like* it."

There were big seedpods in the plant, which Burke also told Jean to eat. The pods tasted less soapy and held almost as much moisture. When they had stripped the plant of all its nourishment, Burke dug up two more yuccas and they devoured the edible parts of those with equal enthusiasm. They also ate a few of the Twinkies, which had dried out so much in the heat that they tasted worse than the yucca roots.

The combination of nourishment and a long rest in the shade brought some color back to Jean's face, though she was still exhausted. It had been almost twenty-six hours since she last slept.

"Lie back in the shade and take a nap," Burke urged.

"We can't. They're coming for us."

She struggled to rise, but Burke held her back. "Sleep for an hour. Then you'll be able to travel again."

"I'm holding you back. They'll catch us because I'm not as strong as you are."

"Don't be silly. I need rest as much as you do."

"No you don't." She looked at him in wonder. "You could go for days without rest. I'll bet you've done it a hundred times."

"Not that often."

"I love you, Ansel."

"Hush up and close your eyes."

Jean put her head on his shoulder and within a minute was asleep and breathing sonorously.

While he watched the desert floor, Burke picked up a stone and began to sharpen the screwdriver. He moved the tip of the tool in tight circles against the hard stone. It was not much of a weapon, but every advantage counted out here.

Burke's thoughts were confused. Jean had said she loved him and the sleepy declaration had filled him with joy. He felt guilty for wanting Jean and for deliberately pushing Maggie to the back of his mind. Was that just because they had shared so much in the past twelve hours? Would he feel the same when—if—they got back to Fort Powell? His heart told him that Jean was in his blood to stay. His conscience reminded him that he had a responsibility to Maggie.

He shifted his thoughts back to the problem at hand. Stopping to let Jean rest had been an absolute necessity even though it cut their lead to about two hours. How should he play it from here? Go up as high as possible and hope to lose them? He wasn't sure Jean could last through the climb. She was strong and very game, but missing a night's sleep would take a heavy toll on her as the day wore on. A one-hour nap couldn't make up for all the fatigue and tension she must be feeling.

An ambush seemed the best way to deal with the three men. Their silhouettes against the white sand in the arroyo came back to him in vivid detail. Arkolotti, small and compact, had reflexes like a mongoose. Williamson was big and heavy, but he moved with the force of an eighteen-wheel semi. Among the three of them Briscoe would be the leader and he was absolutely without fear or pity.

Burke looked at Jean and imagined her in their hands. They'd use her and then kill her without a qualm. I can't let that happen, he thought. I've got to outsmart them. His eyes burned and his shoulders still ached from the effort of pushing the Subaru out of that damned prairie dog hole.

When the hour he had promised Jean was up, Burke rocked her gently into an awakening. "Jean. Time to move on."

Yawning and muttering, she allowed herself to be pulled upright. "Oh God, I'm so tired."

"We've got to climb."

"Climb?" She shook herself and tried to adjust to the brightness of the sun. "Okay, I'm ready."

"Stay right behind me," Burke said. "Hold onto my belt if you want. I'll pick the easiest ground I can find."

"Don't worry about me."

They began climbing higher into the foothills of the Sangre de Cristos.

Briscoe was first to spot the Subaru, and let out a whoop. "There it is! They didn't get many more miles out of her."

Five minutes later they stood around the wreck of the automobile, searching for clues to the condition of its passengers.

"I count ten hits," Arkolotti said.

"A little blood up front," Williamson observed. "Not much. I think Louie cut Burke's arm back at the gas station."

"So we have to assume they're all right physically." Briscoe was disappointed. He'd hoped that Burke or the girl had been hit. "And they're two hours ahead of us."

Williamson stuck his head into the car. "There's an empty clip on the floor. I'll bet he wasn't carrying more than two extras."

"That's the only good news I've heard today." Even though Arkolotti's mouth was parched, he wasn't going to be the first to drink from the canteen. He looked at the foothills ahead and experienced a sinking sensation. Burke would know how to use that terrain to his best advantage. He'll kill at least one of us, Arkolotti thought.

He wasn't the only one to recognize the danger. "We'll move more slowly when we reach the hills," Briscoe said. "Let's take some water now so we'll be in good shape later."

A canteen was passed around. Each man drank a measured portion, put down the canteen, drank again, and then spilled a little water on his head. They checked their weapons and moved out with the strong feeling that very soon now Ansel Burke would stop running and turn to fight.

Chapter 22

Shortly before noon Hank Roper visited the Winston Gallery in Puma. Although it was Saturday, the front door to the gallery was locked and a CLOSED sign had been taped to the glass. Roper knocked on the door and rattled the knob, but no one came forward from within the establishment.

He looked up Maggie Winston's home address and drove there in a rather shabby Ford station wagon he had "borrowed" from the PX parking lot. Some officer's wife was no doubt at MP headquarters right now filling out a stolen vehicle report and trying to explain why she'd left the keys in the ignition. Roper didn't plan to keep the car for long. He needed it only for the visit to Maggie. If things went wrong with her, he wanted to be able to abandon the car.

Maggie's condo was in a stylish part of town. Roper parked down the block and waited until the street was clear before he walked quickly into the complex, located her unit, and went up the private stairway to the door. Dressed in civies and carrying a small canvas satchel, the type known in the army as an "A.W.O.L bag," he pressed the doorbell and waited.

"Who is it?" Maggie called.

Roper had no intention of giving his name. Anyone passing by might hear it. "It's me," he answered, hoping she'd recognize his voice.

"Oh . . . just a minute."

Presently the door opened and Maggie stood before

him in slacks and a V-necked blouse. She was barefoot and holding a glass half-filled with whiskey and ice. Her manner, an aggressive stance combined with a petulant frown, was unfriendly. She swayed slightly. "What the hell do you want? I hope you're not looking for Ansel, because I don't know where he is."

"No, I'm here to see you. And I do know where he is."

"Oh?" One eyebrow arched. "I suppose he's with that red-haired bitch and you've come to gloat about it."

"I wouldn't do that to you."

"The hell you wouldn't."

Roper inched forward. "May I come in?"

"Sure, why not?" She turned and walked away, leaving the door ajar.

Roper slipped inside and followed her into the living room, where he made a leisurely turn. "Very nice. Do you own this place or rent it?"

"I have a lease, which, like the rest of my life, seems to be running out."

"You're in a gloomy mood."

"Why, Sergeant Roper, no wonder you're in a leadership position. You're so *quick*."

"Can I have a drink, too?"

Maggie waved at the bar. "Drunk up—I mean, drink up. Then get out. I've had enough of the army to last me a lifetime."

Roper put down his canvas bag and fixed himself a light scotch and water. He wrapped a napkin around the glass to avoid leaving fingerprints. If Maggie wouldn't listen to reason, it would be simple enough to smash her head open on the fireplace hearth. With a high concentration of alcohol in her blood, everyone would assume she took a fatal fall. Wasn't that how the movie star Bill Holden died? Sure. Those kinds of accidents happened all the time. He hoped it wouldn't come to that. As General Leland had pointed out, Maggie could be very useful right now.

Maggie sprawled in a chair, one leg thrown over the arm. "You know where Ansel is?"

"Yep." He came around the bar and sat down opposite her. "And you're right, Jean Silk is with him."

She flinched as if he'd slapped her face. "Son of a bitch . . . doesn't know a good thing when he's got it."

"I agree."

"Jean Silk." She put a coat of venom on the name. "I knew she was . . . was trouble . . . minute I saw her."

"She's cute," Roper agreed. "But she doesn't have what you've got."

"Damn right." Maggie preened herself with a husky sigh, then gradually slid back into her depression. "Where are they? Some fleabag motel?"

"No, they're way out in the desert. No motels. No restaurants. Nothing." Roper finished his drink and carried the glass into Maggie's kitchen. He washed the glass, found a pot of cold coffee on the stove, and put it on to heat.

"What're you doing in my kitchen?"

"Making you some coffee."

"Get outta there!"

As he came back into the living room, Maggie was struggling to rise from the depths of the chair. He pushed her gently back down.

"Hey! Who the hell do you think you are?"

"Shut up and listen. You and me have some business to discuss."

"Business? What kind of business could I have with *you?*"

Roper picked up his A.W.O.L. bag and opened it. "This kind." He showed her the contents—packets of fifties and twenties, held together with rubber bands. "One hundred thousand dollars, Maggie. And it's all yours, if you'll do one little favor for me."

Maggie shook her head. No, she wasn't *that* drunk. The bag Hank Roper held out was stuffed with money. *Stuffed.* "How much did you say?"

"One hundred thousand dollars. Tax free and untraceable. All for you."

The sight of so much cash transfixed her.

"Put your drink down, Maggie. I want you to understand what I'm gonna tell you."

He zipped the bag shut and dragged a chair up close to her, effectively blocking her movements. Maggie didn't know whether that was intentional, but she sensed danger here. The bag of money, Hank's intensity, the click she now recognized as her door lock snapping into place—all dangerous. Her survival instincts were on full alarm. I must keep a clear head, she thought. "Go on."

"Ansel and his new girlfriend have made enemies. Powerful people. He's into something that's none of his business—never mind what it is—and they've decided he's got to go. Permanently. The girl too."

"I don't understand. On the desert?" Maggie was taking deep breaths, desperately trying to focus her mind.

"That's right. Between you and me, I think Ansel and Jean Silk are already dead." He watched Maggie's reaction and was pleased to see that she didn't try to draw away from him. "But Ansel's a tough guy. He might get away from my friends and make it back to Fort Powell. Stranger things have happened." He shrugged. "Doesn't matter. One way or another, he's finished. My friends just want to make sure no one believes anything he might have said in the last few days, or what he might say if he comes back."

Maggie made an intuitive leap. "And that's what you want me to do? Help you make sure no one believes him?"

"Right." Roper sat back a bit, giving her some room to move. A gesture of trust between potential allies. "You've lost Ansel anyway; you know that. I'm offering you a chance to get even with the bastard for dumping you, and make yourself some big money besides."

One hundred thousand dollars. That would finance my return to New York very comfortably, Maggie thought. And I'd still have Ansel's paintings. Even if he's alive, he couldn't take them back. He's got a contract with me. Those paintings are under my control until they're sold. If Ansel really is dead—and I can't quite believe that yet—I'll be in an even better position. They'll be worth a fortune! And I'll have power of attorney over *all* the money they'll bring in.

She cleared her throat. "Exactly what do you want from me?"

"Are you sober enough to listen?"

"When I talk business, I'm *always* sober."

Roper noted that the slur in her speech had disappeared. "Okay, then." He opened the bag again and took from under the stacks of currency a brown manila envelope with a Department of Defense mailing frank in the upper left-hand corner. "I want you to take this envelope to the FBI office in Albuquerque. Ask for the agent in charge—his name is Devereaux. Tell him you're a friend of Ansel Burke's and that over the past few months Ansel has been leaving envelopes like this one with you for safekeeping. You finally got curious." He dropped the envelope in her lap. "Go ahead, open it."

As she did so, Maggie was aware that she now had gone too far to back out. She was playing Hank Roper's game, and playing it for keeps. What she found was a sheaf of papers about an inch thick. Technical drawings and diagrams of some kind of weapon, she thought.

Two words were stamped across the top of each page: Top Secret.

"Where did these come from?"

"I don't know and I don't care. They were given to me by another friend."

"You have a great many friends."

"Don't ever forget that." Roper was smiling, but his warning was explicit. "I only know this is high-level stuff. The FBI will jump all over it—and you. All you have to tell the Feds is that the words *Top Secret* scared you and so you came straight to them."

"Will the FBI believe Ansel is—what?—stealing and selling secrets? I mean, Ansel has all those decorations. He's a genuine hero."

"The FBI is conditioned to believe the worst about people. Besides, Al Devereaux hates Ansel's guts. He'll go after Ansel out of pure spite."

Maggie didn't care what they believed about Ansel. She was concerned for herself. "If I bring in these documents, they'll think I'm involved, too."

"No way. I told you Ansel has powerful enemies. Some of them are very high up. Just tell the FBI a simple story—the less the better—and they'll let you walk. My friends will see to that."

A new angle occurred to Maggie. "Will this get into the newspapers?"

"Sure, it's bound to—newspapers, television, the whole media circus. That's the objective—to drag Ansel's name through the mud. Make him look like a fucking traitor." Roper moved close to her again. Maggie hadn't yet said she'd go through with it. If she tried to back out . . .

"That's very convenient. The dealer who's putting on Ansel's show in New York has been looking for a publicity hook. He even threatened to cancel the show if I couldn't find one."

Roper allowed himself to relax.

"This is exactly what he's looking for." Maggie was aglow with excitement. "A few years ago an art dealer in London discovered some serigraph drawings by Benedict Arnold. They sold for a fortune and they weren't even any good. *Everyone* will want to bid for Ansel's paintings. I can see the headlines: 'PAINTINGS BY ARMY SPY ON DISPLAY AT HILLARY HOUSE.' This couldn't have happened at a better time."

What a coldhearted bitch, Roper thought. No wonder I like her.

"When do you want me to go to the FBI?"

"The sooner the better. First let's make sure you know what to say."

Roper went for the coffee. They settled down over their cups to rehearse the words Maggie would use with Devereaux and the answers she would give to their questions. Maggie was a quick study. Like all practiced liars, she could fake any emotion and knew how to stutter out answers in a slightly confused, very believable way.

After an hour Maggie began glancing at the A.W.O.L. bag. "Can I have the money now?"

Roper pushed it across the floor with his toe. "Help yourself."

Maggie dug her fingers into the cash the way a farmer turns over virgin soil. "This is beautiful . . . just beautiful."

"Do the job right and there might be a bonus."

"I'll hold you to that."

"I know you will." Roper took hold of her arm. "Come on, let's go in the bedroom."

"I wondered when you'd get around to that." Maggie rose and slipped an arm around his waist. "How do you feel about showers?"

Chapter 23

They climbed steadily up through the foothills for half a day. In the higher elevations they encountered occasional clumps of piñon and juniper. The only respite from the sun came during short periods in which they passed through narrow rock canyons that created crevices of shade. Several times under the steady glare of the sun Jean's vision blurred and she felt faint, but she said nothing to Burke. She refused to cause any delays.

Each hour Burke halted for a ten-minute rest. During those precious minutes Jean threw herself down on the ground and lapsed into a fitful nap until awakened by Burke's hand.

Burke saw how desperately Jean was struggling to keep up and admired her courage. But even courage has a limit. Jean would soon reach hers. He would have to turn and fight while Jean still had the strength to help him. His plan was to find ground that would give them some advantage over their trackers.

"Here, chew on this." He slipped another piece of yucca root into Jean's hand.

"Ugh. I never want to *see* another yucca, much less *taste* one." Knowing it was important to replenish some of the fluids she'd lost, Jean slipped the root stub into her mouth.

"Come on—give me your arm."

"I can walk on my own," she bristled, although she was tottering like an old lady.

Burke ignored Jean's protest and helped her up a particularly steep rise. Time to stop. The rocky hills lacked the best features for an ambush, but he decided to make his stand here anyway.

"Do you think we've lost them?" she asked.

"No, they're probably less than an hour behind." He looked at the sun and knew they'd be overtaken before dark. "We'll stop here."

"Stop? Why?"

"To set a trap."

"Ansel, there are *three* of them. And they've got automatic weapons."

"They're going to find us before nightfall anyway. I'd rather choose the ground myself." He cast his eyes around. "This place has possibilities."

All Jean could see was another plateau in what seemed to be an endless succession of hills. The walls of the hills were steep rock slabs and the plateau was barren. She felt exposed. It seemed an unlikely place to set a trap, but Ansel was looking over the edge with a smile.

"I can make this work for us."

"Make what work?"

He pointed down into the narrow cut they had used to climb up to this plateau. "They'll have to come through there just like we did."

"Ansel—" Jean's voice was choked.

Burke followed her eyes. Down below, three small shapes were moving implacably across a hillside. They were moving swiftly at intervals of at least ten yards. Standard infantry tactic. He had expected that. In this terrain their caution might be turned against them.

"Okay," he said. "The decision's been made for us. We'll have to take them right here."

"Tell me the truth. Do we really have a chance? I have to know."

"We've got a chance. Remember, I know exactly how they think and what they'll do in a given situation."

Jean's spirits lifted. "How can I help?"

"Gather up as many good-sized rocks as you can." He pointed to a hefty stone lying nearby. "Big ones like that. Nothing smaller than a softball. We'll need

at least thirty. Stack half of them here"—he indicated
a spot on the edge of the plateau—"and the rest
farther down, about there."

"All right."

"While you're doing that, I'm going down below. I'll
be back in about ten minutes."

"How soon will they be here?"

"Fifty minutes to an hour." Burke patted her shoulder. "Don't worry, we'll be ready." Jean was wearing a
silver and turquoise bracelet that caught his eye. "Can
I borrow that?"

"Of course." Jean didn't know what to make of the
request. A memento? A talisman? Baffled, she slipped
off the bracelet and handed it over.

"With a little luck, you'll get this back." He put it
into his pocket and hurried away.

Burke climbed back down to the narrow cut below
the plateau. He paced off the length of the cut. About
sixty yards. If they stayed at ten-yard intervals, they'd
all be in the cut at the same time. Arkolotti will take
the lead, Burke decided, because he's their best tracker.
Briscoe will be the center man, he'll want to pull rank
over Harry Williamson. Harry will cover their rear.

He looked up at the plateau where Jean was busily
gathering rocks. Her movements couldn't be heard,
which was a blessing. Small sounds often traveled for
long distances in these rocky hills and canyons.

There was a chance they'd be extremely cautious
and send only one man at a time through the cut.
That's what he would do. But they know they're close,
he thought. They'll be in a hurry.

To make sure they did what he wanted, Burke
stopped at the opening to the cut and dropped Jean's
bracelet on the ground. Then he kicked a little sand
over the bracelet so it wouldn't look so much like a
piece of bait. They'll find it and come up through the
cut at double time, he told himself, rehearsing the
scenario as he wanted them to play it out.

It had better work that way, or Jean and I will both
be dead within the hour.

With that grim possibility haunting him, Burke
retraced his steps and climbed back up to the plateau.

He found Jean sweating and shaking as she built her piles of rocks with the dedication of a squirrel storing up food for winter. "Is this enough?"

"Plenty." Burke surveyed the two piles of rocks. "Let's sit down and rest."

They squatted Indian-style in the shade of a water-melon-shaped boulder while Burke outlined his plan.

"They'll have to come up that little cut down there to follow us. When all three of them are below you, I'll whistle like this." He put two fingers in his mouth and let go with a shrill blast.

"But *they'll* hear your signal, too," Jean pointed out.

"That's what I want. They'll hit the dirt because that's what they've been trained to do. On my second signal, which will be this one"—he whistled twice this time—"I want you to start throwing that first pile of rocks over the side. Don't be fancy about it. Just push them over. And for God's sake don't lean out to see where they land. They're carrying MAC-10s. One round would take your head right off your shoulders."

"I understand. But what if the rocks don't hit them?"

"They probably won't hit anybody. All I want is to make them get up and scramble out of the way. I'm hoping they'll be too busy dodging rocks to use their weapons. Meanwhile I'll be able to get off a few shots at a decent handgun range."

"What about the second pile?"

"They'll try to pull back. I'll whistle *three* times and you push the second load of rocks over the side. If we can make them scramble twice, I'll have a chance to nail all three."

Jean hoped she could do her job correctly. Despite the importance of the plan, her mind was partly on something else. "Why did you take my bracelet?"

"Bait. I dropped it near the entrance to the cut, hoping it'll draw them in faster."

"Oh. I thought— Never mind."

"What did you think?"

"That you wanted to have something of mine to carry." Jean realized she was blushing. "There must have been some locoweed mixed in with the last piece of yucca root."

"I'm sorry I disappointed you."

"You never disappoint me. But you do surprise the hell out of me quite often."

Burke looked at his watch. It was time to put himself in position. "A while ago you said, 'I love you.'"

"You don't have to—"

"I feel the same way. I've wanted to tell you that. The problem is that Maggie's made a real commitment to me."

"I've always had a lousy sense of timing," she said weakly.

He took the screwdriver out of his pocket and thrust it into her hand. "Take this. It's not much, and I hope you won't need to use it."

"So do I." The point of the screwdriver was sharpened to a fine edge. She tucked it in her belt and attempted a smile. "Good luck."

Burke went down the trail into the cut. He moved cautiously along the rock wall to the end of the canyon, crawling the last ten yards on his belly. He saw the three troopers coming up the hillside. Because the terrain was ready-made for an ambush, they moved in a skirmish line with their MAC-10s held at the ready. The sight of them caused Burke's confidence to drop. Look at them, he thought. They've walked almost as far as we have and they still look fresh.

He rolled backward, jumped to his feet and ran to the opposite end of the cut, where a rock shelf protruded from the ground by about two feet. After stretching out behind it, he checked the loads in the Browning and settled down to wait.

"Hold it!" Briscoe called. "Form up over here."

Arkolotti and Williamson jogged over to Briscoe and dropped to one knee. They were sweating profusely. Williamson, in particular, was feeling the heat.

"Look what I found." Briscoe showed them a silver and turquoise bracelet.

"That's just too damned convenient to suit me," Williamson declared. "It's a trap. Burke's trying to suck us into that ravine."

"Gimme the canteen." Arkolotti took it and allowed

himself three swallows. "What do you want us to do, Harry? Flank him?"

"Why not?"

"If he's not in there, if he and the girl are still on the move, we'd lose *hours*," Briscoe said. "We might even lose *them*."

"He's in there," Williamson promised. "One of us could cover this entrance while the other two separate and flank him from both sides."

"We don't have time." Briscoe picked up their remaining canteen and shook it. "Only two quarts of water left. That's not much for three of us in this heat."

"If we go into Burke's trap, there'll be plenty of water. Because there won't be three of us anymore."

"Bullshit." Briscoe had tired of Williamson's repeated warnings. Burke was good—not superhuman. "Even in close quarters Burke is no match for these." He patted his MAC-10. "I say we go through the ravine fast. Arnie'll cover the front door. I'll watch the roof. Harry, you keep the back door closed."

Arkolotti didn't want to go into the ravine, but neither did he relish trying to outflank Burke without support. "Harry, I'm with Joe. If we separate, he could pick us off one by one. I say keep the MAC-10s together. We've got too much firepower for him."

Briscoe turned to Williamson. "Are you ready, Harry?"

After eighteen years in the army, Williamson was accustomed to taking orders he disagreed with. "Okay, let's get it done."

Burke heard them coming at a trot. He didn't dare put up his head. His signal to Jean would have to be based on instinct.

The footsteps pounded ahead, drawing closer by the second. He wanted to draw them all the way in without letting them overrun his position. Finally, when the first set of footsteps seemed almost upon him, he put two fingers in his mouth and whistled loudly.

The sound echoed off the rock walls and down the canyon.

"Drop!" Briscoe yelled.

He heard the three troopers dive into the dirt and pictured them covering the cliffs and ravine with their MAC-10s.

He whistled again. Twice. For a few agonizing moments nothing happened. He feared Jean hadn't understood his instructions. Then he heard a rock crash to the floor of the ravine and the clatter of other hunks of rock bouncing off the canyon walls.

"Pull back!"

Briscoe's voice again.

Burke rose up from behind the ledge to find Arkolotti not fifteen yards away. He fired at the moving target and missed the wiry little trooper by inches, decimating a portion of the rock wall behind him.

Arkolotti, backing away while at the same time trying to watch for falling rocks, returned fire with a long burst from his MAC-10. It went wild, stitching a pattern on the wall to Burke's left.

Burke's second shot was on target. It hit Arkolotti low, just above the groin, punching a hole as big as a fist through his abdomen. Arkolotti screamed and dropped to his knees as if in prayer. Then he toppled over, gripping the wound.

Behind Arkolotti, the other two rose up out of the swirling dust of the rockfall. Briscoe, thirty yards down the cut, was firing up at the spot from which Jean had launched her salvo. Williamson rushed to his side and began firing short, timed bursts.

Burke threw himself behind the protection of the rock shelf as rounds from Williamson's MAC-10 thudded into the barrier. The chatter of the two automatic weapons was magnified a hundred times in the narrow canyon, almost shattering his eardrums.

The three shrill whistles from Burke were lost in the din. Jean didn't have a chance of hearing them. As they fired, Briscoe and Williamson were also moving forward. Burke stuck up his head and risked a snap shot, but fell flat again as a dozen rounds crackled past his ears.

His stupidity angered him. He should have realized his signals would go unheard when the shooting started.

But there was a heavy thunk as another rock hit the canyon floor.

Briscoe yelled something, and for precious seconds the firing halted.

More rocks rained down. Burke saw Briscoe rush forward to avoid them. Their eyes locked and Briscoe ran at him, firing the MAC-10 from the hip.

Burke fired twice, holding his right wrist with his left hand, and scored with both shots. The first pierced Briscoe's cheek, snapping his head back. The second went through his throat. Briscoe's weapon flew into the air. He staggered like a reeling drunk and fell facedown.

Williamson had disappeared. Burke dove to snatch up Arkolotti's weapon. As he raised it, a hail of fire from inside the dust cloud swept over him. He was hit in the chest as if struck by a train. For uncounted seconds he lay clawing at the ground, desperately trying to fill his lungs with air. He began to realize that he wasn't wounded. One of Williamson's rounds had struck the MAC-10, which he'd been holding at chest level, destroying the weapon and knocking him off his feet.

Cursing, he tried to rise, but his arms and legs were useless. Every muscle in his body throbbed from the blow to his chest.

"Tough luck, Ansel." Williamson ambled out of the dust. He bent, still watching Burke, to pick up the Browning automatic and stuff it in his belt. "I warned Joe and Arnie you were trying to draw us in, but they wouldn't listen." He glanced at Arkolotti, curled in a ball with blood streaming from his midsection, and at Briscoe, whose face was no longer identifiable. "I guess things worked out okay anyhow."

"Almost," Burke managed to say.

"Almost don't count, except in horseshoes." Williamson raised the MAC-10. "So long, Ansel. You should never have kicked me in the balls."

Burke looked into the gun barrel, knowing he'd been working toward this moment all of his life. His biggest regret was that he hadn't done a better job of protecting Jean. The prospect of certain death wasn't as frightening as he'd expected. What really shocked him was

Harry Williamson's grin, which had lost its mirth.
Williamson's mouth had gone slack and his eyes had
taken on an unnatural sheen. Bright red bubbles appeared in the corners of his mouth and his huge bulk
began to deflate like a collapsing balloon.

As Williamson toppled forward, Burke rolled away
and struggled to a sitting position. Jean stood there,
both hands pressed to her mouth, staring at Williamson's prone form.

"Ansel . . . I killed him. I actually killed a man."
She closed her eyes to the sight of Williamson, especially the spot on his back where she had driven in the
shaft of the screwdriver all the way to the handle.

"You sure did." He took a long time to climb to his
feet.

"Hold me."

Burke wrapped her in his arms and walked her
away from the corpse.

"I'm so ashamed. I feel I've gone against everything
I believe in, everything my father taught me."

"I think he'd understand."

"Would he?"

"Your father wouldn't have wanted Harry Williamson to put his hands on you—to do the kinds of things
Harry liked to do with girls—and then kill you when
he was finished. In these same circumstances I think
he'd have done pretty much what you did."

Jean was crying. He sat her down with her back
against the rock wall and told her to breathe in and
out slowly. When she had calmed down, he left her
side and began to forage for supplies.

First he picked up the canteen Briscoe had been
carrying and shook it. Good news. It was half-full.
Then he went through the pockets of each of the three
men, looking for anything that might be of help to
them. He took Arkolotti's pocket knife, Briscoe's compass, and Williamson's matches. They had been carrying a rucksack containing several packets of high-
protein tablets, granola bars, spare clips of ammo, two
flashlights, a first aid kit and a flare pistol. He kept
everything except the flare pistol.

Finally he went from man to man, looking at the bottom of their boots.

"Do you want their shoes too?" Jean was glaring at him. "Why don't you take their socks and loose change while you're at it!"

"We need food and water and anything else that will help us. I was checking the soles of their boots because Betsy Palermo's killer left a distinctive footprint." He looked at Williamson. "If it makes you feel any better, Harry Williamson killed Betsy. The sole of his boot matches the boot cast in my desk drawer at Powell."

She didn't speak for a while. Finally she said, "I'm sorry. You looked so cold-blooded going through their pockets and lifting their feet."

"It's a long walk back to Puma. I didn't think you wanted to make it just on yucca roots."

She remained tight-lipped and remote while he finished putting together their kit. He also helped himself to Briscoe's MAC-10, just in case Hank Roper had a second team out looking for them, and recovered his own Browning from Williamson's body.

By the time he was ready to move out, Jean was feeling less rancorous. "I shouldn't have yelled at you."

"Forget it. You've had one shock after another. Having to take a life is the biggest shock of all."

She nodded wearily. "Have I earned my blood stripe?"

"You sure have." He helped Jean to her feet. "Let's get away from here. You'll feel better when you don't have to look at those three. We'll find a shady spot to rest for a few hours and start walking when it's dark and cool. If we travel most of the night, we should reach the highway tomorrow morning."

"Do we have to hurry? I'm exhausted."

"We don't have much water. Besides, I want to get to Hank Roper before he realizes his men botched their assignment."

"Oh, God." Jean slipped back into despondency. "This isn't over yet, is it?"

"It will be soon. Let's walk."

Maggie was surprised to find the FBI office in Albuquerque so busy on a Saturday afternoon. People were streaming in and out of the reception area, where a thick-necked man in a tight suit barred the public from the inner offices.

"I'd like to see the agent in charge," Maggie said. "Agent Devereaux."

"He's busy, ma'am. All the agents are busy right now. Can you come back on Monday? Things should be settled down by then."

"No, I cannot 'come back on Monday.' This is a matter of *national security.*" Hank Roper had told her to use that phrase. "I must see Agent Devereaux right now."

Thick Neck set his mouth into a hard line. "Lady, this better be important."

"It is, I assure you."

He tried to stare her down and failed. "Okay, I'll see if Al can give you a few minutes. Take a seat over there."

Maggie went across the room and sat down on the hardest chair in the world. Clutched under her arm was the bulky Department of Defense envelope Roper had given her. She wiped a sheen of nervous perspiration from her upper lip. A touch of jitters, that's all. She had no doubt about her ability to carry out Roper's scheme. In any case, she had no choice. She'd taken Roper's money and slept with him to seal the bargain. She understood quite clearly what would happen if she failed to carry out her end of the bargain.

"Agent Devereaux will see you," Thick Neck announced.

"Thank you."

"Through there and down to the end of the corridor."

Maggie waited for him to open the door for her. He tried to ignore her, but the awkwardness of the situation worked against him. Finally, with pursed lips, he rose and opened the door. She smiled maliciously and went through.

The FBI staff in Albuquerque couldn't be very large, but every member seemed to be at his or her desk today. The door marked A. C. DEVEREAUX —AGENT IN CHARGE was open. Two men in shirt sleeves were

staring over the shoulder of the man behind the desk—
Devereaux, Maggie presumed—at a computer screen.

"The count is accurate," Devereaux was saying. "All
we need is a cross-check by serial number and we can
transmit this shit to Washington."

"I'll be glad when this one is off our backs," one of
the others said. "I haven't seen my wife in three days."

"Neither have I," said the third man. "In my case,
that's a blessing."

Maggie knocked lightly on the door casing. "Mr.
Devereaux? The gentleman in the lobby said you would
see me."

Devereaux looked up irritably. When he saw Maggie,
his manner changed. He lifted himself gracefully from
his chair, straightening his tie as he did so. "Yes, come
in." He dismissed the others, saying, "Stay with it
until every serial number checks out."

"I'm sorry to bother you at a busy time," Maggie
said.

"That's all right." Devereaux sneaked a look at
Maggie's legs. "Please sit down."

Maggie was glad she had selected the yellow dress
instead of the pants suit she'd considered wearing.
Agent Devereaux was obviously a leg man. She rather
liked his size and the Southern burr in his voice.

"What can I do for you, Miss . . . ?"

"Maggie Winston. I'm not at all sure I'm doing the
right thing by coming to you. But I've been so troubled, so worried . . . and I didn't know to whom I
should turn. Then I thought of the FBI. My goodness,
you are the guardians of the country, aren't you? So I
thought, why not? All they can do is laugh at me, and
that would be better than—"

"Exactly what is the nature of your problem?"
Devereaux asked. "And how can I help you?"

She paused as if trying to pull together her scattered thoughts. From long experience she knew that
Southern men liked to come to the aid of a confused
woman. And Devereaux had that smarmy smile Southern men wear when they begin to think of themselves
as God's gift to the opposite sex. So far so good. "I have
a friend," she began.

"Yes?"

"Actually, he's a client. I'm the owner of an art gallery, the Winston Gallery, on Colorado Boulevard in Puma. My client is a very talented artist who also happens to be a soldier stationed at Fort Powell. His name is Burke. Sergeant Major Ansel Burke."

Devereaux's warmth began to fade. "Burke? I know him."

"Oh?" Maggie looked very much surprised.

"Yeah, and I've heard he does some painting. Is he any good?"

"Yes, Ansel is first-rate."

Devereaux seemed disappointed. "He used to be a first-rate noncom too. Lately he's been acting a little weird. Uncooperative and moody. I had a run-in with him earlier this week, in fact."

"Then I'm not the only one who's noticed a change in Ansel." She leaned forward just far enough to create a more intimate mood. "Ansel is often at my gallery. Sometimes, because he's single and alone, I've invited him for dinner at my apartment. Three or four times he's asked me to hold an envelope for him. Just for a few days." She showed him the gray DOD envelope. "A couple of days ago he gave me this one."

Devereaux's interest finally shifted from her legs to her story. "What's in the envelope? You obviously came here to give it to me."

"I never looked until this morning." She tried to appear somewhat ashamed, which for Maggie was a reach. "My curiosity finally got the best of me. Here, look for yourself."

He took the envelope and pulled out the sheaf of documents Roper had provided. The moment he saw the words *Top Secret* he drew in his breath. "That son of a bitch." He glanced at Maggie. "Excuse me."

"I'm relieved you don't think I was foolish to bring these to you. Ansel isn't only a client. He's a friend. But I couldn't continue to ignore my suspicions."

"Was each of the envelopes just like this one? Did they have Department of Defense printed on them?"

"Yes, that's what made me suspicious. Ansel is in

the army, so of course he'd have official mail. But why would he ask me to hold it for him?"

"This is the only one you've looked into?"

"Yes."

"You said he gave you three or four others. How many exactly?"

"I'm not sure. Four, I think."

A number was written in pencil on one corner of the envelope. Devereaux pondered it. "Jesus Christ, I think I've seen this number before." He picked up his phone. "Charlie, look in your file and give me the phone number of the Russian embassy in Mexico City." He waited. "Okay, go ahead: country code, yes; city code, yes. That's right. Thanks, Charlie."

Maggie was as surprised as Devereaux. She hadn't noticed the phone number. "Is that really the number for the Russian embassy in Mexico?"

"It sure as hell is."

Oh my, Maggie thought. Roper and his friends are very clever. I mustn't take any chances with them. "What does that mean?" she asked, full of alarmed innocence.

"It appears," Devereaux answered grimly, "that our pal Ansel Burke may be giving or selling national secrets to the Russians." He picked up his phone again. "Charlie. Me again. A new case just walked in. Let Leighton and Moffett finish the report on the F.D.N.W.s. Bring everyone else into my office. We'll be working late again, but for once we've got something that's worth our time."

After chow Wolfe Heinzman drove down to the main post and went into Burke's office in Military Police headquarters. Worried about Ansel, Lou Brodsky had asked Heinzman and Amos Biggs to meet him, and he was fidgeting when Biggs didn't show up at exactly nineteen hundred hours.

"Don't worry," Heinzman said. "Biggs vill be here. He just takes more time to fill his big belly at chow than we do."

A few minutes later Biggs strolled into the office, a

toothpick hanging from the side of his mouth. "Hiya, Lou. Wolfe. What's up?"

"Ansel's disappeared, that's what's up," Brodsky blurted out.

"Vat you mean *disappeared?*" Heinzman scratched his bald head. "Settle down, give facts."

"He went off post last night to recon the gas station Hank owns out on Route 41. I haven't seen or heard from him in twenty hours."

"That don't sound like Ansel," Biggs admitted. "He never misses reveille."

"He vent alone?" Heinzman asked.

"No, Jean Silk was with him. She was driving, in fact. And she hasn't been seen since last night either!"

Although Brodsky played that fact as his trump card, Heinzman and Biggs looked relieved rather than alarmed.

"That Ansel," Heinzman sighed. "He gets all the best vimmen."

Biggs stretched. "Think I'll go over to the N.C.O. Club and have a beer. Anybody want to join me?"

Brodsky was shaking his head. "You guys are wrong. They ain't in bed somewhere. They're in trouble. I just know that."

"Come on." Biggs was thinking of Captain Silk's sweet little rear end.

"I'm telling you—"

They looked up as FBI agent Al Devereaux marched into the office at the head of a squad of agents, some of whom were carrying steel straps used by the federal government to seal confiscated file cabinets.

"What the hell is this?" Brodsky demanded.

"I'm looking for Sergeant Major Burke. Where is he?"

"We ain't seen him since last night. He's disappeared. That's just what Wolfe and Amos and me were talking about."

"Disappeared? 'On the run' is the way I'd put it." Devereaux looked to one of his men. "Someone tipped him off. Put his description and the charges against him on the wire. Alert the border patrol too. Burke might try to cross into Mexico and make contact with his friends at the Russian embassy."

At the sound of the word *Russian*, Heinzman's ears went up like a dog's. "Vat's that about Russians?"

Devereaux drew two documents out of his inside coat pocket. "I have a warrant for Burke's arrest. The charge is espionage. And I have a court order impounding every scrap of paper in this office. Where's your commanding officer?"

Brodsky's mouth moved, but no words came out.

"Where is he?"

Brodsky finally found his full voice: "His quarters, I suppose. Ansel's no traitor. You guys are fulla shit!"

"He sold out," Devereaux said coldly.

"No way!" Biggs was surprised at the depth of his anger. He was an easygoing man who usually left confrontation to others.

I can't let Ansel be called a traitor, Biggs thought. He can't be. He was at my *wedding*.

"I know Russians." Wolfe Heinzman spoke in a low but commanding voice. "As a boy I serve in East German army. I see the how the Russians vork. I know the kind of man who is seduced by their promises and their vimmen. Ansel Burke is not one of those."

"I have evidence that he is. You're all friends of Burke, I take it."

They each nodded emphatically.

Devereaux was extremely satisfied with the progress he was making. This was just the kind of case he needed. The notoriety would propel him out of Albuquerque and back to a bigger desk in Washington, where he belonged. The opportunity to put these oafish soldiers in their place—especially the nigger with the great belly—was a nice bonus. "That's your misfortune. You'll be up all night answering questions. Brodsky, get your CO on the phone and tell him to run his ass over here. Tell him the FBI is waiting."

SUNDAY, JUNE 15

Chapter 24

The nuclear weapon inventories coming into FBI headquarters in Washington from the field were screened by a panel of agents with long experience in weapons security. Only one inventory out of three made it through the panel's screening process to the desk of the Director of the FBI on first submission. The other two-thirds were sent back for additional data or clarifications. A few were found to be haphazard or incomplete. In those cases the deputy director personally called the FBI field office responsible and chewed out the agent in charge. Those he spoke to were told bluntly that their jobs were on the line; if their revised reports were still sloppily done, the director would ask for their resignations.

Through this torturous procedure the FBI was slowly completing a physical inventory of every one of the seven thousand Challengers, Halos, and F.D.N.W.s in the country's nuclear arsenal.

Roy McCluskey, Director of the FBI, monitored the entire process, an exercise that filled him with anger and fear. According to the reports he was receiving, nuclear weapons were stored in all sorts of substandard environments. In one case, three nuclear warheads were found stacked on the ground next to a missile silo in Wyoming with only a chain-link fence between the warheads and a civilian road a hundred yards away.

Another team of FBI agents doing an inventory of

Challengers on a SAC base in Alaska discovered eight of the old nuclear bombs rusting away in a damp warehouse. The rust had eaten through two of the bomb casings, exposing their nuclear cores. In a few months those weapons might have begun to leak radioactive gas into the air.

In a third case, a small nuke stored at Fort Benning, Georgia, had been mixed in with a shipment of toilet paper. McCluskey wondered how the U.S. had so long avoided an accidental nuclear explosion or the theft of a weapon. He knew he had proven the vulnerability of America's nuclear arsenal. What he had not proved was that Egypt, and possibly Argentina, had actually gotten their hands on some U.S. devices.

Though it was 8:00 A.M. on a quiet Sunday morning in Washington, McCluskey was already at his desk in FBI headquarters looking for that proof. A pile of field reports in gray folders awaited him. They had come in overnight for vetting and had been approved by the panel. But McCluskey took nothing at face value. He read each report with a cop's skeptical mind.

By ten o'clock he had slogged through half of the pile of reports and was feeling eye-weary and irritable. He flipped the button on his intercom and barked, "Wilma, I'm tired of looking at these damned inventory sheets. Bring me any case files I haven't seen yet."

"Yes, sir."

By the time McCluskey had fired up his favorite pipe and poured himself a cup of coffee from the pot in the corner of his office, his secretary had come in with a computer printout of all new cases under investigation by the Bureau. He'd been forced to ignore other cases, even urgent ones, because of the nuclear weapons inventory. Bringing himself up to speed on other current business might help to clear his mind.

"Sorry, Wilma. I didn't mean to yell at you over the intercom."

"Don't worry about it." McCluskey was the fourth director Wilma Bartles had served, and in her opinion the best of the lot. He knew his business, he had no political ambitions, and he was sensitive enough to actually feel hurt whenever a newspaper or political commentator attacked him. She was sorry to see him so troubled. "There are three days worth of new case files."

"Good Lord, am I that far behind?" He shook his head. "What a way to live."

"You have a stack of phone messages too. But I'm putting off everyone who isn't connected with the inventory project."

"Thanks, Wilma. If I didn't have you to guard the gate, I'd never get any work done."

Before digging into his paperwork, McCluskey devoted a few minutes solely to his pipe. He found great contentment in the aroma of his personal blend of tobacco and the slowly drifting curls of smoke that rose so gracefully from the bowl. Whenever vexed, he retreated either to his wife or his pipe. Both provided him with emotional support. His wife was a wonderful woman—calm, patient, and understanding. But his pipe never said, "I told you so."

Presently he picked up the case files and began going through them. There were a number of cases that on a normal day would have received his close attention. A bribery investigation centering on possible mob-related activities of the Under Secretary of Commerce. Another in a string of brutal bank robberies in the Midwest. The kidnapping of a fur trade heiress from the garment center in New York. Those cases were cop's work, plain and simple.

One new case caught his eye: an army sergeant at an obscure post in New Mexico had been charged by the U.S. Attorney's Office with espionage. Another damned traitor, McCluskey thought. Over the last six months more than a dozen army and navy personnel had been arrested for stealing military secrets and selling them to the Russians. Stories like that were catnip to the media. "This'll make the evening news, too," he grumbled.

Fort Powell.

The name tickled the FBI director's memory. Sure. He'd just read an inventory report from the Albuquerque office. He leafed through the stack of reports and came up with the one he wanted. Special Agent A.C. Devereaux had filed it. Fort Powell was a storage depot for F.D.N.W.s.

He scanned the report. One hundred and thirty-eight nuclear devices were stored in the Restricted Materiel Center at Fort Powell. According to Devereaux's inventory, security measures were excellent and all warheads were in place.

The brief filed by the U.S. Attorney's Office stated that this sergeant had stolen Top Secret manpower and readiness reports for the Third Army area from the G-3 office at Fort Powell and was attempting to peddle them to the Russian embassy in Mexico City. A summary of the sergeant's service record was included in the report. Sergeant Major Ansel Burke. Nineteen years of service. Silver star. Bronze star for valor. Combat Infantryman's Badge. Purple heart with cluster.

And now, after all he'd done for his country, Sergeant Burke was apparently a traitor on the run.

McCluskey shook his head sadly. Why do some of the best ones sell out?

With a grunt of disgust, he flipped through the rest of the new cases until the words *Fort Powell* again jumped out at him. Elizabeth Palermo, an army corporal at Fort Powell, had been raped and murdered. The report only came to his desk because the FBI had jurisdiction over crimes on government reservations. He cleared his desk and placed the Burke and Palermo files side by side with the F.D.N.W. inventory from Fort Powell.

Three separate issues. Or were they?

McCluskey's gut was rumbling. Like all cops, the word *coincidence* made his stomach churn with suspicion.

He reached for his phone and dialed the number of Deputy Director Emmett Avery.

"Avery." Like McCluskey, the deputy director spent most Sunday mornings in the office.

"Emmett, could you come into my office for a minute?"

"Sure, I'll be right there."

"Bring your own coffee."

Avery chuckled. He hated the strong brew produced

by the coffee maker in the director's office. "I intend
to."

A couple of minutes later the deputy director ambled into McCluskey's office and sprawled in a chair
with his coffee cup balanced on one knee. Even on
Sunday morning Avery dressed like a career FBI man—
dark suit, white shirt, conservative tie. He was so lean
that his off-the-rack suits looked elegant on him. In
addition to a fit body, Emmett Avery also possessed
one of the brightest minds McCluskey had ever encountered. And he was dedicated to the Bureau. Most
of the top echelon of the Bureau had been disappointed
when McCluskey was named director; they had wanted
the job to go to Avery. But Avery immediately made
McCluskey feel welcome and offered his total support
from that first day, for which McCluskey would always be grateful.

"Emmett," McCluskey began, "I just stumbled on a
coincidence."

"Uh-oh." Avery knew McCluskey despised that word.

The director pushed the two case reports and the
Fort Powell inventory across the desk. "Take a look at
these."

Avery was a speed reader. In less than a minute he
devoured every fact in the three separate files. "Fort
Powell's had more than its share of problems this
week," Avery ventured.

"Did you see the notation at the bottom of the
Palermo file?"

"Yes, is it for real?"

"That's what I was going to ask. Did you know
anything about that?"

"Absolutely not." Avery was staring at the notation
in disbelief. "Why would Luther Amstel ask us to give
him all evidence related to the murder of an army
corporal?"

"I don't know, but we'd better find out."

"Can I use your phone?"

McCluskey pushed his phone across the desk.

"Weatherby is in today, like the rest of us." Avery
dialed an internal number. "Frank, this is Emmett.
I'm looking at case number L-51149. The girl who was

murdered at Fort Powell, New Mexico. Elizabeth
Palermo. Remember that one? Okay. According to your
case notes, Luther Amstel asked you to ship all the
evidence in that case over to him. And you agreed to
do it. Why?"

Emmett Avery listened in tight-lipped silence to the
response.

"Okay, Frank. Thank you. No, don't worry. You did
the right thing. I just wondered why Amstel was interested in that case. Talk to you later." He put down the
phone. "Amstel called while you were at the White
House and I was making a speech to the California
Bar Association. He told Frank Weatherby that the
Palermo girl was one of his stringers and he wanted to
look at whatever evidence we had in the case. Frank
didn't see any reason to say no."

McCluskey could hear Amstel's smooth voice making the request. "I'll bet he dropped lots of references
to interagency cooperation."

"Yes, that was his tack." Avery sipped at his coffee.
"And I'm sure he made a point of knowing when we
were going to be out of our offices so that Frank
Weatherby had to make the decision."

"It's a minor case," McCluskey said. "We might never
have heard about his interest in it. Thank God Frank
Weatherby documents everything he does."

"Who would want to kill Elizabeth Palermo?" Avery
wondered. "Was she really a CIA stringer? If so, why
were we never told about her? The Bureau is supposed
to be kept informed about CIA informants in the U.S.
And finally, why would Amstel personally take an
interest in the murder of a lowly stringer?"

"Good questions," McCluskey agreed. "I'll add one
more: did Elizabeth Palermo have any connection with
the Field Deployable Nuclear Weapons stored at Fort
Powell?"

Avery whistled softly. "All of a sudden the Palermo
case is a bag of snakes."

"Maybe. Maybe not. We need more information."

"I'll get on it."

"Be discreet," McCluskey warned him. "Luther

Amstel has a hell of a lot more friends in Washington than either of us."

When Emmett Avery had gone, McCluskey turned back to the stack of reports. He read each one with care. But despite all the work he'd put the Bureau through to get this information, he no longer took any great interest in it. His instinct told him the answer to his questions lay in another direction.

At 11:50 A.M. Wilma buzzed him. "President Bryant is on the phone."

"Put him through."

"And Mr. Avery wants to see you again."

"Send him right in."

McCluskey braced himself for what he suspected would be an unpleasant conversation with the President of the United States.

"Roy?"

"Good morning, Mr. President."

"How's the inventory coming?"

"Ninety percent complete."

"Any weapons missing?"

"No, sir. So far every one of our small tactical nukes has been accounted for."

"That's a relief." The President cleared his throat as if to rid himself of fears that had been stuck in there. "When can we make an announcement to that effect?"

Emmett Avery came in and McCluskey waved him into a chair. "Our deadline is six o'clock tonight. I'll send a summary of my findings to the White House by seven o'clock."

"Excellent." The President paused. "I'm beginning to think Luther was right. If Libya's weapon didn't originate here, we can afford to stand back and let the Russians think whatever they want."

"Mr. President, I still believe it did."

"You have no proof?"

"No, sir. Not yet."

"In fact, the inventory that you insisted upon proves just the opposite."

"It's not yet complete."

"Ninety percent complete. That's what you said a

minute ago." The President was beginning to sound testy.

"Yes, sir, but the inventory won't answer every question. I've got a hunch there's a U.S. connection with Egypt and I won't quit until I find it."

"Roy, this government cannot operate on your personal hunches. Give me proof of a U.S. connection or drop the subject."

McCluskey was tempted to confide the nature of his hunch to the President, but decided against that.

"I'm beginning to think your antipathy for Luther has affected your professional judgment," the President went on.

"No, sir," McCluskey said as strongly as he could. "That's not the case."

"Then let's not say anything more about hunches. I'll expect your report at seven o'clock. Don't disappoint me."

There was a loud click in McCluskey's ear. He put down the phone with a trace of a sigh.

Avery frowned. "What did the President say?"

McCluskey recalled a favorite expression of his father's. "He told me it's time to piss on the fire and call in the dogs."

"In other words, he wants a report that clears the U.S. of any involvement with the Qattara attack."

"That's the message." McCluskey was pleased to find that the President no longer had the power to agitate him. "What have you got for me?"

"Corporal Elizabeth Palermo worked in the Restricted Materiel Center at Fort Powell as a data entry operator. Part of her job was to keep records on the F.D.N.W.s stored there."

"I knew it!" McCluskey's fist came down so hard that everything on his desk jumped an inch. "Amstel is in this up to his goddamn armpits."

"You may have a tough time proving it. No one is better at hiding his tracks than Luther Amstel."

McCluskey sat back comfortably, feeling like a cop again. "Everybody makes mistakes—even me. My big mistake was taking this job in the first place. But I've got it—for the time being, anyway—and I'm going to make the most of it. Are you with me, Emmett?"

Emmett Avery was being invited to walk into a fire storm. Few people went up against the Director of the CIA and survived with skin and reputation intact. "I'm with you," he said slowly. "What's our first move?"

"I want you on the next plane to New Mexico. The President doesn't think much of my hunches, but I've got a very strong hunch that Sergeant Major Ansel Burke can tell us a lot about Elizabeth Palermo. Provided you can find him."

"I'll find him," Avery promised. "I just hope he's still alive when I do."

Wilma Bartles went to lunch a few minutes later at a coffee shop near the FBI headquarters. She didn't mind working Sundays. The overtime pay was welcome, and she really had nothing else to do anyway. Wilma was single and alone. Not even a pet, though lately she had been thinking of getting a cat. Cats take care of themselves, a feline quality Wilma admired.

The coffee shop was full of tourists who had just completed the White House tour. She took a seat at the counter instead of a booth, which she would have preferred, and ordered a grilled cheese sandwich and a glass of skimmed milk. Grilled cheese didn't excite her, but she knew it would be served quickly.

When Wilma's lunch arrived, she ate rapidly and paid her check. Then she hurried three blocks down the avenue to the Smithsonian. Her destination was the phone booth nearest the lobby. She dialed an 800 number long ago committed to memory and waited while the call was routed through a series of blind intercepts.

The metallic voice of a computer came on line: *"State your six-digit communications code."*

"855607."

Five seconds of silence followed while the computer checked Wilma's ID. Wilma had no idea where the computer was located, or who received the information for which she was paid. Nor did she care. The checks deposited regularly to her numbered account at Banque

Suisse were all she cared about. After all, a woman alone had to plan for her future.

"Your code is current. State your message. Speak slowly and clearly. When your message is complete, signal by repeating your communications code. You may begin now."

Wilma had rehearsed her message during lunch. Even so, she stumbled when she began. Talking to a computer was something that would always make her nervous. "I, uh . . . worked with the director again this morning. The . . . the inventories are almost complete. No, umm . . . surprises. I mean, no weapons are missing. The director had a call from the President. The director still thinks the weapon came from here in the U.S. The President didn't want to hear that. They argued, but the director promised to deliver his final inventory report by seven o'clock tonight. Let's see . . . what else?

"Oh yes. The director met twice with Emmett Avery. I don't know the subject, but afterwards Mr. Avery had me book him on a flight for Albuquerque. His plane leaves Dulles at two o'clock this afternoon. Uh . . . the director talked to his wife. It sounds to me like he's made up his mind to resign before the end of the year." She stopped for a second. Her control officer had told her that this week she was to gather any information regarding the weapon inventories, McCluskey's personal plans and problems, and his dealings with Emmett Avery. "I guess that's it. 855607."

Wilma replaced the receiver and glanced at her watch. My goodness, it was almost one-thirty. She hated to be late coming back from lunch. Punctuality was one of her obsessions. She despised these young secretaries who didn't care whether they got their work done or not. Wilma believed that an employer had a right to expect eight full hours of work for eight hours of pay. That was only proper.

Chapter 25

Burke used the compass taken from Briscoe's body to shoot a back azimuth and plot their position. They had taken a wandering course through the desert during their flight from Hank Roper's service station. As a result, they weren't as far from civilization as he had feared. He reckoned that Highway 18 was only about twenty-five miles away. A south-by-southeast course should bring them out on the highway near the little hamlet of Pea Patch. From Pea Patch they could catch a bus or hitch a ride to Puma.

At first Jean doubted that she could walk twenty-five miles. She remained shaky from the shoot-out in the canyon, especially the memory of driving the sharpened point of the screwdriver into Harry Williamson's back. Burke assured her that a good rest would put her back on her feet. They lay down in the shade of some rocks and slept until almost 8:00 P.M. Then they started to walk in the direction of Highway 18.

Jean fell into an easy pace at Burke's side. The bright moon and cloudless sky helped her to relax. Ansel's competence gave her additional comfort. What made the trek actually enjoyable was the mantle of intimacy that descended on them. No longer pursued by men with guns, they were free to walk at a leisurely pace and talk without having to look over their shoulders every few minutes.

Jean used the opportunity tell him more about herself. Her childhood on the streets of New York's Lower

East Side. The problems of a girl growing up without a mother's hand. Her father's inability to earn a living as an attorney, caused mainly by his unwillingness to turn down indigent and public service cases. And spurred by his example, her own struggle to become a lawyer.

"I started out following in my father's footsteps just to make him proud of me," she said. "When he died, I discovered that I wanted to be a lawyer just for myself."

"You went to N.Y.U.?"

"Yes. What about you? Did you ever consider going to college yourself, or to an art school?"

Burke could finally talk about his lost opportunity. "It was losing a scholarship that made me join the army. I was nineteen years old and thought my life was over. My life as an artist, anyway. So I said what the hell, I might as well go to Vietnam with everyone else." He shook his head. "A few days ago I saw a bumper sticker that read 'Hire a teenager while they still know everything.' That was me. An obnoxious know-it-all. The world wasn't offered to me on a plate, so I stomped away mad."

He told her about hanging around San Francisco's Embarcadero when he was a boy, drawing facile little pictures of the Golden Gate Bridge for tourists, and his growing hunger for a genuine education in art. He even told Jean how he had hurled all his paints and canvases into San Francisco Bay before going down to the army recruiting office, a story he had never shared with anyone. "Nothing in my life has ever hurt so much as losing that scholarship. It still hurts."

"Surely a lost scholarship doesn't matter anymore. You did become the artist you always wanted to be."

"But look at the years I wasted. All the paintings I haven't done."

"You can't dwell on that."

"Usually I don't." Burke shifted the MAC-10 to his other shoulder. "But on a day like this I see very clearly what I've become: first and foremost, a killer of men." Each word was underlined with a bitter stroke. "Everything else I do is secondary."

"No—"

"You saw me take out Sanchez at the gas station. Craymore in the arroyo. Arkolotti and Briscoe in the canyon. I was in my element back there, doing what I do best. I'll always be better as a soldier than as a painter. How do you think that makes me feel?"

"Ansel, you're selling yourself short."

"I don't think so. Let's take a five-minute rest."

While Jean lay down on the hard desert floor, Burke took out the compass and read the stars to double-check their position.

"You didn't 'take out' the fat one—Harry Williamson," Jean said. "I did that. He would have killed you if I hadn't."

"So?"

She was lying with both hands laced under her head for a pillow. "So maybe you're slipping as a soldier. Maybe you aren't the marvelous military machine you were six months ago. Maybe next year you'll be an even *worse* soldier. When that happens, you'll be at your best as an artist—just what you want. Problem solved."

"I know you're trying to help, but you're making me feel even worse. I'm surprised you win any cases with that kind of courtroom manner."

"I win eight times out of ten. There aren't many male attorneys who can say that."

"Maybe they're just more modest than women attorneys."

They walked on, stopping at regular intervals for rest and water. The night went swiftly. Seven hours later the sun began to rise over the Sangre de Cristos with such curious pink tones that Burke itched to have a brush in his hand.

"It'll be blistering hot soon," Jean said. "I dread that."

"The heat won't bother us today. Do you see that line out there?"

"What line?"

"The dark one, like a thin black thread."

Jean squinted. "Oh yes."

"That's Highway 18."

"My God. I thought I'd never see a two-lane blacktop again."

"Hey, that'd make a great title for a country and western song. "Thought I'd never see a two-lane blacktop again. Doo da. Doo da.' "

" 'Left my sweetheart in Tulsa,' " Jean chimed in. " 'Gonna take that two-lane blacktop home.' "

" 'Been a year since I've seen Tulsa,' " Burke sang. " 'Got those two-lane blacktop blues.' "

"Top Ten," Jean predicted.

"Maybe we can get Waylon to record it."

"Or Willie."

"If they won't do it, we'll get that guitar picker from the Chicken Coop. This song could make him famous."

They worked on the lyrics while they walked. Two hours later, with their feet firmly placed on the blacktop of Highway 18, the tune was beginning to sound a little ridiculous; the words no longer seemed to make sense, either.

"We made it." Jean was full of wonder at their accomplishment. "We walked out of there."

They looked up and down the narrow road, which was barely wide enough to be a state highway. No cars could be seen in either direction.

"I'd better get rid of this." Burke stepped off the road and scooped out a hole in the sand with the butt of the MAC-10. He tossed the weapon into the hole and pushed sand in with his foot until it was buried.

"Which way is Puma?"

"South. A little town called Pea Patch is in the other direction. I'd rather head straight for Puma if we can catch a ride."

"There isn't much traffic on this road."

Burke took her arm and started them both walking toward Puma. "When I was a young soldier, I hitchhiked almost everywhere I went. One thing I learned was that you never catch a ride standing by the side of the road. You've got to keep moving. A hitchhiker standing still looks like a lazy bum."

"Want me to show a little leg when a car comes by?"

"We're looking for a ride, not a gang bang."

The ride was easier to snag than either of them

expected. A few minutes later a farmer in a panel truck stopped and invited them to share his front seat. The back of the truck was stacked with cardboard boxes full of baby chicks. Several hundred tiny heads stuck out of holes in the boxes. The sound of hundreds of baby chicks *cheep cheep cheep*ing at the top of their small lungs was the most irritating racket they'd ever heard.

The farmer, accustomed to the noise, seemed not to notice. During the hour-long ride into Puma he told them more than they had ever wanted to know about chicken ranching, from the high price of feed to the myriad diseases to which baby chicks are susceptible. "I should've gone into turkey ranching," he groused. "Turkeys got constitutions like truck drivers. Never get sick. Eat anything you give 'em. And when Thanksgiving rolls around, why, that's like givin' a turkey farmer the key to the goddamn mint."

To pay for the ride, they felt obliged to frown over the farmer's complaints and compliment his business acumen. When they reached the outskirts of Puma, Burke said quickly, "You can let us out anywhere around here."

"Anywhere!" Jean emphasized.

When they had thanked the rancher and he had driven off in a cloud of *cheep cheep cheep*s, Jean said, "I'll never eat another chicken, even if I'm starving."

"That's no sacrifice. You only eat Twinkies and potato chips anyhow. Poultry has too much nutritional value."

"I used to eat Chicken McNuggets. Never again."

" 'Junk Food Queen Gives Up Chicken McNuggets.' I'll alert the media."

They headed for the sheriff's office. "Len Perkins is usually in his office on Sunday morning. Not because he's dedicated to his job," Burke explained. "He just doesn't like to take his wife to church."

"I'm not talking to anyone until I've washed my face and combed my hair."

"Fine." Burke pointed out Wally's Diner across the street. "Wally's rest rooms are as clean as any in Puma. You go ahead and wash up, then come across

the street. It'll take me a while to explain to Perkins
why I need a search warrant for Hank's gas station."

"I'll see you in about ten minutes."

Burke parted from her and went into the sheriff's
office alone. As expected, Len Perkins was at his desk
reading the Sunday morning edition of the Puma *Union*
and eating jelly donuts. "Hello, Len. I hate to inter-
rupt your breakfast, but I've got a story that'll curl
what straggly bits of hair you've still got."

"I'll be damned." Perkins put down his donut and
rose very slowly with his right hand on the butt of his
holstered pistol. "I'll just bet you've got a story to tell.
You've always had a big mouth, Ansel. But you brought
it to the wrong place this time."

Perkins's reaction surprised Burke. He was always
antagonistic, but this clumsy menace was something
new. "What are you talking about?"

The sheriff jerked the service revolver out of its
holster and aimed it at Burke's middle. "You're under
arrest. You have the right to remain silent. You have
the right to an attorney. Anything you say may be
used against you. If you can't afford an attorney, one
will be appointed to represent you. Now just stand
right there and don't move a muscle."

"Have you lost your goddamn mind?"

"Marv! LeRoy! Get in here!" Perkins smiled nervously. "I don't know why you decided to come back,
but you made one helluva mistake."

Burke looked down the barrel of Len Perkins's revolver. "That's a single action Colt, isn't it? You forgot
to cock the hammer."

"Shut up! I don't have to take any shit from a fucking traitor." He cocked the hammer.

"Traitor? What does that mean?"

"It means you're wanted by the FBI for espionage
and for unlawful flight to avoid federal prosecution."

"Espionage? That's crazy!"

Marv and LeRoy, deputy sheriffs for Puma County,
evidently awakened from naps in the cells behind the
office, came in yawning and rubbing their eyes. They
were larger, slower, even dumber versions of the sheriff.

Marv stared openmouthed at Burke. "You got him, Len. *You got him!*"

"Damned right I do. Wasn't easy, either. He came in loaded for bear. Cuff him, LeRoy."

LeRoy moved ponderously toward Burke.

"Don't walk between us!"

"Sorry, Len." LeRoy came around behind Burke and wrestled his arms back, then put on the cuffs.

"Make sure they're tight." Perkins didn't begin to relax until he heard the cuffs click solidly.

"They're tight. Hey, he's carrying a gun." LeRoy pulled the Browning automatic out of Burke's side pocket and sniffed at the barrel. "This piece has been fired lately."

"This is a mistake," Burke said. "Or a frame-up."

Perkins grinned at his deputies. "How many times have we heard that one?"

"Plenty," Marv said.

With Burke cuffed and disarmed and the deputies prepared to back him up, Perkins swaggered forward. "You been looking down your nose at me ever since you came to Fort Powell. Acting like your shit don't stink, and all the time you're selling secrets to the Russkies."

"That's a lie." Burke put his back against the wall, bracing himself. When Perkins threw the punch, he twisted so that the sheriff's fist only glanced off his ribs.

"Hold him."

Marv and LeRoy rushed to obey their boss. When they had pinned Burke against the wall, Perkins stepped in and threw another punch. This one landed solidly. Burke coughed and gritted his teeth, determined not to give Perkins the satisfaction of another sound. As the blows rained down on him, he tried to detach his mind from the beating. How had Hank Roper managed to get him charged with espionage? Who was behind him? What kind of evidence did they plant?

His legs weakened and the handcuffs bit deeply into his wrists. Just when he thought he might drop, Perkins stopped swinging his hamlike fists and stood back, sweating and grinning.

"You marked his face," LeRoy said.

"So what?"

"You always told us not to mark the face of a prisoner we work over."

"Ansel's a special case. He's a traitor. Nobody's gonna criticize us if a traitor gets a few bruises. We had to subdue him, didn't we? He was violent when he came in."

"That's right," Marv vouched. "Violent."

" . . . not a traitor."

"The FBI says different. Marv, wipe his face."

Burke leaned against the wall while Marv went for a wet washcloth, which he used to wipe blood from Burke's mouth.

"I'll take him to Fort Powell myself," Perkins announced. "Marv, you drive. LeRoy, call the FBI field office in Albuquerque. Talk to Special Agent Al Devereaux. Inform him that I captured Ansel Burke and I'm bringing him in. And call the Puma *Union* while you're at it. Tell them to send a reporter out to Fort Powell and to call the wire services and television stations." He looked at Burke as if he were a Christmas present. "You're a big story, Ansel."

Burke was tempted to tell Perkins what he was going to do to him one day, but thought better of it. He needed his strength. The FBI would listen to him. Even Devereaux would recognize a frame-up when he heard the whole story. "Get me out of this place," he said through swollen lips. "It stinks almost as much as you do."

Jean came out of Wally's Diner to see Ansel being pushed out the front door of the building across the street. His face looked battered and his wrists were handcuffed behind him. The sheriff and another man in uniform were handling him roughly.

She stopped in her tracks, then started across the street at double time. Ansel was being led to a police car. Their eyes met and he was able to shake his head before being pushed into the back of the car.

Confused, Jean returned to the curb. Ansel looked out the side window and shook his head again. Obviously he didn't want her involved in whatever was going on. She didn't understand, except to sense that Ansel thought she could be of more help as an attorney than as an involved party.

She watched helplessly as the police car pulled away from the curb and headed in the direction of Fort Powell. When the car disappeared, Jean looked around as if trying to find her bearings.

There was a phone booth on the corner. She rummaged up some change from her pocket, called the Fort Powell provost marshal's office, and asked for Sergeant Brodsky. When he came on the line, she said: "This is Jean Silk. I didn't know who else to call about—"

"Captain Silk?" Brodsky sighed deeply. "Jesus, I was beginning to wonder if you were still alive. Are you all right? Is Ansel with you?"

"He was until a few minutes ago. I just saw him being taken out of the Puma County sheriff's office in handcuffs. Sergeant Brodsky—Lou, what's going on?"

"Perkins has him? Goddammit, I wish Ansel had called me. Where the hell've you two been?"

"That's a very long story."

"Where are you now?"

"Puma. In a phone booth outside Wally's Diner."

"Get off the street," Brodsky urged. "Go inside the diner and take a booth at the back. I'll get there quick as I can."

"First tell me what's going on."

"Somebody framed Ansel. Set him up to look like a traitor. Those dumb pricks from the FBI—excuse me—have charged him with espionage."

"That's impossible!"

"No it ain't. They're out to get Ansel. Ruin him so nothing he says sounds true. If you've been with him, I got a hunch you're in trouble too."

"Are there charges against me?"

"No, ma'am."

"Then I can help him. He'll need a lawyer."

"First we have to make sure you're safe. Go into

Wally's. I'll collect a couple of Ansel's friends and be there soon."

"All right. Thank you, Lou."

Brodsky wasn't accustomed to having an officer use his first name. He didn't know quite how to respond. "You watch yourself, Captain Silk."

"I will."

Jean went into the diner and took the most inconspicuous booth she could find. She was numb. Roper and his friends were awfully smart. They had made sure that if Ansel survived in the desert, he'd be discredited when he returned. Gradually the smell of real food penetrated Jean's black mood. It was Sunday morning and she hadn't eaten a real meal since Friday evening. She had some money, so she ordered breakfast: a Coke, onion rings, and a piece of chocolate cake.

The waitress looked her over jealously. "I don't see how you keep that cute figure, honey."

Thirty minutes later, as she was finishing breakfast, Lou Brodsky came into Wally's Diner with the bearlike sergeant major she had met at the Chicken Coop, a black man with a huge gut, and little Sean Feeney. When they slid into the booth with her, Jean felt like a child surrounded by anxious relatives.

"Ve are delighted to see you alive," Wolfe Heinzman said.

"I'm alive because of Ansel. We were almost killed by Hank Roper and his friends."

"I knew it," Brodsky growled.

"I'll have a beer," Biggs called to the waitress.

"We don't serve beer until two o'clock."

"Coffee." Biggs sighed. "For all of us. I'm Sergeant Amos Biggs," he said to Jean.

"There ain't one of us who thinks Ansel Burke is a spy or a traitor." Sean Feeney dug a cigarette out of a crumpled pack. "But they got him cold. Funny, I'm the one who oughtta be in the stockade. Not Ansel."

"Where did the FBI get the idea Ansel is a traitor?" Jean was still confused by the turn of events.

"From that bitch—excuse me—that girl friend of his." Brodsky squeezed his hand into a fist. "I'd like five minutes alone in a room with her, but she's already left town. Closed her gallery and went to New York, the way I heard it."

"Maggie Winston told the FBI that Ansel is a spy?"

"Not only told them," Wolfe said. "Evidence vas given to them by Miss Vinston. Top Secret documents she claims Ansel left at her apartment. The FBI thinks Ansel has been selling secrets. They claim to have found a connection between Ansel and the Russian embassy in Mexico City."

"My God." Maggie really was a viper. Why hadn't Ansel seen that? "Where did she really get the documents? From Hank Roper?"

"That's what we think," Biggs said. "But we've got no proof and nobody wants to hear from us anyway. We're nothing but grunts. Our CO has washed his hands of Ansel. In fact, Sloane hardly comes out of his office anymore."

"Vat happened Friday night?" Wolfe Heinzman asked. "Vere haff you two been since then?"

Jean related the entire story as slowly and completely as she could: the visit to the service station, their flight into the desert, the final shoot-out in the narrow canyon. The most difficult part to tell was the death of Harry Williamson. She stated the facts concisely, still unable to think about what she'd done without feeling ashamed.

The four men in the booth evidently did not share her belief in the sanctity of human life. Approval and admiration dominated their expressions.

"Didn't I tell you she's dynamite?" Sean Feeney looked around at his companions. "First she saves me from a trip to Leavenworth, then earns herself a blood stripe. Do you know another broad who could have done that?"

Wolfe smiled at Jean. "You have great courage."

"Sounds like Ansel hasn't lost his touch, either." Biggs ticked off names on the tips of his blunt fingers: "Sanchez. Craymore. Briscoe. Arkolotti. They were all heavy hitters. I served with Arnie in the old Sixty-ninth, y'know. In fact, it was Arnie who introduced me to Carta Blanca beer."

The conversation began to make Lou Brodsky nervous. "Let's not talk too much about this. We got five senior N.C.O.s A.W.O.L. from Fort Powell. As far as anyone knows, they're just off on a drunk together. If the FBI knew what really happened to them—that Ansel pulled their life-support plugs—things would only go worse for him."

"I read in the *National Enquirer*," Feeney said, "that all FBI men gotta wear jockey shorts. It's some kinda weird regulation. And they gotta have their peckers checked every week for V.D. You know, the old short-arm inspection."

The others stared at him.

"I'm just sayin'," he went on, "that you can't expect a bunch of guys in shorts that are too tight, guys always worried about the next pecker check, to do their jobs the way they should. So maybe we'll have to do it for them."

Wolfe Heinzman scratched his shaved head. "I surprise myself to say this, but Feeney makes sense. Ve must prove Ansel innocent because the FBI vill not."

"Damn right." Feeney was proud to have led the discussion to a crucial point.

"How?" Biggs asked. "Ansel's got most of the pieces to the goddamn puzzle, and he's locked up."

"The first thing to do," Jean said, "is find out where Ansel is being held. I'll establish myself as his counsel. They've got to let him talk to an attorney."

"When Hank and his friends find out you're still alive, they'll come after you," Brodsky predicted. "They've gone too far to quit now." He gave her an old soldier's wink, full of malice and guile. "What they don't know is that we're gonna give you round-the-clock protection."

"Nobody vill touch you," Wolfe promised.

Feeney and Biggs nodded solemnly.

Jean realized that some people would consider her protectors only a few degrees more respectable than those who threatened her, but she found their presence comforting. "Thanks. I'm going to need your help as much as Ansel does."

Chapter 26

Burke had been inside the Fort Powell stockade hundreds of times to pick up or deliver prisoners, and thought he knew it well. Now he realized you could never know a stockade until you were a prisoner yourself. Everything about the place, from the narrow cells to the institutional smell and the drab prison uniforms, was newly suffocating.

Sheriff Perkins had taken Burke straight to the stockade, where the desk sergeant at first refused to book him. "There's got to be a mistake," the desk sergeant said. "This is Sergeant Major Burke. He *runs* this joint."

"Not anymore. You must've heard there's a warrant out on him."

"Sure, but I figured that was just another army fuck-up."

"There's no mistake, sonny. Book him."

The desk sergeant twisted uncomfortably. "Sorry, Ansel. I guess I don't have any choice."

"That's okay, Denny. Let's get it over with." Burke began removing things from his pockets and placing them on the booking counter.

His personal possessions were catalogued and he was taken to a dressing room where his clothes were exchanged for prisoner's denims and a pair of unpolished army boots. He was fingerprinted and photographed. The doctor looked him over and pronounced him fit to be put in with the general stockade population. But that wasn't done. Instead, he was put in an isolation cell that contained only a bunk, toilet, and wash bucket.

The booking drill was familiar to Burke. He had walked prisoners through it many times. The procedure required no thought on his part, which was fortunate. His brain still wasn't functioning. He felt sick in both mind and heart. Driving to the post, Perkins had taken delight in revealing that Maggie Winston had fingered him for the FBI. She "broke the case," as Perkins had put it, by turning up on the FBI's doorstep with a package of Top Secret documents that she claimed he had left with her for safekeeping. At first Burke refused to believe him, but Perkins had too many convincing details.

Why would Maggie do that to me?

A hundred possibilities churned through his mind, none of them reasonable. Maggie *wouldn't* do it! *Couldn't* do it! But she had. Depression settled over him like a cloak.

Looking back, he realized there had been sufficient clues. Infatuated with her, he had pushed them from his mind. Now he took them out and examined them: the waspish tongue; the quiet contempt she had shown for good people like Lou and Wolfe; the dollar signs in her eyes when she looked at a piece of art. Maggie had a cold and calculating side he'd chosen to ignore.

Money, loot, dough—whatever you called it, the subject preoccupied Maggie. Hank must have put Maggie up to this crazy story. And money would have been Hank's lever. Perkins said Maggie had left Puma for New York, which probably meant that Hank had financed the new gallery she wanted to open there.

And she'll be showing my paintings!

Shit-oh-dear.

He stretched out on the bunk and tried to consider his situation more objectively. Hank, and whoever he was working for, put together this frame-up in a hurry. First they had to get hold of some Top Secret documents, then talk Maggie into taking them to the FBI, and even rehearse Maggie on her story—all in the space of a day. Maggie had already left town, surely with the FBI's approval, but she couldn't just drop her bag of evidence and run. Sooner or later she'd have to testify in open court where a lawyer as smart as Jean could take apart her story. Hank must know that.

So the frame-up was just a way to get him out of circulation for now. In the long run, they couldn't afford to let him live.

From down the cellblock a guttural voice called out, "Burke! We got'cha now!"

The frame-up was also a perfect way to discredit him.

"You have to come out of that cell sometime, Sergeant Major. When you do, we'll be waiting for you."

He was glad Jean had gone into Wally's Diner. There was no reason for her to be connected with him, except as an attorney. What would Hank do when he found out Jean was still alive and on the outside? He'd want to silence her. That worried Burke, though he knew Lou and Wolfe would take care of her once they heard her story. She'd be okay under their protection. Hank wasn't the only one with tough friends.

"Hey, Burke! You ain't never coming out of this stockade alive. You know that, don'tcha?"

He tried to ignore the catcalls from the other cells. By now every prisoner in the stockade knew he was in here. Since he'd sent a lot of them away, they'd be anxious to get their hands on him. From that viewpoint, the isolation cell was a safe haven.

"Get ready, Burke! Get ready to die."

He closed his eyes and tried to get some rest.

Four hours later Burke was awakened and taken to an interrogation room on the second floor of the stockade. Waiting for him was Special Agent Al Devereaux, dapper in still another expensive summer suit.

"Hi ya, old buddy."

"I told you before—don't call me that."

"Doesn't matter what you want."

"No? I want a lawyer. And I don't have to talk to you until I have one."

Devereaux waved off the request. "Your rights are protected. You'll get a lawyer. I just thought you might want to talk to me first. Get this thing off your chest, you know?"

"I don't have anything on my chest."

"Sit down." Devereaux took the chair across from him. "I'll get you an attorney right now if that's what you really want. But when you leave this room, you won't go back into isolation. I'll see that you're thrown in the tank with all those hard cases you put away. How'd you like that, tough guy?"

Burke looked at him impassively.

"I mean it. I talked to General Leland and he's agreeable. In fact, it was his idea."

"The lawyer I want is Captain Jean Silk of the J.A.G. office here at Fort Powell. I've got the right to see an attorney. You know it and so do I."

Devereaux's smile was beginning to look shopworn. "Don't be such a hard-ass."

"You aren't listening." Burke stood and moved to the door. "Without my lawyer, the interview is over. Send me back to my cell, or into the tank, I don't care which. I'd rather fight the stockade rats than talk to you."

"Okay!" The FBI man heaved himself to his feet. "Captain Silk's waiting out at the desk. Goddamn lawyers all have radar. I'll get her."

Burke went back to the scarred wooden table in the center of the small room and sat down. He didn't believe Devereaux was part of the conspiracy. Devereaux was just a bureaucrat with his eye on a promotion; he'd believe anybody who could help him win a bigger job.

A few minutes later Jean, in a fresh uniform with captain's bars gleaming on the shoulders, was ushered into the interrogation room by Devereaux. She didn't look nearly as fresh as her uniform. "Hello, Sergeant Burke." Her tone and demeanor were cool and formal. "I understand you want me to represent you."

"That's right."

"I'll see what I can do for you." She sat down across from him, opened an attaché case, and took out a notebook. "Special Agent Devereaux intends to tape-record this interview. He has a right to do so."

"Fine."

"You don't have to respond to any questions unless you wish to. Do you understand that?"

"Sure." Burke was relieved that Jean had fallen so smoothly into this charade. It wouldn't do either of them any good to let Devereaux know how deeply they were involved with each other.

Devereaux put a fresh tape on a reel-to-reel recorder and spoke into the mike in his pleasant Southern voice. "This interview is taking place at 5:00 P.M. on June 15 in the stockade at Fort Powell, New Mexico. Three people are present: myself, A. C. Devereaux, special agent in charge of the Albuquerque field office of the FBI; Sergeant Major Ansel Burke, U.S. Army, and Captain Jean Silk, U.S. Army, his attorney."

"I'd like to make a statement before we begin," Jean said. "Sergeant Burke has lacerations around his right eye and lips and a swollen mouth. The flesh around his eye and mouth are also discolored. He's obviously been beaten."

"Not true," Devereaux said quickly. "Sheriff Perkins of Puma County told me Sergeant Burke was armed and violent at the time of his arrest and had to be subdued."

"I wasn't violent," Burke said. "Perkins and his deputies worked me over for the fun of it."

"Your comment is on the record. Let's get on with the questions," Devereaux suggested. "Sergeant Burke, the primary purpose of this interview is to inform you officially of the charges the U.S. government has lodged against you—espionage and unlawful flight to avoid prosecution."

"Not guilty. Can I go now?"

"You aren't funny. For the record, would you like to state whether you have ever taken Top Secret documents from the G-3 section of this post and provided them to a foreign power or to any individual?"

"Absolutely not."

"Did you give a package containing such documents to a Puma art dealer, Miss Margaret Winston, to hold for you?"

"No. The only things Maggie ever held for me were my paintings. I'm sorry I let her have those."

Devereaux glanced at the next of his prepared questions. "Have you ever made personal contact with the government of the U.S.S.R. for any reason?"

"No, never. Anyone who says I did is a liar."

"What about the Russian embassy in Mexico City?"

"What about it?"

"Have you ever made contact with that embassy for any reason?"

"Nope."

"Have you ever accepted money from anyone in exchange for information about U.S. military plans, personnel, or weapons?"

"Never." Burke's patience had run out. "Can't you recognize a setup? Don't you know what this is really about? F.D.N.W.s."

Devereaux cleared his throat portentously. "Where did you hear that phrase?"

"Betsy Palermo worked at the Restricted Materiel Center. Part of her job was to track the inventory of the F.D.N.W.s stored out there. Someone paid her to falsify the inventory. That's why she was killed."

"Are you talking about the girl who was murdered out here the other day?"

"That's right. If you took the time to look at the evidence you 'confiscated' from me, you must have seen how much money she's banked. Betsy was working for Hank Roper, the sergeant major who runs the N.C.O. Club here at Fort Powell, and he's probably working for the spook who runs the R.M.C. They're trying to make me look like a traitor because I found out what they're doing."

"And what is that?"

"Peddling nukes. I think they've stolen some of those devices from the R.M.C. and stored them close by. Hank Roper owns a gas station out on Route 41. It's a control site used to electronically monitor the storage depot where the nukes are hidden. I wouldn't be surprised if the warhead used in Egypt came from Fort Powell. I went to Sheriff Perkins this morning for a warrant to search the bungalow behind the station. Instead, the asshole arrested me."

The FBI man shook his head. "You must be high on dope."

"I think you should give my client the benefit of the doubt," Jean said evenly. "Sergeant Major Burke is a nineteen-year veteran with a spotless record."

"Until now." Devereaux was almost smiling again as he switched off the tape recorder. "A search warrant for a gas station? On what grounds? Your client concocted this lamebrained story in an attempt to muddy the case against him."

Jean wouldn't give up. "If the idea of missing nukes is so 'lamebrained,' why have you been making an inventory of Field Deployable Nuclear Warheads?"

"That's none of your business." Devereaux hadn't intended to confirm his recent assignment, even by inference. Lucky thing he'd switched off the recorder. He rewound the reel and took it off. "You can have a few minutes alone with your client." His Southern accent had become more pronounced and his demeanor more gracious. "And if you'd like to discuss the case further, I'd be delighted to do so over dinner this evening."

"No thank you."

"Whatever you say." Devereaux started to slip the tape reel into his coat pocket, then decided not to risk stretching the fabric of his suit. "Call me if you change your mind. I know some of the best restaurants in Albuquerque."

"I'm sure you do."

"I'll tell the guard to give you a full ten minutes."

"Thanks." When he left, Jean vented her anger by slamming her briefcase shut. "Where did the FBI find that incompetent?"

"The University of Alabama backfield."

"I should have guessed." She reopened her briefcase, then shut it again as a way to put off saying what was on her mind.

Got to get it out in the open, she thought. Out and disposed of. "Ansel, I'm sorry it was Maggie they used to frame you. I know how much that must have hurt."

Burke shifted in his chair. "I was numb for about an hour. Practically in a coma. Now I'm just sore—mostly at myself." He managed a rueful smile. "I made a royal jerk out of myself over Maggie, didn't I?"

She maintained a tactful silence.

"You look tired, Jean."

"I've had a busy couple of days."

"Get some rest."

"I will. First I want to show you what Lou Brodsky and I discovered this afternoon." She took a slip of paper from her briefcase. "Do you remember telling me on our walk back to Puma that the key to this puzzle is in what happened to that couple, the Hallidays?"

"That's right. I heard Harry Williamson and Hank Roper talking about the Hallidays. They murdered those kids. Did I tell you the diagram on their computer screen looked like a system of caves?"

"Yes, and the Hallidays were spelunkers."

"Right. I'm guessing the Hallidays stumbled on the place where those warheads are stored. That's why they were killed."

Jean brandished the slip of paper. "I think I know where that place is. This afternoon I asked Lou Brodsky to take me to the sheriff's impound yard. They still have the dune buggy the Hallidays rented the day they died. Perkins and the rental car company have been in a tangle over it; the company thinks the county should pay for the days the dune buggy was in impound and Sheriff Perkins refuses. I talked my way into the impound yard and searched the car. This was in the glove compartment."

Burke took the slip of paper and read it with a mounting sense of excitement:

Tuesday, May 6, 11:15 a.m.
My wife and I are exploring caves within the mountain known as Rattlesnake Peak twelve miles north of Puma and three miles off Highway 41 near Hassayampa Creek. We intend to complete our exploration by five p.m. Should this note be found after that hour, ask the local authorities to send help for us.

Bob Halliday

"I see. The Hallidays left a safety note in the car and Hank's men didn't find it after they killed them. Hassayampa Creek." Burke visualized the area. "Right down the road from Hank's gas station. Goddammit, I should've guessed! No use having a monitoring station unless you can get to the storage site fast if something goes wrong."

"What should we do with the note?" Jean wondered. "Give it to the FBI?"

"Devereaux won't believe the deaths of those kids have any connection with his nukes. Why should he? He made his count and none seemed to be missing. Hank must have left dummy warheads in place of the ones he took. No, Devereaux won't help us. How do you think he'd look if we proved his damned inventory wrong?"

"Then what can we do with this information?"

"Use it ourselves. That's why I have to get out of here."

"Getting you out will take time, especially since they're moving you to Virginia tomorrow night." Jean already had given thought to legal strategy. "I'll follow the day after, and by next week we should have enough evidence to counter these ridiculous—"

"Virginia? I'm not going to any detention center in Virginia. That'd give Hank time to cover up everything he's done."

"But Devereaux said that tomorrow night—"

"He doesn't know this stockade the way I do. I'm getting out of here tomorrow morning at ten o'clock, if you'll help me." Burke suddenly realized he couldn't ask Jean to do what he had in mind. How could he put her at even greater risk than she'd already faced? "Forget it. Crazy idea."

She sat down across from him. "What's your plan?"

"Never mind. I'll come up with something else."

"I have a *right* to know what you want to do. According to Lou Brodsky, I'm in as much danger as you are. He's guarding me as if I were the Mona Lisa."

Burke smiled over the only piece of good news he'd heard all day. "God bless the old-timers. You can always count on them."

"You're avoiding the subject. Ansel, nobody knows better than I do just how savage these people can be. They've got to be stopped. I've already had to kill a man. So you might as well tell me what else you want me to do."

Burke stared at his knuckles, something he often did while making a hard decision. "Okay," he said finally. "But your Bar Association won't like it."

Deputy FBI director Emmett Avery emerged from the 727 into Albuquerque International Airport feeling groggy and slightly unfocused. Despite all the air travel he'd done in his life, he never enjoyed it. At least this was a day flight; 90 percent of his trips seemed to be taken at night.

It would be a few minutes before the baggage came down the chute onto the carousel, so he found a phone and made a credit card call to FBI headquarters in Washington, D.C.

"This is Deputy Director Avery," he told the central operator. "Please put me through to Roy McCluskey."

After a moment, a voice said, "Director McCluskey's office. Wilma Bartles."

"Hello, Wilma. Emmett Avery." He glanced at his watch. "It's past eight o'clock there; long day for you."

"Oh yes, it has been. I'm just about to leave, but the director is still at his desk. How was your flight?"

"Tiring."

"Oh, dear." Wilma clucked sympathetically. "I'll put the director on straightaway."

After another brief interval, Roy McCluskey's deep voice boomed over the phone: "Emmett! How're you doing?"

"I just arrived in Albuquerque. Thought I'd check in with you before driving out to Fort Powell. Did anything happen while I was flying down here?"

"Yes! The local police arrested that sergeant major. Seems he walked right into the county sheriff's office, bold as brass."

"To give himself up?"

"I don't know."

Avery made a guess. "To ask for help?"

"That's a possibility. He may have some answers for you. Al Devereaux is interviewing him right now."

"Have you talked to Devereaux?"

"No, and I don't think I will. Not yet. Do you know Devereaux?"

"Just by reputation."

"Exactly. He's not one of the bureau's best."

Avery tried not to take offense at that remark, but as deputy director he had to bear some of the responsibility for the poor quality of agents McCluskey's predecessor had recruited. "You're right," he admitted.

"I haven't sent the usual telex to let the field office know a member of the director's office is coming on their turf. You're solo."

"Just like the old days. Sometime I'll tell you about the year I spent undercover with the teamsters."

"I'd like to hear it." McCluskey's voice dropped so low that his next words were almost a whisper. "Be careful, Emmett. We're going head-to-head with Luther Amstel. Call me first thing tomorrow morning."

"I will. So long, Roy."

Avery collected his one piece of luggage and went to the Hertz counter, where he rented a Ford LTD. The clerk gave him the keys and marked the route to Fort Powell on a map.

"The town of Puma's about an hour west of Albuquerque," she said. "And Fort Powell is just south of Puma."

"Thanks, I'll find it."

The rental cars were parked in an area across the access road. Avery walked out of the terminal and was crossing the road when the whine of a car engine caught his ear. He had looked both ways before stepping off the curb, but a big old dilapidated Oldsmobile with a University of New Mexico sticker on the bumper came out of nowhere. As he hurried toward the opposite curb, the Olds veered toward him. Avery broke into a trot. The Olds tracked straight for him. He dropped the suitcase and ran, knowing with icy certainty that he'd never reach the safety of the fenced-in area where the rental cars were parked.

The Oldsmobile was traveling at more than fifty

miles an hour when it hit Avery at the level of his left
hip, throwing him all the way over the fence he'd been
trying to reach. Avery screamed as he plunged onto
the concrete surface of the parking lot. For a dozen
agonizing seconds he fought to draw air into his lungs,
then gave himself up to the ultimate abyss.

By the time people came running to the site of the
accident, the Oldsmobile had disappeared.

Jean was surprised at how young Lieutenant Walter
Sloane looked. He can't be more than twenty-three or
twenty-four, she thought.

His manner, however, was as brusque as a church
elder's. "Why did you want to see me, Captain?" Sloane,
who was wearing civilian clothes, glanced irritably at
his watch. "At seven o'clock on a Sunday night?"

Vaguely dizzy, she closed her eyes.

"Are you all right?" Sloane jumped to his feet. "Let
me get you some water or tea. You look terribly tired."

"I guess I am." Jean opened her eyes and willed
herself to sit up straight. "Please don't trouble yourself about the tea."

"Have you had dinner?"

"Yes, a candy bar."

"My God, that's not enough. Let me take you over to
the Officer's Club. You need a hot meal."

"No time . . ." She gripped the desk. "Please let me
go on."

Sloane reluctantly returned to his chair. "Why did
you ask to meet me in my office tonight when you're
exhausted? Wouldn't tomorrow morning have done as
well?"

"No. You see, I'm working on a very important case.
I'm an attorney with the J.A.G. office here at Fort
Powell and I'm representing Sergeant Major Burke."

"Burke?" Sloane drew away from her. "Why do you
want to see me? I've nothing to do with the case
against him."

"Weren't you surprised when your sergeant major
was charged with espionage?"

"Yes, certainly—a terrible thing. I hope he's cleared,
of course. Sergeant Burke and I have had our differ-

ences, but I don't believe he's the kind of man who
would turn against his country." Sloane twisted the
West Point ring on his finger so hard that the flesh
underneath began to redden. "Has Sergeant Burke
ever said anything to you about me?"

Jean opened her briefcase and took out a manila
envelope. "He instructed me to find this in the place
where it was hidden and give it to you."

Sloane stared at the envelope as if it contained a
letter bomb. "Did you look inside?"

"No, Ansel asked me to give it to you unopened."

Sloane undid the flap and peeked inside, then closed
and sealed it at once. "How can I believe that?"

"Because it's true. Ansel Burke isn't a liar. Neither
am I."

"No, he isn't." Sloane became softly bitter. "He's
honest . . . tough . . . loyal. Men look up to him. Women
admire him. Ansel Burke is everything my father
wanted me to be, and I guess I hate him for that." He
focused his rheumy eyes on Jean with some difficulty.
"What do you want from me?"

"Ansel needs your help."

"How could I help him? And why should I?" He
tapped the envelope. "Did you know that Burke threatened to use this to destroy me?"

"No." Jean was afraid Sloane was going to break
down. He seemed on the verge of tears, or something
even worse. "I only know that Ansel needs your help
to get out of the stockade tomorrow morning."

"Get out?" Sloane was quick to grasp her meaning.
"What are you talking about?" He again began to
twist the ring. "If Burke is innocent, why should he
have to do something like that?"

"Terrible things are happening at this post. Haven't
you realized that?"

"I'm not stupid." Sloane impulsively tossed the manila envelope into the empty wastebasket and torched
it with his cigarette lighter. The flame burned slowly
until it reached the chemically treated photographic
paper, which went up with a *whoosh*. "Burke is being
prosecuted because he wouldn't stop investigating the
murder of that girl. He tried to tell me what was

behind that; I wasn't in the mood to listen. All I know
is that you can't go against the power structure, Captain Silk. Not in the army."

"Will you listen now?"

Sloane looked unhappy. "If you insist."

Jean told him why Betsy Palermo had been killed,
offering as evidence the large sums of money she had
spent or put away in various banks, and repeated the
information Ansel had developed on Hank Roper and
the fake captain at the Restricted Materiel Center.
Sloane had not known that nuclear warheads were
stored at Fort Powell, or that an inventory had been
made in connection with Egypt's attack in the Libyan
army. Jean also told him about the deaths of the
Hallidays and showed him the note she had found in
their rented dune buggy. To underscore the savagery
of the opposition, she described the fight at Hank
Roper's gas station and their flight into the desert.

That particular revelation was the most disturbing
to Sloane. "Do you mean all those senior N.C.O.s aren't
A.W.O.L.? They're dead? Burke actually *killed* them?"

"He had no choice."

He wagged his finger at her. "You're going to end up
in the stockade with him."

"I can't worry about that right now. Lieutenant, we
have to find the warheads stolen from this post."

"Go to the proper authorities. If nuclear warheads
really have been stolen, that's a question of national
security. We're just Military Police."

"We've tried that. The FBI doesn't believe Ansel. In
time he'll prove everything I've said. Right now we
don't have the luxury of time. This is a high-level
conspiracy. We've got to stop it ourselves before it's
covered up."

"I'm not saying I believe your story. But if you think
you know where stolen warheads are being kept,
couldn't you go after them without Ansel Burke?"

"Would you want to go without him?"

Sloane admitted to himself that he would not want
to undertake such a mission without a man like Burke
on the point. He felt ashamed that he'd never be able
to command men with Burke's authority. I'm a fraud,

he thought. While I'm off in the shadows satisfying my
urges, people like Burke and this lawyer—this *girl*—
are fighting the real battles. "Let's say, just for the
sake of argument, that I believed your story. Exactly
what would you want me to do tomorrow morning?"

When Jean outlined Ansel's plan, Lieutenant Sloane
became more frightened than ever.

"I can't allow such a thing to happen. I'm the acting
provost marshal!"

"That's exactly why we need you."

"My father—"

"Lieutenant, for once in your life do something just
because it's *right*."

Burke's plan was so audacious Sloane could find no
words to describe his fear of it. To take part would be
to end his career in immediate disgrace. He lingered
over that fact. Did his army career still matter? Did it
really? Wasn't it headed toward a shabby conclusion
anyway? Sooner or later his sexual habits were bound
to be discovered; he simply could not leave his dogs
alone, they provided the only love available to him in
this vicious world. Wouldn't it be infinitely better to
end his so-called career in one grand defiant gesture?

Perhaps he could still save himself by seeking a
psychiatrist's help or resigning his commission. But if
he did that, could he live with his father's inevitable
contempt?

Jean saw that Sloane was carrying on a heated
debate within himself. She could only hope the best
side of him would win.

"If I resign my commission," Sloane said, more to
himself than to Jean, "I'll be nothing. A cipher."

"I beg your pardon?"

"There's no way I can save myself." Sloane raised
his sad eyes to Jean. "So I might as well do what I can
to help Sergeant Burke." He raised a cautionary finger. "On one condition: I'm going with him to that
mountain."

"Lieutenant, that's a deal."

General Leland stood over the architectural model
of the home he was restoring in Baltimore. He wasn't

sure the trees were placed just right. The eight tiny
model oak trees lining the miniature driveway seemed
to be sitting too far back. He moved them carefully.
Yes, much better. He recalled that as a boy he'd rigged
up a swing on the tree nearest the house. Those were
grand days. He could hardly wait for his home to be
restored to its former glory.

"You were crazy to send Roper to kill Emmett Avery,"
said Captain Dan Miller, who was pacing the floor of
the general's office.

"Orders," Leland replied. "He was coming here to
talk to Burke."

"That sergeant's the one who has to be taken care
of."

"Obviously," Leland agreed. "But he's a difficult man
to kill."

"One lousy sergeant."

"And the girl," Leland reminded him.

"The operation's coming apart. I've seen it happen
before." Miller waved the glass of bourbon Leland had
given him as a sedative for his nerves. "Somebody
makes a mistake and everything starts to unravel."

There was a knock on the door and Leland said,
"Come in, Sergeant Roper."

Although Roper was wearing civilian clothes, he
saluted General Leland out of habit. "Sir, you don't
have to worry about that visitor from Washington. He
had a nasty accident outside the airport."

Miller moaned. "That was the Deputy Director of
the FBI! Do you have any idea how much heat we're
going to take?"

"It was an accident," Roper said. "Hit and run. The
cops'll find the car behind a dorm at the University of
New Mexico. Empty beer cans on the floor. Pot in the
glove compartment. They'll blame it on some kid who
was flying high."

"You won't fool Roy McCluskey." Miller gulped down
some of his drink.

"I've been told that McCluskey is on his way out as
FBI director." Leland left the model and went behind
his desk. After checking his watch, he picked up the
phone and dialed an 800 number. When the connection was made, he said, "Bluebird. 758826."

Miller and Roper looked at each other, both curious about the identity of the man from whom General Claude Leland took his orders.

"Yes, this is Bluebird." Leland smiled. "How are things going there?" He glanced at Miller and Roper. "No, I'm not alone right now. Yes, our visitor had a serious accident at the Albuquerque air terminal. That should give us time to cover our tracks." He nodded. "I agree, that's only prudent." He paused and listened intently. "Well, we've accomplished a great deal already. Very well. Don't worry, everything will be cleaned up on this end."

After Leland put down the phone, he stared at his desk top for a few moments while sorting out facts in his mind. "We have our marching orders," he said finally. "Priority one: shut down the monitoring station and the storage site. Priority two: move the balance of the units to the backup site."

Miller was relieved. "Does that mean we're not going through with the sale to the Arabs?"

"The exchange is postponed, not canceled. Now tell me about the backup site."

"It's a warehouse in Denver." Miller drained his glass. "This clothing company was going broke, so I bought their warehouse. There's a fur vault just right for storing our kind of merchandise. Good climate control and a seven-inch steel door. Security isn't as good as the mountain, but it'll do for now."

Leland's eyes moved to Roper. "You're in charge of the logistics of the move."

"Everything's laid on, sir." Roper looked at his watch. "The computer'll be taken out of the bungalow behind the station tomorrow morning. At the same time we'll go for the units inside the mountain with an air-conditioned truck. Be out of there by noon and in Denver by midnight." He grinned at Leland and Miller. "Burke can do all the talking he wants after that."

"I still want Burke and the girl disposed of," Leland said.

"Burke is being sent to a federal detention center in Virginia tomorrow night." Miller went to the small refrigerator in the corner of Leland's office and began making himself another drink. "There are two Mafia types in there; very tough individuals. They've been promised pardons, money, and new identities in exchange for ridding us of Sergeant Burke."

"Good. He may not even live that long. I've had him taken out of isolation and put in the stockade tank along with the riffraff he sent there. Now what about Captain Silk?"

"I'll do her," Roper volunteered. "Right now Ansel's friends have got her covered around the clock, but they can't do that for long. Shit, they're only ordinary grunts. They've got regular duty."

"I'll see that they're assigned additional duties. They'll be kept too busy to watch over her." Leland thought about open items. "Miller, what about security between here and Denver?"

"Six free-lancers are coming in tonight. Colombians. Top men in their field. They'll ride in separate cars in front of and behind Roper's truck all the way to the Denver city limits. They've got orders to peel off there. Only four people will know the location of the new storage site, including the three of us."

"Do your free-lancers have any idea what will be in the truck?"

"Hell, no. They've been told they'll be riding shotgun for a drug shipment, which is their primary business. And you don't have to worry that they'll get ideas about a rip-off. They know they're doing business with the CIA. They can't afford to double-cross us."

"Then we're in good shape." Leland saw that Roper and Miller were less satisfied. "Don't look so grim. We're not in this alone, you know. Our friends in Washington can't afford to let this operation be exposed."

"It's fine to have powerful friends," Roper agreed. "But it's your enemies that count. I won't feel comfortable until Ansel is dead and buried."

MONDAY, JUNE 16

Chapter 27

At a little past 6:00 A.M. on Monday morning, the phone rang at Roy McCluskey's home in Alexandria, Virginia. He snaked his hand out and managed to pull the receiver into bed without disturbing his blankets. "Hullo," he grunted.

"Sir, this is agent Al Devereaux in Albuquerque. I'm sorry to bother you at home."

"That's okay." McCluskey pushed back the blankets, sat up, and looked at the bedside clock: six o'clock in Washington; four in the morning in Albuquerque. "What is it, Al?"

"A man has been killed here by a hit-and-run driver. It took a while for the local police to focus on his ID. Sir, I'm sorry ... The dead man turned out to be Emmett Avery."

"What?"

"The deputy director is dead. Hit and run. I didn't even know he was in town."

"Where did this happen?"

"Right outside the airport."

"What time?"

"A little after five o'clock yesterday afternoon."

McCluskey closed his eyes. It must have happened right after he had talked to Emmett on the phone. "Has Mrs. Avery been told?"

"Not yet. When the local police got around to looking at his ID, they called me. I couldn't believe it, so I

came down to the morgue to look at the body. It's
Avery, all right."

God damn them, McCluskey thought.

"Sir?"

"I'm here."

"As I said, I didn't even know the deputy director
was in Albuquerque. That's why I thought the police
had made a mistake; we usually get a telex when a
VIP is expected on our turf." Devereaux sounded
aggrieved.

"You say it was a hit-and-run accident?"

"Yes, sir."

"Any witnesses?"

"Yes, and the police have already located the car; it
belongs to a student at the university."

"Al, hold on for a minute. I'll be right back."
McCluskey put down the receiver and gently shook his
wife's shoulder. "Ellen? Wake up, hon."

"Umm, what is it, Roy?"

He waited until his wife had struggled to a sitting
position. "I've just had some bad news. Emmett Avery
has been killed by a hit-and-run driver."

"Oh, my Lord. Does Kate know?"

"Not yet. I'm going over there in a few minutes to
tell her."

His wife threw back the blankets. "I'll come with
you. She'll need someone, her kids are away at school."

As Ellen began to dress, McCluskey picked up the
phone. "Listen carefully, Al. I don't believe Emmett
was killed by accident. I sent him to New Mexico to
look into the Burke case, not knowing at the time that
Sergeant Burke would turn up so soon. Somebody found
out why Emmett was in Albuquerque and made certain he didn't get a chance to talk to that sergeant."

"Murder?" Devereaux sounded dubious. "The witnesses
said it was a drunk driver, and some pot and empty
beer cans were found in the car. Sounds more like
vehicular manslaughter to me. Some kid flying high."

"No, we're dealing with clever people. Have you
interviewed Burke yet?"

"Yes, sir. I did a prelim to advise him of the charges
last night."

"What did he say? Give it to me net. I want to get over to see Mrs. Avery as soon as possible." As McCluskey listened to Devereaux's account of the interview with Ansel Burke, his jaw muscles clenched until they were tight enough to snap. "You didn't see any reason to investigate his countercharges?"

"No, sir. You'd have to meet this Burke to understand why. He's a hardhead. Always giving people trouble. I wouldn't believe word one from him."

God save us from idiots, McCluskey thought. "Al, I want you to send me by courier the tape recording of your interview with Burke; I want it in my hands by ten o'clock this morning, Washington time. Then go back to Fort Powell and double-check the F.D.N.W. inventory. Take your whole staff with you. This time make sure each device is identical. They may have pulled a switch on you."

"Sir, I don't think so." Devereaux's voice trembled.

"I hope to God you're right."

"Uh, what about Burke?"

"Leave him in the stockade for now. If he turns out to know more than we do, we'll pull him out of there fast. Call me at Bureau headquarters when you've got some news. One more thing, Al. Keep your mouth shut about Emmett's death not being an accident." He hung up and hurried to dress himself.

The next several hours were the most depressing in Roy McCluskey's life. As chief of police in San Francisco, and then as FBI director, he had brought more than one unfortunate woman the news of her husband's death. But this was the first time he had ever lied to a widow. Looking directly into Kate Avery's eyes, he told her Emmett had been killed in a hit-and-run car accident in Albuquerque, probably by a drunk driver. He hated himself for the lie, even as he realized he had no choice. If his suspicions were true, no one else must know who really caused Emmett Avery's death—not even Emmett's own wife.

He left Ellen to help Kate Avery with the inevitable phone calls to children and relatives and drove to his office at Bureau headquarters in a foul mood.

Despite the long overtime she had put in on Sunday,

Wilma Bartles was at her desk outside the director's
office when he arrived.

"Good morning, sir."

On an ordinary day McCluskey would have returned
the greeting and gone on past into his office. Today he
paused and looked at her with more interest: Wilma
Bartles, age forty-eight, if he remembered correctly;
unmarried; no close relatives; twenty-odd years with
the bureau. "Wilma, I want you to send out a telex
right away."

She quickly picked up a pencil.

"I regret to inform you," he dictated, "that Deputy
Director Emmett Avery died last night in Albuquerque, New Mexico, from injuries sustained when he
was run down by a speeding car. Mr. Avery was one of
the most respected men in the bureau. His loss dimin-
ishes us greatly. Funeral arrangements will be announced later today."

Wilma Bartles went pale.

"Did you get all that, Wilma?"

"Yes, sir. Yes. Oh, that's terrible news."

"Send the telex to all division chiefs and district
administrators, then come into my office."

McCluskey placed himself behind his desk and waited
for Wilma to come in.

"Sit down," he said when she appeared.

The expression on the director's face alarmed Wilma.
"The telex has gone out. Is anything, wrong sir?"

"I want to share some confidential information with
you. Mr. Avery's death wasn't an accident. Someone
purposely ran him down."

"That's awful!" Wilma sat rigidly at attention, her
heart pounding.

"You and I were the only ones who knew that I sent
Mr. Avery to New Mexico. In fact, you even knew the
number of the flight he was on."

Wilma kept her knees locked together and her eyes
downcast.

McCluskey was an old hand at interrogation. He
knew that some people break under heavy questioning
while others buckle under the pressure of silence. Wilma
would fit into the second category. He stared at her in

silence, his beefy arms crossed on the desk and his expression larded with distaste.

When Wilma could no longer stand the silence, she said rather shrilly, "Are you accusing me of something?"

"I'm giving you an opportunity to speak up, Wilma. This is the *only* chance you'll be offered. In five minutes I'm going to pick up the phone and call the U.S. Attorney. I'll ask for a warrant to search your house and seize your bank accounts. The internal squad will be digging into your activities. The IRS will also be called in. If you've done anything wrong, every agency in Washington will take a piece of you."

She began to blubber.

"You've been with the Bureau long enough to know what that means. Oh, your pension will be forfeit, too." McCluskey glanced at his watch. "Four minutes."

"Please . . ."

"Please won't do it. Emmett Avery is dead."

McCluskey watched coldly as she began crying into her handkerchief.

"All right," she said presently, refolding the handkerchief to find a dry spot. "Good heavens, you're treating me like a criminal. All I've done—ever done—was pass on some harmless information once in a while. And never to a foreign power. Heavens! What do you think I am?"

"I don't know what you are. I only know what you've done. How do you pass on the information?"

Wilma told him about the phone booth at the Smithsonian, the six-digit code, the metallic computer voice. "It was the CIA that approached me. Not some Russian, if that's what you're thinking. I'm a loyal American. My people came to this country in 1795." She cried some more. "I just didn't want to be poor when I got old, that's all, not poor as well as lonely. Is that so awful?" She sobbed more loudly. "You wouldn't destroy me for something like that, would you?"

"How long have you been doing this?"

"For three years, maybe a little more."

Ever since Luther Amstel became Director of the CIA, McCluskey thought. He picked up the phone and dialed the number for internal investigations. "Clint,

this is the director. Come upstairs right away. I have
someone who wants to make a statement to you. Yes,
it's terrible about Emmett." He was always amazed at
how fast bad information traveled. "Don't bother knocking, just come straight into my office." He smiled wanly.
"No, Wilma won't bite your head off."

He turned Wilma over to internal investigations as
quickly as possible. There was much to do and very
little time. At least he now knew what to look for. The
pattern was established, all he had to do was look in
the right places and talk to the right people.

Over the next few hours he dispatched a dozen of
the Bureau's best agents to gather the facts he needed.
His office took on the atmosphere of a war room, with
agents coming in to give him bits of information and
going right out again on new assignments. Everyone
in the building knew there was a brand-new flap on,
but no one could pin down its exact nature. McCluskey
kept the various pieces of his investigation compart-
mentalized. He intended to be the only one holding all
the facts.

When the tape came from Albuquerque, McCluskey
locked himself in his office alone and played it back.
The outrage in Burke's voice sounded genuine. Burke
had a good voice, strong and forthright—no bullshit
there. And he could think too. His thoughts were presented with persuasive logic. Why the hell Devereaux
didn't act on Burke's suspicions was a mystery to
McCluskey. Devereaux was an asshole, of course. But
a Bureau asshole and therefore untouchable. He also
liked the woman's voice, and sensed more than a professional attachment between her and Burke. She was
cutting Devereaux to pieces and he didn't even realize
it.

McCluskey played the tape twice. When he had di-
gested each fact and analyzed every nuance, he began
to make a list of points in the order he would present
them to the President. Only one fact was missing—the
big one: have nuclear warheads been taken from the
stockpile at Fort Powell?

For another hour he chafed. Then his new secretary,
hastily drafted from the word processing center, an-

nounced that Devereaux was on the phone. He snatched
it up. "Al, what's the verdict?"

"I'm afraid there are ten warheads missing." Devereaux sounded dazed. "We found devices in every case,
but some turned out to be fakes. Very good fakes," he
emphasized, desperate to protect himself. "Same weight
as the real things. Same design. You can hardly tell
the phonies from the genuine articles. I'm sure you'll
understand why my first—"

"Shut up and listen. Go to the stockade and get
Sergeant Burke. He may have some idea where the
missing warheads can be found." McCluskey snorted.
"He sure as hell knows more about it than you do. I
want him flown to Washington immediately under
protective custody. And Al, continue to keep your mouth
shut. Impress upon your staff that this is a matter of
the highest national security. If there's a leak, I'll bust
your ass."

"Sir, I resent—"

"Do your resenting on your own time." McCluskey
put down the phone with a sense of accomplishment,
but no elation. However the day ended, there would be
one big loser—the United States of America.

Chapter 28

At 9:30 A.M. First Lieutenant Walter Sloane, dressed in army green fatigues, spit-shined combat boots, and wearing a holstered .45, appeared in front of the stockade desk sergeant. "Good morning, Sergeant. I want to see Ansel Burke."

"Good morning, sir." The desk sergeant picked up his prisoner ID file and frowned. "Uh, Ansel—I mean, Sergeant Major Burke—is being held by the FBI."

"Yes?"

"Well, sir, they left instructions that no one was to question Sergeant Burke except a federal officer."

Sloane began to show the impatience for which he knew he was already well known. "They obviously didn't mean the acting provost marshal." He whipped out a pen and notebook. "What's your full name and serial number?"

"Staff Sergeant John A. Eustace, RA 433298."

Sloane wrote that down. "Do you doubt my authority, Sergeant Eustace?"

"Oh no, sir. I'm just trying to follow the FBI guidelines."

"Sergeant Burke may be an FBI prisoner, but he is still a sergeant major in the U.S. Army. I don't want to question him. I'm only interested in last week's morning reports. They're a complete mess and I need Burke's help to clear them up."

The desk sergeant felt he had done enough for the FBI. Federal agents come and go, and after they were gone he'd still be here serving under this West Point asshole. No use getting Sloane more pissed off than he was already. "Whatever you say, sir." He pressed a button and the door leading into the corridors of the stockade swung open. "Corporal Johnson, the provost marshal wants to see Ansel Burke."

The corporal on interior guard led Sloane down a corridor to the section of the stockade known as the "tank." Though all prisoners slept at night in separate cells, those who weren't taken out in the morning on work details were herded together in the tank until after evening chow.

The tank was a rectangle of floor-to-ceiling steel bars about thirty yards wide by eighty yards long in which perhaps twenty prisoners were now lounging. They were the stockade's hard cases, men considered too dangerous to be allowed outside on work details.

"Burke!" the corporal yelled. "Front and center!"

On the opposite side of the tank, Ansel Burke sat cross-legged on the floor with his back to the bars. He uncoiled himself, wincing a little, and came forward favoring his left leg.

"Hello, Lieutenant."

Sloane nodded curtly. "How did you get those bruises on your face, sergeant? And what's wrong with your leg?"

"The sheriff and his deputies gave me the bruises; they worked me over before bringing me in yesterday. When I was thrown in the tank, some of the stockade rats thought they'd settle old scores. Too bad you weren't here after breakfast, you missed a pretty good fight."

Sloane noticed that a few of the other prisoners were nursing their own sets of scars and lacerations. One man was even unconscious in a corner. Sloane's West Point training had instilled in him a respect for military justice that did not countenance kangaroo courts. He turned on the interior guard in a rage. "Why didn't you break up the brawl?"

"Sir, me and the other interior guard were busy with another fight at the opposite end of the wing. These guys mix it up all the time. We can't be everywhere at once."

"Starting tomorrow I'm adding two more interior guards." Sloane belatedly realized he would not be the acting provost marshal after today. "Oh, never mind. I want to talk to Burke in the exercise yard."

"In the yard? Sir, you're supposed to use an interrogation room for interviewing prisoners."

"I'm taking Burke into the exercise yard," Sloane repeated. "Are you going to stand there all day?"

The corporal quickly unlocked the door to let Burke into the corridor and led them to an exit that opened onto an exercise yard with a twenty-foot wall at the end. The yard was empty now. It was open to the prison population only from noon to 1:00 P.M., and 4:00 to 6:00 P.M.

"That will be all for now," Sloane said. "Come back in half an hour."

"Yes, sir." The corporal withdrew hastily to avoid another chewing out.

"Let's walk," Sloane said.

The outside air smelled wonderful. Burke filled his lungs as he fell into step next to Sloane. "Lieutenant, I know you're putting your career on the line. I wish I could think of something better to say than 'thank you.'"

"Save your thanks. I'm helping you only partly because I believed Captain Silk's story. I just want to put an end to your blackmail."

"Blackmail? I told Jean to give you all the pictures."

"We both know you can get more of those photos from your buddy at Fort Sill. I want your promise that you'll ask him to destroy all photos and negatives." He smiled with a trace of self-mockery. "If we get out of this adventure alive, which I doubt."

"That's fair enough." Burke examined the two guard towers facing the exercise yard. Because all other prisoners were in the tank or out on work details, there were no guards in either one right now. "I think we'll get out of the stockade alive. What happens afterward is another story."

They stopped near the wall and Sloane took out a pack of cigarettes. "Do you want a smoke?"

"No thanks."

Sloane removed a cigarette from the pack with shaky hands. "I'm a little nervous."

"So am I."

"You hide it better than I do."

"I've had more practice. Look, you're right when you say there was a touch of blackmail in getting you to do this. I have leverage and I used it. But you're a West Point man. You believe in the army. I didn't think you could stand by for very long while a crowd of crooks made trash out of it."

The notion that his sergeant major might still hold some genuine respect for him made Sloane feel taller and stronger. To cover the rush of gratitude that overcame him, he looked at his watch. "Five minutes to ten. Do you think your friend will be here? On time?"

"Feeney will be here." Burke smiled to himself. "He wouldn't miss this party for all the whiskey in New Mexico."

After breakfast Sean Feeney faked a crippling stomach ache and was given permission to return to barracks. He went to his bunk and lay down. He was nervous and thirsty. The thirst was easier to cure than his nervousness. From the bottom of his footlocker he took a bottle of Jack Daniel's and helped himself to a bracer. Usually he didn't drink until afternoon. Tried not to, anyhow. But today was special.

At 9:25 Feeney again dug to the bottom of his footlocker, this time for a clean shirt. He changed into the one fatigue shirt from which he had not removed his corporal's stripes after the court-martial. If he was going to die today, which was possible, he wanted to be wearing his stripes.

The bottom of Feeney's footlocker contained a variety of items disallowed in barracks by army regulations. Whiskey, for one. And a personal handgun. He unwrapped the oily rags from a P-38 pistol he had picked up on a tour of duty in Germany, loaded the weapon, and slipped two extra clips into his pocket.

Feeney put the bottle of Jack Daniel's and the P-38 into a brown paper bag and went across the company compound to the motor pool, where the tanks were parked.

About half the tanks had been taken out on maneuver. The one he wanted was there, a brand-new Abrams M1 medium tank with laminated armor and one of the new 120 millimeter smooth-bore guns. The captain was waiting for the other two Abrams M1s to arrive before putting this one into service, but it was fully gassed and mechanically checked out.

He went to the armory and took the bottle of Jack Daniel's out of the sack. "Hey, Eddie. Want a drink?"

The armorer shook his head. "You're stone-crazy, Sean. No, I don't want a drink. And you'd better put that bottle away before the old man sees it. Ain't you supposed to be sick?"

"I'm feeling better. How about giving me a half a dozen sabots for the new M1? I'd like to try out those suckers."

"Are you nuts?"

Feeney took the P-38 out of the bag and pointed it at the armorer. "I'm serious as hell, Eddie. Break out a case of sabots and carry them out to the M1 for me."

"No!"

"I'm not fucking around. Do it, and do it fast. I'm on a schedule."

The armorer hesitated until he concluded that Sean Feeney's threat was real. Then he unlocked the door to the weapons room and, under Feeney's gun, picked up a case of six 120-millimeter sabot armor piercing shells. Feeney marched him out to the new M1 and told him to put the case up on the turret. He then locked the armorer in his office and ripped out the phone line.

Feeney loaded the sabots into the ammo rack behind the gunner's seat. The sabot was a new type of ammunition for a tank gun. Because the 120 was smooth bore instead of rifled, the sabot had stabilizing fins on the rear end, making each sabot resemble a three-foot-long dart. When the shell was fired from the cannon, the lightweight casing, or sabot, would break away in the air, allowing the missile to streak to its target at maximum speed.

He switched on the ignition and the powerful turbine engine turned over. Seconds later the tank was rolling out of the motor pool and heading down the road leading to the main post.

No one who noticed the tank thought anything about it. Rolling armor was a common sight on the dirt roads around Camp Funston and Custer Hill. Feeney knew he wouldn't attract any real attention until he reached the main post where tanks were off limits because of the way they chew up roads.

At 9:46 he was only a minute behind schedule as he turned the tank onto a back road leading to the main post and increased speed to forty miles an hour. The hatch in front of the drive's compartment was down and the driver's seat raised so that Feeney's head and shoulders were out in the open. When the action started, he'd lower the seat, close the hatch, and use the periscope to see where he was going.

He was well onto the main post now, passing the chapel and the Bachelor Officers Quarters. A few people gave the M1 curious stares. One officer even looked with outrage at the deep ruts the tank treads were making on the road surface. But no one signaled Feeney to turn around or tried to stop him in any way.

Post headquarters appeared on his left. Feeney grinned as he passed under General Leland's office and crossed the quadrangle facing the stockade. He was in MP territory now and finally drawing attention. An MP ran up and shouted "Where the hell do you think you're going?"

Feeney tromped on the gas pedal and left the MP in his dust. The stockade was a city block long. He approached on an angle and drove the tank around to the side of the stockade. There was a Buick poking along in front of him. The driver heard the roar of the tank's engine, but didn't recognize the sound. He finally looked in the rearview mirror and saw a tank behind him, its huge gun pointed directly at his rear window, and sped away.

The stockade walls were thirty feet high and made of three-foot-thick concrete reinforced with steel bars. He found the two guard towers that overlooked the exercise yard and stopped the tank in front of the wall.

"Time to button up." He lowered the seat and closed the front hatch, then slipped into the gunner's seat and put on his helmet. With a flick of his thumb, he traversed the gun until it was pointing at the wall. "Lock and load," he chirped, sliding one of the sabots into the breech of the 120.

His watch read 9:59. He moved the safety latch covering the trigger of the 120 and poised his thumb over the button. "Now we'll find out if this new ammo's any good."

Burke and Sloane had placed themselves at the far end of the exercise yard, as far away from the wall as they could manage.

"It's 9:59," Sloane said. "Are you sure he's coming?"

"I hear the tank engine."

Sloane cocked his head and heard the rumble, too. My God, he thought. We're actually going to do it.

The door opened and FBI agent Al Devereaux came striding across the exercise yard with the corporal of the guard at his heels. "Sloane, what the hell are you doing with my prisoner? I left orders that no one could talk to him except me."

Sloane looked nervously at Burke. "What'll we do?"

"When the wall goes, we go."

Devereaux looked somewhat less self-important than usual as he came up to Burke. "Sergeant, I've got orders to take you to Washington."

"Sorry, I've got other plans." Burke wished Feeney would get on with it.

"Other plans? Look, I don't give a shit—"

The ground shook as an explosion at the opposite end of the exercise yard knocked both Sloane and the corporal of the guard off their feet. Devereaux stumbled, but kept his balance.

"What's—"

Burke slugged Devereaux and dragged Sloane to his feet. "Come on!"

The wall had collapsed at its center into a pile of rubble from which clouds of dust were billowing like a desert storm. From out of the dust emerged the spearlike barrel of a gun. An M1 tank climbed to the top of the rubble and perched there like a mechanical king-of-the-hill. The crashing weight of the tank caused another section of the wall to collapse.

A hatch opened and a helmeted head popped up. "Hey, Ansel, want a lift?"

"Open the other hatch!"

Feeney obliged him and reached down to help Burke and Sloane up onto the turret. They scrambled aboard. Burke pushed Sloane headfirst into the tank, then lowered himself and pulled the hatch shut above him. "Let's roll, Sean."

"Lemme put one more hole in the stockade, so's the other yardbirds can get out, too."

"No!"

"Well, shit." Feeney threw the tank in reverse and backed out of the destruction he had created.

Sloane had never been inside a tank. He felt claustrophobic and more than a little nauseated. Gases from the firing of the 120 lingered in the tank and he wasn't wearing a helmet like Feeney's, which was equipped with sound baffles and a breathing apparatus. Just as bothersome as the gas was the heavy aroma of whiskey that permeated the small compartment. He was shocked to see the tank driver drinking out of a bottle of Jack Daniel's.

"Corporal, that's strictly against army regs!"

Burke took the bottle and helped himself to a drink. "Feeney just blew a hole twenty feet wide in the stockade wall. They're not going to hang him or us any higher for having a couple of drinks afterward." He thrust the bottle at Sloane. "You look like you could use one yourself."

"Well . . . I see your point." Aware that he was in danger of letting his customary priggishness take hold, Sloane gingerly drank some of the whiskey.

The tank was rolling massively toward the main gate at maximum speed. People had come running. Two MPs were kneeling on the quad with rifles raised.

"Time to button up again." Feeney lowered his seat and slammed shut the front hatch just as rifle fire broke out. The 30-caliber rounds bounced harmlessly off the tank's turret and armored skirts, which were

made of laminated plates of steel and titanium. "Ansel,
these new sabots are in-fucking-credible. Did you see
the hole I blew in that wall with just *one* of these
babies?" He kept his eyes fixed on the telescope. "Hold
on, we're going through the main gate." He grinned.
"And I do mean *through* the main gate; they closed the
sucker on us."

Burke braced himself, but the M1 crashed through
the barrier as if it were made of matchsticks. More
small-arms fire ricocheted off the tank, then faded
away.

Sloane finally recognized Sean Feeney. "Now I know
you! You're the corporal who used your tank to knock
down that house of prostitution."

"You flatten one whorehouse and you're marked for
life," Feeney grumbled.

"Sean, they're bound to follow us." Burke had to
shout to make himself heard above the engine. "And
they won't have a tough time doing it. This thing
leaves pretty big tracks."

"In five minutes we'll be crossing the Camp Funston
tank range," Feeney shouted back. "There's nothing
but tank tracks out there. Ours'll be just one more set.
When we leave the tank range, we'll turn east to meet
up with the others out on the desert."

The full impact of what they had done was finally
coming home to Sloane. "What if you're wrong? What
if there aren't any stolen warheads inside that mountain?"

Burke smiled at him. "Then we're all in deep shit,
Lieutenant."

General Leland instantly recognized the sound of an
artillery piece firing. He'd heard it thousands of times.
But here on the main post?

He swung his chair around and looked across the
quad toward the stockade. A cloud of dust was rising
from along the north wall. A moment later a tank
raced down the road right under his window toward
the main gate.

A single word jumped into Leland's mind: *Burke*.

To confirm the thought, his clerk rushed in to make

a breathless report: "Sir, there's been an escape from the stockade. Somebody in a tank blew a hole in the stockade wall. Nobody knows yet how many prisoners got away. It's pure confusion over there."

"I can see that." Leland was watching jeeps full of MPs drive off in different directions, each group sure it knew which way the tank had gone. And what would happen if they actually caught up with the tank? They couldn't stop it. Nothing short of an air strike or an APC equipped with an armor-piercing rocket launcher could stop one of the new M1s.

Leland picked up his hat and hurried out of the headquarters building to his car. This wasn't a simple escape—Burke had something else in mind. Could he know where the warheads were hidden? That seemed impossible. But so much had gone wrong that he couldn't take that chance. He had to warn Roper.

Chapter 29

Luther Amstel's limo deposited him at the north entrance to the White House at a quarter to one Washington time. The prospect of victory buoyed him so much that he alighted from the long black Chrysler and walked up the steps with hardly a trace of his usual limp.

Before going up to the Oval Office, Amstel made his customary detour to Jim Canon's cubbyhole. Though he personally disliked the press secretary, he usually found Jim Canon to be a useful bellwether of the President's thinking. Today Canon was slumped in the chair behind his typewriter, a cigarette burning unnoticed in the ashtray, the phone ringing unanswered.

"Something wrong, Jim?"

Canon looked at Amstel with distaste. "Yes, something's very wrong. You're getting your way, as usual."

"What's that supposed to mean?"

The press secretary ripped a sheet of paper from his typewriter and passed it over. What Amstel read was the rough draft of a presidential statement that came very close to endorsing Egypt's use of the nuclear weapon. By implication, the statement would also lend weight to Argentina's argument that it needed a nuclear deterrent to defend itself against aggression from Cuba. "Does the President intend to issue this statement today?"

"I'm afraid so."

"I know you disagree. But I think time and events will prove the President right about this."

Canon gave a shrug of defeat.

Amstel left the press secretary to his melancholy thoughts and took the elevator up to the second floor, where he was immediately ushered into the oval office. His exhilaration was kept under strict control; President Walter Bryant hated nothing more than the notion he had been manipulated. Amstel's benign Father Christmas smile was securely in place as he approached the President. "Good afternoon, sir."

"Luther, thank you for coming at such short notice. Sit down."

"Hello, Luther."

Amstel was startled. He hadn't noticed the hulking figure of FBI director Roy McCluskey sitting in the shadows. "Oh. Hello there, Roy. I didn't realize you were going to join us."

"This is Roy's meeting," the President said.

"I see." Amstel was finding it increasingly difficult to suppress his euphoria. "Are you here to admit you were wrong about where Egypt's nuclear weapon came from?"

"No."

"Bad news, Luther." The President looked miserable. "Roy has proof that it did come from our stockpile."

"What? That's impossible!"

McCluskey shook his head. "I'm afraid not."

"I don't understand." Amstel leaned forward, trying to read the President's expression. "A few minutes ago I was in Jim Canon's office. He was preparing your statement in support of Egypt."

"I asked him to do that earlier, before Roy came in. Excuse me for a moment." Bryant picked up the phone. "Put me through to Mr. Canon. Jim? How far along are you with that statement? No one's seen it except you? And Luther Amstel. Good. Run it through the shredder and forget you ever worked on it. Understand? That's right, I've changed my mind. I'll explain later. And, Jim, thanks for hanging in here with me. I need you."

As Walter Bryant put down the phone, Amstel felt his victory slipping away without understanding why.

"Luther, I asked you to come over here because Roy has raised some very serious charges against you."

"Charges?" Amstel's benign expression turned to cold disdain. "For God's sake, Roy, who the hell are *you* to be making charges against *me*? Apparently you still don't know how things work in this town. The FBI doesn't have the clout to carry on an investigation of the CIA. Go ask any congressman or senator on the Hill."

Roy McCluskey lumbered to his feet with the clumsiness of a man who has never really understood his own strength. "I'm not in the mood to play political games."

"Neither am I, and I refuse to listen to—"

"Be quiet," the President snapped.

Amstel was alarmed by the President's peremptory tone. "Sir, I won't let myself be subjected to this man's ravings."

"You'll sit there and listen," Bryant promised. "And then you'll answer my questions. Go ahead, Roy."

McCluskey was pacing the floor. "Many years ago," he began, "you were a student at the Virginia Military Institute. Your roommate and best friend was another cadet named Claude Leland. The two of you graduated and went off to the Korean War together as young second lieutenants. At Inchon beach you got that leg wound, Luther, and had to leave the service. But Claude Leland stayed in the army."

"I picked up more than a lame leg at Inchon," Amstel reminded him. "I was awarded a silver star, and don't you ever forget that."

"Leland is now a brigadier general in command of Fort Powell, New Mexico, and still your best friend. You take vacations together and exchange phone calls and letters frequently." McCluskey showed the President a photo of Amstel and Leland dressed in hip boots and plaid shirts. They were holding up a string of trout while grinning foolishly into the camera. "Fort Powell happens to be one of the storage depots for Field Deployable Nuclear Warheads. And I confirmed this morning that ten warheads are missing from the depot."

Amstel licked his lips. "Are you certain?"

"I am."

"Well, I'm sorry to hear that ... and surprised, of course. But there is no way that Claude Leland could be connected with such a thing. Those warheads may have been lost, misplaced—anything might have happened to them. Your report to the President stresses how sloppy and unsecure our nuclear storage program has become."

McCluskey pounced on that. "How do you know what was in my report?"

"I don't really *know*. I've just heard rumors."

"You know exactly what I said because you've had a spy in my office. My own secretary."

"That's ridiculous," Amstel blustered.

"Wilma Bartles has admitted it. She's given us the phone number she uses to contact the CIA and even her six-digit CIA code. We used it to get through to your computer this morning, just to check her story."

"I know nothing about that."

"Yesterday afternoon my secretary called your computer and reported that Emmett Avery was on his way to Fort Powell. When Emmett arrived in Albuquerque, he was run down and killed by a 'drunk driver.' Or so I was supposed to believe."

"I'm sorry to hear about Avery. But it's ridiculous to blame me. Accidents involving drunk drivers happen every day." Amstel glanced at the President and saw that he believed every word McCluskey was saying. Stop being defensive, he told himself. "Roy, you're embarrassing yourself. Yes, Claude's a good friend of mine. And he does command Fort Powell. Does that make him personally responsible for some missing weaponry? Of course not! You're operating on speculation."

"Okay, let's have a few more facts." McCluskey flipped through a folder. "Leland has come into some big money lately, enough to allow him to buy and lavishly restore an old estate in Maryland."

"I'm sure there's a logical explanation for that,"

Amstel said smoothly. "Nothing mysterious about wanting a retirement home, is there?"

"And it's an open secret in the CIA that you've been running an agent yourself, which no director since Richard Helms has done. The code name for the agent is Bluebird. Is that true?"

Amstel nodded complacently. "I am in the intelligence gathering business, Roy. Running agents, whether directly or through intermediaries, is what I do."

"At V.M.I. you and Leland were in a choral group called the Bluebirds. Another coincidence?"

"Yes." Amstel tried to press a handkerchief to his sweaty upper lip without appearing to look nervous. How had this damned cop found out so much about his days at V.M.I.?

"Here's one more interesting coincidence. One of your case officers, Daniel Weathers, has been absent from Langley for several months on special assignment to you. It turns out that Weathers, who these days is calling himself Captain Daniel Miller, was put in command of the storage depot at Fort Powell by General Leland."

What made me think this man wasn't good at his job? Amstel asked himself.

"A young woman who worked in the storage depot was murdered earlier this week. She had a lot of money stashed in various bank accounts. And five senior N.C.O.s at Fort Powell have disappeared; they've been spending a lot of money lately, too. You and your friends didn't just *give* those nukes to Egypt and Argentina. You sold them. So stop waving your silver star at me."

Bryant had been listening with mounting agitation. "Luther, I don't want to believe what I'm hearing. It's bad enough that you've turned against your country— but for *money?*"

"I would never sell out this country!"

"What else would you call it?"

Amstel couldn't bear to have the President of the United States think that he would sell out his birthright for a few miserable dollars. "Yes, all right, I suppose there's no longer any point in denials. You know most of it already." He found himself stammering. "It was my—my plan. But everything I did was—you've got to believe this—*for* this country."

Bryant could only stare at him.

"Yes! Yes! *For* the country." Amstel looked from the President to Roy McCluskey. "Someone had to do it. Don't you see? We've stopped the Russians cold in the Mideast by giving Egypt the bomb. And now we've checkmated the Cubans in Latin America, too. They won't dare make a move on that continent now that Argentina has a nuclear deterrent. Don't you see? It's— There's no reason to be afraid, we've got the advantage."

"Advantage?" The President was pale with rage. "You've brought us to the brink of nuclear war!"

"Sir, until just a little while ago you were ready to take advantage of Egypt's action."

"You convinced me the weapon came from elsewhere. Now that I know the U.S. is morally in the wrong, how can I do anything to capitalize on what's happened? That would take the lowest kind of cynicism." Bryant slammed the flat of his hand down on the desk top. "Don't you understand what you've done? You're a traitor! And you've made every American an accessory to mass murder!"

"No!" Amstel shook his head violently. "That's unfair. You're putting the wrong interpretation on what I've done."

McCluskey was at the moment more interested in obtaining information than in arguing morality. "Luther, how many warheads did you channel to Egypt?"

Amstel could have stood up under torture, but a charge of treason coming from the President of the United States struck at his very core. No one could believe that of him, could they? He was known for his patriotism. He wanted to marshal his arguments, make them see the logic of his plan. But his resolve crumbled under Walter Bryant's merciless glare. In his supreme self-confidence, he had forgotten just how much power and authority stood behind the man in the Oval Office. "Two . . . just two."

"And Argentina?"

"Again two."

"Have you sold warheads to any other countries?"

"No, not yet. There was an agreement struck with the Saudis, but no delivery. And I resent the word *sold*. I couldn't do this alone. I've had to make use of some unsavory people. Most of the money went to them."

"Where are the other six warheads?"

Amstel was suddenly frightened. He heard the whiny note in his voice and hated himself for it. The look Bryant and McCluskey exchanged frightened him even more. They had decided his fate even before he came into the Oval Office.

"Where are they?" McCluskey repeated.

"We built a vault inside a mountain—deep inside. A cooling system . . . everything."

"Where?" McCluskey persisted.

"Near Fort Powell. About . . . about fifteen miles from Puma, near the place where Route 41 crosses Hassayampa Creek. They're in there, all six warheads." He immediately corrected himself. "No, they're being moved today to Denver."

"May I?" McCluskey inclined his head toward the telephones on the President's desk.

"Go ahead."

McCluskey dialed his office and was told that the special agent in charge of the Albuquerque field office was waiting for him on the other line, and that he sounded hysterical. "Hysterical?" McCluskey feared the worst. "Switch me over to him right away."

Devereaux's voice was quaking. "Hello? Is this the director?"

"Yes, Al. What's happening out there?"

"It's crazy! A few minutes ago Burke broke out of the stockade. I was right there, he knocked me down. He used a *tank*. Someone blew a hole right through the stockade wall. By the time I got to my feet, Burke was *gone*."

McCluskey breathed easier. He had been afraid Devereaux was going to tell him some even worse news about the warheads. "Which way did Burke go?"

"I don't know. Nobody knows! The stockade's a madhouse. The whole post has gone wild. The acting provost marshal and the sergeant sitting in for Burke have disappeared. The prisoners started a riot and General Leland drove away in—"

"Leland? What direction did *he* go?"

"Uh, I'm not sure. Somebody said he went east."

"Al, get your men together and take them out Route 41 to where it meets a creek—Hassayampa Creek. There's a mountain nearby. Six of the missing warheads are hidden inside that mountain."

"Hassawhat?"

"Hassayampa. Get a goddamn map!"

"Which mountain?"

"I don't *know* which mountain. All I can tell you is that it's close to that creek. Hell, just look for the damned tank! That's where Burke's gone, I'd bet on it. And for Christ's sake, don't shoot at him. In case you haven't figured it out yet, Burke is on *our* side!"

"But he's an escaped prisoner. I told you, he had a tank blow a hole in the stockade wall."

"I don't give a shit if he blew up the post headquarters! He's trying to get those missing nukes back and he's got the firepower to do it. Find him! Help him."

"Yes, sir."

"And put someone on this line. Keep it open."

"Yes, sir. I'm on my way."

McCluskey put down the phone, suddenly embarrassed at the language he'd used in front of the President. "I'm sorry, but things are moving fast out there."

"I gathered that," the President said dryly.

"The MP sergeant major at Fort Powell figured out what was going on long before anyone else did, so General Leland had the man thrown in the stockade. He broke out and I think he must know where the warheads are, because he took a tank out into the desert."

"Good Lord."

"I'd like to keep this line open to Fort Powell."

"Of course. I want to know what's happening down there from minute to minute."

"I think I should leave now," Amstel said, rising slowly.

"Yes," the President agreed. "We won't be needing you anymore, Luther."

Amstel had used the intervening minutes to regain some of his self-confidence. "You'll have my resignation by the end of the day. It will be diplomatically worded. I'm sure you would like to have me arrested and prosecuted, but I suggest you forgo any legal action. It would be traumatic for the country to air this episode in an open court."

Walter Bryant had never hated anyone so much. "Right now, Luther, I just want you to get out of my sight."

"As you wish." Amstel limped out of the oval office with as much dignity as he could muster. Free from the President's determined probing, some of his inner strength returned. Part of his objective had been accomplished, and he was still holding a few cards. Poor Claude Leland was finished. But you will survive, he promised himself.

He went directly to the north entrance and got into his car. The sanctuary of the official automobile made him feel better. It's silly, he thought, but for a moment I doubted they'd let me out of the White House alive.

There were papers in his office that he didn't intend to let Bryant see. He decided to call ahead and have his assistant gather up his personal files before the President thought to impound them.

His hand reached out, but the car phone wasn't in its usual place. Frowning, he looked around for it. No phone. And the footrest he used for his bad leg was gone, too. Gradually he realized this wasn't his limo. It was a black Chrysler. Same year, same model—but a different car.

"Arthur?"

The driver was not Arthur. The man didn't turn around and Amstel couldn't find the button to make the glass partition between the front and backseats slide away. There were no control buttons for the windows, either. He rapped on the partition, then banged on it with his fist. But the driver would not turn his head.

Amstel realized they weren't driving toward CIA

headquarters in Virginia. They were on a side road heading . . . toward Maryland?

"Stop the car!" He pounded the partition with his fist. "Let me out of here right now!"

The driver might have been a robot for all the attention he paid.

Amstel pushed on the door, rammed it with his shoulder, shook it, but could not make it open. In his fury, he ripped off a shoe and began beating at the window with the heel. The window was shatterproof and unyielding. Still he beat on it, until he was gasping for breath and crimson in the face. "Let me out!"

No one could help him. They were driving along quiet country roads with few houses in sight. He saw two little boys walking at the side of the road and screamed for help. Unable to hear Amstel, they thought he was only waving hello and so they waved back with big smiles.

The cool efficiency of the driver was terrifying. He looked neither right nor left as he guided the big Chrysler through the back roads to whatever destination his superior had selected. What destination? And who was that superior? Roy McCluskey, of course. Amstel realized with growing dread that having Emmett Avery killed was a huge error. The FBI, especially with an old-time cop like McCluskey in charge, would never let the murder of one of their own go unpunished. What do they have planned for me? An accident similar to the one I arranged for Avery? Suicide?

The shoe dropped from Amstel's hand and he slumped against the leather cushions, feeling out of breath and utterly helpless. I'm going to my death, he thought, his mouth so dry he could hardly swallow, in a bloody limo.

Chapter 30

The tank plowed across the desert in a straight line, leveling every lonely cactus in its path. At a point close to Highway 41 the turbine engine closed down and the massive piece of armor came to an abrupt halt in front of a small group of people crowded into two open jeeps.

"Hey, Sean, vat takes you so long? Ve been here thirty minutes."

Burke jumped down from the turret and wrung Wolfe Heinzman's hand. With Heinzman were Lou Brodsky and Amos Biggs. Jean stood a little off to the side.

"I'm right on my fucking schedule," Feeney protested. "Excuse me, ma'am."

"You can say anything you want today, Sean." Jean came up to Burke and kissed him in such a practiced way that the others thought they had been doing a lot of it. "I was worried about you."

"No problems." He put his arm around her as if that were the most natural thing in the world to do. "Gabriel's horn was nothing compared with Sean and his tank. Okay, form up over here. Amos, I see you're still drinking on duty."

Biggs was nursing a can of beer that he made no effort to hide. "I figure you aren't gonna bust me today, Sarge."

"No, I owe you too much. I owe all of you."

"The hell you do," Brodsky growled. "We don't like what's goin' on around here either. I did a drive-by on

368

Route 41 about an hour ago. Two of Hank's men were carrying gear out of the bungalow behind the gas station, and there's already some vehicles out by that mountain. They're pulling out, Ansel."

"Ve got new players, too," Heinzman reported. "Last night I'm vatching N.C.O. Club and six men go in through the back entrance to see Hank. Civilians. But they don't act like civilians. They're in our business I think, even if they don't vear uniforms."

"Five of Hank's best men are dead," Burke said. "He has only Sam Veck and Nels Jansen left from his original group. If he's moving the warheads to a safer place, he'd need help. Are Veck and Jansen at the bungalow?"

"Affirmative," Biggs said. "And there are eight men out at the mountain, counting Hank."

"Is Captain Miller one of them?"

"Affirmative again."

Burke smiled. "Then we've got everybody bottled up at one place or the other." He looked over his own group, feeling a strong bond with each of them. Only Lieutenant Sloane stood aloof from the group, so Burke gestured for him to come over. "The lieutenant's going to the mountain with us. He's the ranking line officer here, so we'll take our orders from him. That might even make a difference in how the brass looks at this operation when we're court-martialed."

No one objected to taking orders from Sloane: that's the army. Nor did anyone doubt that a court-martial would swiftly follow today's events.

Sloane's West Point training served him well at this moment. The young officer stepped into a ring of men whose years of combat experience eclipsed his theoretical knowledge and began issuing orders in a firm voice. "We have two objectives: the bungalow and the mountain. In both cases we have to be careful how we use our firepower. A wild round hitting a nuclear warhead just might set it off. Private Feeney—" Sloane noted the hurt on Feeney's face. "*Corporal* Feeney, that means you won't be able to make much use of the 120."

"Shit, sir. I'm just getting good with it."

A trace of a smile crossed Sloane's face. "Maybe next time. Sergeant Heinzman and Corporal Biggs, take the jeep with the mounted fifty-caliber and hit the gas station. Try to bring in those two troopers alive. They can help prove Sergeant Burke's story about army involvement in this business."

"Yes, sir," Heinzman replied.

The troops held Wolfe Heinzman in almost as much esteem as Ansel Burke. His respectful response gave Sloane that special rush of excitement that comes from commanding troops in the field. He'd heard about that feeling from his instructors at the Point, but had just about given up hope of experiencing it for himself.

"Sergeant Brodsky and I will take the other jeep. Burke, you and Captain Silk will be in the tank with Corporal Feeney. Go straight in with the tank. We'll come in fast from Highway 41 to cut off any vehicles trying to escape in that direction." He glanced at Burke to see if he agreed.

"Good plan, Lieutenant." Burke turned to Wolfe Heinzman and Amos Biggs. "I doubt that Hank has any nukes stored at the gas station. Even so, don't spray too much lead around."

"Ve be perfect gentlemen." Wolfe grinned.

Biggs belched.

"Any questions?" Sloane looked around. "That's it, then. Let's go."

Burke took an M16 and an ammo belt from Brodsky and clapped the old soldier on the shoulder. "Good luck, Lou. Take care of yourself."

"See ya in the stockade." Brodsky laughed, full of youthful vigor. "You won't even have to change clothes to go back."

Feeney and Burke helped Jean up onto the tank and showed her how to slither down inside it.

"I'm glad I wore old jeans," she said. "It's so *oily* in here."

"New tanks are always oily." Feeney sniffed the foul air. "Don't that smell beautiful?"

"Delightful." Jean moved closer to Burke, which wasn't hard to do in the cramped compartment. When

Feeney turned over the engine, she said, "Up lance. Down visor."

"That green lieutenant might make a good officer some day," Feeney shouted. "If he lives long enough. And if they don't court-martial his ass into Leavenworth."

"How fast can the new M1 go?" Burke asked.

"Fast enough to turn every knob in your spine to mush."

Roper would want to get those warheads out of the mountain as quickly as possible. "Goose it, Sean. We don't have much time."

"Okay, Sergeant Major. Hold on, and say good-bye to your insides. They ain't never gonna be the same again." With a leprechaun's grin, Feeney gave full power to the turbine engine.

As the tank rapidly picked up speed, Jean and Burke grabbed for handholds. Soon they were flying across the desert floor with a series of crashing jolts that made them feel they were riding a twister.

General Leland drove straight out Route 41 past the gas station. As he passed, he saw two of Roper's men carrying the last of the monitoring equipment out to a van. Thank God something was going right. Half a mile later, he crossed over Hassayampa Creek and turned his new BMW into the desert. The undercarriage scraped against so many rocks that he was afraid the expensive toy would never be the same.

But that was the least of his worries. Somewhere out in the desert a madman was driving a tank toward this mountain.

The route he took wasn't really a road, just the most level stretch of land between the highway and the mountain. After about two miles he saw a cluster of cars sitting in the shade of the mountainside. Before he reached the spot, men popped up on each side of the road and covered him with automatic weapons.

Leland hit his brakes, causing the BMW to skid sideways to a rough stop. "Don't shoot! I'm here to see Miller!"

Miller came running up from the van. "It's all right, let him out of the car."

The gunmen backed off.

"What are you doing here?" Miller demanded. "These Colombians don't know you, but they do know a general's stars when they see them."

"Burke is on his way here—in a tank!"

"In a *what?*"

"He broke out of the stockade. Someone used a tank to blow a hole in the wall." The court-martial proceedings of a few days ago popped into his mind. He recalled Sean Feeney's insolent face, remembered in detail the charges against the man. "Feeney! I should have sent that scummy little man to Leavenworth when I had the chance. Where's Roper?"

"In the vault."

"How many of the warheads have been taken out?"

"Five. They're in the van. Roper went down a few minutes ago to get the last one and shut down the air-conditioning system."

The staccato rattle of distant gunfire made them turn toward the highway.

"The gas station." Miller licked his lips. "Something's gone wrong there." Before he could decide what to do, the grinding sound of a heavy engine came from the opposite direction. "What the hell is *that?*"

"The tank." Leland raised his arm. "There!"

At first they could see only the turret and cannon. Then the tank came over the rise in all its noisy magnificence, bearing down on them with frightening speed.

"Fire on it!" Miller screamed, waving to his men.

"You'll never stop it with small arms." Leland pushed Miller toward the van. "Get the van out of here! I'll destroy the last warhead myself."

"How?"

"There's a deep sinkhole in the caves, quicksand at the bottom. I'll throw it down there. Hurry!" He jostled Miller into the van and ran for the mountain. The Colombians were firing their automatic weapons at the tank and the air was filled with Spanish profanity.

Leland reached the entrance to the cave and looked

over his shoulder. Miller had started the van and was pulling out.

The ground level entrance to the cave system was concealed behind a sliding stone door and camouflage netting. Leland pushed aside the netting and squeezed past the stone barrier. The specter of capture and public disgrace filled every corner of his mind. He had to dispose of the last warhead. If Miller could escape with the other five, there'd be no real proof against him.

"Roper! Where are you?" The passageway was longer and dimmer than he remembered.

"In here."

At last Leland stumbled into the vault, so cool and dry that it felt like a movie theater in the summertime.

Roper was down on one knee carefully fitting the last warhead into an aluminum case. He took one look at Leland's face and asked: "What's wrong?"

"Burke's here!"

"How?"

"That friend of his, the stupid little corporal from the tank corps, used an M1 to break him out of the stockade. The tank's right outside!"

"How many men does he have with him?"

"I don't know. I heard gunfire coming from the gas station too. We've got to throw this warhead down the sinkhole."

Roper finished enclosing the device in its case. "What about the others?"

"Miller's taking them away in the van."

"I hope to hell Ansel doesn't fire on the van. We'd all go up in the same mushroom cloud."

The walls and floor of the vault trembled slightly as the muffled sound of an explosion seeped into the vault.

"Tank gun." Roper was calculating the odds and didn't like them. Miller was an administrator, a case officer. Alone he was nothing. Ansel would have no trouble scooping him up. Miller and the F.D.N.W.s would be all the proof Burke needed. He picked up the heavy case and thrust it into the arms of a surprised General Leland. "Here you go, General. It's all yours."

"What are you doing?"

"You can have the honor of dumping this thing while I get the hell out of here."

"You can't leave me to do it alone! I'm not sure where that hole is; I've only been inside the mountain twice."

"Just follow the passageway and stay to your right." Roper picked up a MAC-10 and slung it over his shoulder. Underneath his shirt was a belt containing the "fuck you" money he had suspected he might need. Between the money belt and his bank account in the Bahamas, he wasn't worried about dying a pauper. He was only worried about dying.

"Wait—"

Roper ignored General Leland as he hurried out of the dimly lighted cave. All he had to do was get clear of this damned mountain and nobody would ever find him.

Feeney brought the M1 to the mountain from the east so the sun would be at his back and in the eyes of whoever was out there. He also throttled down the engine so they wouldn't be heard until they were practically on top of Roper and his people.

Being an infantryman instead of a tank jockey, Burke found it frustrating to have to look at the world through a periscope. When he did sight the cluster of men and vehicles, he pounded Feeney on the shoulder. "There they are! Two o'clock."

"I got 'em." They came over a rise and Feeney let the tank have more power. No need to run quiet now. The enemy had seen them and was firing.

As rounds bounced off the tank's steel plates, Jean said, "That sounds like *popcorn*."

"Popcorn's a lot healthier for you." Burke swung the periscope and saw General Leland running for the mountain as the phony Captain Miller was trying to pull away in a Dodge van. The small-arms fire was coming from different spots around the perimeter. "Sean, put a round from the 120 into the side of the mountain. That might send some of them running."

Feeney was happy to oblige. "Load for me, Ansel."

Burke grabbed one of the sabot rounds from the

ammo rack and loaded it into the breech of the 120. When the round was seated, he rapped his knuckles on the back of Feeney's helmet.

"Put your fingers in your ears," Feeney warned. "This is gonna make one helluva noise."

Jean did as she was told and closed her eyes for good measure. The 120 fired with such force that the tank recoiled, throwing Jean against the steel wall behind her and driving the air from her lungs.

"Are you all right?" Burke shouted.

She nodded dumbly.

"Traverse to your right," Burke said to Feeney.

Feeney complied and Burke was able to catch a glimpse of General Claude Leland wedging himself through a hidden opening at the foot of the mountain. He was torn in two directions. He wanted Miller and he wanted Leland too. He wasn't awfully suprised to find the general here. The son of a bitch had always thought he could make his own rules.

"Sloane and Brodsky coming in at nine o'clock," Feeney reported.

"I'm going outside."

"Watch yourself, Sergeant Major."

"Jean, stay with Feeney."

"Don't give me orders," she snapped back. "I'm a captain and you're only a noncom."

"You picked a great time to pull rank."

He threw back a hatch and pulled himself up and out of the tank in one motion. The blast from the cannon had created a swirling sandstorm that provided good cover. He rolled off the front skirt and hit the ground running. As he came out of the sand cloud, a man appeared on his left. Burke fired the M16 on full automatic and the man staggered and fell.

"Lou, stop the van!"

Brodsky steered the jeep directly at Miller, who was trying to negotiate the van along the sandy trail. At the last moment Miller turned the wheel sharply to avoid a collision, taking the van into deeper sand. Its rear wheels spun and the engine stalled.

Burke was running in that direction when two more of Miller's men popped up in front of him. He hit the ground as a burst of fire crackled over his head. Suddenly he was drawing so much fire that all he could do was burrow in and hold his breath.

Behind him the 120 fired again and another chunk of the mountainside exploded, raining down a shower of rocks. Burke rolled over several times until he was safe behind a slight rise. There was as much firing as ever, but the enemy had shifted to a different target—Brodsky and Sloane.

No easy way to do it. Burke jumped to his feet and ran forward. Two of the opposition were firing at the jeep from behind one of their own cars. He shot the closest one in the back and jinked to his left as the other spun around. They fired at each other simultaneously, but Burke was a moving target. His burst caught the man at waist level.

"Ansel!" Brodsky yelled. "Drop!"

He threw himself down as someone else opened up on him. The burst went wild. Way off the mark. A moment later, after voices shouted back and forth in Spanish, a car engine started and one of the vehicles drove off into the desert.

The silence that followed was funereal. Burke walked cautiously across the open space to where Brodsky had run the van off the road. The jeep was pocked with bullet holes. Brodsky was sitting on the ground with his back against the jeep and both hands pressed to a bloody leg wound.

Lieutenant Sloane lay dead next to him.

"How bad is your leg?"

Brodsky shrugged. "I've been hit worse."

"Where's Miller?"

"Ran off into the desert like a pregnant cow. But I hit him. I think he bought the farm. Them Latinos opened up before I could make sure. Sloane did okay, Ansel. He knocked off one of the Latinos, but the bastards had too much firepower for us."

"I'll see about Miller." Burke had to walk only fifty yards out from the jeep to find Captain Daniel Miller lying facedown with three holes in his back. He put a finger to Miller's carotid artery, then retreated to the jeep, keeping a careful watch for any stragglers who might have been left behind.

"You put a nice tight pattern into that so-called captain. He's not going anywhere."

Brodsky merely nodded. "Y'know, I was just starting to like the kid."

Dead, Lieutenant Walter Sloane looked even more like a youngster. Burke wondered if the boy finally had done enough to make his father proud of him. He went around and opened the back doors of the van. Inside sat five large aluminum cases. He pulled one over and opened it carefully. The case contained what resembled a standard artillery shell, except that the payload was a small nuclear device stenciled all over with red warning notices.

Feeney and Jean came running up from the tank.

"Ansel, I saw Hank Roper try to skin out," Feeney reported. "That's why I fired a second round from the 120, to drive him back into his hole. It worked, too. The son of a bitch decided he didn't want the mountain coming down on his head."

Jean knelt beside Brodsky and gave him a handkerchief to press against the wound. "You're losing a lot of blood. We have to get you to a doctor." She glanced at Ansel. "Is the lieutenant dead?"

"I'm afraid so." Burke grabbed Brodsky around the waist. "Sean, help me get Lou into the van. Jean, take the van back to the post. Go straight to the provost marshal's office. Get help for Lou and tell them to be careful how they handle these nukes."

"You're staying here?"

"Hank and General Leland are still inside that mountain."

Jean appealed to Feeney. "Sean, make him come with me. He's done *enough*."

"Ma'am, I can't make Ansel do nothin'. He outranks me." Feeney grinned at her. "Hell, everybody outranks me."

Burke put Jean behind the wheel of the van and kissed her. "Go. I'll see you at the post."

"You'd better." Jean put the van in gear and gently

gave it some gas while Burke and Feeney pushed it out of the sand.

When the van was rolling free and on its way to Highway 41, Burke felt a lot better. Jean was a handful. Keeping her safe was a full-time job.

"You got a real woman there, Sergeant Major. Maybe she ain't got quite as many curves as the other one, but she's always gonna be there when you need her."

"Sean, for once in your life you're making sense."

Feeney took out his P-38 and pulled back the slide. "I'm ready to help you flush out those bastards."

"Stay with your tank."

"Ansel, that ain't fair!"

"As long as you're covering the exit, they've got no easy way out."

"Hell, there's probably six or seven ways to get out of the caves in this mountain."

"This is the one they use, the one they know the best. They won't want to take another route. Do you have a flashlight in that bucket of bolts?"

Feeney scrounged up a flashlight from the toolbox and passed it over grudgingly. "You could use some backup in there. You're tough, but you ain't Rambo."

"Give me twenty minutes. If I'm not back by then, do what you want."

"That's a dangerous order to give an unstable old drunk like me. Good luck."

"Thanks for the use of the tank, Sean."

"It's brand-new, needed a shakedown anyway." Feeney climbed back into the M1 and put up the front hatch. There was a light machine gun in the tank, which he mounted on the bracket outside the hatch and swung around to cover the cave entrance.

To ease the waiting, Feeney returned to his bottle of Jack Daniel's. It would be his last drink for a long, long time. The army might let you get away with knocking down a whorehouse or two, but not with blowing a hole in the stockade.

Soon after Ansel Burke entered the cave, a curl of dust rose slowly from the direction of Highway 41 and began to expand. Feeney slid into the tank commander's seat and pressed his eyes to the periscope sight,

turning the controls to six-power magnification. What
he saw coming across the desert was a line of ten to
fifteen cars: MP jeeps; police cars; and what looked to
Feeney like several of the plain black sedans favored
by the FBI.

"Holy shit."

Feeney knew he could easily stand them off with the
tank. Blow them to hell, if he wanted. But Ansel
would be pissed if he did that. Besides, this was a
great excuse to leave the tank and follow Ansel into
the cave.

He slid down from the turret and ran for the entrance.

Burke crept through the low tunnel with his M16 at
the ready, wondering who the hell was yelling up
ahead. The last thing he expected was to walk into the
middle of an argument. Was that Hank's voice? Yes, it
was. And Leland's.

". . . outta your fucking mind!"

"Just stay back."

"The sinkhole—that's the place for it. You said so
yourself."

"What happened to your famous 'cool,' Sergeant
Roper?"

"Just let me get the hell out of here, then do what
you want."

"Stay right there! I'm warning you, I'll do it right
now."

Burke slid around a corner into a brightly lighted
chamber. He swept the room with the M16, but neither Hank Roper nor General Leland made any move
against him. They faced each other from opposite sides
of the vault. Hank's weapon lay on the floor at his
feet. The general was on his knees in front of an open
aluminum case from which he had removed the Field
Deployable Nuclear Warhead. The device lay nestled
in his arms like a baby. It looked different from the
one Burke had seen in the van. The cover had been
removed, revealing the interior of the nuclear device.

"Welcome, Sergeant Burke. Put down your M16."

"Do it!" yelled Roper, whose face was slick with
sweat.

"As you can see," Leland continued, "I've taken the cover off this device. Are you familiar with the term *critical mass?*"

Burke's mouth dried up. "Yeah, I think so."

"Very good. Do you see the two red rods?"

In the center of the device was a pair of red rods about the length and width of two pencils. They pointed at each other across a gap of about six inches. "I see them."

"When the two rods come together, they create a critical mass. Followed by a nuclear explosion. Not a large nuclear explosion by today's standards, but a blast big enough to turn this entire mountain into a handful of dust."

Without a word, Burke put his weapon down just as Roper must have done.

"He's gone nuts!" Roper croaked.

Leland looked cool and in perfect control of himself. His regular features were unruffled. "All I have to do to cause a critical mass is push this spring, which will bring the rods together. Do you see it? Usually the spring is activated by a timing mechanism calibrated to ten-thousandths of a second. The shell is set for a particular range. When fired from a howitzer, the nuclear charge is automatically detonated in the air above the target. This is one of the simplest nuclear weapons in our arsenal, which is why it was chosen for distribution to our less sophisticated allies."

Keep him talking, Burke thought. "So that's how they work. I've always wondered. You must have done a hell of a lot of research."

The compliment caused Leland to preen himself. "Yes, I have."

"So the Egyptians did use one of ours?"

"Of course. It was bright of you to figure that out. We fooled the President of the United States, the Congress, the media, the FBI—everyone except you. That's why I was waiting for you. I'm going to set off this device, Sergeant Burke. And I wanted to make sure you went up with it."

"You don't have to do that," Roper whined. "We can still get clear. I've got enough money put away for both of us."

"Money." Leland spat out the word. "That's all you think about."

"You took plenty for yourself!"

"Yes, but money was never the point." Leland turned earnestly to Burke. "You understand, don't you? By giving these weapons to Egypt and Argentina, my friends and I have done more to stop communism than anyone in the last twenty years."

"Who's going to believe you weren't in it for the money?" Roper shouted. "You must have taken half a million."

"You're right," Leland admitted sadly. "No one would believe me. Which is why escape is pointless. My reputation means more to me than my life. By bringing this mountain down on us, I'll wipe the trail clean. There will be no one left alive to implicate me."

Roper was inching toward the exit from the vault, which caused General Leland to laugh.

"Go ahead, Sergeant Roper. Run! Do you really think you can outrun a nuclear explosion?"

"If you set that thing off," Burke said, "you won't be around to defend yourself. Even without Hank and me, there's enough evidence to implicate you. Do you want the media trashing your name after you're dead? Wouldn't you rather be here to tell the world why you did all this?"

"That would be a persuasive argument, except that I have friends, one good friend in particular, who'll see that my reputation survives intact." His expression hardened and a final cloud of madness passed over his eyes.

A gunshot echoed through the vault and Leland's right arm whipped to the side. He stared at a bloody stump. All that remained of his hand dangled by a few strings of flesh. Injured rage bubbled up into his throat as he groped for the spring with his remaining hand.

Burke and Roper simultaneously dove for him. Leland scooted back, dragging the warhead along. There was another shot fired and Leland bucked like a wild bronco.

"I've got it!" Roper's hands closed on the device. He shrieked in pain as the two radioactive rods snapped forward, pinning one of his hands between them. "My God! Help me! My hand's burning up!"

The smell of searing flesh made Burke gag. He forced himself to hook his thumbs on the opposing poles and force the rods back to their original positions. "Sean, put something between these damn things!"

"What?"

"Anything! Give me your pistol."

As soon as Feeney thrust his P-38 into the gap between the radioactive rods, Burke let them come slowly forward until the tip of each rod rested firmly against gunmetal. It was only after he took his hands off the warhead that he realized they were shaking wildly.

Roper lay on the floor next to General Leland, holding his damaged hand close to his body. "I never had a burn like this. My hand's on fire. Ansel, I can feel the pain all through me, like a hundred bayonets. What's happening to me?"

The back of Roper's hand was as twisted and blackened as the roots of an oak tree. Burke looked at it and felt sick again. "Radiation burn."

"Sweet Jesus," Feeney murmured.

"Am I gonna be okay?" Roper stared around blearily. "Get me to a doctor, will you? Please. I'll pay you anything."

Burke and Feeney lifted Roper up between them and dragged him toward the exit from the vault, anxious to put distance between themselves and the malignant piece of high technology on the floor.

"I told you to stay with the tank," Burke growled, to take his mind off Hank's disfigured hand.

"Well, shit, if I could take orders I'd be a bird colonel by now. Hey, I showed General Leland that Sean Feeney is good for something more than knocking down a whorehouse, didn't I?"

"You sure did, Sean. You showed everybody."

MONDAY, JUNE 30

Chapter 31

By 6:00 P.M. most of the art galleries on East Fifty-seventh Street had closed for the day. The Hillary House was an exception. Two panel trucks were double-parked in front of the gallery to allow caterers to carry in food and drink through the front door. Inside, Maggie Winston directed a frenzy of activity, showing the caterer where to set up the refreshment table while at the same time giving orders to a pair of insouciant young men who were moving lights around on overhead tracks.

"Champagne on the left. Punch bowl in the center. Food to the right. No, I want the flowers at each end of the table. George, move that light to the left. And do you have an ivory gel? A bare spotlight looks so *harsh* on that particular canvas."

The young men giggled as they adjusted the light.

"Much better, thank you." Maggie prowled through the gallery like a suspicious cat, inspecting the presentation of each painting in the show and assuring herself that the refreshments and other arrangements would satisfy the most discriminating guests.

Donald Hillary came down the steps from his office wearing the formal gown of an eighteenth-century Chinese mandarin, which caused the young men moving the lights to applaud.

"Thank you, George. *Merci,* Andre." In the long Chinese gown, Hillary moved as if on wheels. "Do you like it, Maggie?"

"Yes, but why Chinese when we're showing a new Western artist?"

Donald Hillary rolled his eyes. "This is called counterpoint, darling. I don't intend to be lost amid all these macho images, magnificent as they are."

Maggie understood that Donald was slightly irritated over her impending success. Despite the fact he would make a great deal of money from introducing Ansel Burke's work to the New York critics, Donald knew that he was promoting Maggie too. Hence the Chinese attire, which was meant to overshadow the red Halston gown she had purchased for the opening. "Do you have your order book handy, Donald? I believe we're going to move some paintings tonight."

"Darling, the folds of my gown hide *many* fascinating objects." He winked and moved to the refreshments table, where he stole a strawberry from the top of a cake and popped it into his mouth.

The caterer came up to Maggie scowling. "A policeman wants us to move our trucks and we're not completely unloaded yet."

"Give him this." She slipped a hundred-dollar bill into the caterer's hand. For such a sum, a New York City patrolman would reroute traffic all the way up to Sixty-third Street. To Maggie, that was part of New York's charm. Everything was for sale.

She took one last tour around the gallery, studying each of Ansel's paintings with the zeal of a stockbroker reading the Dow Jones. They were, as Donald had said, magnificent. Ansel had talent to burn. Maggie regretted the fact that he'd never give her another painting to sell, but at least she had these. They'd be enough to build on.

"Satisfied?" Donald was at her side.

"Yes, you've given them a very good showcase. I suppose I should thank you."

"No need. We'll both do quite well." Donald glanced at his watch. "My goodness, look who's come early."

Maggie immediately recognized the older couple coming into Hillary House as Charles and Sandra Elliott, the wealthy Massachusetts couple who had come into her gallery in New Mexico.

"Hello there, Donald," Elliott said. "Miss Winston, a pleasure to see you again."

"We've been looking forward to this." Sandra Elliott eagerly studied the paintings.

"You're a bit early, the champagne hasn't even been poured yet," Donald said, "but you're welcome nonetheless."

"There it is." Elliott pointed to the painting of the old Colt revolver. "That's the painting that caught my eye in New Mexico."

"Yes, I know." Sandra Elliott looked from Donald to Maggie. "I was shocked when I saw on television that Sergeant Burke had been arrested for *espionage*. Good Lord, I thought, with all that talent why would he have to sell secrets to the Russians?"

"Sandra, the man has since been cleared and released," Elliott reminded his wife.

"Yes, and all those headlines certainly won't hurt this show, will it?"

"We're just glad Ansel was cleared," Maggie said smoothly.

"Will he be here tonight?"

"No, he's still in New Mexico."

"What a pity." Sandra Elliott suddenly noticed that her husband was already circulating through the gallery. "I'd better watch Charles or he'll buy everything in sight. He can be so impulsive. Excuse me."

As soon as the Elliotts were out of earshot, Donald whispered, "When Charles Elliott gets impulsive, he writes checks for six figures."

"Let's hope he loses Sandra in the crowd."

Donald peered at her. "Are you certain Sergeant Burke is still in New Mexico? I wouldn't want him showing up here and causing some kind of scene."

"Don't worry, there's nothing he can do. I had my contract with Ansel vetted by an attorney. We have every legal right to sell these paintings. There's nothing Ansel can do about it."

"Ah, more guests. Time to start circulating. Maggie, both the *New York Times* and *Art World* will be here tonight. You can have the bitch from *Art World,* but

leave the lovely young man from the *Times* to me.
This is my gallery, pet."

"I understand, Donald."

Donald Hillary moved away with his hands hidden
in his sleeves like a true Mandarin.

The Elliotts' reference to Ansel had disturbed Maggie's
sense of equanimity. The whole episode leading up to
and following Ansel's arrest had given Maggie fre-
quent cause for anxiety. Having taken the money from
Hank Roper to betray Ansel meant that she had to
stand by her story. When Ansel was arrested, she
thought the matter would end there. He would be
charged, tried, convicted—end of story.

The immediate publicity following his arrest did
just what she and Donald had hoped, focusing the
media's attention on him and bringing his name to
prominence.

Then a few days later came the big shock: Ansel was
released from custody, and *cleared* of all charges. To
make matters worse, the Director of the FBI personally made the announcement that new evidence showed
Ansel to be innocent of all charges.

Maggie headed straight for her attorney, who assured her that no one could touch her for bringing
those papers to the FBI as long as she had done so in
good faith. She assured him that was the case. Fearing
that Ansel might come for his paintings now that he
was free, Maggie also asked him to look at her contract with Ansel. It was a valid document. Signed by
both parties and notarized. In effect, the contract gave
Maggie power of attorney over the paintings and pro-
ceeds from the sale of the paintings.

For the last two weeks Maggie had continued to live
in fear of a confrontation with Ansel. Fortunately, it
never occurred. He hadn't even tried to contact her,
either by letter or in person.

Her other fear was that Hank Roper might confess
to having paid her to take those papers to the FBI.
Maggie subscribed to the *Puma Union* in order to stay
in touch with what was happening there, and was
rewarded with an obituary. Sergeant Major Henry H.
Roper, U.S. Army, had died in the Puma County hos-

pital "following a short illness," whatever that meant. So he was no longer a threat.

Another item in the *Union* caught Maggie's eye. Also in the Puma hospital was Sheriff Len Perkins. He had been found behind the sheriff's office severely beaten "by person or persons unknown." For some strange reason, Sheriff Perkins refused to say who had beaten him.

It was Maggie's nature to be suspicious. Hank's death was cryptically explained. Ansel's name faded from the story when President Bryant gave Egypt and Argentina twenty-four hours to return the nuclear warheads stolen from the U.S. or face a formal declaration of war. Both countries immediately complied. Though the media had dropped Ansel in favor of the hotter story, she suspected that Ansel, and perhaps even Hank Roper and Sheriff Perkins, had been part of that story.

The newspapers had also hinted there might be something irregular about the death of CIA director Luther Amstel, who had been found at his summerhouse in Maryland, a victim of a stroke.

Maggie didn't even want to think about what part she may have played in those events. And besides, the whirl of activity surrounding the mounting of the show soon occupied all of her time and energy. Within a few weeks she managed to forget—or at least to rationalize away—any guilt she may initially have felt.

The real culprit was New York. How could anyone become mired in the past when there was so much going on *today*. Maggie loved being back in the city.

Glancing at her stunning reflection in the nearest mirror, Maggie felt that New York was quite lucky to have her back. And the city had demonstrated its gratitude. She had been to three "A list" parties since her return and enjoyed a brief affair with a French diplomat. On the basis of her connection with the Ansel Burke show, she had signed up two promising new artists. And with part of the money Hank Roper had provided, she had signed the lease on new gallery space in Soho. Soho wasn't Fifty-seventh Street, but it was becoming a more important art center every year.

Everything was working out just as she'd planned.

"Hi, Maggie!"

She waved to a VIP, pleased to have been singled out by him. The gallery was beginning to fill up. Champagne corks were popping and people were staring at Ansel's bold and colorful images with *ooh*s and *ahh*s on their lips. Maggie circulated with perfect instincts, never staying with any one person for very long unless it was someone of prestige.

Donald grabbed her arm. "I've just sold 'The Dreamer' to Stuart Wellington."

"Full price?"

"Absolutely."

Maggie patted Donald's cheek. "You should always dress in Chinese robes, my dear. Everyone is talking about how wonderful you look." Maggie was about to add another insincere compliment when, to her absolute horror, she saw Ansel Burke come into the gallery with that little redheaded lawyer from Fort Powell at his side.

"What's the matter?" asked Donald, whose social senses were acute.

Maggie didn't know what to say. Or do. Finally she said, "Ansel just came in."

"Where?" Donald searched the room and saw a tall, wide-shouldered man in old denims and an army jacket making his way through the crowd in a rather rude way. With him was an attractive young lady dressed just as casually. "Oh my God, what does he want?"

"I don't know." Maggie was thinking fast. She had her contract with her, just in case. And the two private security guards on duty reported directly to her. With those factors in her favor, she greeted Ansel Burke and Jean Silk with a frozen smile. "Ansel! I'm so glad you could be here. You too, Miss Gingham—I mean, Miss Silk. So many people want to meet you, Ansel. Would you like me to introduce you around?"

"No, we won't be staying long." Burke looked at his paintings with pride. "They do look pretty good up there, don't they?"

"They're wonderful," Jean said, impressed all over again by Ansel's talent. "I especially like the one of the old rancher."

"You do? Then it's yours."

"If you're talking about the one called 'The Dreamer,' it now belongs to Mr. Stuart Wellington," Maggie informed him. "By the way, this is your host, Donald Hillary."

Donald took his right hand out of the mandarin sleeve and extended it. "So glad to meet you, Sergeant Burke. Your talent is most exciting. In my humble opinion—"

"The painting isn't yours to sell, Maggie." Burke found he didn't hate her after all. Like a snake, she was too cold to hate but too treacherous to ignore. All he wanted was to take his paintings back from her. "None of them are."

"That's ridiculous," Donald scoffed. "You have a contract with Miss Winston that gives her the right to sell these paintings in your name."

"Have you looked at the contract?" Jean had been looking forward to this moment and intended to savor it. "I mean, looked *closely?*"

"My lawyer read every word," Maggie snapped. "It's iron-clad."

"I wasn't talking about the words. Did you look at the notary stamp?"

Maggie produced her copy of the contract and opened it to the last page. "It's just a notary stamp, like a million others."

"Not quite." Jean smiled at Burke. "Shall I show her why, or do you want to do it?"

"You're the lawyer, you show her."

Jean pointed to the date on the notary stamp. "If you recall, you and Ansel had your contract notarized by Sheriff Leonard Perkins of Puma County, who also picks up a few extra dollars as a notary public. Unfortunately, Sheriff Perkins is a very careless administrator, as well as a rotten sheriff. He let his notary license run out without getting it renewed. As you can see, his notary seal is out of date. I read the contract six times myself before I noticed that small fact."

"So what?" Maggie demanded. "That means nothing. It's just an oversight. A technicality."

"Lawyers make entire careers out of just such technicalities." Jean produced another legal document. "Your contract is invalid because it was improperly notarized, and I have here an order from the Superior Court of the State of New York directing you to deliver these paintings into the hands of Ansel Burke."

"No! I won't!" Maggie screamed, causing heads to turn.

"You have no choice." Jean slapped the court order into Maggie's hand.

She threw it on the floor. "Get out of here!"

"We're going, but I'm taking my paintings with me." Ansel began removing canvases from the wall.

"Stop! Stop that!" Donald Hillary rushed up to Burke, who brushed him aside as if he were a pesky mosquito.

The security guards came forward. Before Maggie could order them to eject the intruders, Jean picked the court order off the floor and explained its significance to the guards. Many of the people in the gallery, attuned to what was going on, pushed forward to take sides. Maggie shouted obscenities while the catering staff continued to pop champagne corks. The guards looked at each other and backed off.

In the center of the fracas, Burke and Jean calmly continued to remove paintings from the walls, carry them outside to their rented van, and return for more. A few of the men in the crowd, angered by Burke's rough dress and behavior, considered trying to stop him, but were cowed by his obvious physical power and intimidating manner.

Donald Hillary clutched at Burke's arm. "You're throwing away a fortune! I can sell these paintings for you, every one of them. And for top dollar!"

"Not right now, thanks. Jean and I want to look at them for awhile before I sell any."

Charles Elliott stuck a card in Burke's jacket pocket as he went by. "Call me, I want to talk to you."

"You can't do this!" Maggie was sobbing. Someone had stepped on the hem of her gown and torn it. Her world, her entire future, was collapsing around her. She was aware that some hateful people were enjoying her anguish, laughing at her behind their hands. "Get away from me! Leave me alone!" she shouted at them.

With pushes and shoves, Maggie made her way through the gallery crowd and out onto Fifty-seventh Street. She ran toward Madison Avenue weeping hysterically and vowing never to set foot on this street again.

"We've got three weeks leave. Where do you want to go?" Burke asked, once they were on the Henry Hudson Parkway and driving north toward New England. "Vermont? New Hampshire? Maine?"

"Maine," Jean decided. "You might find something you want to paint in one of those old fishing towns. They're lovely in the summer."

"I already know what my next subject's going to be."

"Really?" He had said nothing about painting since all the turmoil at Fort Powell had settled down. As far as Jean knew, he hadn't even done any pencil sketches. "What is it?"

"You."

"Me?"

"In the nude."

"Are you crazy? I'm an *officer*. You can't go around painting officers in the nude. What would happen to military discipline if sergeants started asking their superior officers to take off their clothes and pose? Besides, I'm not so sure I want to be painted in the nude." She was serious now. "How long would it take?"

Burke gave Jean's question the deep consideration it deserved. "Years."

"Well, that's different." She slid down and let the summer air sweep over her through the open window. "I accept."